Lucia tuned out th‍ ‍d
stood, making sure her‍ ‍-
ing beneath her skin.‍ ‍a
tight nod and walked‍ ‍d
down the hall. The nev‍ ‍t
slowly picked up speed. She would outrun the panic attack
that clutched at her chest. Following nothing but the eddies
of Aether, the wood-paneled walls blurred as she passed. Far
and farther still, until she left the last passing stranger and
found a door that wasn't locked. She wasn't going to lose
it in front of people. She wasn't going to lose it at all. Inside,
a library. In her anger, the Aether sprung from her hand and
slammed the door shut behind her, air thick with ink and old
paper, leather and cloves, and blessed, blessed silence.

"Who is chasing you?"

"No one. I'm just starved for a good book."

"Help yourself." He motioned to the stacked shelves.
The flash of his smile drew her eyes down to his lips. Gods.
He'd never even kissed her. Was she so undesirable? So
untouchable that she inspired no lust, no passion? Well,
fuck it. Rising on her tiptoes, she had the brief glimpse of
his lips parting in surprise, his eyes widening before she
took what she'd always wanted from him.

Anger gave way to heat. Aether sparked where their lips
met. If he hadn't been holding so tightly to her arms, she
would have fallen backward. He didn't give her the chance.
The Aether shocked down every nerve ending straight to her
core, and suddenly she was wet and aroused and wound
tighter t'

He se

"Wh

She

*I think.*

was like

this far.

**Books by Kira Brady**

*Hearts of Fire*: A Deadglass Novella

*Hearts of Darkness*

*Hearts of Shadow*

*Hearts of Chaos*

**Published by Kensington Publishing Corporation**

# KIRA BRADY

# Hearts of Chaos

## ZEBRA BOOKS
### KENSINGTON PUBLISHING CORP.
http://www.kensingtonbooks.com

ZEBRA BOOKS are published by

Kensington Publishing Corp.
119 West 40th Street
New York, NY 10018

All Kensington titles, imprints and distributed lines are available at
special quantity discounts for bulk purchases for sales promotion,
premiums, fund-raising, educational or institutional use.

Special book excerpts or customized printings can also be created to
fit specific needs. For details, write or phone the office of the
Kensington Special Sales Manager. Attn.: Special Sales Department.
Kensington Publishing Corp., 119 West 40th Street, New York, NY
10018. Phone: 1-800-221-2647.

Zebra and the Z logo Reg. U.S. Pat. & TM Off.

First Printing: March 2014
ISBN-13: 978-1-4201-2458-3
ISBN-10: 1-4201-2458-7

First Electronic Edition: March 2014
eISBN-13: 978-1-4201-3413-1
eISBN-10: 1-4201-3413-2

10 9 8 7 6 5 4 3 2 1

Printed in the United States of America

*To Ryan, Juniper, and Hawthorne:*
*God blessed the broken road that led me straight to you.*

*To Sherida and Collin:*
*For their unwavering belief in my writing,*
*and for raising the best hero a girl could ask for.*
*Thank you!*

# Acknowledgments

Thank you to Joy Adare, without whom this trilogy would never have been written. Thank you for talking me through the hurdles and for knowing exactly what I wanted to say when I couldn't find the words. Thank you to Joy and Marni Folsom for plotting assistance.

Thanks to Sherida Stewart for reading every draft for me, even on a tight deadline.

Thank you again to my editor, Peter Senftleben, for believing in the Deadglass Trilogy. It's been an awfully big adventure.

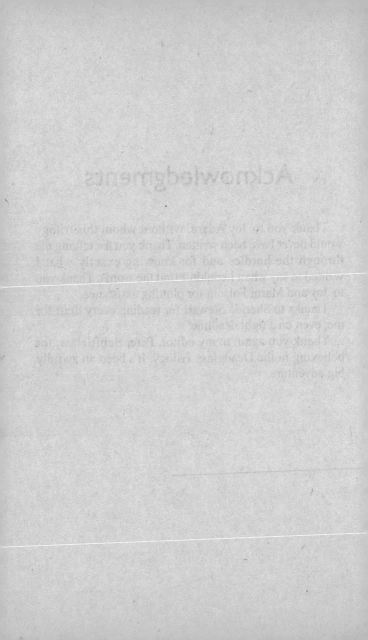

# Chapter One

*To the land of no return, the land of darkness,*
*The place where dust is their nourishment, clay their food.*
*They have no light, in darkness they dwell.*
*Clothed like birds, with wings as garments.*

—From *The Descent of the Goddess Ishtar*
   *into the Lower World*

Lucia knelt on the blood-soaked lawn of Kite Hill and let the shouts of victory wash over her like an acid rain. A stain of crimson crept up the skirt of her white gown. Strands of her snowy hair plastered across her vision as she held Johnny's limp hand. A drop of rain splattered his high cheekbone, and she wiped it away with her white sleeve. Innocent, virtuous white. She should have pulled black Kivati battle gear from the Aether like he had, except it hadn't protected him from the aptrgangr's ax. His black battle shirt stuck to his lithe, muscled torso where the blade had entered. He lay on his back, limbs akimbo, just one of the sea of bodies scattered broken across the once-green parkland. His hair, ebony as a crow's wing, was still in a sleek queue. Tears blurred her vision. They were all there—Kivati shape-shifters, Drekar dragon-shifters, human soldiers, and the demigod Kingu's possessed bodies—united and equal in death as they'd never been in life.

Not two feet away lay another body—aptrgangr, those who walked after death. Mud streaked the man's thick gray overalls. Coal dust creased the worn edges of his face and decay ate the skin of his cheeks. He'd been dead a long time—since long before the battle that had turned this hill to a graveyard. But this death had finality to it. His body lay mercifully still, ax dropped an arm's length away. The wraith that had possessed it until a few minutes ago had been banished beyond the Gate, where it belonged.

All along the hillside and down past the still-burning cylindrical towers of the Gas Works, the Aether shimmered with the exodus of souls. It should be a shining, beautiful thing, but some of the mortal decay seeped up from the bodies to twist, as a foul taint, through the fabric of the universe. The Aether had been broken since the great Unraveling seven months ago. A rogue Kivati had brought down the Gates between the Land of the Living and the Land of the Dead, unleashing a legion of souls and the Babylonian demigod Kingu into the Living World, and collapsing civilization in a rain of skyscrapers and steel.

Once freed, Kingu had gathered an army of the undead and marched on Seattle seeking Tiamat's Heart, which would give him the Babylonian Goddess of Chaos's god powers. If Lucia hadn't disobeyed the Raven Lord, blackmailed Lord Kai, and led Kivati warriors to join the battle, Kingu might have won. If she hadn't, Johnny might still be alive and it'd be only the soul-sucking Drekar and humans lying on the battlefield with their mouths open and their guts ripped out. The past and the present, the destruction of the Unraveling and the dead of the Gas Works, overlapped in her vision, and she felt the familiar beginnings of a panic attack squeeze her chest. Not again. Not *here*.

"It was a good death," a deep voice said above her.

She wiped her eyes and glanced up, hoping to see a lean, dangerous face looking into hers, the proud nose and intense, violet-black stare of the Raven. But it was only Kai. She squeezed Johnny's limp hand. "I killed him."

"Every warrior from the Western House who came knew what he was getting into. They fought for their honor and freedom. They died protecting the Kivati way. Don't take that away from them."

She gave a hopeless little laugh. "When did blackmail become the Kivati way?"

"Hey." Kai pulled her to standing and pinned her with his Thunderbird gaze. The violet bands around his black irises that marked him as a Kivati shape-shifter expanded. "You're all right, little warrior." His broad frame blocked out the sight of the hill and his fingers sent trills of Aether to lick around her skin. She heard nothing but the soft wind and his voice until her pulse slowed. "Shock is normal. This is your first battle, and you did your people proud." He wrapped his leather jacket around her, and she clutched it to her chest. Tall, muscled, and imposing like all the Thunderbirds, Lord Kai had been the only one who would risk the Raven Lord's wrath to come here. He might lead one of the four Kivati Houses, but he wasn't decent. No tailored suit could mask all that wildness. His hair was a mane of black curls and a bandolier hung desperado style across his chest. He did forbidden things just to prove he wasn't anyone's pawn, including sleeping with one of their sworn enemies, the Drekar Astrid Zetian. But if the Raven Lord, Emory Corbette, found out about Zetian, he would probably kill Kai. So it had been easy for Lucia, once she'd known his secret, to blackmail Kai into risking his men in battle fighting Kingu. There was honor in dying for the Kivati. There was none in being killed for fucking a soul-sucker.

Lucia knelt by Johnny, closed his eyes, and said a prayer to the Lady to guide him home. "He didn't get much of a reprieve."

"Seven months can seem like a lifetime to a man with a second chance."

"Corbette was merciful."

"Only for you."

She glanced across Lake Union to where dusk backlit the ruined towers of downtown Seattle. The battle had taken place at the Gas Works, an old coal gasification plant that jutted out into the lake with an excellent view of Queen Anne Hill to the southwest. She could just see the yellow walls of the palatial Kivati Hall at the top of the hill hunkering down against the night. Crows from all over the city streaked the sky black as they returned to roost on the parapets and the surrounding hilltop trees. "You better pray he'll be merciful again," she told Kai.

"You got balls of steel, Crane." Kai loomed over her. He leaned down, his velvet voice a seductive purr only loud enough for her to hear. "But I'm not going to be the one on my knees. You'll use every trick—and I mean *every*—to deflect Corbette from the truth. You better not wuss out on me when the Big Bad turns his screws in your sweet, little fingers. You take my secret to your grave."

She swallowed. Would Corbette hurt his fiancée? The prophesied Crane who was supposed to lead their people out of the darkness? She'd just undermined his rule by leading his warriors to battle against his orders. He couldn't afford to be merciful. She felt the Aether, the shining water that filled the space between molecules of air and earth, wove the fabric of time and built the Gates, heat.

Kai squeezed her arm as he flashed her a look beneath thick lashes. "Loose lips . . ."

"Got it." She straightened her spine and pulled the leather jacket around her shoulders like a shield. The jacket was permeated with the warmth of Kai's body and the calming scent of fir. She lifted her chin as Kivati shape-shifters in their totem forms shot into the air above Kivati Hall and flew toward Kite Hill. The two Thunderbirds were magnificent. Giant birds with silvery wings the size of a pterodactyl, they ate whales and could pull fiery thunderbolts from the Aether with a twitch of their fingers. A reverent hush floated across the field as men caught sight of the two beautiful creatures. Behind them flew a dozen man-sized Crows with their majestic midnight wings and cruel beaks.

But Lucia couldn't tear her eyes away from the true danger—the Raven. Awesome. Terrible. Aether crackled over his feathers and pulsed out to warp the air around her. She watched his approach as if it were a steam train barreling down on her. He landed on the hillside, and torchlight glistened off his ebony feathers as he Changed. Aether shimmered over him like a blanket being shrugged off, and when it slipped away a man stood in the giant Raven's place. Terrifyingly handsome, like a crack of lightning hurled from the Sky God's staff, he was dark and brooding and altogether arrogant. The Thunderbirds had a height and muscle advantage on him, but every inch of his frame was sleek power. Everything about him was sharp: pitiless black eyes ringed by a violet band, a hooked nose, a severe line of a mouth. He was dark everywhere she was light, with skin the color of driftwood and hair

blacker than coal. He'd pulled his clothing from the Aether
when he'd Changed, his usual three-piece perfection of a
midnight suit, silver studs in his cuff links, silver rings
in his ears. But he'd forgotten to tie his necktie, and his
shirt hung open to expose the vulnerable line of his neck.
There his pulse beat steady, controlled. And why shouldn't
it? Impeccable, immovable Emory Corbette would never
appear in public as anything less than perfect. He might
have been an automaton, all robotic movement with no
capacity for human error. No heart.

Except the Aether crackled from his skin. All the
Kivati shifters on the battlefield bowed their heads in the
face of his dominance.

"I did the right thing," she blurted. "We won. The city
is safe."

"Not here," Corbette said.

"I'm not sorry for it." Her voice rose. "Don't punish
the others. They were under my orders."

"And since when do you give orders to my Thunderbirds?"

She clutched Kai's jacket to her. The thick leather was
no shield for the Aether writhing from the Raven Lord.
He took a step toward her. The noise of the soldiers and
the cries of the wounded faded to static. How many times
had she wished for him to lose his self-control? To come
down to her level—mortal, imperfect, touchable? But
here he was with his necktie undone and anger sparkling
off him like a Death Valley sun. She was terrified. Her
totem Crane beat inside her. *Fly*, it crooned. *Fly!*

"Follow the Crane to destiny," she recited.

"Haven't you left enough ruin in your wake?"

A deep sob broke in her throat. The last line of the
prophecy said, *for behind her lies ruin*, and Lucia had
certainly caused destruction. Seven months ago her blood

had brought down the Gate to the Land of the Dead. She pulled the jacket sleeves to hide her hands. Her scars had healed—she'd never scarred easily—but the memories still woke her screaming in the middle of the night. Would the image of this battle be the next one to wake her in the dark?

"You are cruel, my lord."

Corbette's eyes tightened. "That was uncalled for." The violet band of his iris expanded, threatening to drown the black. "You make me forget myself." He held out his hand, but she stepped back.

"You expect me to be the Crane, don't you?" Had he ever looked at her as Lucia and not the prophesied Harbinger? The panic attack threatened to come back full force. She beat it down. She'd wasted too many months feeling sorry for herself. Lifting her chin, she gave him her haughtiest glare. The look was ruined by a tear that slipped free, but she pushed on. "Well, no one can follow me if I don't lead. Kingu marched on the city, and I made the call."

"I see."

"You chose to stay and guard Kivati Hall. I chose to join the Drekar and humans in the fight here. They needed us."

"You chose to join our ancient enemies instead of following my orders."

It sounded crazy when he said it.

He took a step closer, and his voice dropped to grind like the rocks of the seabed. "Did you mean to replace me on the madrona throne, then? Should I call my second and meet you at dawn?"

Her eyes widened. The transfer of power required a fight to the death, the animal way for dominance. Grace Mercer had taught her to throw a few punches, but there was no way she would survive two seconds in the ring with Corbette.

"No?" He circled her, a predator playing with his prey. The hairs on the back of her neck rose as he took a breath at the base of her neck. "You smell like him."

"It's not like that!"

"I think you'd find the weight of the crown would ground your poor fragile wings, little bird."

She clenched her teeth. He'd never spoken to her like this. He'd always been unfailingly polite, if a trifle cold. This new Corbette was seductive, but even more dangerous. "Then why marry me if I'm so fragile?" she chewed out. "Maybe you should find someone better suited to kissing your ass."

His nostrils flared. "You wish to end our engagement?"

"Please." With that cruel lie spilling off her tongue, the rest of the world snapped back to life. An all-too-real hush fell over the Kivati warriors surrounding her, silent as a catacomb.

Corbette didn't blink. His lips pulled back in polite smile. His anger dissipated, the cold searing his features again into the self-controlled alpha they knew all too well. He gave a sharp bow. "As you wish." His shoulders relaxed. He turned to Lord Kai. "Please return Lady Lucia to her parents. They have been worried about her."

Kai nodded.

Lucia watched the exchange while the Aether in her veins turned to ice. It was . . . over? Just like that? She hadn't meant to challenge Corbette's rule. She just wanted to be worthy of that stupid prophecy and mean something to her people. Something real, not an empty title. Corbette's easy dismissal reinforced all her worst fears: he'd never really wanted her. He'd wanted a figurehead, a pretty, powerless poppet to sit at his side and agree with his every whim. The hope that he had seen something more in her—Lucia, not the Crane—fractured in a million pieces.

She wished the ground would open and swallow her whole.

Corbette turned away from Lucia before he lost control of his mask of emotions. She was no longer his responsibility. He might never see her again, never watch her Change to the graceful white Crane with the flash of red at her temple, never have to interrupt his work to go chasing after her. He was free of her upsetting influence. Free of her beguiling ways. Free of the fog that she laced through his brain like some fairy light leading weary travelers off course. He wouldn't have to look at her every morning over the breakfast table and grit his teeth as she tossed his carefully laid plans on their head.

Inside, the Raven screamed. Corbette held himself back as he glared at his Thunderbird general, Lord Kai, errant head of the Western House, when what he really wanted to do was gut the man for taking his fiancée into danger and then marking her for all to see with his jacket around her shoulders. *Former* fiancée. He'd been thinking of her as delicate for so long that he'd failed to realize the moment she'd become a threat to his rule.

Directing his thoughts through the Aether, he sent Kai a message: *Meet me at the sacred circle at dawn.* The direct challenge to his authority had to be met with swift punishment. Even if Kai had done the right thing. Kai's face tightened, but he nodded. Only one man could be alpha. Only the strongest and cleverest could hold their people together.

Ye gods, wasn't the Spider tired of weaving his fate threads in such a painful tangle?

*You can't lead*, his father's voice echoed in his mind. *You have no heart.*

But what would he do with Lucia? He'd built the Kivati up from nothing, fought off the Drekar for over a century, protected their sacred powers with everything in him. He'd endured a lifetime of darkness and death with one hope guiding his hand: that the Harbinger of Destiny would finish the Drekar off once and for all. When that day came, when the Kivati lived in peace and stability, only then would he be free to relax his guard.

He recited the Spider's prophesy in his mind, looking once again for what he'd missed.

> *In an age of Darkness, the Crane will bring a great light. The people who lived in the land of the shadow of death will rise up, and the Harbinger will lead them. Cast off your shackles, oh Changers! See, oh you blind ones! Follow the Crane to destiny, for behind her lies ruin.*

How could the Lady have picked a weak young girl to vanquish their enemies? Lucia was no warrior. She could barely Change her skin. It would have to be her husband who wielded the sword. Corbette had determined that it would be him, but she hadn't been content to sit by his side and be a calming presence. She was a willful, distracting, infuriating young woman. Yet the Spider's words were clear: whomever she chose as a mate would lead their people into the future.

He didn't have the luxury of letting her decide. Could he force Kai to take her after this rebellious display? He needed someone unquestionably loyal. Kai's brother,

Jace, would have been perfect. Unfortunately it was the black sheep brother who'd survived the Unraveling. Corbette's life had been full of hard choices, but this last threatened to break him. Lucia might be happier with Kai. A man closer to her age. A man who shared her rebellious streak.

Corbette was not that man. He would never change for her, and she would never settle down.

Aether rushed through him, dizzying and hot. Corbette pulled the fraying edges of his self-control tightly around him before he lashed out. His vision fractured red. He had to get out of here. Away from the exodus of souls. Away from people he would hurt when the tainted Aether whipped out of his grasp. Away from Lucia.

"Will," he said to his second in command, "take over."

Will stepped up immediately and began barking out orders. "Kai, take her home now. Lucia, Change. Be quick."

Corbette turned his back, unable to watch Lucia's slow, painful Change to Crane. The Harbinger should have more raw power. The Raven wanted to soothe her, but Corbette couldn't afford that weakness. If he hadn't been the Raven Lord, tasked with protecting thousands of shape-shifters and the Gate between worlds, he might have tilted back her delicate pointed chin and kissed the fear from her mind. But too many lives depended on him. The best thing he could do was find her a keeper. Some-one else.

"Emory—" Will called after him.

"I'll see to Asgard," he growled, voice full of Aether.

*You can't lead*, his father's ghost whispered in his mind. *You have no laughter, no joy, no compassion.*

Leniency for the Drekar had been his father's downfall. Corbette wasn't about to relax his guard even if this Regent showed different colors.

Corbette left Will to direct his men to comb the battle-field for survivors. He stepped over bodies of the dead and skirted the corpse of a giant dragon, the empty shell no longer dangerous, the entity within simply gone. Drekar had no souls to pass through the Gate. What would it be like to cease to exist? To be barred from the Land of the Dead and the Lady's grace? He couldn't fathom it; his world revolved around serving the Lady to protect the balance of the universe. A quest he'd failed when the Gate that separated the Land of the Living from the Land of the Dead had fallen under his watch. Would the Lady still let his twin souls through the Gate when his mortal clock ran down?

Soldiers and healers worked to clear the hill of the injured and dead. He passed by stretchers, then burning trees, then the great ditch where the Drekar Regent had tried to fight off the approaching army by dropping the towers of the Gas Works from the air. As soon as he passed out of view beyond the trees, he bent over and retched his guts out.

The demigod Kingu and his wraith army had lost. Kai's men had saved the day. Corbette hadn't endangered anyone with his own out-of-control powers. Now that Kingu was defeated, maybe the Kivati would have some measure of peace in which to rebuild. Maybe he'd finally be able to find a woman to rule at his side.

Not Lucia. His hands curled into fists, talons breaking through his fingertips to pierce his palms.

When he had himself under control, he climbed Kite Hill. At the top he found Leif Asgard, the Drekar Regent, who held his woman to his side while he watched his men light bonfires to burn the dead. No bodies could be left whole to tempt the wraiths to pilot them. Kingu's force might have been defeated, but there were always more ghosts who refused to pass beyond the Gate when it was their time to go. The ghosts who stayed became wraiths, unable to taste or smell or touch unless they took over a living body.

The Regent's human mate, Grace Mercer, growled when she saw him. Short, pretty, and pugnacious, she was a handful that would keep Asgard good and busy. Her hand flew to the knife at her hip, but Asgard held her back. "You rat bastard! Letting us fight your battles for you, huh? What would happen if we'd lost? Kingu would have taken you down next. There's no excuse—"

"If I had come, I might have posed a greater threat," he said.

"Kivati and Drekar aren't in danger from wraiths."

"But how about a demigod? Or even a demigod with the Tablet of Destiny? If Kingu had managed to possess me, you would have lost for sure. Is that a chance you're willing to take?" He felt the violet in his eyes flare out to the killing edge. Asgard's woman had fire, but she was smart enough to back up.

Asgard ran a hand through his blond locks. Like his brother Norgard, he looked like a Viking berserker. He'd fought taking the Drekar crown after the Unraveling. So far his actions set him apart from his notorious brother, but one Dreki was the same as the next. A soul-sucking, evil lot of them. It was only a matter of time before the man slipped up. "Why is that? We needed your Thunderbirds and their thunderbolts. We almost lost."

"But you didn't," Corbette said. "You had the troops of the Western House under the direction of my best general. I don't see the problem."

"What are you going to do to Lucia?" Grace asked warily.

Corbette tilted his head. "As I'm not in the habit of harming women and children, nothing."

"She's not a kid anymore."

He let his short bow hide his wince. "I know. Regent. Miss Mercer."

"Wait, Corbette," Asgard called after him. "There's a problem."

"Is there?"

"Astrid Zetian turned to Kingu's side during the battle."

Not surprising that the Regent's adviser, the only female Dreki in the territory, had turned, Corbette thought darkly. The Drekar were a barely cohesive group, each one waiting to stab their leader in the back and take his place. One more reason to remind his Thunderbirds the price of loyalty. The strict hierarchy of the Kivati didn't leave room for traitors, except maybe for Kai's Western House. But his men had their uses.

"Her body is missing," Grace said. Drekar could regenerate unless beheaded.

"Where are the Tablet of Destiny and Tiamat's Heart?" Corbette asked. "You promised you had them well in hand."

Asgard turned away. "Lost in the battle."

"I see," Corbette said. Aether lashed through his body with the force of his anger.

"I can vouch that Kingu was destroyed," Grace said. "I bound him and broke him apart. But Tiamat's Heart . . . I tried sending it back across the Gate too. I failed."

He speared her with the Raven's glare. She met his eyes and shook her head. Surprising. Few shape-shifters could stand his dominance, but this human woman wouldn't be cowed. If she was the one showing Lucia how to fight, it would explain Lucia's insubordination. He had to admire courage.

"You don't sense the Heart somewhere in the Aether?" Grace asked.

"No." But how could he be sure? The Aether was twisted and tainted and uncontrollable. Who could say that the Babylonian Goddess of Primordial Chaos wasn't now swirling around their heads?

"Tiamat's Heart contains all her god powers and manifests as a very powerful wraith," Grace said. "If the Heart gets hold of the Tablet and a body, Tiamat could resurrect herself. She would be unstoppable."

He turned his glare back to Asgard. "You stole the Tablet from our safekeeping and refused to share the location of the Heart. Now you tell me Chaos is almost inevitable. And you have the gall to ask for our trust and participation?" His vision swam red. The Raven came to the fore, and the need to Change rippled over his skin.

"We still need to work together," Asgard said. "Now more than ever. The humans have only Edmund Marks to lead them, and his religion won't allow him to see reason. We needed you to stop Kingu. We will need you more if Tiamat rises. We need to set up a task force."

"Name the date, and I will send my emissary." The Lady willing, he'd have enough time to find a strong enough fourth Thunderbird general to keep the Kivati together if something happened to him. He had only three experienced leaders for the four Sacred Houses—William, Theodore, and Kai, and the latter had just openly disobeyed him. That made two he could count on. He needed to shore up the leadership structure and fast, or the Kivati risked splintering at the first sign of trouble.

Lucia. He let the image of her drift through his mind

and tip his control over to the Aether. Feathers burst through his skin in a flash of light, and he rose into the air. Rage reddened his Raven vision, and he streaked across the sky in a blaze of thunder. A kinder man would let her choose. He couldn't afford that luxury. The entire fate of their race depended on it.

# Chapter Two

"Get up, Lucy!" her sister yelled through the closed door. "You can't hide in here forever."

"I just fought a demigod," Lucia muttered. "I can do whatever the hell I want." She rolled over and buried her head under the pillow. Thin rays of sun fought their way through the crack between the drapes.

There was a loud thump, followed by muffled swearing. Another thump and a loud, ominous crack. The brass lock broke through the wood of the door frame and the traitorous door burst open. "Lady be damned," Delia swore. "When did you become such a yellow-bellied coward? You've been doing so well too." Delia stomped over and tore back the drapes. "You're missing the sun. In November!" Her sister was a sun worshipper with the misfortune to have been born in the Pacific Northwest. There was no sin so great as staying inside on a sunny day, especially during the long, dark, wet season. "I swear, Luce, if you go back to moping, I'll kill you myself."

Moping? She hadn't seen *Delia* on the battlefield. Lucia dug her fingers into the pillow, but Delia wasn't content with pulling back the ivy-embroidered drapes.

The telltale squeak of her armoire doors signaled Delia's true quest. She shot up. "Get your dirty paws off my clothes!"

"What do you need them for? It's an absolute crime to let art like this molder away." Delia sighed wistfully. "I could hate you. Beautiful, pampered, be-frocked, and you don't enjoy any of it. If I were the Raven Lord's wife, I would never wear the same outfit twice."

"There are people starving in the streets. You are so self-absorbed."

"And how does hiding away in your bedroom help any of them?"

"I'm not hiding! Besides, I'm not the Raven Lord's wife." Lucia fell back in bed and held the pillow over her face. She wished she could shut out the memory.

"Not yet."

"Not ever."

"Lucy, Lucy, Lucy." Fabric rustled in the armoire as Delia searched through the dresses. "You know nothing about men."

Lucia held herself very still.

Delia sighed again. "I don't mean that, sweetie. Rudrick wasn't a man. He was slime. Every moment you spend letting what he did keep you from happiness is a moment he wins. Don't let him win. He isn't worth the spit on the soles of your boots."

"You don't know—"

"Lady be! You wouldn't talk to me for months. Do you think I didn't suffer knowing how he hurt you? But you just have to move on."

Lucia set her jaw. She'd heard it before from her mother and aunts and cousins and well-meaning strangers. *Move on. Choose to be happy.* Like it was so simple.

"Wow. This teal is to die for. How come I've never

HEARTS OF CHAOS 19

seen you wear this dress? It would be awesome with my eyes." Delia, with the same tact she always showed, moved on. "Or your eyes, I guess. Though mine have more green in them. Yours are just too blue. You should let me wear it."

"Go ahead. Just go away."

"I did that last time, and I'm sorry for it. I won't do it again." The mattress sagged as her sister sat on it. "Look." Delia lowered her voice. The magnolia tree outside scraped against the windowpane. Come spring it would be full of large white blossoms, but now it was only a jumble of gnarled branches. Year-round it was the perfect place for crows and other birds to perch and watch and listen. Aether-strong Kivati could connect their consciousness to animals, and birds made the best spies. If Kivati were listening in, the thin walls of the old house wouldn't muffle loud voices. "Mom and Dad are beside themselves that you broke the engagement. Even if it was your choice, no one understands why a girl, especially one with a certain . . . history . . . would turn down the most powerful match in the land for a disreputable Thunderbird. Personally"— Delia leaned close—"I'd let Kai rock my world any day. You have such an enviable choice. But why choose at all? Just imagine both of them together."

"Delia!"

"Come on. Imagine it."

"No!"

"Pity." Delia sighed.

Heat rushed to her cheeks. She hadn't, but now that Delia suggested it, images flooded her brain. The strict Corbette and debauched Kai and her and . . . "Okay, okay. I'm awake!"

"Seriously, though, people are talking about you."

"You barged in here to tell me that? What else is new?"

"It's different this time. You allied yourself to Corbette's top general and joined the Drekar against Kingu. You've done a one-eighty again. After the Unraveling, you were so quiet I was worried you were broken."

That made two of them. "I couldn't stand by and watch Kingu win," Lucia protested. "How could you? How could anyone?"

"And that's why I back you and Kai in the race."

Lucia stared at her sister. Delia had the same oval face but tanned skin. Sleek black hair, thick black lashes, and hazel eyes set her apart from Lucia's paleness, especially after Lucia's hair had grown in white after the Unraveling. She was glad Delia hadn't gone anywhere near the battlefield. Worse than being there herself would have been seeing someone she loved in danger. "What race? The battle is over."

Delia shook her head. "It's only just begun."

"I'm not siding with Kai against Corbette."

"That's not what it looks like."

"But it's the truth!"

"Truth is relative, Luce. We've been at the edge of revolution for a long time. The stifling edicts of the Raven Lord—"

"They keep us safe."

"Do they? They didn't stop the Unraveling. They didn't defeat the Drekar. They haven't stopped our blood from thinning and fewer and fewer Kivati being able to connect to the Lady's sacred powers."

"What would you suggest?" Lucia asked.

"Open up to the wider world. Why should we hide in the shadows? The Kivati are the last bastion of magic. We shouldn't have to hide from the humans."

"Now you sound like Rudrick."

That brought Delia up short. She raised her chin. "Is that what he told you?"

Lucia looked away. "Corbette pinned his hopes on me. The Harbinger. The Crane. I can't lead the Kivati into a bright new tomorrow. I can barely Change my shape. Rudrick seemed so persuasive."

Delia hugged her. "He was scum of the earth. Forget every word he said."

"Even if you're saying the same thing?"

Delia pulled back. "I would never tell you to sacrifice yourself for the Kivati! I love you. If it were a choice, I'd tell everyone else to fend for themselves. You're my sister. You're irreplaceable."

"Thanks, Del." She wasn't so sure her mom and dad felt that way. They'd been pushing her on Corbette since the first moment she'd walked out of the woods after her spirit quest with the totem of Crane.

"So you haven't given up Corbette?"

"The engagement is off. Corbette was so relieved. His whole body relaxed like I'd been an albatross around his neck and he'd finally cut the chain. I've never been so embarrassed." Tears welled in her eyes, and she wiped them away.

"Gods, Luce. I'm sorry." Delia folded her in another hug. "But can't you see? You have nothing to be ashamed of." Lucia gave a choked laugh. "You don't! You've always been so strong. I know I'm the ditzy sister. I've always been a little jealous of you with all the attention, but you took more than your share of public censure. I'd never have stood up to all that. And you disobeyed Corbette! You led the most disreputable Thunderbird and the Western House against a demigod!"

"But nothing I do makes things better. My blood killed half our people and decimated our world. More died in this last battle because of me, and now you're telling me I'm on the forefront of a revolt. Who would lead without Corbette? Me? You've got to be kidding me. Every time I try to help, people die."

Delia stood and strolled back to the armoire. "Well, you can't stay in here. People will think you're hiding again. Make up your mind quick, and make a stand: Team Kai or Team Corbette."

"I'm not trying to throw him off the throne!"

"But you could. He's losing support and fast. You've got to put on your best dress and wave it like a red flag."

"That's treason," she whispered.

Delia's smile turned serious. "Only if you lose."

Lucia studied her room: the pale pink roses on the wallpaper; the vanity with its finger-thin spindle legs; the row of porcelain dolls, hair and makeup and frilly dresses still in mint condition, never played with, never loved to pieces like normal dolls. Her mother had designed this room to be everything the perfect Kivati lady should be: elegant and dainty and demure.

She'd never been that girl. It was too late to start now.

"I'm wearing the teal," Lucia said.

"Good. I wanted the lavender anyway."

With her sister's help, she dressed. Lace and silk instead of leather and bone, but it was battle gear just the same. Her stomach knotted up in the soles of her feet, she left the cocoon of her bedroom and emerged into the low boil of revolution.

Insubordination must be punished. "Say it again," Corbette commanded.

"I fucked Astrid Zetian," Kai bit out.

Corbette wondered how Lucia had found out. It had

taken him an hour to break the truth from Kai's lips. He brought his half-shifted hand across his Thunderbird general's chest. The talons carved shallow cuts that welled quick with blue-crimson life. Kai clamped his teeth but couldn't keep the roar of pain silent. Both men had stripped to the waist. They wore the red sash of formal challenge around their waists. The blood flowed down to the sash and was swallowed up.

"My trusted Thunderbird general," Corbette said. *My friend.*

"I betrayed the honor of the Kivati by sleeping with the enemy." Lines of strain etched Kai's face. Blood trickled from a dozen gashes across his tanned skin. "I led my men against Kingu and his army of the dead, which was—"

"Joined—again!—with our ancient Drekar enemies. Do you wish to be one of them? Where is your allegiance?" Corbette growled. They fought in an ancient circle made of bone and ash. Three witnesses—Corbette's second, Will; Kai's second, Theo; and the Sprit Seeker—watched from behind the burnt line. The circle had been dug one foot into the soil and lined with rocks. Those who had died here never left; their bodies had been burnt and their ashes rubbed into the thick perfect circle of ancient magic.

"I am loyal to you," Kai said.

"And your third sin . . . ," Corbette whispered.

For a moment Kai faltered, then his features hardened. "Lucia chose her own path."

Red fire shot across Corbette's vision and a burst of Aether singed the tips of his fingers.

Kai used the distraction to launch himself at Corbette's middle. Kai's bulk should have taken him down, but no one could match Corbette's manipulation of the Aether.

He dug his toes into the earth and connected to the beating heart of the world. The blood pulsing in his ears echoed the beat, and he drew in the gossamer threads of the fabric of the universe. The slippery Aether bucked in his grip as he struggled to keep his rage in check. Sweat dripped down from his hairline. He neared the edge and his vision flickered black and violet, strange oscillations in the air as the Aether and all its connections funneled through his body. He threw a loop of Aether to catch the larger man around the middle and hook him off his feet. Kai shot backward and hit the invisible barrier of the sacred circle. His wild mane shot out like he'd stuck his fingers in an electrical socket, and he collapsed to the ground.

Corbette's vision cleared. With heavy steps, he walked over to where his Thunderbird general lay on the ground. "She is the fate of the race. She is not at liberty to choose her own path." If any of them were.

The Aether wall dispersed, and Theo and the Spirit Seeker moved to Kai's side. A sun break illuminated his slowly rising chest. The Spirit Seeker waved her hand over Kai, and with a smooth lick of Aether—so different from Corbette's brutal hold—the Thunderbird woke.

Will came to stand next to Corbette. The Thunderbird, head of the Southern House, had been his closest adviser since boyhood and had helped Corbette put back together the Kivati after his joke of a father had let their ancient enemies, the Drekar, move into their territory. Gray threaded his hair. The light lines on his square face made him look distinguished. The faint scar down his cheek, intimidating. Will had seen more battles than the other Thunderbirds combined. He was a ruthless adversary and loyal to a fault. "You let him live."

Corbette forced his breathing to slow. "What would you have done, Will?" He watched Theo, the third

Thunderbird general and head of the Eastern House, help Kai up. A web of bruises spiraled across Kai's back over the intricate tattoos that lined his spine.

"Your father would have—"

"I know what my father would have done." Corbette turned away. His father had set these events in motion. Halian should have killed the Dreki Sven Norgard when the damned soul-sucker had first shown up with his Norse followers, but he had wanted to join the wider world and the riches that went with trade. He'd been a jovial man, loved by his people and humans alike. His selfish desires had put the future of the race in jeopardy. That first battle had burned the city to the ground and cost Halian his life. It had taken Corbette a century to rebuild, only to watch his kingdom be destroyed in the Unraveling. If Halian had only had the self-control to do what was needed . . . none of this would have happened.

Corbette was doomed to spend eternity cleaning up his father's mess. He had to keep a tighter rein on his people, even if that made him seem heartless. His father had always said he was a disappointment. *The feeling was mutual, Father.*

Corbette stepped out of the circle and released his mental connection to the heart of the earth. Climbing up to the edge of the line of rocks, he looked down over the crumbled remains of downtown Seattle, and Will followed him. Queen Anne Hill occupied critical ground in the middle of the city. Directly to the south lay the crater that had opened up during the Unraveling. He could feel the Aether twisting up from the Spider's sacred caves beneath the city, and it reeked like fish left out too long in the sun. From the west, the wind blew in from Puget Sound. This morning sun wouldn't last; already clouds covered the horizon. He took a deep breath of sea air and let the salt cleanse the smell of blood from his nose. "I can't afford to lose another Thunderbird."

"You can't afford to look weak. The people are restless. They will only follow the strongest of the pack. You need to cut all dissent."

"And Lucia?"

"Her most of all. She must be contained." Will followed Corbette's gaze down to the crater. The sea waves nibbled at the edge of it, some pouring down into the bucket at high tide. "She is the Harbinger, but so far all she's brought us is destruction."

"What would you have me do?"

"Clip her wings."

Gods, he despised that thought. Rudrick had almost done it for him, and Corbette had hated to see her so listless. Every night he replayed the scene of the Unraveling in his mind: rushing through the sacred underground caves as the earthquake shook the floor out from under him and finding the heap of beautiful girl collapsed a few feet away. Her blond hair had flowed like a river of silk across the trembling dirt floor. Red had stained her white gown. Her virgin's blood had opened the Gate. He'd been too late to save her.

He would carry the slash on his soul into the Land of the Dead with him. There was no magic that could remove his great dishonor. He realized, to his shock, that he missed the girl who had driven him mad with her insubordination. But that girl didn't fit into his tightly controlled world. What could he do with her?

Will shifted his weight. "You carry too many burdens, my friend. Let me shoulder some for you. Lucia is a liability. You should leave some part of your life for your own desires. Take a wife. A woman who will be loyal, who will make a hearth and home that will revive you when the burden of rule is too great. You don't need to deny yourself that small gift."

"Any woman by my side becomes a target for my enemies."

"Lucia was never a good match for you. Her Aether skill is weak and she's willful. You need someone peaceful. Someone who will stay put. If she follows orders and stays home—which the Crane is obviously incapable of—your mate won't be in danger. Kivati Hall is impenetrable; we can protect her there. A woman would help ground you. The Lady never meant a man to live alone."

Corbette could see the woman Will would pick for him: a biddable, pretty young thing who would smile and entertain and never disagree with him. Grace and charm and soothing calm. Everything he'd once thought he wanted, but now it sounded stultifying.

He turned to watch the waves of Puget Sound stretch out in shades of cerulean and steel. He could follow it north, out into the open ocean, and let the wind carry him to distant possibilities. *Change*, the Aether called, but he turned from the wild sea. "I let Kai live because I can't afford to lose another general. We need four strong Thunderbirds to keep the Houses secure, and we only have three. If someone finds both the missing Tablet of Destiny and Tiamat's Heart, we will need every scrap of manpower we have."

"And Asgard said Zetian is missing? Can we trust Kai to fight with us in that case?"

"I believe the Thunderbird's heart is in the right place, even if his dick isn't."

Will caught his arm. "Are you sure you're not letting your emotions rule your judgment, just like your father did?"

Corbette shook off Will's hold. Aether whipped around

him, whirling and frothing like a snowmelt river around a boulder. The Aether was a river of shimmering, massless liquid that filled the universe. Since the Unraveling, it wasn't right. No longer conducting electricity was the least of the problems this created. It surged through him, wrong, tainted, and sorrowful, and he could no longer depend on his power to manipulate it. How could he put the world right again? "The Crane is the key to it all, but I just can't see how the Lady intends us to use her."

"Let me take care of her for you."

"Lock her in a cage like some exotic bird?"

"I'll marry the girl. I'll keep her leashed. You won't have to worry about her anymore."

And watch his most trusted adviser bed the woman he had planned to marry? He was a man of honor and discipline, but he wasn't a saint. "I have it under control," Corbette said. He resisted the urge to rub his temple as a migraine stabbed through him.

Will raised an eyebrow. "And the rebellion?"

"I have a plan to tie up our loose ends." May the Lady grant him strength to see it through.

Kivati Hall was overrun with people. They spilled out of the palatial mansion, past the cedar porch, and onto the green lawns. Even the slight drizzle didn't chase them away. Ladies and gentlemen in their Sunday best, only slightly worn about the edges from the months of postapocalyptic hell. Kingu had been defeated, and everyone wanted to see and be seen. Life could finally return to normal. The majesty and grace of the Kivati people had not been cowed.

"Eyes up," Delia hissed. "They're here to see you.

You met Kingu on the battlefield. Don't let these geese intimidate you."

Lucia raised her chin, pasted on the ghost of her old haughty smile, and steeled herself for sharp cuts. The field was awash with striped umbrellas and bright splashes of yellow rain boots. As she passed beneath the spirit bells chiming in the wind and entered the imposing wrought-iron gate, a whisper spread through the crowd like wildfire. She started to sweat. She had expected public censure, but the expressions that greeted her were about half-and-half. Some nodded in approval. Others turned their backs in scorn. Lucia raised her chin and held Delia's hand as she strolled down the long brick walk to the mansion's front doors.

Lady Alice, Corbette's notorious sister, met her on the porch. Alice was the only Kivati Lucia had ever heard of willingly taking a Drekar mate. She didn't know if Alice had been threatened with death; all she knew was that Alice and Brand had fled Seattle and stayed away for over a century. They'd only returned after the Unraveling. Her Drekar mate wasn't welcome at the Hall, but Lucia had seen him before. He was everything one would expect from a Dreki: built, blond, and beautiful. Alice was tall and strong, with a sharp nose like her brother and long black hair with a hint of auburn. "I need to talk to you."

Delia tried to extricate her hand, but Lucia squeezed it tight. She didn't want to be alone with Alice. She didn't trust the gleam in the other woman's eye.

"Let's go inside," Alice said. Lucia followed, but dragged Delia beside her. She was nervous about Alice's intentions, but even more curious. Alice hadn't been seen in the Kivati territories since the Great Seattle Fire, when her father had been killed and Sven Norgard had burned the city to the ground. Afterward, Corbette had forbidden her name to be mentioned. Lucia had never known she existed until recently.

Alice led the way to the conservatory. Inside, the air was humid. Flowering trees and exotic ferns crowded the tables. The roof and three walls were glass panels between a lattice of iron. Suspended from the ceiling was a miniature iron railroad track; a tea train, puffing peppermint steam, ran between the kitchens and the small round tables in a clover loop. The train stopped at each table to unload its fare. Each car held a different delicacy: cucumber and ginger sandwiches, cinnamon cookies, and scones with huckleberry preserves.

This afternoon every seat was occupied, but Alice glared at some teenagers in the corner and they fled. She snapped her fingers, and a waiter cleared the table. Lucia closed her gaping mouth. She'd imagined Corbette's sister to be the perfect Kivati lady—elegant, polite, and proper. But Alice had all of Corbette's arrogance and none of his care for decorum. "Sit," Alice ordered.

Lucia sat with Delia beside her.

A woman from the next table turned to her. "You did well, Crane." The others from her table nodded in agreement.

"Didn't think you had it in you," a man said. "It will be good to have a new direction."

Lucia smiled tightly. Most of these people hadn't talked to her since the Unraveling. Overnight she'd become something of a sensation. Not an object of pity anymore, but a figurehead of a growing movement she didn't want.

She was not trying to overthrow Corbette. She would not.

Farther down the room, she saw some of her cousins sitting with their parents—Milo, who'd not yet gone through his first Change, and Estelle, a girl only a little

younger than Lucia. Estelle had gone on her vision quest
and come back empty-handed. No totem gift from the
Lady. No sacred powers, weak or otherwise. Every year
there were more kids like her who didn't make it, one of
the reasons Corbette insisted Kivati marry Kivati, to keep
their sacred blood and sacred powers pure. Milo waved.
Estelle usually ignored her, jealous of Lucia's Crane, but
now she was watching her thoughtfully.

Lucia wished she had some great wisdom to impart.
She knew the feeling of being a disappointment all too
well. Aether-weak with a long-awaited totem. Maybe it
didn't matter what gifts the Lady blessed you with, but
the choices you made. Her gifts certainly hadn't helped
her in the battle with Kingu—the Crane wasn't a fighter.
She'd used a secret to blackmail Kai, completely without
honor or gifts, and that little action seemed to have set a
bomb off in Kivati Hall. Around them, Kivati lords and
ladies openly debated the future of the race. For the first
time in Lucia's life, the blind obedience that Corbette
wielded was nowhere to be seen.

"Tell me," Alice said, drawing attention back to her.
"How did you convince Kai?"

Lucia only smiled and pushed the button in the middle
of the table to call the tea train. The fickle sun had returned to its November roost behind the clouds. A raindrop
or two splattered the glass ceiling. The train arrived with
a burst of peppermint steam, and the tea caddy dropped
down from the first car to fill her cup.

"You can trust me, Lucia," Alice said. "What is your
next step? I'm not a pawn for my brother, if that's your
concern. We've never seen eye-to-eye on important issues,
and anything—or any person—who upsets the status quo
is of interest to me."

"No offense, but you've been gone for a long time to

suddenly express deep interest in the affairs of the Kivati."

"I've kept well informed. The Crows are not loyal only to Emory."

Lucia slowly measured two scoops of colored sugar into her cup. "Watching is not the same as actively participating."

"What do you think this is, a democracy?" Alice laughed. "Emory crafted the perfect dictatorship, and he made it very clear what he would do to my mate if we ever returned. There's been no room for dissent for a hundred years." She leaned forward. "Until now."

Lucia took a fortifying sip of tea. She glanced to her sister. Delia stuffed a huckleberry scone in her mouth. No help from that corner. "Maybe I'll look for a mate." Delia choked, and Lucia had to pat her on the back. "Or not. I want to be useful to the Kivati. I'm not happy sitting on the sidelines and watching our people suffer."

"That's what I wanted to hear," Alice said. "So what do you plan to do about it? Join with Kai? Ally with a Dreki and really shake things up?"

"Good Lady, no." Lucia surprised herself. What did normal girls do at eighteen? Maybe she could go to college. Get a job. If there still were colleges and jobs post-Unraveling. Maybe she should *build* a college so that Kivati women with weak or nonexistent Aether skills like her wouldn't be held back by the Kivati's stranglehold on tradition and antiquity. What a thought. Her mother would have a coronary.

"Give her a break," Delia said. "She just earned her freedom. Let a girl play the field a little."

Alice set down her teacup. "I'm as much for women's emancipation as the next feminist, but people need to know if you're not going to marry because . . ."

"Because I'm damaged goods?" Lucia bit out.

Delia squeezed her hand. "Be free, Luce. It's a new beginning. No dead Babylonian gods marching on the city. No restrictive engagements tying you down."

Lucia had a brief image of Corbette tying her ankle and wrist to the massive four-poster bed, the crimson of the silk bindings like a slash of blood against the dark mahogany and his midnight sheets.

And then the daydream faded beneath the real memory of the ritual in the Sacred Caves beneath the city. Her limbs tied to the stone altar. Her lifeblood flowing in rivulets into the ceremonial trough to make the Gate come crashing down.

Stop it. *Stop it!* The Raven Lord didn't want her anymore, and no wonder, when she couldn't think of a man without panic. She'd worked so hard with Kayla, the healer, to fuse the broken rents in her spirit. Grace, the aptrgangr hunter, had taught her to fight so she'd never be a victim again. And now Emory Corbette, who gave up control for no man, had set her free to choose her own path. A gift, precious as an ice crystal. She should be grateful.

She cupped her hands around the tea mug, but there wasn't enough heat in the whole pot to warm her.

The tables nearby had been eavesdropping, and the usual polite conversation turned heated. Buckner, the head of the Cougar clan, actually thumped on his table to get his point across. The china tinkled like a death rattle. His pretty young mate threw up her hand to stabilize the teacup from spilling on the baby nursing at her breast. They had no reason to welcome change, but the Coyote who was their dining companion stood up and growled.

"Don't be naive," Alice said. She waved off the sandwiches. So did Lucia, her appetite gone. A splatter of rain hit the windows overhead. The train engine gave a little hiccup of steam and chugged off to the next table. "The Gate might be closed, Kingu might be defeated, but the Kivati are not safe by a long shot. I want to know what my brother is up to. Do you actually believe he let you go? The Harbinger?"

"What do you mean?"

"He hasn't been himself, but you'll still have to pry control from his cold dead hands. Emory will crush this dissent, and he will be ruthless. He's just biding his time. You look like you're shacking up with Kai—"

"I'm not!"

"Doesn't matter. You positioned yourself against him, and he's coming for you."

"He would never hurt me."

Alice set her teacup down. A bit of tea spilled over the rim. She set her hands carefully in her lap, and Lucia realized they'd been shaking. "I'm his flesh and blood, and I've been banished for over a century. You might be the Crane, but you're nothing but a tool to him."

Lucia felt cold down to her bones. "What do you know that you're not telling me?"

"Find yourself a strong ally and quickly."

A huge black bird crashed into the windows and rattled the ceiling of glass. The glass cracked at the point of collision and split like a forked thunderbolt down to the ground. A second later another bird followed, and the two rolled across the curved roof, clawing and screeching and stabbing with their knifelike beaks. The room erupted. Ladies in pastel afternoon gowns and lords in dark three-piece suits rushed to the windows to get a better view.

"What's going on?" Delia asked. "Is that . . . Rafe?"

Lucia sucked in a breath as a crimson stream of blood shot across the windows. Long black feathers stuck in the leaded seams and across the smear of red. Rafe was one of Kai's Crows in the Western House. Was this the first bloodshed between Kai's and Corbette's supporters?

Alice didn't move.

"You know," Lucia accused. "What is it?"

"My brother pulled an ancient Kivati rite out of the history books. It's a challenge: brawn, brains, and heart."

"But Corbette is the strongest," Delia said. "That's why he's king. He'd win any challenge."

"He's not going to enter," Alice said. "He's going to find a new head of the Northern House to replace Jace Raiden and tie up all his loose ends with one fell swoop. The new head will be completely dependent on Emory's support until he brings the loyalty of his House under wing."

"So he'll firm up the hierarchy of the Kivati with a new general, but what do you mean, 'all his loose ends'?" Lucia asked. "What else?"

"You will crown the victor of the tournament," Alice said, "and as part of his prize for winning, he gets your hand in marriage."

Lucia felt her blood run hot and cold, ice and hellfire dancing along already tight nerves.

"So figure out who you can live with and start making connections," Alice said. "Because you don't want Emory picking out your husband for you. You have a tiny sliver of leeway to influence who wins the tournament, but you've got to start pulling strings now."

Lucia thought she might be sick. "How kind of him," she said, tongue firmly in her cheek, "to give me any say at all."

# Chapter Three

Lucia tuned out the buzz of neighboring tables and stood, making sure her face didn't reveal the tempest brewing beneath her skin. She gave her dining companions a tight nod and walked away, out of the conservatory and down the hall. The news was already spreading. Her feet slowly picked up speed. She would outrun the panic attack that clutched at her chest. Following nothing but the eddies of Aether, the wood-paneled walls blurred as she passed. *Away*, she thought. That was all that mattered. Far and farther still, until she left the last passing stranger and found a door that wasn't locked. She wasn't going to lose it in front of people. She wasn't going to lose it at all. Inside, a library. In her anger, the Aether sprung from her hand and slammed the door shut behind her, leaving her in a dimly lit room, air thick with ink and old paper, leather and cloves, and blessed, blessed silence.

That bastard. She hurled her small purse against the far wall, where it bounced off the sturdy row of books and fell to the ground in a scattering of change. "Gaaaaaaaah!" He let her think she was free. Free to make her own decisions and free to choose her own path and free to find love. But no. How silly of her. Of course the Raven Lord couldn't leave her well enough alone. Of course the man who loved control more than his own mother would try to manipulate her into doing exactly what he wanted. He didn't come right out and arrange a match for her. That would be too lowering. By calling the tournament, he gave her the appearance of freedom, while still getting exactly what he wanted: her tied up and off his hands.

Lady damn him!

She turned around and ran smack into a black waistcoat. Firm, which meant it hid muscle. Black, which could mean any number of men. But the telltale scent of ink and cedar was enough to make her stumble back. Corbette. His large hands seized her arms and kept her standing. He had long fingers, like a pianist, and square nails. Blue and black lines ran across skin. She expected to find diamond cuff links, but in a rare show of skin, he'd taken off his jacket and rolled up his sleeves. He had the forearms of a man who dug coal for a living with the ink-stained fingers of a poet. As body parts went, the forearm was not the most seductive, but never before had she felt quite so weak at the sight of so much strength.

She could feel his pulse vibrating through his hands into her bones, and the blood in her body pulled along to its piper's tune. Her heart sped, her breath hitched. A little stumble and a stutter that gave her away. The threat of panic faded completely, replaced with emotions of a hotter kind.

And still, she hadn't looked up into his face.

And still, he hadn't spoken a word.

But the moment stretched. How could she not have noticed the room was occupied when he heated it with his presence? Of course, there was no room that he didn't own.

There was no man, woman, or child in all of Kivatidom that didn't call him lord and master.

The Crane inside her stretched as tendrils of Aether rolled down his skin and into hers. Little pulses of life and magic. Little furls of heat.

He shouldn't have this effect on her. He saw her as nothing more than a tool.

Rage curled tightly in a ball in her chest. She pulled her lips in an irreverent grin, surprised that the old expression slipped smoothly over her features like an old love. She'd been good at needling him once. She could do it again. Never let the bastards see you cry.

She looked up into eyes screaming with violet, the pupils so black they were nothing but pinpricks into the Spider's realm. Cold and sharp and hungry.

Whatever sarcastic comment she'd been about to say went numb on her lips.

He broke the silence first. "Who is chasing you?"

"No one. I'm just starved for a good book."

"Help yourself." He motioned to the stacked shelves. The flash of his smile drew her eyes down to his lips. Gods. He'd never even kissed her. Was she so undesirable? So untouchable that she inspired no lust, no passion? Well, fuck it. Rising on her tiptoes, she had the brief glimpse of his lips parting in surprise, his eyes widening, before she took what she'd always wanted from him.

Anger gave way to heat. Aether sparked where their lips met. If he hadn't been holding so tightly to her arms, she would have fallen backward. He didn't give her the chance. The Aether shocked down every nerve ending straight to her core, and suddenly she was wet and aroused and wound tighter than a spindle.

He set her away from him.

"What was that?" he asked, voice like uncut diamonds.

She touched her lips with a shaking hand. "A kiss." *I think.* Lady be, if that was what one kiss between them was like, maybe it was a good thing they'd never made it this far.

"Ah." He released her and took a wide step back. His straight ebony hair tufted out from his sculpted jaw. If the Drekar were angels of light, he was the prince of darkness, and he looked truly mad in this moment.

"Is that all you can say?"

"Lady Lucia—"

"Lady!" How could he distance them after a kiss like that?

"Always."

Corbette watched her eyes flash fire. Lady be praised, the battle with Kingu hadn't taken what was left of her spunk. If anything, it had restored it. She hadn't been herself since the Unraveling.

Neither had he.

He hadn't drunk more than a finger of gin to take the edge off, but after that blast of Aether he felt a full three sheets to the wind. He couldn't trust himself around her. With that anger bubbling to the surface she was once again the girl who'd driven him half mad, except now he couldn't delude himself. She was a woman. Not the woman he'd thought he wanted. Not the calm, peaceful, elegant influence that'd make a good queen.

She was a woman he couldn't get out of his head. Wrong for him. Wrong for the Kivati. And, good gods, he wanted her. The tournament had to happen. Will was right: she had to be contained and off-limits to him. Once she was safely wed, her mate could protect her. "You've heard the news," he said.

Her hands balled into her skirt.

"As the Crane, it's your responsibility—"

"You didn't even have the courtesy of asking me."

"It's not about you."

"My marriage isn't about me?" Angry pink splotches appeared on her high cheekbones. "Of course not. What am I saying? It has never been about me."

"That's not true—"

"Gods!" She spun and walked to the edge of the room. He watched her hips sway away from him. He liked the view too much, but she was off-limits. Turning again, she stalked part of the way back.

"You have your pick. The tournament only helps you decide from the strongest and smartest of the pack," he said.

"What if I don't wish to marry?"

He paused. "You must." *Because I can't have you.*

She threw her hands up with a growl. "Haven't you ever wanted to rebel?"

"Never."

"You've never wanted to throw off everyone's expectations and live only for yourself? Think what you might do if you weren't the Raven."

"But I am—"

"You could do anything. There would be no one and nothing to tell you what to say or think or do. You could be free."

"You think someone told me to do this work? I chose this path." He stepped closer to her and let her feel the power in his body. He moved for no man. Every action he'd ever taken had been a carefully measured risk. "This is my vocation. I hold this responsibility because there is no one else to do it, and the work is great. Thousands depend on me. Of course I feel the weight, but there is honor in serving my people. Would I trade it all for the ability to cut loose and drink till dawn and gamble my fortune away? Would I give up—"

"Control."

"—*responsibility* in order to waste my life away in petty, selfish, narcissistic pleasure? Never in a million years." Lifting her delicate chin with his finger, he forced her to meet his eyes. She held the dominance in his gaze for a long heartbeat, then looked away. Leading the force against Kingu had restored some of her self-confidence. He wished he could have been there to see it. "Those of us destined to lead must put our own desires aside for the good of the whole. We can't afford to be selfish. I learned that the hard way from my father. We sacrifice, but we get something infinitely better in return: the knowledge that our people will be healthy and whole. You and I are cogs in the Lady's great spinning wheel. It's enough to know that our efforts won't be in vain." It had to be enough.

His words dimmed the spark in her eyes. She dropped her gaze to his chest.

"You can do this, Lucia."

"Yes, Lord Raven."

"Good." He dropped his hand before he could reach for her. The woman destroyed his carefully calibrated peace of mind. How he'd ever thought he could marry her and stay sane was a mystery.

"Smile, darling," Constance said, brushing a stray wisp of hair from Lucia's face and tucking it behind her ear. "This show is for you."

Lucia gave a tight-lipped smile. Her mother was happy Lucia had agreed to show up, and she still harbored the illusion that Corbette planned to swoop in, win the contest, and redeem her eldest daughter. On Constance's other side, Lucia's father, Milton, gave a steady rundown of the contestants, their net worth and their political and Aether power. If her mother had allowed it, he would have been placing bets on the winners like horses at the Kentucky Derby.

Sunday evening spread pink and gold across the sky, bathing Queen Anne with the promise of new hope. The steep hill overlooking the crumbling downtown could have been plucked right from the turn of the twentieth century. The Queen Anne houses in pastels and ginger-bread that gave the hill its name wound around and over the hill like lattice frosting on a wedding cake. The imposing Georgian mansion splashed yellow and white against the blue. The wide cedar veranda and long grassy lawns were packed like a carnival—balloons, kites, and kettle corn included.

Lucia stewed. She barely saw the muddy ring where three combatants fought for her hand. Muscle and skin and testosterone . . . and it was all for her. The tournament would run for a week. Today was a show of physical prowess. Tomorrow, cunning. Tuesday would be the test of heart.

"You have to admit, this is pretty cool," Delia said. "When have you ever seen Kivati showing off their skills in the open?"

All along the edge of the park, overlooking Elliott Bay, Kivati showed off their Aether skills. Earth workers blew cannonballs of dirt across the bay toward Alki and coaxed roses from the ashen ground. Water workers called sculptures of ice from the frozen waves and dashed their opponents' creations against the rocks. Kivati with air power swooped in totem form across the sky, diving and tearing at each other. Feathers rained down on the lawn. The Thunderbirds hadn't started pulling thunderbolts out of the air yet, but they'd probably wait until nightfall when the blue blasts of condensed Aether sparkled and singed against the night sky.

"Never in my life," Constance said. She wore her best dress, ready to impress the contestants as the mother of the bride. Her skin and hair shone, but her eyes were tight. "Never have we lived so openly."

"So why don't you look more relaxed?" Lucia asked.

"A long life of conditioning. Be secret: be safe. You have it so good, Lucia. You don't know what it was like growing up outside the shelter of Kivati Hall. An outsider, always on the run. Your grandparents would have called you spoiled, free to sit here, nice gowns and soft fingers. When I think of Sarah's sacrifice—" Constance broke off and took out a white handkerchief to dab her eyes. Her mother's sister had been kidnapped and killed by Drekar right before Lucia's birth. She hated to talk about it. "You have a chance to make something of yourself. To be something and prove everyone wrong. Don't mess it up."

Milton patted his wife's hand. "Enough of that. Look how many warriors are out vying for her hand. We'll be rid of her soon enough." Her father had been half joking, but her mother burst into tears and turned to sob into his jacket. He glared at Lucia from over her head, brown mustache twitching. "Before this day is through, love, I'm sure Lucy will have a pick. The strongest warrior of the lot. She'll be safe, don't you worry."

"But she doesn't ever l-listen!" Constance cried. "She throws away everything we've sacrificed for her."

"There, there," Milton soothed.

Lucia turned away. Her parents were right on one aspect: this was worth fighting for. To be free with their Lady-blessed gifts. To live openly with their totems. To be safe walking down the street unescorted without fear of assault or kidnapping from their enemies, as her aunt Sarah should have been safe. The Kivati way deserved to be protected, and Corbette had to be applauded for saving it from the wreckage of his father's rule. Without him, the Kivati ability to Change and touch the Aether might have died out long ago. Corbette fought against that bleak future, a never-ending quest. But she didn't think the old protectionist ways would work in the new post-Unraveling world. The Kivati needed to be leaders in rebuilding civilization, not separate and secluded like they'd been in the past.

Delia cheered at something in the ring, and Lucia turned back to the combatants. "If Georgie were here—"

"Georgie is dead," Lucia said. *I killed her.*

Delia paused. "Yes, well, Georgie would have loved this. Maybe she's still watching from the other side of the Gate." Georgie would've been leaning over the banister whistling catcalls and making rude jokes. Lucia missed her. Georgie would've been the first person to comfort Lucia after the Unraveling. She would never have given her distance and space and left her alone to fade away in spirit if not in body. But Georgie, like so many others, hadn't survived the Unraveling, and Lucia had been left alone to mourn her friend with the black mark of her death on her conscience.

Lucia had spent far too much time trying to be perfect to please Corbette and her parents. She'd almost forgotten who she'd once been—the girl who popped gum and sang off-key in the Raven Lord's presence just to get him to notice her, the girl who'd evaded her guards and snuck out to the Drekar's illicit club, the girl who took risks just to prove she was still her own person.

She couldn't go backward, but she didn't have to be

the perfect Kivati lady she'd been trying to be either. It was time to forge a new path. Without Corbette. Without her parents' hard-to-win approval.

"What's the score?" she asked as she studied the ring.

"The Bear clocked the Crow and has the Thunderbird pinned. He's big, he's mean, but I'd never have thought he'd have it in him to best a Thunderbird general."

Lucia sucked in a little breath. Not the Bear. He'd been one of Rudrick's.

"Don't worry," a deep voice said behind her. "Theo's just messing with him."

Lucia turned in her seat to find Lord Kai looming over her. The sky illuminated the red tones in his dark mane. Ladies always whispered that the Thunderbird was handsome as the devil and twice as wicked. She'd always been a little afraid of him. Unpredictable, he was. Improper. Kai would never keep himself in check if he were engaged to a girl. Sensual, dangerous Kai wouldn't let such an opportunity go to waste.

He took her hand and bowed over it. "Good morning, my lady."

"Hi." She smiled. Next to her, Constance scented danger, stopped crying, and straightened up. They wanted her wed, didn't they? The strongest warrior next to Corbette was Kai, but *safe* he wasn't. The Blessed Lady seemed to be pushing her in a certain, disreputable direction.

Kai gave her his wickedest piratical grin, and kissed the back of her hand. If she wanted to stick it to Corbette, she had to look no further. She could put herself firmly in the rebel camp, be a banner maiden for overthrowing the old ways. With Kai at her side, they'd dismiss all Corbette's propriety and control. Everything he'd worked to build, every drop of blood he'd shed for their people, she could turn it all to dust.

"Aren't you entering?" she asked. Her father gave a choked grunt.

Ignoring her parents, Kai put a hand over his heart. "Would you like me to? I'm touched." He leaned forward so that his voice rumbled in the air between them. He had eyes for her and her only; it was a thrill. "Give me a token of your esteem, and I'll clear the ring for you."

Nerves danced along Lucia's spine. This was a dangerous game. Maybe Corbette was right and that first kiss was forgettable—she wouldn't know, would she, without kissing another man in comparison? If there were any man domineering enough to compare Corbette to, it would be Kai. Closing the distance between them, she gave Kai's lips a light touch. "A kiss for good luck." There were gasps and cheers from the surrounding crowd.

Kai arched a brow. "You call that a kiss?" He seized her upper arms and dragged her close, so that her breasts pressed into the hard planes of his chest, and landed a hard, fierce kiss on her mouth. His tongue swept out through her shocked lips, and all she could do was tremble as he sent the Aether sweeping across her nerve endings. Ye. Gods.

He stepped back. "Now you've done it, my lady. I can't help but win."

Lucia could only stare as she tried to catch her breath.

He cast a look at the balcony above and something dark flashed across his features, but it was there and gone in an instant. She wasn't sure she hadn't imagined it. He shrugged out of his shirt, eliciting a squeal from Delia, and, with a rakish grin, entered the ring. Theo had just finished knocking the Bear out, as Kai had predicted he would.

"Theo, how 'bout you stop playing around? These fine people didn't come out for a picnic."

Two men dragged Benard away, and Theo shook Kai's hand. The audience perked up at seeing two Thunderbird generals in their prime. This was what they'd been waiting for. The undercurrent buzzed with rebellion. She could taste danger on the soft west wind.

"If Kai wins," Delia whispered, "there will be no going back."

"Would that be a bad thing?" Lucia asked.

"Only if you're sure you don't want Corbette."

"I don't see him in the ring fighting for my hand."

Kai flipped Theo with a move that was barely visible to the human eye. This contest was physical only—no shifting, no manipulation of the elements. Theo was tired from previous bouts, but Kai's torso showed recent wounds too.

Lucia glanced back at the Hall. Corbette stood on the balcony with his black greatcoat blowing out in the wind like wings. His hair whipped around his face. His stern nose and handsome face were cast in shadow. He didn't watch the fight in front of her. His gaze locked on her own, and he gave a little nod.

He'd seen. She felt a moment's panic. He'd seen her kiss another man, one of his trusted generals, no less.

But wasn't that what she was here for? He'd tasted her kiss and let her go as if she were a spawning salmon. That shock of Aether was one-sided. Instead, he almost pushed her into the arms of his adversary. He'd made a spectacle of her, let their private pain radiate across the Kivati. She could do no less than take his challenge seriously. He didn't want her? Fine. She would forget all about him.

Turning forward in her seat, she watched the Thunderbirds circle each other on the lawn. Both were brawny.

Both sported the intricate Thunderbird feather tattoos on their backs to remind them of their totem while in their human skin. Most Kivati youth were inked after they completed the totem ceremony. Her skin had rejected the ink and was now bare as those with watered-down blood, those not Lady-blessed enough to Change, like her cousin and the healer Kayla. It had seemed like an omen at the time; she was Crane, but not-Crane.

She didn't need ink to remember the Crane, but watching the shirtless Thunderbirds go at it made her feel unfinished somehow. How could she forget her role when every moment of every day she was told how lovely and perfect and priceless she was? Watched, by everyone, with jealousy and pity as they waited for her to do Great Things? The phantom scars on her wrists and inner thighs itched.

Kai caught her eye and winked. Theo took that opportunity to jab with his right fist, but Kai saw it coming. The smack of fist on flesh echoed in the early evening air.

Kai and Theo were too evenly matched to knock about. They circled and circled, playing up a jab here and there just for the audience. She tried to imagine picking Theo over Kai. A drop of sweat trickled down her back beneath her corset.

"Lady be, did you see Corbette's face?" her mother whispered. "I don't think he's given you up after all. He's going to enter; I just know it."

Lucia shook her head. She wanted nothing to do with him. Standing, she pulled her handkerchief from her pocket, and threw it at the grappling Thunderbirds in the ring. Theo caught the flash of white out of the corner of his eye, and Kai used his distraction to deliver a brutal uppercut. Theo slammed into the wet ground in a shower of dirt. Kai caught the handkerchief before it fluttered to the ground. He raised it to her with his wicked smile teasing the crowd, then placed it to his lips and inhaled. She smiled, since all eyes were on her. "Bravo," she said. The crowd cheered.

"Who else fights for the glory of the Lady?" Kai asked. No one stepped forward.

"It looks like I have a champion, then." She reached for the laurel crown sitting on a velvet cushion at her feet.

"Wait—" Constance put a gloved hand out to stop her.

Murmurs spread through the crowd, and Lucia looked up to see who might be crazy enough to challenge the strongest Thunderbird.

Corbette stood at the entrance to the contender grounds.

Corbette found himself standing at the edge of the crowd without truly knowing how he'd gotten there. He'd watched the tournament with growing black rage until he felt weighted down like a submersible on the ocean floor. His ears buzzed. He was aware of shocked noises around him, but he hadn't realized he intended to enter until his hand landed on the gate to the fighting ground.

He felt a vibration through the Aether that signaled a message from one of his Thunderbirds. Only powerful Aether mages could send messages directly through the Sparkling Water of the Universe. He paused, one hand on the latch.

*What are you doing?* Will demanded.

Corbette had no response. He really, truly, had planned to give her up. She'd said she didn't want him, and he didn't want her messing up his plans either. His mind flashed unbidden to the scene in the library. She'd kissed him. A woman didn't kiss a man she had no interest in.

The Aether stream from Will turned sour. Too late

Corbette realized that he'd shared that memory with the Thunderbird. He stifled the connection and tipped his head to the ash cloud in the south, where Mount Rainier used to be visible on the horizon. "To the glory of our goddess," he murmured. The two snow-covered humps of the mountain had been said to be the Lady's milky breasts. The mountain had erupted during the Unraveling. The top half turned into a cloud of hot ash that was still falling on the trees and houses.

Corbette stripped off his coat and shirt. He entered the ring, and bowed to Lucia. She stood with her lips parted, eyes wide, face pale. What was he doing? But it was too late to back out. The Raven screeched inside him. His totem had never wanted to let her go.

Kai growled low, and Corbette turned to him. "There's no Aether in this contest," Kai said. A muscle flexed in his jaw.

"Then you might have a chance," Corbette said. "But I doubt it."

Kai rushed him. Corbette let his mind fall into the Raven's presence. The Raven swooped his human form beneath Kai's arm and danced beyond his reach. All of a sudden a blast of Aether shot from the direction of Puget Sound. It knocked him off his feet, but caught him up before he could hit the ground. His body was a conductor, and the Aether held him rigid in its raging tides. Kai, less Aether-sensitive and in attack mode, drove a sharp uppercut that rocked Corbette back on his heels. The Aether broke around him, and he crashed to the ground, stunned.

The audience gasped. Above him, Kai's face drained of color. He stared at his fist, then searched the hushed crowd, then turned back to Corbette. Corbette could only lie there and will the breath to come back to his lungs.

What had happened out at sea? Only one thing was certain: something terrible was coming this way, and his Aether powers—hitherto unmatched—didn't hold a candle to it.

Lucia stared at Corbette. He'd fallen from a punch he should have seen coming. How could their leader fall?

Corbette coughed. "Good show," he said to Kai, voice hoarse. Aether rolled from him, heating the air, sparkling over the skin of the watching Kivati. The urge to Change called to Lucia. He wiped the trickle of blood off the corner of his mouth. Aether power wasn't measured in the physical portion of the tournament, but Corbette couldn't turn it off. It washed out from his pores and swirled around his crouched body.

"Get up, damn it," Kai muttered.

Corbette stood so gracefully it seemed like the Aether floated him up. The sparkling water churned around him. His hair fanned out from his neck. "Lady Lucia," he said, voice deeper than a roll of thunder, "please crown the victor."

She fumbled for the laurel wreath and dropped it. Kai didn't wait around. By the time she bent to retrieve the crown and stood back up, he was gone.

The crowd didn't part as readily this time for Corbette to make his retreat. It was no longer a game.

"What's wrong with him?" Constance asked, growing increasingly hysterical. "He . . . he has to take Lucy. Who will protect her? He can't leave her!"

"Listen to them." Milton motioned to the crowd. "Animals can't follow a weak leader. Once the Alpha is old or injured—"

"He can't do this," Lucia said. "Just to get rid of me? He'll lose his throne too." Responsibility, he'd said. He'd made it very clear in the library that he'd never give up his rule for her.

"Maybe that's his plan," her father said. "Look at him. Maybe he set this whole thing up for a clean transfer of power. It'd be the only way to stop a rebellion from shattering the Kivati into warring tribes. Maybe he doesn't plan to survive."

"No," Lucia denied it. She watched him walk, tall and proud even though his pack had turned on him. He strode past her, eyes straight ahead. He wasn't even going to acknowledge her? She bit her tongue to keep herself from moving forward. He was so alone. "Emory Corbette doesn't know the word 'defeat.'"

He was driven determination down to his marrow. It had long been joked that when it came time to join the spirit world, Corbette would crisply tell the Blessed Lady that he was too busy to go. There was no mountain he couldn't climb, no ocean he couldn't swim. Intimidating as hell, but comforting too. In the dark days after the Unraveling, she'd seen Corbette's strength and determined to pull herself together. If he could rebuild their people from the ashes of the Great Fire, if he could fight the unceasing war against the Drekar and not lose hope, if he could enforce a bastion of Victorian civilization amid the encroachments and seductions of the modern age for thousands of arrogant shape-shifters, then nothing—no, nothing—could threaten their race. She—all of them— believed victory was inevitable, because Corbette would will it to be so.

But Corbette's abrupt defeat spread fear through the crowd. Intuitively, she knew that without him, the strict hierarchy that he had imposed would break down as Crow turned to Crow and Cougar to Cougar. The large totem tribes would break away, leaving unique totems like

Hummingbird, Whale, and Crane to fend for themselves. She couldn't let that happen, she realized. Even if no prophesized powers of Crane had manifested yet, she had to start acting like a leader. She couldn't sit by and let Corbette dictate her future anymore. She stood up and pushed past her parents. "Let's go, Delia."

"Where are we going?" her sister asked as she hurried to catch up.

"You wanted a revolution? You got one."

Kai let the Change burn through him and he collapsed in his human form on the beach at Discovery Park. The islands of Puget Sound hunkered down against the night like giant tortoises, each one bearing its own little world on its back to swim through the starry universe. He grabbed a handful of rocks as he jumped to his feet and flung them at the offending deities.

"Gods damn you, Jace!" Neither his brother nor the gods answered him. He yanked the Aether and made the wind pick up an eighty-foot beached log and hurl it out to sea. The uncaring ocean swallowed it with only a hint of sound. "You get back here and fix this!"

He threw a boulder with the wind, but it wasn't as satisfying as letting out his anger physically. He needed his hands on someone. Punching, kicking, dodging. Letting the sweat and blood and flesh take this frustration that swelled under his skin. By thunder, he wanted to kill someone.

But not Corbette. Not for the throne. Not for a woman. Especially not the prophesied Crane Wife.

Lucia wasn't so bad. Any other girl who'd been pampered and petted from age thirteen would have become a self-centered bitch, but Lucia had managed to keep herself grounded. She had a little rebellious streak that he could appreciate, even if she didn't have the backbone to back it up. He didn't have much use for fragile, delicate women. Didn't want to waste time tiptoeing and kowtowing to some drama queen.

He thought the Unraveling had driven that last spark of defiance out of her, making her into the perfect doormat for Corbette's ruthless rule. If only she hadn't caught him in the alley with Zetian, she would never have been able to blackmail him. It was one thing to risk his life dancing naked with a psychotic dragon. It was another for Corbette to find out. Kai wasn't so much afraid of banishment or death as he was of his brother's ghost coming back from the dead to kick his ass. Jace had died for the Kivati. Kai owed it to him to stay and rebuild their people.

Besides, when Lucia had come to him with her proposition that he lead his Western House against Kingu, she'd had a familiar determined light in her eyes. He had to keep her alive whether she wanted to battle a demigod with her own two hands or march into the Land of the Dead itself. Jace had died trying to free Lucia after she'd been kidnapped by one of Kai's own men.

The weight of his guilt pushed Kai down to his knees, and he dug his hands in the freezing tide. Could he see himself in Lucia's bed? With the prophecy hanging above their heads ready to fall like an ax? Could he see himself on the madrona throne? Gods damn him. He disagreed with Corbette's rules, but he didn't want to take his place. Jace would have done it. Jace had always been a better man. The better twin. Light to Kai's dark, good to his bad. The more Jace went right, the more Kai went wrong. And it suited Kai. He'd never envied his brother for the mountain range of responsibility he'd shouldered at an early age. Jace had even dragged Kai along when it became apparent at thirteen that they would be some of the strongest Kivati born in a century. Kai had never intended to stay this long. He'd fought for the general role only to appease his brother, not realizing that he'd be stuck toeing the straight and narrow long after Jace had flown on.

*Why'd you set off on adventures where I can't follow, bro?*

The salty waves of Puget Sound lapped the beach. Ten yards in front of him, the water splashed. Too big to be a fish, but black and silver and sparkling like scales. He pushed to his feet. Nothing good swam in the water. "Show yourself," he ordered.

Sinuous coils broke the surface. A giant serpent floating in on the tide. Instinct urged him to Change and flee the evil that stalked the shore.

Just what he needed.

Kai let the tips of his talons break through his skin. He caught the Aether to him, ready to Change. Between his fingers the Aether coalesced. It buzzed like the golden glow inside a Leyden jar. He waited for the ripple again and shot the thunderbolt. The bolt hit with a crackle and crash. Ripples of what looked like lightning splashed out, and the creature roared. It shot from the deep water straight into the sky, a slender dragon more serpentine than bestial. Its silver-tipped scales and three horns were as familiar as the gold whiskers and almost dainty claws. Astrid Zetian, the imperial dragon adviser to the Drekar Regent. The malevolence in those silver eyes didn't scare him. He'd fought her before and won.

He'd fucked her before too. Was still making up for that bad decision.

"You're supposed to be dead," he called up to her. He watched the silver dragon hover in the air for a long moment highlighted by the moon behind. The Lady provided. He needed a fight, and he couldn't image a better adversary than this pumped-up dragon harpy. A little part of him had to admit that her dragon form was as beautiful as her human one. She did it for him in a kinky, love-thy-enemy sort of way. The memory of that one colossal mistake still woke him hot and bothered in the middle of the night, which only reinforced his belief that the wrong brother had died. Jace would never have been turned on by their mortal enemy. But Kai was not a model Kivati, and never had been.

Lucia wouldn't have been able to blackmail him if he were.

He'd thought Zetian had died in the battle with Kingu. But it was impossible to kill a Drekar unless one cut his head off. Immortal and soulless, the creatures had been doomed to roam the earth forever alone. Unless the rumors about the new Drekar Regent were true, and he'd really found his soul mate in that caustic fighter Grace Mercer. The hill had been rife with speculation that Grace had actually joined her soul with the monster. They would die together and pass on through the Gate into the world beyond. Together forever. He wondered if Alice and her Dreki, Brand, had done the same thing. Two Drekar in the Land of the Dead? Lady be damned.

Kai let his anger shoot through him to embrace the Change. The Lady Moon lent her energy as he shed his human skin and the Thunderbird took over. Twenty-foot wingspan, cruel, hooked beak. Hawk eyes of green and blue with sharp focus. The night winds buoyed his feathered wings and he shot toward his adversary, talons out. The dragon was smaller than his Thunderbird form, but she slithered like an eel away from his attack. A high shriek echoed from her vocal chords.

*Laugh it up,* he thought. *You just made my day.*

Fighting Drekar was a hard thing; their magic blood

healed in moments, so the only way to beat them was to keep them so busy defending themselves that they didn't have any free energy to heal. He tried that technique now, but every move, she blocked him. It was like she could read his mind. Eerie. Uncanny. When was the last time he'd had a real fight?

She banked hard, and he overshot his next attack. Where had she pulled that from? She landed on his back and clawed her way across his wings. Pain ripped across his skin. Fuck. She was stronger, quicker than last time. His body protested. The pitter-patter of feathers and scales into the ocean below looked like falling stardust.

He threw her off and tried to retaliate, but she dodged again.

Gods, but she was hot. He'd die before he admitted it. There was no one to see him get his ass handed to him. Bested by a woman. By a soul-sucker.

The Aether ripped over the water in the next instant like an electromagnetic pulse from a small atom bomb. It catapulted him head over heels, forcefully stripping the feathers and skin from his bones, a shock of pain and surprise as his Thunderbird form was ripped from him without his consent. And then he was human and falling.

The black water rushed up at him. A scream shook his eardrums. He had only a moment to close his mouth before he was hit with a force so great he blacked out.

Kai woke when the freezing water gushed into his nose and mouth. The salt burned down his throat. He thrashed until his fingertips found the surface, and he kicked his way out of the frozen tomb. He coughed water out of his lungs and treaded ice while he tried to find his bearings. Shock and the icy November sea—gods, he was cold. Embarrassed too. Not even a raw youth lost his hold on the Aether enough to have his totem form ripped from him. Who or what could do such a thing to him? Not even Corbette was that strong.

Which meant there was some monster worse than a Dreki here in the black water with him. With ice in his veins, he managed to swim to shore and pull himself out onto the rocky beach.

He searched the Sound and gray sky for a sign of the Dreki, but the moon showed softly lapping waters and empty air. She couldn't have done it. Drekar couldn't manipulate the Aether; they could Turn between man and beast, but nothing more.

"Get a grip," he told himself. He shook the water from his mane and pulled clean, dry clothes from the Aether. He could dry his hair too, but fatigue made his bones brittle. He felt bruised. He hadn't managed a single hit on the demon dragon. Fuck him.

How had the Kivati lasted this long in the war against the Drekar if one lowly soul-sucker could kick his ass? And Zetian, even. She was ancient and powerful, but they'd wrestled before in both forms—

"Sorry, Jace," he whispered to the night sky.

The deserted beach mocked him. The only set of footprints was his own. It was like he'd imagined the whole thing, phantoms from the past plucked from his mind to torment him for his betrayal, his failure.

He heard a faint splash behind him. He turned. The moon illuminated a woman rising from the water like Venus from the foam. Naked, buxom, and powerful, she was the hottest thing he'd ever seen. Her smooth black hair cascaded around her shoulders to kiss her pelvic bone. Her catlike eyes were accentuated with thick lashes as if she'd been born outlined in kohl. Her perfect breasts peaked in the cold of the sharp autumn night. Her coral lips parted just enough to be inviting.

She shouldn't have such an effect on him, when he'd tapped that already, but he'd learned nothing. He couldn't move as she floated out of the sea, a siren damning him to a watery grave. He'd dash his brains out on the rocks just for a taste of her. The soft curve of her belly led down to slender hips and the sleek pelt hiding her femininity. Man alive. *Her kind killed your bro, remember?* He needed to unstick his tongue from the roof of his mouth, but she pushed all his buttons: she was smart, hot, and dangerous as a cracked Gate. He could fight her all he wanted, but she would win. And the look in those all-seeing eyes said she knew it.

Fear iced up his spine while heat rushed to his dick.

He had to get out of here. Self-preservation first.

What would Jace do? He'd sacrifice himself for the Kivati. Die trying to kill this gorgeous creature. Jace wouldn't be tempted to sin.

Kai swallowed. He took a step forward.

Zetian's tongue slowly wet her lips. She kept walking toward him with that slow, rolling gait that made all her feminine parts jiggle nicely.

"You ran out on Asgard," he said. Stupid, stupid. He had to leave. He had to make her mad so she would stop coming toward him.

"Hmmmm," she hummed deep in her throat.

His brain shot him a picture of her making that noise while his dick was in her mouth. May the Sky God smite him. "You want to start this again? A rematch—human skin to human skin?" He flexed. Even soaking wet, even with those curves, he was easily twice her weight. If he could just keep his mind on track and out of the gutter, he could finish her off.

Not like that. Lady be damned.

Zetian was at arm's length now. He could reach out and

cup those peaches in his palm, but he wasn't sure he could throw a punch when it mattered. And it did matter, because she was his worst enemy, and he had some honor left to him. Really. He did. He didn't move.

"I like you." She butted up against him and rubbed her head along the underside of his chin like a cat. She made another deep, lust-filled noise in her throat that sounded like a very large, rather aggressive purr. He expected her claws to come out any moment. Instead, she reached her arms up and wrapped them around his neck, plastering her icy body to his. Her skin was still wet and slick with salt. The water soaked through his clothes. He seized her arms and rubbed hard and fast. It was part chivalry and part deviltry, but she laughed and shrugged him off. And then her claws did come out, but only to tear the fabric of his shirt until the ribbons of good linen floated to the dusty sand.

"This isn't a good idea," he said. His hands closed around her shoulders and back, but whether to immobilize her or to draw her close, he didn't know. His fingers dug into the curve beneath her shoulder blade. He could shoot out his talons and bury them between her ribs. He should. She sunk her teeth into his bicep. "Fuck!" Pain shot up his nerves. Finally, the fog cleared from his mind. He shoved her hard.

She tumbled back into the sand, limbs splayed, hair tangled with the seaweed like a mermaid washed to shore. She laughed up at him. "I like the taste of you, little bird warrior." One long, clawed finger beckoned. "We will make such pretty babies to eat the world."

"What? You're out of your mind." He backed away slowly. "You're a soul-sucker. Damned to eternity. Filth." He spat.

She looked down at her gorgeous, goddess body and

lingered at the apex of her thighs. She tilted her head quizzically. "This body appears pleasing to me." Her eyes shot to his crotch. "And it appears pleasing to you. Come." She beckoned again. Her smile curled seductively. "Let me see if it's as pleasing to touch as it is to look at." The way her lips caressed the word "touch" had to be illegal in fifty states.

He didn't think his dick could get much harder, but even the shame of being attracted to a Dreki couldn't make it see reason. He coveted. Hatred only spiced the proposition.

Fuck.

He thought of the tournament. Of Corbette on the ground with blood trickling from his lip. *Responsibility*, the memory of his brother hissed in his mind. This woman and her kin had killed his brother and countless of his friends.

He turned his back on her. His feet plodded through the sand, carrying him away from temptation. A moment later he hit the sand with a hundred pounds of angry female digging her claws into his back. Her scream filled the night, part rage, part desire. Rolling, he tried to throw her off. He threw out his elbows and rammed his back against the nearest jagged edge of driftwood. She just laughed and wrapped her legs around his waist.

"What did you eat, woman?" he grunted. She was much too strong.

"Harder, harder, little pet," she whispered in his ear. "Show me your claws. Show me your power, poppet. You cannot break me. But I want to see you try."

He slammed his head back and hit her in the forehead. She broke her hold for a moment, and he dislodged his back from her claws. He rolled over and planted a fist in her gut. Such a slender thing, and—Lady forsake him—

he'd never hit a woman. But this wasn't a woman. She
was a demon in disguise, and the pain seemed to startle
her more than hurt her. She snapped her legs around his
waist and squeezed. They rolled down the rocky beach
toward the water, sand and salt bitter on his tongue. His
eyes watered. He tried to rip her off, but she was like a
noose. The harder he fought, the tighter she got, and,
fuck, now he couldn't hide the bulge that grew up against
the V of her thighs.

She laughed and sliced her claws down his back to cut
through the waistband of his trousers. The cold of the
damp pebbles cut his ass when she flipped him. She held
him down with the strength of her thighs, ripped back the
cut fabric separating them, and impaled herself on his
shaft. *Spirits haunt me.* He couldn't move as all the blood
rushed south. The wet heat surrounding him pulsed with
the beat of her heart. Mesmerizing pleasure shot up his
nerve endings and across his skin. Zetian rose above him
and threw back her head, her hair a ribbon of blackest
black against the night sky. She turned her heart-shaped
face to the Lady Moon above with a deep, satisfied moan.
She was glorious, a goddess fucking in the moonlight.

"Yes, this," she moaned. "I missed this. I'm so very
glad you were waiting for me to rise. There are some
things worth waiting millennia for." Her silver eyes cut
back to him. Unearthly light swirled in their depths, and
as she slowly levered herself over him, shooting paralyz-
ing sensation over his heated skin, the small voice of
reason started screaming in the back of his brain.

*This is not right.* But it felt so good. *She is not Zetian.*

A question penetrated the haze of lust. She slammed
herself down, grinding her pelvis against his. His eyes
rolled back in his head. "Zetian." He grabbed her hips to
stop her. "What game are you playing?"

She bent over him and shook her breasts in his face. His fingers slipped on the smooth skin of her hips. "Do you love this 'Zetian'?"

"No!"

"Your cock says different."

He grit his teeth. "What is with you? You always talk about yourself in the third person?"

She gripped his hands and drove him deeper. "I like you, warrior. I've been trapped in a weak, human shell for too long. But now I'm in control. Ah! Sweet, sweet sensation. This body pleases me. This body is fertile and strong."

His eyes shot open. "Fertile? Hell, no. Who are you?" Her silver eyes reflected the moon. "Astrid Zetian, adviser to the Drekar Regent?" Or something else?

"Adviser?" She laughed and pinned his wrists to the sand. "I am queen."

"I think someone beat you to it."

"I am queen, and I need a consort."

He thrust up to meet her hips. She moaned, wanton, wild, louder until it echoed against the stars above. A bolt of blue flame shot out of her to light the night sky like a beacon. A bolt of Aether lit through his body from the place they were joined to scald the inside of his skin. As if one of his own thunderbolts had turned on him. Pleasure and pain rocked him, an orgasm so strong and so terrifying that he almost blacked out. Again.

What. The. Fuck.

It wrung every thought from his body, leaving him worn as a millstone. This wasn't Astrid Zetian. Her svelte body, but not her mind. Drekar couldn't manipulate the Aether, but this woman straddling him had done just that. Who was strong enough to pilot a dragon?

He was suddenly very, very sick.

"Tiamat," he whispered.

She turned her face back to him. Aether crackled across her lovely face as she smiled. "Yes, you'll do quite nicely, warrior. It's been millennia since I walked this earth with my own body. This one . . ." She held up her hands to examine them. Claws shot out of her fingertips, and her eyes gleamed. ". . . is extraordinary." She dropped her hand and trailed a claw lightly down his face. "You like it, don't you, Kai Raiden? You are strong. I lost two pantheons of useless children, but, as you mortals say, third time's a charm." She bent over him and whispered in his ear. "Together, darling, we will birth a new army and take back this glorious world and the next."

He was in deep shit.

# Chapter Four

In the topmost turret of Kivati Hall, Lucia leaned against the window and watched small groups of Kivati peel off into the brewing storm. Already the four sacred Houses with mixed totems, each led by a Thunderbird general, were starting to crack. It was only natural, she supposed, for their Animal spirits to cling to their species mates in time of crisis. Corbette's strict House system had gotten rid of tribal infighting, but without him it wouldn't last. Not unless a strong leader stepped up to take his place.

At the foot of the hill, the Space Needle rose like a towering tombstone, representing every failed futuristic dream that lay beneath the rubble of the Unraveling. The Unraveling had thrown civilization back in time, not forward. Space travel, nanotechnology, atomic power, and genetic manipulation were nothing more than pipe smoke in the dark when the Aether frothed and Babylonian goddesses rose from the dead.

The Kivati had been ready. Thanks to Corbette, they'd never really joined the twenty-first century anyway. He'd built them a sanctuary from the outside world and kept them sheltered and closeted and—gods, but she was growing to hate that word—*safe*.

Safety was stifling. If she never took great risks, how would she ever know how much she was capable of?

Delia sat near the fire taking notes. "So we have Lady Acacia to speak to Cougar and Lady Alice for Owl, but who can we appeal to in Crow?"

"If only Johnny was still alive."

"No, no one would have listened to him. He was dishonored. We need someone with cred."

"Maybe Great Uncle Lonan?" Lucia listened to the distant strains of violin and drums from deep within the Hall. Despite the chilling end to the contests that day, the celebration party went on as planned. "We need to hurry so we can get down there and start making alliances."

"Plan first. You can't just waltz into the ballroom and expect everyone to listen to you."

"I need credibility."

"Right. Now the prophecy is a good place to start. People know you have a claim to lead them, even if they don't like it much. We should talk to the elders who were alive when the prophecy was made. They might take it most seriously."

"Are you sure that Aether blast didn't come from Corbette?" Lucia asked again. "Maybe he tried to cheat by drawing the Aether to him. Or maybe he just lost control . . ."

"If you hadn't been staring so hard at his naked chest, maybe you would have felt it."

Lucia felt her cheeks heat. She'd never been as sensitive to the Aether as her sister was. She had to concentrate hard. "If we could find other people who felt what you felt, maybe we could convince them Corbette didn't give up."

"But if you don't believe me, we're not going to be very convincing. Besides, are we trying to strengthen Corbette's rule or replace him?"

"I'm not strong enough to lead. Who could do it?" Lucia curled her hand into a fist and turned away from the window. This room—the Princess Suite—was where she lived when she wasn't at her parents' house. If she wasn't going to be a pawn for either of them, she needed to find her own place. "People are forming their own alliances while we wait up here. Let's go down and start slowly casting our net while the iron is hot. Del, please get the scarlet gown."

Delia's eyes lit up. "That will certainly get everybody's attention." Her sister helped her into the very low-cut scarlet gown with silver thunderbolts embroidered at the neckline and hem. Lucia had planned to wear it to the grand ball at the end of the tournament, but why wait? She needed its confidence now. Her sister helped her twist her long white hair back in a simple wrapped pony-tail. The brilliant splash of white against the scarlet was the reverse of her totem's coloring. No one could ignore the Crane in this dress.

Delia gave her a nod. "That'll do. You should talk to Lord Douglass first. The Thunderbird won't know what hit him in that dress."

"He would be a powerful ally." Lucia slipped ruby earrings in her ears. Once she would have loved wearing this dress, but after what Rudrick had done to her, she felt overexposed showing so much cleavage. She needed to take back her body and find the sensual, passionate nature that she'd been born with. The growing storm outside seemed to have taken up residence in her belly. She couldn't show fear; the animals would tear her apart.

Lucia paused at the door to her room. "This is it, Del."

"You'll do great." Delia squeezed her tight and planted a kiss on her cheek. "We're never alone. May the spirits of our ancestors guide us."

Lucia made her way down the grand staircase with her head high. The mansion's lights had been dimmed. Outside, the storm grew, so loud that she didn't hear the angry words coming from the foyer until she was almost upon them. She slowed as she realized it was Corbette and Kai. Her footsteps softened on the stairs. They argued about a woman. Were they talking about her? Corbette's back was to her. The biodiesel light illuminated angry scratches down Kai's cheeks.

"—and then she said she was here for the throne. She would build a new Babylon and a third pantheon to replace the one she lost," Kai said.

"Did she actually call herself Tiamat?" Corbette demanded. "Could it be another deep water spirit, or a powerful ghost?"

*Tiamat! It couldn't be.*

"No." Kai ran his hands through his hair. Will came running from a nearby study bearing a glass of golden liquid. He shoved the glass into Kai's shaking hands, and Kai tipped it back with a single swallow. He coughed. The color started to return to his face. "She spoke of her body like it didn't belong to her. Zetian—I've fought her before, and she wasn't this good." He locked eyes with Corbette, and an understanding passed between them. "I've known her intimately, and she's not the same woman."

Corbette hesitated a beat. "I see."

"She fights like an immortal, and her Aether control

would give you a run for your money. Zetian was a formidable adversary, but she couldn't touch the Aether except to Change. This new, improved version, she fights like a demon and fuc—"

"Lady Lucia," Will hissed.

The three men's eyes shot to her. Busted. Lucia raised her chin and stood away from the wall. She cleared her throat. "And she fucks like a goddess, is that right, Kai?" Lucia felt her face flame the color of her gown, but she glided down the staircase, swan-necked, shoulders back. Her etiquette teacher would be proud.

Kai stared at the ground. Corbette swore. Will only gave her a stony look.

"Go back to the ballroom, Lady Lucia," Corbette ordered.

"No."

One thick black eyebrow rose. It was all he usually had to do to send his minions cowering. She was done with that.

"I have just as much right to know as you do," she said. "I risked my life to defeat her. I have the right to know if I failed."

"It's for your own good," Corbette said. There was no trace of warmth in his voice. No hint that he'd once held any affection for her.

"I'm not a child anymore."

His eyes briefly flicked down to her gown's revealing neckline and hip-hugging skirts. "I can see that."

She swallowed the F-U on her tongue. "They are my people too."

"Silence." He held his hand up. Kai and Will both stared at her like she'd grown an extra head. "You aren't a warrior. You are a spiritual leader and your role is here."

He gestured back to the ballroom. "If Zetian is a threat, we will eliminate her. You are not to go—"

"If there is a new threat, the Drekar and humans need to know about it," she said.

"Absolutely not. The Drekar had both Tiamat's Heart and the Tablet of Destiny, and they lost both. This is their fault. We will contain it ourselves," Corbette said.

"After all that's happened, how can you say that? Who fought Kingu? We can't leave them unprotected."

"The soul-suckers would leave us in a heartbeat."

Lucia curled her hands into fists. She wished she could knock that arrogant look off his face. "The Drekar and humans fought when it mattered, to protect all of us. You were the one who stayed and hid like a yellow-bellied coward."

Aether crackled in the room. Lucia felt the hair on her arms and neck rise. Sweat beaded on her forehead. But she couldn't back down. Corbette and the two Thunderbirds stood stock-still. They stared at her like she'd Changed into a dragon, scaled and soulless and damned. With all that power and testosterone in the room, she should be running for cover.

"I forbid you—" Corbette growled, violet rings in his eyes expanding to cover the black.

*Fly!* the Crane called inside her. She raised her chin. "I don't think you have that right anymore, do you, Raven? Because Animals will only follow the strongest alpha, and I distinctly remember Kai knocking you down."

Kai's mouth dropped. Will took a step forward, a thunderbolt beginning to form between his fingers.

Corbette threw his hand out and pulled Will back. "Don't touch her."

"You can't let her—"

"I'm still in charge here." His eyes were completely

violet. Grim lines set around his mouth. He fought for control. The Change rode him. Aether rippled over his skin.

She'd never seen him so out of control, and it terrified her. All of his energy was focused on keeping himself in human form. She backed away slowly.

"Corbette?" Will said. "Emory, are you all right?"

Kai caught her eyes and nodded his head toward the door. She could stay and try to follow the original plan, or she could use Corbette's brief spell to get a head start out the door.

She chose the door, escaping down the front stairs and out into the stormy night. Grace Mercer, Queen Consort to the Drekar Regent, was her friend. She had to be told about Tiamat. Grace deserved to have a fighting chance of what was coming after her, and her allies had proved themselves saving the city from Kingu. It was the right thing to do. Shaking, Lucia called the Aether to her. It buzzed over her face and down to her slippered toes, but her body didn't Change. Her skin stayed human, her feathers nowhere to be seen. Lady be, she was a disgrace.

But she couldn't waste another minute. Corbette would return to his senses, and then he'd come after her. Running through the rain toward the front gate, she found one of the guard's steam-powered bicycles idling and unattended as he spoke to another guard some ways off. Hiking up her skirt to her waist, she threw the bulk of the wet fabric over one arm, straddled the bike, and gunned the engine. The guard called after her, but she drove through the imposing iron gates, leaving him in a cloud of steam and smoke.

The crows rose from the trees in a black mass to follow her. As if she didn't know how to lose them. She'd been sneaking out since she was old enough to fly. Waterlogged leaves slipped beneath her tires as she drove west down to where the Interurban hugged the foot of Queen Anne. The old highway had been cleared after the Unraveling, and now it was the only major thoroughfare that bisected the city north to south. She hit it and turned south. The Needle Market sprang up on either side of the boulevard—stalls and tables and the tent city that grew like creeping moss to swallow neighboring blocks. It was hopping even at midnight. The curfew that had protected the city dusk till dawn was over now that Kingu and his wraith army had been defeated.

She lost the crows in the crowd and joined a caravan down into the bowels of the ruined city. If anyone would tell her the real scoop about Tiamat, it was Grace. Even before the mercenary had married the Drekar Regent, Grace had had her ear to the ground for the latest supernatural happenings. Lucia hoped Grace was in her small tattoo parlor in Pioneer Square, and not at the Drekar Lair with her new husband. Pioneer Square was relatively neutral territory. There was brave and then there was stupid; venturing into the Drekar Lair to find Grace definitely fell into the latter category.

Luckily, as she swerved into Flesh Alley, she saw Grace pulling the door shut. The short half-Asian woman with blue-black hair watched Lucia park with a wary look. "What's wrong?" Grace asked.

Lucia swung herself off the bike. She was drenched, her skirts stained with dirt and oil. "Tiamat."

"Tell me everything." Grace opened her door again and ushered Lucia through. "But tell me as you change clothes. There was an alarm from the temple. We have to hurry."

Thank the Lady Grace didn't tell her she would just get in the way. No-nonsense Grace never coddled her or told her to go back home; she was the only person Lucia knew who wasn't afraid of Corbette. Grace saw her. Not a figurehead. Not a victim. Not a fiancée or a princess. Not a powerless little girl in need of protection.

Grace showed her inside, handed her a towel, and lent her sweatpants and a T-shirt. The pant legs were too short, but the waist fit since she'd lost so much weight over the last year.

"If Tiamat's here, I want to fight," Lucia told Grace as she dried off and dressed. "I didn't sit back when Kingu attacked, and I'm not going to now. It's like they've forgotten what happened less than a week ago. I was on that bloody field. I might not have made much of an impact, but—"

"But you showed up and you brought warriors with you. You saved my ass, Lucy, and I thank you. But fighting isn't the only way."

Lucia pulled her ruined slippers back on and paused. "It's the only time I feel powerful. I matter in that moment."

Grace opened her black hoodie jacket to where her tools were nestled in pockets sewn into her black leather corset top. Sharpened iron railroad stakes to slow down aptrgangr—the walking dead—were next to the hollow silver needles she used to ink protection runes. A short running iron and a dagger hung from her waist. "Physical strength isn't the only type of power. Neither is military authority or weapons or money. These weapons can slow down aptrgangr and banish the wraith back beyond the Gate, but they're not my greatest tool, not by far." She pulled a small brass spyglass from beneath her top. It spun on the chain, and light from the biodiesel lamps glinted off the gears and tempered glass. "This is. The Deadglass is soft power. It pulls back our preconceived notions of reality to let us see beyond the veil. It provides true wisdom, and wisdom, without throwing a single punch, can stop armies and end wars."

"Weak power."

"No. Violence is predictable. Violence begets violence begets violence, till the rivers run red. But the Deadglass disrupts our predictable actions by forcing us to look at the world in a whole new way. What is hidden becomes visible. What doesn't exist suddenly exists. Don't discount soft power when you're trying to find your personal power again. You don't need to seek out violence to have agency. Soft power is wisdom, compassion, intellect, spiritual guidance—"

"All the virtues of the Crane." Lucia swallowed the bitter note in her voice.

"And don't discount them." Grace led the way out of the shop into the dusky twilight. Torches lit the strange storefronts down the alley—an apothecary and spell store, a weapons dealer, an occult bookshop, and a small turreted House of Ishtar where three of Ishtar's Maidens practiced their "devotion" when they weren't serving at the main temple. She pulled the chain over her head and handed the Deadglass to Lucia. "Take it. It'll protect you a lot better than a knife."

Lucia slipped the chain over her head and followed Grace a few blocks east to the Drekar-owned temple of Ishtar, the Babylonian goddess of love, sex, and war. Grace and the Drekar might say they were more like geisha, but the Kivati called them high-class hookers. Their religious devotion to their art was all for the glory of their goddess. Wherever there was a significant Drekar population, there was a temple, because the human Maidens also provided souls for the Drekar to feed on.

The rain had eased to a light drizzle by the time Lucia

and Grace arrived at the temple. It occupied a historic brick mansion a few blocks east of Pioneer Square. Usually it glowed with welcoming gaslight, a bastion against the oppressive darkness, calling sailors to worship at the altar of sex. A barbaric fence made of human bone surrounded it. Tonight all the lights were out.

"What would Tiamat want with the House of Ishtar?" Lucia asked.

"How much do you know about the Babylonian creation myth?" Grace asked.

"Only the basics."

"Tiamat and Apsu were soul mates, the primordial salt water and fresh. They birthed the first pantheon of gods, one of whom killed Apsu. Tiamat birthed a second pantheon of monsters—including dragon kind in her own image—to avenge her murdered husband and gave her lover, Kingu, the Tablet of Destiny to wage war against the gods. Using the Scepter of Death, Marduk killed her and her demon army, and cursed the Drekar to a soulless immortality. Because Tiamat had waged war in revenge of her husband, her heart was ripped out of her body and forced to roam the Land of the Living, forever parted from her mate." Grace paused at the gate and traced one of the carved runes with her fingertip. "Her heart had her powers, but they were bound. I think she slipped through history searching for a way to undo the binding until she got trapped inside me."

"How did she get out?"

"The old Regent, Norgard, found me right after she'd been trapped by my natural shields. He put the first rune on me," Grace said. Lucia remembered the lines of blue-black ink that until recently had snaked across Grace's skin. "I put more on, binding and unbinding and working so much magic to keep the thing from breaking out of me that the old binding broke down. Her heart was trapped inside me, but I didn't know it until Kingu came looking for it."

"Norgard didn't know either?"

"I had pretty strong mental shields, and he only strengthened them." Grace's lips pressed together. "There isn't a pit in hell deep enough for that fucker."

Lucia looked away. She understood only too well. Rudrick belonged in that same pit. But Grace had kept fighting and moving forward, and now she was practically married to a soul-sucker. Lucia had always wished to be more like her, except the soul-sucker part. How could Grace tell her to find agency in weak power while she strolled the night brandishing an arsenal of weapons? She was so tired of being told how she should act as the prophesied Crane; she didn't need to hear it from Grace too.

"Don't pity me," Grace said, mistaking Lucia's silence. "I got my revenge and my happily ever after. Who knows what would have happened if the universe had stuck me on a different path? Would I give up Leif if it meant I never had to crawl through hell to get here? Never in a million years."

"How sweet," Lucia said, because there was really nothing else to say. There was only one man she'd ever wanted, and no matter how hard she tried to convince herself he was all wrong for her and mad besides, she'd have better luck joining a nunnery. She had to change the subject. "So Tiamat and Ishtar . . . ?"

"Ishtar, being the Goddess of love and all, felt sorry for Tiamat and Apsu. After the battle, the Drekar were stripped of their souls and cursed to walk the earth forever craving the souls of others to survive. But Ishtar gave them a way out—if they can find their soul mate."

"You really bound yourself for eternity to Asgard?"

Grace drew her bone knife and pushed through the gate. "Yup. Let's go in the back."

The black windows looked foreboding in the gloom. Part of her wanted to be back in the warmth and safety of Kivati Hall, where the ball still twirled and her people still danced in ignorance of the new threat. What would it take to find permanent peace and freedom for her people? For herself?

"Why here?" Lucia whispered.

"Ishtar gave Tiamat her aid, both her army of the dead and her sacred courtesans. Makes sense that Tiamat would go to Ishtar's temple for resources. She'll be disappointed if she's looking for the warrior maidens of old, though." She put her finger to her lips and motioned for Lucia to follow. They crept around the house and in through the kitchen door. Inside, the house was black as the outside.

Lucia hoped the maidens were still alive. Zetian—or Tiamat—had let Kai live. But why?

Muffled chanting rumbled from beneath the floor.

*The ceremonial chamber*, Grace mouthed and led the way through the house. The walls were paneled in rich brocade and red silks. Every room was sumptuous, decorated to seduce the eye and lure the patron to forget his conscious worries. They passed through rooms filled with hors d'oeuvres plates and half-drunk mugs of mead. It looked like the party had been interrupted. There was no hint of the patrons who had been enjoying these earthly delights. The food was lukewarm.

Grace creaked open a servant's door and led the way to the back stairs. They were narrow, but sound, and led into the basement, where peepholes had been drilled through the thin walls. What kind of debauched ceremonies did

Ishtar's sacred whores perform down here? Her imagination jumped to provide the image of a buxom, blond Maiden in a white robe going down on a muscled, naked man. The man had raven-black hair and eyes ringed in violet. His hunger made the violet expand to swallow the coal-black pupil. His stern face relaxed, his lips parted, as the Maiden took him in her mouth. He wore nothing but the silver rings in his ears, and his stomach was a flat rock of muscle. A downy fine trail led down from his belly button—but there her memory ended and supposition filled in. Sculpted thighs and . . . she jerked her mind back from the precipice. *Don't go there.*

What would it take to unwind the Raven Lord? What kind of woman could bring him to his knees and make him beg? She almost knocked into Grace, who had stopped at the foot of the stairs. Grace put a finger to her lips and motioned to two peepholes in the plaster. The chanting was louder down here. High voices rose in an unintelligible language. The Aether flooded the air like the horizon before a thunderstorm.

Lucia softly rose on her tiptoes to peer into the room.

Inside, the chamber was alight with a thousand candles. Maidens of Ishtar in flowing white robes stood in a circle around the outer edge of the oval room. In the center, just like in her daydream, rose a yew altar with a sacrificial stone. A man lay across the stone. His arms and legs were chained to the four corners. She didn't need a closer look to know that deep grooves would ring the stone to bring his blood to a trough at the foot. Her mind flashed to a similar stone in a similar sacrificial chamber. Reflexively, she clasped her wrists where her phantom scars burned.

She searched the man's face, but she didn't recognize him. The stranger was naked. A woman stood over him with a familiar crescent-shaped piece of jade, the edge sharpened to a blade. Lucia's stomach threatened to turn over. In the right hands, the Tablet of Destiny could be used to rewrite one's destiny. Lucia hadn't met the woman who wielded it before, but she would know her anywhere: the only female Dreki in the territory, Astrid Zetian, with the high forehead of her Norse mother and the cat eyes and black hair of her Mongol father. Gorgeous and willowy, she was a Dragon Lady and took no prisoners. There was no indication that she was anything other than Zetian, except the room buzzed with an Aether storm no dragon could call. But maybe with the Tablet she could.

"Ishtar!" Zetian called, voice thick with the sparkling water of the universe. "Fulfill your promise to me. Aid me in my hour of need. Give me your army to be my eyes and ears. Handmaiden of death, return to me what was lost. Heal that which was cursed. Take this man, oh goddess of war, and send him into your sister's kingdom to bring me back her Scepter. Take this offering and give me the Enkidu!" She sliced down and across with the dagger, and the man's throat sprayed red. The Maidens' hum grew. Lucia resisted the urge to vomit. She'd been on the battlefield and seen worse, but this felt different. This was torture, not self-defense. This was a ritual killing to power some dark magic. The Aether bucked.

She watched in horror as the blood spread over his skin as if it were being drawn across with an invisible paintbrush. The dirt floor around the altar began to bubble. Earth sprouted up. Writhing slowly with a life of its own, the clay drew together and climbed up the sides of the altar toward the man's jerking body. At first touch, his torso arched off the stone. The chains held him down as the earth penetrated his skin and disappeared into his body. Together the dirt and his blood-slicked skin mixed to form a red-brown mud. It weighed down his limbs, and his torso dropped back to the stone. And still the earth rose to fill his shell, and the Aether twisted, and the Maidens hummed. Concentrating, Lucia could feel the spell take shape even if she couldn't see the tangled webs that formed the undeath.

Grace tugged at the chain around Lucia's neck. Lucia took the hint and pulled the Deadglass from beneath her shirt. Fitting it to her eye, she adjusted the gears on the side until the brimming supernatural world came into focus and light—that which was taken on faith suddenly became truth. A soft power, Grace had called it. The Deadglass gave eyes to those who walked in ignorance of the supernatural, much as the Crane was prophesied to lead the blind.

Through the glass, she could suddenly see the swirls of sickly water that frizzed around Zetian's body. A Dreki should appear a shadow, empty of soul, but Zetian blazed. She was so bright, she was hard to look at directly. Power glided off her. If this was what the ancient humans had seen, no wonder they'd deified the immortals like her. There was no refuting the truth: Tiamat's soul burned in Zetian's body. Was there anything left of the Drekar adviser? Did she fight for control of her own body as Grace had? Or had this new Tiamat, free of her bondage by the power of the Tablet of Destiny, squashed the Dreki's mind like an ant?

Tiamat broke the chains and the clay man sat up. He moved robotically. It was different from when aptrgangrs possessed their puppets, clumsily learning to draw the tendons and muscles of their new marionette; this was a programmed machine. He was meant for one use only, and when he satisfied that purpose he would return to the earth from which he had been made. His skin took on a hardened sheen like pottery in the kiln, set but shatterproof. He would be almost impossible to kill until his mission was complete. The clay man pushed himself off the stone and stood. The maidens stopped chanting.

"I seek the Scepter of Ereshkigal, clay man," Tiamat said. "The Scepter that was used to kill my corporeal form and take death away from my dragon children. I won't live in fear of my sister and her Death. It is time the gods had a taste of what I suffered. I will eat their precious children and take the two Worlds back to be mine. Chaos will reign again. Go. Fetch the Scepter and bring it back to me."

The clay man moved smoothly. When he was still, he was still as the mountain rock. When he moved, he moved like a mudflow: fast, smooth, and dangerous.

Lady save her. Lady save them all. Kai spoke true. Tiamat seemed to have full control of Zetian's body and was able to manipulate the Aether for godlike spells. It was worse than Kingu, who had never achieved full power when taking over a human body. If Tiamat got control of the Scepter, she would wield the power of life and death for the whole world. She would be able to wipe out whole civilizations and bring back the dead. No one could stand up to her. They would all be lost.

Zetian watched the clay man go, and then turned to the cloaked Maidens. "Come, daughters. We will move our party to a place worthy of our illustrious selves. There are warriors aplenty to serve us. My Thunderbird is waiting."

Lucia pulled back from the wall. Her knees locked. Kai was waiting for Tiamat? She stumbled on the first step. She couldn't believe it of him. Kai had seemed so shaken by his run-in with the goddess. But if he had been anticipating her arrival, he was a better actor than any of them knew. Teaming up with Tiamat would be the ulti-mate card if he wanted to overthrow Corbette. It wouldn't be the first time he'd fallen in bed with the enemy, but was he a traitor?

Lucia retreated up the narrow staircase with Grace behind her. It seemed much longer and darker this time. Or maybe her muscles simply were in shock. She expected the frantic beating of her heart could be heard throughout the mansion. Any moment Zetian would rip through the wall and find them. She tried to hurry. Tried to keep her slippery grip from failing her on the banister. She had to get back to Kivati Hall and warn Corbette.

She escaped out the kitchen door in time to see the clay man leave by the front and race off in the direction of the crater. His joints were well-oiled pistons. His smooth gait was like an air train speeding over rough terrain. The Gateway hummed far below their feet in a chasm half filled with water. Through that Gate and into the Land of the Dead, he would make his way to the Lady of Death and her Scepter.

"We have to stop him," Lucia said.

Grace pushed her and they fled down the stairs into a nearby alley for cover. "Hurry then. The fate of the world depends on it."

# Chapter Five

"Me?" Lucia asked.

Grace grabbed her sleeve and pulled her down the street. They had to get away from the House of Ishtar before Tiamat discovered them. "Lucia, I've read the prophecy. The land that lives in the shadow of darkness? That's another name for the Land of the Dead."

"No, it's this world. Haven't you noticed? The Unraveling—earthquakes and volcanoes that turned the air black with ash. The lights and electricity doused. Dead who stalk the streets and wraiths that terrorize the living. Soul-suckers . . ." Lucia waved around to the ruined city. Panic started to bubble up. Go back into the crater? Was she crazy? "If there was a land in shadow and darkness, this is it."

"It's all about the Gate. You can't ignore the signs. The Unraveling, Kingu's release, and now Tiamat's servant to get the Scepter. Nothing will be made right again until somebody goes through that Gate and fixes it once and for all."

Lucia shook her head and took a step back. "The Raven is the only one with the power to travel between worlds.

You can't ask me to go back down there. You weren't
there. You didn't see the Gate bulging out with angry
demons and wraiths. It didn't break around you—Lady!—
no." Her hands shook, palms sweat. Her breath, too fast,
seemed to clog in her throat. She stuffed her hands in
her armpits and clamped down. She'd come so far, but
the memories were still too fresh. "Corbette can do it. The
Thunderbirds. You! You know how to fight the dead."

"Hey, I understand what you went through, but the
prophecy says—"

Lucia shook off Grace's hand. "I can't pass through
the Gate."

"Your blood opened the Gate."

"I can't go back down there!" Her heart galloped in her
ears. The alley started to spin. She pushed past Grace and
stumbled. She hadn't had a panic attack for months, but
she was fooling herself if she thought she was over it.
Gods, Grace was right—someone had to go after the clay
man. But what use would Lucia be if she freaked out at
the mere thought of seeing the Gate again?

The Deadglass bounced painfully against her breast-
bone. Her panic drove the Aether to her, wild and uncontrolled as a spirit storm. The Change ripped through her.
First, her skin peeled back from her muscle to let her long
white feathers unfurl; then her leg bones shattered into the
long thin legs of the Crane. Her beak led her into the air
as her wings caught an updraft. The Change had never
been so painful or so fast. Almost unthinking, emotion
ripped it through her, a mad shattering of ligaments and
cells. Aether crackled from her body. Was this what Corbette felt on a daily basis? How could he stand it? No
wonder he kept himself so tightly wound, if the uncontrolled flow of Aether through his body threatened to rip
him apart.

She spiraled up, leaving the brick streetscape far behind her, and sped to Kivati Hall. Crows rose from their roosts in the trees, screeching the alarm. A few Crow guards and Theodore, in Thunderbird form, flew into the air at her approach. They searched the air for sign of her pursuer. A thunderbolt crackled from Theo's wing. She crashed into the front doors of Kivati Hall. Her muscles ached. Her breath caught in her throat. She had to focus to force a Change back to human form. For a moment, she didn't think she could do it, and then Kai was there and Lady Alice and Will.

Kai crouched next to her and brushed back the tangled hair from her face. She jerked away from his touch. "What is it?"

"Tiamat," she croaked.

His face tightened, and he dropped his hand. "Where? Tell me!"

"Clay man. Gate," she said. Her vision swam. She tried to get the words out, but they tangled together, locked in her throat. Her mind was still enmeshed with the Crane. Human speech wouldn't form on her tongue.

"Calm yourself, child." Lady Alice shrugged out of her stole and covered Lucia. She drew her against her bosom and rocked her gently. Lucia curled into the heat of her body. She was so cold.

"What happened?" Will demanded. "Where have you been?"

"Let the girl breathe, Will," Alice said. "All of you. I said give her room!"

Lucia found her tongue. "Tiamat killed a man and turned him to clay. She sent him through the Gate to recover the Scepter of Death. Where's Corbette?"

Will crossed his arms. "He's already gone." He turned and started barking out orders. "The city isn't safe. Call back the warriors and lock down the Hill. No one should be out tonight. If Tiamat—"

"No," Lucia struggled away from Alice. "Get everyone out. She's coming to the Hall! She's coming for Kai." Kai's nostrils flared. "Where's Corbette? He has to stop her. She talked about a third pantheon and saving the Drekar from their undeath. She plans to build a new Babylon and take over both worlds. Where is the Raven Lord?"

Kai swore.

"You have to answer, Will." Lady Alice turned on the Thunderbird general. An undercurrent of anger sparked between them. "Don't pretend you don't know. He wouldn't just put you in charge and leave his duties. Not Emory. He doesn't know the meaning of the word retreat."

"He's already on his way through the Gate," Will said.

"But he doesn't know about the clay man!" Lucia shouted. "Someone has to go after him!"

Will's eyebrows drew down. She'd never seen him look so somber. "You don't understand. If Tiamat has returned, we can't risk touching the Aether. Any message we send will be intercepted. She can't know he's gone."

"Why would he go through the Gate?" Alice demanded.

Will turned away. He clasped his forearms behind his back. "He felt the blast of Aether when Tiamat rose and knew he couldn't match her power. In his dreams, the Raven has been showing him the path through the Gate for some time now, and the Aether blast made him realize that he must follow his totem's lead. His answers lie on the other side of the Gate."

"Now? This is no time for a spirit quest!" Lucia said.

"Bullshit," Alice said. "Emory wouldn't abandon the Hill at a time like this."

"It couldn't wait. Haven't you seen it in his eyes?" Will spun to face them. "He knew as soon as Kai told us about his 'encounter'"—his mouth drew back in a sneer—"that his totem had been trying to tell him the means of defeating Tiamat must be through the Gate. He will find whatever it is. Don't worry. The Raven can pass between worlds. Kivati Hall is prepared for a siege. We'll outlast anything Tiamat can throw at us until he gets back."

Lucia struggled to her feet. "He doesn't know what he's looking for."

"The gods will show him. It's not our place to demand answers from them. That is the way the spirit quest works. You know that. When you went on your vision quest, did you demand the Lady answer your call?"

"Yes!"

"No. You simply went with an open heart."

Alice stormed to the open doors to stare out into the night. In trousers and a billowing shirt in pale blue, her long black hair hanging free to her lower back, she looked fiercely independent from her brother's rule, but quite like him all the same. Brash. Arrogant. She rapped her knuckles against one massive oak door. "How can you tell me that my compulsive, controlling brother would abandon the Kivati in the face of a monster?"

"He didn't abandon it, Ali," Will protested. "He left me in charge. I will protect you."

"May the Lady help us all." Alice stepped back from the doors. She looked meaningfully at Lucia. "Well? What are you waiting for?"

Will's eyes widened. "She can't go after him."

"Let me—" Kai started, but Alice blocked his path.

"You will not lead Tiamat after Emory. She's coming for you. You aren't going anywhere," she said.

Lucia saw what she had to do. There really was no one else. The Thunderbirds and strongest warriors were all needed here to defend the hill if they had any hope of survival. No one could be spared to go after Corbette. No one but her. "Yes. I'll go." She tried to pull the Aether to her. It shushed against her skin like silk, but wouldn't catch.

"Tell him hello for me!" Alice said and shot a wave of Aether at Lucia. It dug in like the blade of a knife and gave her the extra power she needed to Change. Her human skin crumbled to let the Crane burst through. She shut her eyes against the pain and rose into the air. Looking back, she saw Alice blocking Will from following her. Kai watched from the doorway. She shot through the air toward the crater. *Don't think about it.* Anything but the memories of her last time deep beneath the city streets. Instead, she thought of Corbette, of his sharp profile and angry brows, of his sleek muscled torso when he took his shirt off to fight, of that rare elegant curve of his mouth when he found her amusing.

Plunging through the low cloud cover, she raced to the crater, folded her wings, and dropped down into the cavern. She couldn't let herself take a breath; the fear would suffocate her. Down into the belly of the sacred earth, she fell. Dark swallowed the dim sky overhead until the earth closed over her like the mouth of a great whale. *Don't look. Don't look.* Waves crashed against the base of the crater. Hungry, grasping. She shuddered, but dove into the black maw, lined with earth stained red with her blood. So much blood.

Shaking so hard she could barely keep aloft, she landed on a rocky outcrop a foot above the surface of the salt water and Changed. Painful, slow, but the Aether didn't abandon her. She made it.

"Corbette? Can you hear me?" No answer but her own voice echoed back at her. He'd already gone under. The thought of being crushed under all that water and rock sent spirals of white cascading across her vision. She remembered—gods, she remembered. The blood and the pain and the betrayal. The earthquake that had crashed the rock around her and shaken the marrow from her bones. The despair as she'd felt her lifeblood seep away to fuel the opening Gate. Corbette's black eyes finding her, locking onto her, never letting her go. She would have crashed out on a maelstrom of loss, but he'd anchored her to the Living World like a clothesline in a blizzard. There had been madness, and then there had been him. He'd drawn her back, one frozen finger at a time, until her soul had poured back into her injured body and the shadows had fled from the broken corners of her soul. He'd been there for her, and she couldn't imagine a world where he wasn't waiting in the wings to save her again.

He needed her now. She couldn't avoid the rolling water. She had to find him before the clay man did.

With a deep breath, she dove beneath the waves. The shock of frozen cold assaulted her. After a beat, she reoriented herself and kicked down and under, finding the tunnel Kai had told her about. Her lungs burned. Cranes were waterfowl, but not meant for narrow passageways and angry salt seas. Fear fueled her body, and then she was through and into the magic-infested burrow of the Spider's lair.

Corbette pulled aside a thick curtain of spider silk with the point of his cane, and a cloud of dust rained from the roof. He'd brought a torch and a rucksack full of food and supplies. He didn't know what it would be like on the other side of the Gate, but he was prepared for anything:

a blizzard, a demonic storm, an army of ghosts. What he
wasn't prepared for was the small, wet woman who
charged into his back, almost knocking him down.

"Corbette? Corbette! I found you."

He caught her; hands found bare skin and long,
wet tresses covered in spider silk. "Good gods, Lucia,
you're . . . you're . . . ." Wet. Cold. *Naked.* He wanted to
draw her to him to warm her and stop her shaking. The
torch, which had dropped but not burnt out, illuminated
her pale limbs and the shadow between her thighs.
Startled, he froze. Lady be. He'd said good-bye, at least
in his mind. He never thought he'd touch her again, and
now here she was, a siren in the dark, naked and alone
and—gods, did he mention naked? "What are you doing
here?"

"The clay man. Tiamat sent"—she took a huge shaking
breath—"Ereshkigal's Scepter and . . ."

"Shhh, calm yourself." He rubbed his hands down her
shivering arms. Her skin was so smooth, her limbs so delicate. The Raven was a visual creature, but the man
craved touch, and the temptation of her skin was too
great. He yanked her clothes from the Aether to shield her
from his sight. Too late, he realized the last clothes he'd
seen her in had been the scarlet gown. The sudden flash
of red and silk, the tightening of her waist and thrust of
her small breasts as the corset materialized, sent his
senses reeling. He set her away from him and took a long
step back. He was only a man, and she was forbidden.
"Now tell me from the beginning."

Her fingers flew to a chain around her neck that disappeared beneath her gown between the valley of her
breasts. She held on, her breathing labored for a long
moment as she adjusted to the weight of petticoats and

silk. "We went to the Temple of Ishtar and watched Zetian, with Tiamat inside her, kill a man and turn him to clay."

"The Enkidu. They were used in ancient Babylon as bodyguards for the royal family. Gilgamesh took one on his journey to the underworld."

"Will she make more? It was gruesome." Lucia wrapped her arms around herself.

"I don't know. Tell me the rest."

"Zetian—Tiamat—sent him through the Gate to bring back the Scepter of the goddess of Death. She means to overthrow the gods and take over both worlds. She will be all powerful."

Every word was rent out of his nightmare, but this was the waking world. He'd failed to protect the Gate, failed to protect the woman under his care, and now the Babylonian Goddess of Primordial Chaos sought to rule his world and the next? Even Halian's mistake hadn't been so great. If his father had only killed the Drekar when he'd had the chance, all this could have been avoided. He searched his brain for the moment when his protocols had begun to break down. Chaos was the opposite of everything he worked for. Safety, security for his people. There was no room for mistakes. No space for unpredictable people who didn't toe the line. He picked up his cane and shouldered the rucksack. "Yes, Tiamat will likely make more Enkidu to protect herself and her spawn. Thank you for your assistance. Please go back now. Quickly. Tell the others what you told me, and don't leave the Hall again. Not for anything—"

"Don't you understand?" Lucia grabbed his sleeve as he tried to turn. "She said Kai was waiting for her. The clay man went to get the Scepter while Tiamat joins Kai at Kivati Hall. When I left, she was on her way with all of Ishtar's Maidens from the Temple."

"You think Kai disloyal?"

She bit her lip. "Don't you?"

"Given recent actions, isn't that the pot calling the kettle black?"

"I was right to help the Drekar against Kingu! Tiamat is much worse—"

"And she is the mother of all dragons. The Drekar can't help but heed her call. But Kai? I don't believe he would turn, not for anything. Still, Kivati Hall has withstood a Drekar siege before. Go back and tell Will what you've told me."

"He knows—"

"Then return to the Hall and, for the love of the Lady, follow directions for once. You must listen to me: cut all ties with the Drekar. They will flock to their Goddess." He took her hand and searched her eyes. "We must eliminate them before they can join Tiamat's plans."

Her jaw tightened. "Not all of them will follow her."

"Of course they will. It's in their nature. You don't know what they're capable of. You've been sheltered from much of the bloodshed."

Her lips pulled back to show her even white teeth. She didn't look so delicate anymore. "The Gate fell because of one of us," she snapped. "My blood opened it. My blood destroyed the world. Sheltered? Look at me, Corbette. See me. All you see when you look at me is some broken, pretty thing. I don't even recognize myself! There is more to me than that, and I'm not going to spend the rest of my life trying to atone for some sin that's not my fault. I can't be that fragile, sensitive Lady you seem to want. Every time you look at me I see the disappointment in your eyes—"

"Not for you—"

"And I can't bear it. I'm sorry the Crane chose me.

I'm sorry I didn't live up to your expectations from the beginning. But, damn it, I've faced down the Gate breaking and Kingu's army and snuck past the Goddess of Fucking Chaos, and I'm not going to blindly follow your orders."

Gods, she thought this of him? He'd only thought of his own failure, his own response to her that reminded him all too sharply of his lack of control as a raw youth. He had put her off to give them both time to adjust to their new roles. He'd thought his instinctive draw to her would cool off. He'd believed she would grow into her powers eventually. He'd wanted to wait until things were settled with the Drekar, until they had safety for their people, peace to get to know each other away from the war. He'd thought they had time. He'd been wrong.

"The Drekar must do as their mother goddess commands," he said. "Think if our Lady demanded sacrifice from us—could we refuse? No."

"A brave man would do what is right, will of the gods or not."

"Well stung, Lady Crane."

"I'm coming with you."

"No."

She let go of his sleeve and raised her chin. "I can help—"

He barked a laugh.

Her nostrils flared. "Tiamat will have reached the Hill by now. There is no other direction to go. If you send me back, you send me straight into her arms."

Corbette stared at her, white hair plastered back from her too wide blue eyes, dress the color of sin set off by her moonlight complexion. She ruined every one of his plans. He searched his brain for somewhere safe to stash her, but there was nowhere but the Hill. How could he bring her

through the Gate and into death? Everything he'd worked
so hard for was crumbling like grains of sand. Winding a
hand through a long strand of her hair, he pulled her close
and let her see the wild in his eyes. "Then you shouldn't
have come, Lucia."

"You needed to know about the Scepter. You must stop
the Enkidu." Her pupils dilated. Her fingers tightened on his
sleeves. He could smell her fear. He could smell her arousal.
He'd never handled her roughly like this, and it excited
her. He wasn't sure who was more surprised, he or she.

And that made him angrier, because he'd never treated
her with anything but kid gloves, but she still knew his
animalistic nature was capable of less civilized brutality.
She should demand more from him. He demanded more
from himself.

"If you can't go with me and you can't go back, you
must fly, little bird. Fly fast and fly far and leave this
cursed land behind you." His voice broke. This land was
part of his blood. It had been the home of his mother and
his mother's mother all the way back to the first Kivati
who'd traveled these shores and joined her spirit with the
first totem animal. Everywhere he looked, he saw the
Lady: the earth was Her womb, and the oceans Her tears;
the mountains Her breasts and the stars Her hair. Her
heart beat in the deep core of the planet with the promise
that the Kivati would never be forgotten.

He'd never left fate to the gods. "If I don't return from
the Land of the Dead, and Tiamat takes Kivati Hall, it will
be the end of the Kivati. Maybe this is what the prophecy
meant, that you will be the last. You must escape, Lucia."

"Alone?"

"Promise me, Lucia Crane. You must survive." She
nodded her head a fraction, and he took that as assent.
He crushed his mouth to hers in one last good-bye. The

Aether he'd been holding back rushed through him in a wave of heated energy. It blew back the spider silk in a phantom wind and struck every nerve ending between them like flint. Spirits preserve him. Her lips lit under his touch, a firecracker in July, and everywhere they touched sparked with a thousand stars. She tasted of sea salt and moonbeams. He meant to say good-bye, but instead he poured every regret, every abandoned hope for their romance into that kiss and lost himself.

She shocked him with the anger he tasted from her lips. Scalded him with this taste of what might have been. Teased him with the press of her breasts against his chest, the widening of her stance just enough for him to slip his knee between the skirts of her gown. He found the V of her thighs. It was soft and waiting, a heaven he'd only glimpsed in his dark dreams, not the proper way he'd imagined it in the light of day. What he wanted, and what he should want. In the dark, in the dreamscape, in the Spider's intoxicating silk, there were no clear lines between right and wrong. There were no censuring eyes, no rules to uphold. Who would see if he gave in to the wild inside him? Who would know if he bore her down to the wet, rocky earth, on a bed of silk, and buried himself inside her?

And if he didn't survive, if his Thunderbirds lost the Hill to Tiamat, if this was indeed the end of it all, he might die easier knowing that his seed would live on. The Raven had long insisted he take her to mate. Only the man had held back. Propriety. Decorum. But at the mouth of the Gate to the Land of the Dead, those rules of civility melted away. He wanted her. Her bold tongue said she wanted him too.

All of a sudden, she screamed.

He looked up. A giant spider the size of a Volkswagen Bug clung upside down to the tunnel ceiling. It had fangs

the length of his body. It held itself very still, sparkling
silk clinging to every hairy leg, and watched him with
giant, multifaceted eyes. Stand still or run?

A drop of venom dripped down one long fang.

"Run!" He pulled her after him, away from the tunnel
entrance. She tripped in her slippers and constricting
skirts. He cursed himself. Why hadn't he dressed her in
some black battle dress, pants and boots and practical
leather? There was no time to Change. They tore through
curtains of spider silk and the Aether clung to their skin,
pulling them into the dreamscape, but the monster chasing behind kept their feet moving. The shimmering silk
bathed the tunnel in a dim glow, barely enough to see the
darker shadows in their path or the gaping black of the
tunnel ahead.

Then the ground dropped out beneath them, and they
fell through a hole in the tunnel floor and out into the
open air.

Lucia's skirts slid up to tangle her body and obscure her
vision. She felt Corbette lock his arms around her as they
shot into the open air, free falling into space. She got a
sense of a vast cavern, with no walls as far as the eye could
see, and then the roof of the tunnel disappeared from view
into a sparkling, churning Aether of light swells and
moonbeams. It was like the vast curvature of space above.
No connection to the earth but Corbette's iron grip,
holding her, smelling of musk and cedar and safety.

The sound of rushing water echoed from below. Lucia
glimpsed a vast stretch of curving land, and then they
were falling, falling, falling.

She pressed her head against Corbette's chest, but kept
her eyes wide open. A river of black rose up, the barrier

to the Land of the Dead. Humans had many names for it—Styx, River of Lost Souls—but whatever name it went by, it remained the first and last barrier to living bodies passing through to the world where they didn't belong. She had just enough time to take a deep breath before they plunged into the freezing water.

Pain stripped her body, worse than her worst Change. A pain so great it seemed like her soul was being ripped from her chest. She had to fight not to open her mouth and scream. The velocity of their fall carried them under, and the water wrapped them in its heavy embrace.

Lucia was torn from Corbette's grasp. The pain made her delirious. She didn't know which way was up. Water soaked her heavy petticoats and skirts, and they tangled around her legs, ballast in the water. Her dress dragged her down. She would drown. She panicked. Her lungs burned.

*Help*! she screamed inside her head, pouring everything she had into sending Corbette a message through the Aether. She'd never been able to before, but surely the threat of drowning was enough to spark her weak power.

The Aether didn't move for her. Not so much as a trickle. She shouldn't fear water; she was Crane, for the Lady's sake. Her panic should force the Change and free her from her murderous gown. She reached out, but she found nothing. No trace of the sparkling water that was her birthright. No Crane beating inside her.

She couldn't hold her breath any longer. Liquid seeped into her mouth, and instinctively she coughed. No air. No light. No Aether. She choked on the river of death.

Drowning was a quiet affair. Welcoming, freezing. *Be quiet*, the river crooned. *Be peaceful.*

Her helplessness fueled a rage inside her. *No*, she told the river. She wouldn't be complacent in her own demise. She fought her skirts, tried to find the ties that would free her.

And then someone grabbed her hand. Corbette's mouth was suddenly on hers, and he was feeding her a breath. Lady of Life. She felt the ties snap and his blade against her skin. The sharp edge scraped her in his haste, but the pain jolted her oxygen-deprived mind. He helped wrestle her out of the fabric and dragged her to the surface. Her head broke water. Oxygen. Sweet, sweet oxygen. Her greed for it was so great she couldn't force the water first from her lungs. She thrashed.

"Easy, easy now. I've got you." Corbette towed her on her back in a lifeguard's hold. He dragged her to the shore and up onto a hard, rocky beach. Her chest heaved. She couldn't stop coughing. It felt like she'd swallowed the entire river. Only once she was safely out of the river's reach did he collapse by her side, her icy skin white as snow next to his sun-tinted arm. Their breath steamed in the cold. They lay side by side for a long moment, treasuring each breath of clean, easy air.

"Thank you," Lucia whispered.

"I couldn't Change." His voice was hoarse.

She rolled her head to the side and looked at him. His wet black hair was plastered to his neck. He'd ditched his suit jacket and wore only wet wool trousers and a slick white linen shirt that clung to his soaking body. His hands were fisted against his sides. Why hadn't he dried himself with the Aether? Why hadn't he pulled fresh clothes and sluiced the water from his hair?

"You can't Change?" she asked, as the impact of that thought hit her, another blow stole a precious breath. "You can't touch the Aether."

He stared at the strange swirling sky. There was no sign of the tunnel they'd fallen from. There was nothing to indicate they were underground at all.

She sat up and rubbed her arms to get the blood

flowing. Lady be, she was so cold. What she'd taken for driftwood and rocks turned out to be metal scrap. Giant pipes and half-buried machinery and, beneath her fingers, ancient coins, bent fasteners, and small, lost buttons.

Something was deeply wrong. She tested herself. All her limbs seemed to be in order. Nothing broken, just bruised from the impact of hitting the water. A few scrapes from the slide and a thin line of blood where Corbette's knife had cut the gown from her back. But when she reached inside herself for her totem self, her Crane, she found nothing. No trace of the bird spirit that had been her constant companion for the last five years. "The Crane is gone."

"Yes."

"You don't feel the Raven inside you?"

He swallowed and shook his head.

"The pain when we hit the river." Lady, Lady. Without her totem, was she even Kivati? She wrapped her arms around herself. "Are we dead?"

Corbette was silent a long moment. "Not yet."

"Gods, it feels like I've been skinned alive." For all that she resented the prophecy, she loved the Crane. Without it, she was less. She was practically human. It was amazing Corbette, with Aether in his veins instead of blood, hadn't died on the spot. "How do you stand it?"

Slowly, he sat up. "I stand it because there is no other option." He turned to look at her, his black eyes unfathomable. "We must set ground rules."

She became keenly aware that she wore next to nothing: a ripped shift, bloomers, and stockings. Lacy things suited to a boudoir, not a dark beach at the border of Death. Ties and ribbons, designed to be undone. She was soaking wet too, and the fabric clung to her body like a second skin. They were two half-clad people on a beach without a soul in sight. No witnesses. She remembered that kiss in the tunnel all too clearly. She felt some color leech back into her cheeks. "What sort of rules?"

"We can't have an incident like before."

"An incident?"

"No touching. You're in an emotionally vulnerable state—"

She bristled.

"—and we can't let our animal natures get the best of us. Look what happened." He gestured around to the barren river. "You almost died. Twice. We must have our wits about us, and for that you must follow my lead. If I say run, you run, no questions."

Lucia felt her blood boil. "I don't see the Raven anywhere, so I'm not sure where you get off giving me orders."

He stood and pulled her up. Even without Aether crackling from his being, his body was imposing. Tall and strong, he could force her to do his bidding if he stooped to physical intimidation. He never had before. "You're right. My totem is gone, I can't touch the Aether, and there is no sign of the Gate."

"I'm not afraid of you."

He didn't move, but danger radiated from every pore. Even stripped of his magic, he could crush her like a bug. It became apparent that he was also keenly aware of the state of her undress. The wet wool of his trousers rose in interesting places.

She took a hasty step back.

"Big words, little warrior," he said, voice dark as chocolate. He tilted his head in the Raven's curious half bow. "You will follow my lead, and maybe we will get out of this alive."

# Chapter Six

Corbette's head felt strangely light. He watched Lucia from outside himself, this beautiful, bedraggled girl that he'd taken to death's door. He'd never seen her so mad or so vibrant, and it took every inch of his willpower not to take her in his arms and kiss her into willful submission.

But he was not himself. The Aether, so long a storm through him, his bane and the source of all his power, was gone, leaving him like a bone-dry riverbed. Never had there been a punishment so damaging or so soul-wrenching. This he would have wished only on his worst enemies. His second soul had been completely stripped from his body. No wonder evil filled Sven Norgard and his dragon kin. Without a soul, the vessel of the body was primed and waiting to be filled. Sin rushed in.

"Corbette—" she began.

"Emory. I am not the Raven. Not anymore." His totem, his power, his very identity—all gone in the space of one long slide into darkness. One final mistake in a long series of terrible mistakes. He turned from her so she couldn't see the anguish in his eyes.

"Look!" she said.

A bird cry came from overhead. Glancing up, he saw two birds: a white crane with red feathers at its temple and a raven, black as soot. They flew west, away from the river. "Raven!" he shouted and ran after them. His totem gave him no notice. He tried to reach through the Aether, but it was like trying to catch starlight. Picking up a rock, he hurled it at the bird. The rock missed by a mile and clattered down to the beach. The Raven simply flew on as if he didn't exist, as if they hadn't spent more than a century sharing one body. "Raven!" he screamed. He dropped to his knees. "Raven!"

A gentle hand touched his back. He shrugged her off. Now he really had nothing to offer. Without the Aether, without his totem, he might as well be human. Weak, vulnerable bits of clay. Lady damn them.

He couldn't protect her. He couldn't even protect himself.

Lucia gave him space. "Let's follow," she said after a long moment. "Hopefully they'll show us the way to the Gate."

Corbette rose. It was cold on the river's shore. He realized he was shivering. His wet clothes had begun to itch. He couldn't fathom this discomfort. To not pull dry clothes from the Aether—it was unthinkable. And Lucia—he could do nothing to ease her cold, freezing state either. What would he do if someone attacked them? He had dropped his knife after freeing Lucia from her waterlogged skirts. His cane with its hidden sword and the rucksack had vanished beneath the waves too.

Leaving the river behind, they followed the beach west. Garbage littered the landscape. There was no plant life or pleasant smell of mulch and green things growing. Instead the air had a metallic tinge. He detected oil and rust and the dust of long-forgotten corners. His vision had altered. No longer did he have the crisp, far sight of the Raven. The distance seemed blurry, the ground beneath his feet strangely far away. He was so used to sight being his primary sense that he was off balance. And his feet— never had he walked so far on human legs. For a hundred years, he'd had wings. There had been no need to develop hard soles to walk over uneven, junk-filled earth.

As they hiked, they passed half-buried souvenirs of bygone eras. He started to identify the flotsam and jetsam. Roman goblets made of lead. Harpoons still rusted with blood. An early rigid diving suit with a copper helmet and iron belt. Small, partly smashed silver balls that he realized were bullets.

Silence lengthened the walk. He kept his eyes on the sharp bits of discarded metal and not on the scantily clad damsel in distress with her pert nipples and watery eyes. He didn't know himself in this state. He couldn't trust the passion in her eyes any more than the fear.

She walked a distance behind him. He could feel her anger scalding his back. She could stew all she liked as long as she followed his orders when the time came.

The birds led west to the base of two mountains, where the landscape truly turned into an antique junkyard— smashed Model Ts; a four-masted schooner with its hull caved in; and an entire steam train, each car brimming with cast-off metal and wire and broken gears.

Between the two mountains was a thin sliver of a canyon, no more than a crack between the stone. Ancient symbols had been carved into the limestone at each edge. As they drew near, they found two stone giants blocking their way. They stood watch, the eternal sentinels of the dead. At first, Corbette didn't think they were alive, but when he tried to walk beneath their crossed spears, they animated and barred the way. He watched uselessly as the

Raven and the Crane flew through the narrow gap and disappeared from view.

"Only the dead may enter here," one giant said. His voice was the whisper of wind through the mountain pass.

"The Raven may pass," Corbette said.

"Only the dead may enter here," said the second giant. Her voice spoke of the womb at the beginning of the world and the blood they would all return to.

Corbette tried to call the Aether to him to blast his way through the Gate. He grit his teeth against a roar of frustration. His powers were gone. A creak and scratch answered him, the sound of two rocks sliding together, and he realized the giants laughed at him. "I seek the Queen of the Spirit Realm. Both worlds are in danger. Tiamat has risen."

"What do we care of mortal tidings?" the first giant asked.

Lucia came to stand by his right shoulder. "Stay back," he told her.

"You need a gift," she whispered.

"Let me handle it."

"Who is that behind you?" asked the second giant. "Be on your way. Only the dead may enter here."

"But the Raven walks between the worlds," Corbette said again. "You have to let me through."

The giant shook her head. "I don't see the Raven. Do you, Upshantmaan?"

"No, wife" said Upshantmaan. "Just a man."

"Just a man. Go!" The female giant pounded her stick on the ground, and rocks fell from the mountains above. Corbette dove to cover Lucia with his body. The earth shook.

Lucia clung to his shirt. "You're doing it wrong. Give them a gift!"

"I have nothing!"

"Tell them a story."

"Who is that with you?" the female giant asked.

Corbette scowled. "I know what I'm doing—"

"Do you? I might not have done well in Aether studies, but I listened in folklore class. In every folktale around the world there must be an exchange. A gift for passage, and there's nothing the gods love more than a story. So get off your high horse and let me do this." Lucia pushed him off. Standing, she faced the giants dressed in little more than wet lace. She threw her white braid over her shoulder and lifted her chin. "Noble guardians, I bring you a gift! A story to ease your long wait."

Tensing, Corbette waited for the giants to start another avalanche, but they stood expectantly.

"In the beginning," Lucia said, "there was darkness. The land was dark and the sky was dark and the sea was dark. Raven flew between the worlds, and saw the humans and animals shivering in their lodges in a sea of mud. He flew out of the realm of the birds, the spirit realm, and found a single long house glowing with the light of a hearth fire. He waited until three young maidens came out, the Sky God's daughters: first the pale Lady Moon, then the bright Lady Sun, then the Dark Lady who sparkled with a million tiny souls. The Moon was too pale. The Sun was too blinding. But in the darkness of the third maiden he found a light that would unlock the joy of a thousand stars."

Corbette watched Lucia. Her spine straightened, her elegant hands danced with the words, and her face softened, inviting, as she wove her tale. Her voice took on a melodic quality he'd never heard her use, and for the first time he could see her as a Spirit Seeker.

"So Raven turned himself into a droplet of rain and

slipped between the Lady's lips and down into Her belly. She returned to Her father's house and gave birth to a baby boy—Raven—reborn as the Sky God's grandson. Inside the lodge he found the secret box where the Sky God had hidden his tools: fire, spindle, and glass eye. He knew the world needed light and heat, so he opened the box, grabbed the tools, Changed back to himself, and flew out through the fire hole in the roof. The Sky God in a wrath burst through the front door and chased Raven through the sky. The fire burned Raven black as coal. He dropped the fire, the spindle and the glass eye, but still the Sky God came after him, and there was no place in the dark and the mud for him to hide. The Dark Lady took pity on him, for she had loved the babe he'd pretended to be. She threw herself between Raven and her father and Changed to make a safe place for Raven and all his people to live. Her milk-filled breast became the mountains and her tears the sea. Her shining soul fire became the molten core of the planet, and her womb the fertile valley of the earth. She renamed Raven and his people the Kivati—those who Change—and told Raven that because he'd risked all to make the world a better place for humans and animals, he would forever be responsible for their keeping. She gave him the Sky God's tools: fire to heat the lodges, which Raven taught to the humans; a spindle to weave the Aether and the glass eye to see the Aether's sparkling webs, which Raven kept for himself. Forever after, the Kivati, humans, and animals have had a place to live, and when they grow weary of flying, they return to the bosom of the Dark Lady. Even in the darkest night, when we, Raven's children, close our eyes, we can still see Her sparkling water calling us home."

The giants were crying. Upshantmaan went to his wife and held her. "Go, go! Do not speak to us anymore."

Corbette had to clear his throat. It had been a long time since he had heard the origin story so eloquently told. Lucia had a gift. Maybe not weaving the Aether, but there were other ways to bring people together. She bowed to the giants and walked on through without a backward glance. He hurried to catch up with her. When they'd passed through the narrow gap and the stone giants were out of sight, he spoke. "I didn't know you were a story-teller."

"The things you don't know about me could fill an ocean."

He forced himself to swallow his surprise. Perhaps he owed her an apology. He'd watched her for years, but he'd never made the effort to get to know her: the real girl, thoughts and feelings and peculiarities. If anything, this journey would provide time to remedy that. He just had to figure out how to start.

Death didn't arrive in a thunderstorm. Death walked up the Hill and through the Kivati front gates. The guards were helpless to stop her, and no alarm sounded before it was already too late. The worst part, Kai reflected as he watched Zetian stroll confidently through the front door like a monarch returning home, was that the Kivati had been warned. Corbette's dreams. Kai's run-in—he wasn't calling it more than that. Lucia's frantic message that Tiamat was here, now, and coming their way.

But no one had thought Kivati Hall would fall without a single shot.

And so their castle became their coffin. But no one re-alized it soon enough.

Lord William Raiden was the first to die. Unbendable
as steel, Will's right and wrong were carved in the cliff
face, not like Kai's in the sand where the tide moved the
line as it saw fit. Will took one look at Zetian and ordered
the women and children out and the men to fire. Zetian—
Tiamat—smiled. A slow curve of her lips as if the prospect
of blood excited her. She raised one jewel-encrusted hand
and a ball of Aether coalesced, blue with the fire of the
gods. The ball she created was like his thunderbolts, but
so much more. His thunderbolts materialized and were
gone, with only seconds between the zap and the fizzle,
but hers stayed strong.

"In the beginning," she said, madness in her eyes,
"there was Chaos. So shall there be again, when the Gates
fall and the two Worlds join as one. You will sacrifice
yourself for me, and your children will sacrifice themselves for me, and your children's children. All will serve
Chaos, and the earth will call out for blood, until darkness
covers the land." Tiamat tossed her ball of blue fire into
Will's chest. His body absorbed it. Every hair shot
straight out and his arms were thrown up, frozen for a
long second as the energy burned through him. Blue fire
radiated across his skin. His mouth opened in a silent
scream, his eyes rolled back in his head, and then William
Raiden was no more, just a charred bit of ash to float in
the air of the room.

Lady Alice, standing at Kai's elbow to witness the
atrocity, swore, and Kai, never one to sacrifice himself
meaninglessly, heard himself say, "I'll buy you time."

The screams and pounding of running feet dimmed to
static. Kai swaggered forward. He knew it for a swagger,
because it involved his whole body, oiled hips and a lazy
smile and just enough cock-sure to let his audience know
he was willing and ready to turn that vertical dance into

something of a horizontal nature. He didn't turn to see if
Alice made it out, or which warriors fled and which made
a stand, or who might glare daggers at his back as he
waltzed up to the enemy. It was important for the lady to
know that he had eyes only for her. And he did. Zetian-
Tiamat was a firestorm of Aether, beautiful and brilliant
in the soft gaslight of Kivati Hall. He'd always imagined
the gods and goddesses to manifest in a more ethereal
nature, but Tiamat was an earthy sort. Energy seemed to
radiate up from her toes, drawing from deep within the
earth. He had to admit Zetian was truly beautiful. Hair
black as a raven wing. Lips like coral from the sea. Her
figure was slender and features dainty, but her eyes
blazed power, and he had reason to know that body wasn't
as delicate as it pretended. She could beat him in a fight,
and the knowledge both shamed him and drew him in.

If he didn't know she was Drekar and deranged Babylonian goddess, if he hadn't seen her kill Will only seconds
ago, in another galaxy, in another life, he'd put all his
energy getting into her bed.

But because she'd killed and would kill again, he still
put all his energy into getting into her bed, because he
knew what she was after, and he could distract her until
the others got away.

*You figure out what needs doing, and then you get it
done*, his brother used to say. But Jace had always been
the better twin. Ironic, now, that Kai's less virtuous skills
were finally useful to the Kivati.

"Tiamat, love," Kai said. He let his eyes wander down
her silk-clad figure and back up to her face. The red
sheath dress looked as if it had been stolen from a High
Priestess of Ishtar, and she wore gold bracelets up to her
elbows.

Her hands were stained red with clay.

# Chapter Seven

Through the narrow gap of the Gate to the Land of the Dead, Lucia found a lush jungle rising out of the scrap metal and discarded artifacts. Almost Jurassic, with giant mangrovelike trees that tangled together from a briny bog. She recognized none of the plants, but could easily imagine an allosaurus pushing its way through the thick brush. The path was wet. When there was a path.

"I always thought the way was clear through the other-world," Lucia said. Now that the adrenaline from facing the giants had passed, she found herself shivering again in her wet underthings. The silence of the woods was full of menace. No bird song. No scurry of animals. Just wind tussling the canopy. "I thought the Aether lit a shimmering path to show souls the way."

Corbette pushed a branch away and helped her over a gnarled root the size of a giant's foot. "Maybe the Land senses we don't belong here. It looks like there was a path, but it's been overgrown with this rubbish."

The plastic casings of printers and laser discs piled on top of small altars and offerings to long-forgotten gods.

She found books too, some so burnt only the spines were left. "What are all these things?"

"Ideas that have died. Inventions that are obsolete. Abandoned plans and paths and beliefs. The discarded flotsam and jetsam of the Living World."

"The forest feels dead. Nothing moves. It's creepy."

"A dead forest in the Land of the Dead? Imagine that."

He didn't have to sound so patronizing. "But it doesn't feel right," she insisted. "This isn't the way it's supposed to be."

Corbette crooked an eyebrow at her. "And why do you think that, fair Lucia? Dreams are the province of the Harbinger. You never told me you dreamed of this place."

"I didn't." But she'd dreamed of deaths. During the worst of the Kivati-Drekar war, the nightmares had been so bad she'd become an insomniac for fear of sleep. "I just have this strange feeling. Like I've been here before." Beneath the junk, the swamp whispered to her. If she concentrated very hard, she could almost sense a heartbeat within the thick twisting bark of the mangrove. The forest wasn't completely dead after all, but the pulse was so faint. Just the barest flicker of life, like an ancient crone waiting for the dark.

Corbette pushed on ahead. "We need to keep moving. If what you say is true, the Enkidu has a good lead on us."

Bristling, she followed. "So where does Ereshkigal live?"

"The Lady of Death lives in a palace, but I don't know what it looks like. The legends say there are seven gates to pass through before you reach her, but myths are rarely clear. Those gates could be physical or metaphorical."

"Tests," she said. "The gods always test the hero to see if he is worthy of entrance."

Corbette's shoulders stiffened, but he pressed on. What

was it she had said that bothered him? Was it fear that they
might not pass, or fear that they might be found lacking?

"The Kivati haven't trespassed into the spirit realm in
recent memory," he said. "Think of your legends, then.
They might give us some hint of the tasks to come."

Their passage was labored. Gnarled roots snagged
their feet. Massive trunks of trees that had grown together
blocked the path for what seemed like miles. The discarded metal made every step hazardous. Lucia still wore
her slippers, but they were made for dancing. The thin
soles tore easily and let her feel every sharp rock.

The long roots of the giant mangrovelike trees grew
one on top of another, raised from the earth, almost like
small, forgotten cages that the forest had reclaimed.
Every so often she thought she heard someone crying.

Neither of them were used to scraping in the mud like
this. Only Kivati children and the non-winged had to
walk. The Raven would never stoop to trudge in the mud
when the air was so much faster, cleaner. She'd had more
practice walking because of her weak grasp of her totem.
But here they were without totem or Aether. Stripped
down to their single components. Simple and ordinary
and altogether unremarkable.

Not the infamous Raven Lord.

Not the anticipated Crane Wife.

Corbette offered his hand to help her over the next
hurdle. She placed her hand in his, and the spark of skin
on skin shocked her. Stumbling, she landed against his
hard chest; her breasts flattened against him, her lips
parted as she found herself inches from his mouth. He
smelled like dirt and sweat and wet linen, but in an earthy,
wild sort of way that agitated her senses. She'd been
trying not to touch him. Trying hard to be good and give
him the space he so obviously wanted. But her body had

other plans. He didn't push her away. Pressed against him like this, she could feel his shallow breathing and raised heartbeat and all that lean muscle. With her history, it was amazing so much testosterone and power didn't make her run screaming into the night.

Quite the opposite. He was primal and male, and the thought of moving against him, of closing that small gap between their lips, sent heat twirling low in her belly to the crux of her thighs.

"Lucia," he said in a hushed breath.

"Yes?"

"You're not making this easy for me."

Well then. She stepped back. "I tripped."

He made a low noise in the back of his throat. Frustrated? She'd show him frustrated.

And why was she trying to behave around him? After all her pep talks about being herself, around Corbette she went right back to trying to please him. Trying to be some perfect, proper lady. To make this easier for him.

Why in the name of the four sacred winds would she do that? Easy! She'd never had it easy. If all this time he had been able to smother the spark between them, certainly he didn't need help now. She raised her chin and gave him a perfectly normal, innocent smile.

His eyes widened.

Perfect.

"Carry on then," she said and turned to climb over the next hurdle in her path. The whisper of a cry came again from the direction they were heading. She pulled herself up the next mass of tangled wood that had grown over a horse-driven plow and a Roman chariot, but couldn't quite make it over the top. She was stuck half dangling from a tree, giving Corbette an excellent eye-level view of her barely dressed ass. He let her struggle for a long moment.

Lady be. A blush stained across her cheeks. "A little help please?"

"Lucia—" he growled.

"What?"

"Nothing." His hands descended on her rear end and gave her a hearty push. Hello, big, hot hands! He could brand things with those weapons. He launched her over the offending barrier, but she could still feel a handprint on either cheek.

She slid face-first down the steep embankment. Her fingers grasped for purchase. She caught herself just in time before she connected with one of the giant root balls.

On the far side, Corbette gave a muffled oath. "Are you all right? Answer me!"

*Let him stew*, she thought. Her nose landed an inch from the latticework of the roots. Air whooshed through the spaces between. Up close it looked even more cage-like. And there it was again—the little cry, almost human. It was a bird, she was sure of it.

Inside the root ball, something moved.

She jerked back. "Corbette?"

"On my way," he grunted. She could see one of his hands over the top of the barrier.

The thing in the root cage moved again. A little bird chirruped. Was it trapped, or did it live in that dank hole? She pushed to her feet and peered inside. A blue bird shivered in the narrow dark. It didn't have enough space to open its wings. "How did you get in there?" she asked it. The bird tilted its head and gave her another sorrowful *chirrew*.

She dug her fingers between the slats in the roots, planted her feet, and pulled, but it wouldn't budge.

"Lucia!" Corbette came over the top of the slope. "What are you doing?"

Ignoring him, she searched the nearby forest for a tool of some kind. She found rusted blades and steel chains and shards of glass buried in the mud. A scythe poked out from between two roots. Lady of Luck. Pulling it out, she returned to the cage and set about hacking it with the rusted blade. When she'd loosened the bars enough, she took one in each hand and yanked. The wood gave way in her hands, and she tumbled backward into the mud. She'd ripped a sizable hole between the root bars of the cell.

The bird hopped to the edge and flew out. It landed on a branch in front of her and stretched its wings. It was really a beautiful shade of blue. Not anything local to the Pacific Northwest. Yellow feathers were nestled between the royal blue on its wings. It looked at her, black eyes piercing, and launched off the branch right at her face. She screamed and covered herself, but the bird Changed in midflight. Aether swirled around the small body, and then a handsome blond woman in a gorgeous blue cloak stood in front of her.

The woman took Lucia's hand and fell to her knees, sobbing. "I'd almost lost hope." Her voice was the same pitch as the *chirrew* of the bird. "You came—"

Lucia tried to pull her hand away. "You've mistaken me for someone else."

"No. No, the Crane would come. I've been lost and locked there for eighty years. But the others said you would come and lead me out of the darkness."

Lucia went still. It was her vision quest all over again—returning from the woods to find great expectations and impossible hopes. "You are mistaken. I've led a whole world to ruin."

"You have changed my world." The woman rose. "Sometimes one needs only light a single match to vanquish the darkness."

Corbette came over the top of the root wall and slid down to meet her. "Madam," he said, giving the woman a polite bow. He deftly took Lucia's place, so fast and so smooth that she didn't realize he'd blocked her until she was staring at his back. "Gentle lady, how did you get here?" he asked in a voice of midnight silk. His dangerous voice, the seductive croon hid the viper within.

He saw danger. Maybe she shouldn't have freed the lady bird. Maybe the woman was trapped here for a good reason. Damn it. Lucia was always rushing in without thinking things through.

The blue lady wasn't fooled. She tilted her head so she could see around Corbette and spoke directly to Lucia. "How can I repay your kindness?"

"Nothing," Corbette said. "She needs no reward."

"Right," Lucia said. Did he think she was an idiot? She knew better than to accept a favor from a spirit.

The lady paid no attention to Corbette. She simply walked right through him like he didn't exist. The light of the forest showed through her, but when she put her cold hands on Lucia's cheeks, they felt very solid. "Ask me a question."

"No—" Corbette said.

But Lucia couldn't look away from the woman's pale blue eyes. The cold hands on her cheeks anchored her head in a strange embrace. "Where will you go now?"

A thin smile streaked across the woman's face. She dropped her hands. "You don't judge my past, only my future." She held up a finger when Lucia would protest. "I follow the shining path to join the spirits of my ancestors. Don't be afraid. I'll give you a gift for your kindness." Corbette moved to stop her, and the lady's smile slid off. Her eyes shone with a cold light. "Don't insult me. The dead are not powerless." The blue cloak slid from her shoulders. It solidified into rich wool with a trim of brocade. Beneath the wool, the woman was naked. She picked up the cloak and spun it out and around Lucia before she could protest. The wool embraced her with the warmth of a down jacket. It covered her from neck to toe, hiding her damp underthings from view.

"Thank you." Lucia clutched the coat closed at her chest. She was half afraid Corbette would take it from her. He could try. "May the Lady speed your journey."

The woman smiled a real smile. Light shimmered over her translucent form like a blanket covering her body, and in a flash she was a small bird again, unremarkable in shape or species except for her bright yellow feathers. A dandelion of the feathered realm. The blue of the cloak was gone. The bird took off, rose above the jungle canopy, and disappeared.

When Lucia turned back to Corbette, his black brows clashed together.

"What?" she said. "You can't tell me you wouldn't do the same."

"Not if it interfered with my mission."

She pursed her lips. "How do you know this isn't part of our mission?"

"Our mission is to find Ereshkigal, steal her Scepter, and get back home before Tiamat destroys what's left of the city."

"Steal?"

"You think she's just going to hand it over?"

"How will we outrace the clay man or an enraged goddess with or without our wings?"

"We will do it because it must be done. I refuse to entertain any alternative." Turning, he stomped off through the forest. She hurried just enough to keep him in her sight. The bulk of the cloak inhibited climbing, but the warmth was well worth it.

The bird woman wasn't the only trapped bird spirit in the glade. Lucia stopped counting at fifteen and lost sight of Corbette a few times. He waited impatiently. None of the other birds spoke to her when she broke their cages, but she could tell by their trills that they were all glad to be free. A few dropped long tail feathers for her on the way out, and these she wove into her drying hair so that she shimmered with crimson, orange, and aquamarine. With the cloak, feathers, and dark wood, she felt like a fairy huntress on a quest. Step by step, some of her old anxiety crumbled away. She didn't have to be the maiden in a tower anymore. She was muddy to her eyeballs and climbing in her underdrawers and feeling altogether disreputable. Like Maid Marian, setting the villagers free. Everything about it had a topsy-turvy air. She'd left Kivati Hall and its expectations and restrictions far behind. Here in the Land of the Dead, the worries of the Living World shucked off like a snake's skin. She could do what she wanted. Be whomever she liked. She just had to figure out who that was.

She found herself humming a little tune as she followed the scowling leader through the wood. Corbette stormed through—uncombed hair, silver earrings, and rumpled clothes—a ship captain far from his beloved sea. Following him, she could daydream without his too-seeing eyes. Her dreams held mermaids and ladies ravished in the wood by a Black Knight.

As if he heard her daydream, he turned at that moment. The violet ring of his eyes was thick with danger. If they had still been in the Living World, Aether would have crackled from his skin and charged the air with his power. This Corbette held none of that charge, but every inch of his dominance.

She fought the urge to lower her eyes.

He was still an imposing, dangerous man. She shouldn't misjudge him. He would never be tame.

Lord Kai woke to the sound of banging on his door. He rolled out of bed and landed in one smooth jump on his feet, fully awake. This was it. Tiamat must have decided he was expendable. Maybe she'd found Grace's rebel camp. Maybe . . .

The pounding came again, and a voice. "Kai Raiden! Kai, hurry your ass—"

In two strides he was at the door, hand half-Changed to Thunderbird talons, and he pulled it open to find Lucia's mother. His heart skipped a beat. "Is Corbette back?" The Raven Lord had been gone a month already.

"No." Constance had chosen to stay behind, much like he had, and she looked like she'd aged a decade. She was shorter than her daughter and thinner than she'd ever been after four weeks living under Tiamat's thumb. Stress made her skin tight across her cheekbones. He wondered how much it showed on him. He'd never had much interaction with Lucia's mother, and she had always struck him a little too concerned with appearances and social climbing for his taste, but she'd stayed. Anyone who'd had half a chance had tried to escape. Anyone sane.

"What's Tiamat done now?" he asked.

"Did you know about the children?" Constance grabbed his arm and pulled him down the hall.

"No. What is she doing?" He tucked his shirt into his pants and tightened his belt as he raced to keep up with her.

"Tiamat has started a new series of experiments."

Kai felt bile rise in his gut. The bitch goddess had become obsessed with cross-species breeding and genetic manipulation. She sought to create the ultimate warrior army by forcing Drekar and various totemed Kivati to mate while adding power and occult magic to the process. Apparently her first two pantheons had simply sprung from her giant womb as fully formed adults, but over the millennia her powers had waned until she had to make babies the old-fashioned way.

"She's not willing to sit on her heels as she waits for her forced unions to produce fruit."

"If Kivati and Drekar can even mate—"

Her hand tightened on his arm. "They can."

"When? I don't know any—"

"They can!" She shoved him back against a silk-paneled wall, startling the hell out of him. "Don't let down your guard."

"What happens to a half-Drekar, half-Kivati abomination? Why haven't we heard of any—"

"The babies disappear like the moon marked."

"You mean they're left on Mount Rainier for the elements?" Kai studied the older woman's face. The biodiesel lamps cast haggard features in an unattractive light, but she'd been beautiful once. Before Tiamat. Everything good was before Tiamat. The shadows shifted over her like long-buried secrets. He suddenly wondered how well he could trust Constance.

Constance gave a sharp nod, and released him. "They

are just babies! Innocents. There is more dishonor in hurting a child than in raising one with Drekar blood."

"Babies? As in more than one?"

"I—" She looked both ways down the hall to make sure no one was listening, but they were alone. "My parents raised us far outside the shelter of Corbette's protection. You have lived among your own kind your whole life. Don't let that blind you to what is and is not possible. Just because you haven't seen it with your own limited perception—"

"Who? Who birthed such a monster child and hid it from Corbette?"

Constance's face blanched. He suddenly remembered that Drekar had abducted her sister. Sarah was supposed to have died trying to escape after almost a year in captivity. Had it been closer to nine months? He started counting years, measuring ages of the youth of the Kivati who were close to Constance's family. Constance herself had arrived with a husband and newborn in tow when he was twelve.

"If that's true, a Drekar could sire a child and sneak it right into the heart of the Kivati," he said. "Do these creatures even have souls?"

"Yes! They are no less Kivati by the circumstances of their birth," she spat. "More blessed by the Lady than you or I."

"How do you know?"

"I know."

No wonder Constance had tried to push her daughter to make friends in high places if she was harboring a soul-sucker's fledgling somewhere among them. "And what of the Aether? Would such a child be able to touch the shimmering water? Would it heal unnaturally fast like the Drekar?"

"Listen, you must hurry," Constance hissed, digging her fingers into his arm. "Forget the past. The real viper is on our throne right now, and she's experimenting on our own flesh and blood. Tiamat has decided to see what she can do to increase the power of Kivati children. She ordered Lady Acacia to deliver her daughter ten minutes ago."

Kai felt his stomach roil. He needed to know whom Constance was protecting, but she shamed him; Tiamat was the real threat. "I'll do what I can, but distracting Tiamat will only put it off."

"You have to get more people out of here."

"Lady be damned, can't you see I'm trying?" He schooled his features before he pushed past Constance into the throne room to find a sobbing Lady Acacia being held back by two Drekar thugs. Resplendent in red and gold silk, Tiamat sat on the throne looking like the Virgin Mary in a Russian icon. A shaft of sunlight illuminated her head and golden crown, and Acacia's angelic toddler sat on her lap. She was dangling a diamond necklace worth a small fortune in front of the girl. The toddler gave a nervous glance at her mother, but the lure of the rainbows through the jewels and Tiamat's seductive coos kept her quiet.

"You are a very lucky little girl," Tiamat told her. "I'm going to give you this pretty, pretty"—the toddler reached for it, but Tiamat pulled it away—"and something even better: in my blood there is power. How would you like to be like me, little poppet?" Tiamat bared her nipple and drew a claw down her breast to scratch a long line of blue-black blood. She took a gentle hold of the back of the toddler's head and guided her forward. "There, there, my pet. I'll be your mother now."

* * *

The jungle gave way to mudflat. A slick plain of endless brown. The sky was an inverted bowl of thick dark clouds, which butted together like a herd of black sheep. Corbette almost missed the obstacle course of the woods, but at least here there were no caged souls. There was nothing: no trees, no plants, no houses or people to break the monotony of mud. It sucked at his boots as he walked. A long, slow slog. He was better off than Lucia. She'd lost one slipper in the mud. The brown seeped up her new blue coat and into her long, tangled hair. She should look bedraggled, like something tasteless the mountain lion had dragged in, but her white hair shone against the dark sky and the bright feathers she'd twisted into her hair were a beacon of color in a gray world. The blue of the coat brought out her gorgeous eyes. She was covered in mud, exhausted, hungry. She was the most beautiful thing he'd ever seen.

And also miserable. He'd been less than friendly to her since she'd surprised him in the caves. Punishing her when he was mad at himself was beneath him. "Penny for your thoughts?" There. That wasn't so hard, was it?

She cast him a sidelong glance. "Have you ever been in love?"

Good gods. Never a dull moment with Lucia. "I gave my heart to the Kivati long ago."

"Seriously? In over a century you've never had a romantic relationship? I don't believe you."

He grimaced. He owed her honesty at least. "Nothing significant."

"What about the insignificant ones? Why didn't you

get married long ago? Isn't that what you're always saying is the duty of the Kivati? Procreate so we don't die out?"

"Do you always ask so many questions at once?"

She pulled the cloak tighter around her shoulders. "We've got time. Endless mud in every direction. Or when you asked for my thoughts, did you think I'd been pondering the weather all this time? 'Lovely weather we've been having, isn't it?'" she joked. "'Ripping day for a hike.'"

He kind of liked this sarcastic version of her. She'd been hiding for too long. "There were two," he admitted.

"Two what?"

"Women whom I thought of marrying."

"Oh." She sounded almost disappointed. He glanced at her expression. She was biting her lower lip. "What were their names?"

"Evangeline and . . ."

"And?"

"Lucia." He sped up, suddenly tired of this conversation. He kept his eyes on the flat horizon, the line between black-brown and black-gray so thin it could cut butter. He was half afraid it would disappear on him, leaving this strange dark sky and dark land in a looming fishbowl of mud. At the corner of his eye, Lucia was a bright splash, like a winter rose that cut through the snow. He didn't want to know what she thought of his admission. Relief that she'd narrowly escaped a lifetime shackled to him? Or disappointment? He wasn't sure which would be worse.

"So what happened?" she asked.

He raised an eyebrow.

"With Evangeline."

"Same thing that always happens. War. Blood. The safety of the Kivati comes first. It's too much for most women to come second."

"The world is too dark a place for happily ever afters?"

"When Tiamat is defeated and the Drekar driven out, maybe then there will be hope for me." He let a smile he didn't feel curl his lip.

"Not all Drekar are evil."

"Don't start. I've heard it all from Alice, and even my sister can't convince me that my entire life of war has been in vain because 'not all Drekar are evil.'"

"Not all Kivati are good." Her voice broke him.

He steeled himself against the memory of her blood spilling down her wrists and across the white robe. "I'm sorry. I would eliminate Rudrick from existence, beyond either world, Living or Dead, if I ever got the chance." They trudged on in silence. Something about this place made him attribute emotions to the landscape. If the last forest had been fear, this mud plain was despair. The Aether was gone from him; he could no more send a thunderbolt to dry this damnable mud than he could light a match.

He hated the thought of Tiamat raging through his territory while he slogged through the mud, unable to do anything to stop her. Had she reached Kivati Hall yet? Was Will managing to hold her off? Had Asgard and his Drekar joined her yet? Or did the Drekar Regent oppose his Dragon Mother, as Lucia hoped for? It seemed too good to be true. He hated this feeling of impotency being so far away from the action. He could do nothing to help his people but trudge on until he claimed the Scepter.

Glancing over at Lucia, he was struck again by the picture she made: skin and hair the color of the Lady Moon, the feathers in her hair a bright shock of blue, red, and yellow. Such odd coloring for a Kivati. Too fair, too Scandinavian, and the name—Lucia—the patron saint of light venerated by the Drekar's followers. What had her parents been thinking? He'd always preferred her naturally dark hair to the blond she'd dyed it as a teenager, but the white it had turned since the Unraveling brought out her otherness. Now she matched her totem. He couldn't look at her and not see the Crane.

He'd watched her wriggle in her wet, lacy drawers for hours. No blue cloak—however fine—could banish the memory. Without the Raven, he was just a man. Fallible. Weak. His fingers itched to throw the blue wool from her shoulders and take her down into the mud to breathe some life back into this weary land.

A dangerous daydream, but a happier one than imagining what his people were facing back at Kivati Hall without him. How many familiar faces would fly past him on his long trek through the Land of the Dead?

"Is that a house?" Lucia woke him from the endless slog. He snapped his gaze to where she pointed, and there, on the horizon, a bump poked up, a darker shadow against the dark horizon. House might be too generous a term, but it was shelter and it was something other than endless mud.

He felt a quiver of foreboding when he saw smoke coming from the chimney. "It might be a trap."

"It looks dry," she said. "It's getting dark."

He glanced up and saw that she was right. She had a better feel for this land than he did. His brain was too tied to the orbit of the living sun, but here in the dimness it was harder to tell that this thing that passed for day was coming to a close. "Stay behind me," he ordered. "If I say run, run. Let me do the talking." She made a low noise that sounded suspiciously like a crude insult. He let the edge of his lip twitch. How had he ever convinced himself that she was delicate?

The shack was scarcely bigger than an outhouse, with

a comically long stovepipe chimney and three sagging stairs that led up to the front door. A window on one side was blocked by a shade, but a thin band of light showed at the bottom sill like a streak of yellow paint. The smoke drifted out without a wind to move it. He caught the scent of sage and myrrh and thought of the burial rites of the Kivati.

"Be ready to run," he said. She lifted her chin. The red feathers braided into her white hair gave her the coloring of the Crane. Even stripped of her totem, she couldn't ignore her birthright. But he had to look past her attractive outer appearance if he wanted to know more about the hidden mind inside. She marched on without complaint. He knew few pampered Kivati ladies who would have done the same in her shoes. She had the heart of a warrior.

He made himself mount the stairs before he could do something foolish.

The stairs creaked under his weight, a sigh of giants. His boots left muddy footprints on the cedar steps. The owner must fly in and out through the window, because there wasn't a speck of mud on any of them. Corbette knocked. After a long moment, the door was pulled open. A man stared back at him. A mirror, only this reflection was older. Black hair unruly to his nape; hooked nose and carved cheekbones; the thin build of a flier; the familiar large eyes, crinkled at the sides. Wrinkles like the ghost of laughter. The reflection's eyes in death were blacker than jet, more like absence of color, a hole in his eye to another dimension. Corbette felt the floor drop out beneath his feet.

"Emory," the man said.

"Hello, Father."

# Chapter Eight

"Reached the end of your rope, have you?" Halian Corbette asked.

"I don't know what you're talking about."

"Nonsense. No one comes to the Land of the Dead unless they're all out of options. Don't bristle at me, boy. It's the truth, ain't it?"

Corbette forced himself to relax his shoulders. He needed a moment to collect his thoughts. His father. Here. In the Land of the Dead, in a field of mud. He'd never thought to see the old man again. After more than a century, he should be able to meet his father man to man.

*Hello, Father, how have you been? Pleasant weather we're having.*

*Hello, Emory, so good to see you after so long. I've missed you.*

But nothing had changed. The first words sent him back to being nothing but an angry adolescent. He tried to find something polite and neutral to say, but the only thing that rose on his tongue was the old accusation: *You should have killed the Drekar when you had the chance.*

"Let me take a look at you." Halian turned him by his

shoulder as if he were no more than nine. His father's
black eyes dug beneath Corbette's skin, where the old
resentment festered. "You've grown into your nose, I
see." Halian nodded and released him.

Corbette tried to unclench his teeth. He would usually
give a look that leveled his opponent, even better than a
cutting remark in response to such a backhanded compli-
ment, but he only managed a tight-lipped smile.

Then Halian caught sight of Lucia. "And who is this
beautiful creature?" His critical gaze smoothed out between one blink and the next, replaced by a radiant smile.
Charm oozed from his pores. He dropped into a deep bow
and swept Lucia's hand to his lips. "My lady, you grace
my humble abode."

Lucia smiled in return, and her look cut Corbette like
an arrow. Did she ever smile like that for him? It was
genuine. An ease in her shoulders and warmth in her eyes
that she never showed him. For him, her smiles were all
polite, her spine and shoulders stiff as a whalebone corset.
He could taste her fear, even when she tried to hide it
behind a saucy swagger.

"Well, don't leave the lady out in the cold, boy. Didn't
I teach you better than that? Come in, come in," Halian
said. He ushered them through the door. Corbette hesitated only a moment. His first instinct was to flee, but he
needed to find out what his father was doing here and one
look at Lucia told him that she needed the warmth and
food offered even more. He couldn't drag her back in the
mud just to assuage his own pride.

Inside, the little shack was a twist of perspective; what
looked like one room from the outside was, in reality, a
large, well-appointed lodge in the old style. Though from
the outside the building seemed square, inside the walls
were smooth and round. A fire burned in a pit in the

center, and the smoke drifted up through a hole in the
roof. Cedar boards trimmed the roof and thick woven
rugs of red and green covered the dirt floor. On the walls
hung ceremonial masks of Kivati totems: Crow, Coyote,
Bear, Wolf, Fox, Owl, Eagle, Thunderbird, Whale,
Cougar, Frog, and Hummingbird. They hung at regular
intervals, broken by two empty hooks.

Corbette forced himself to make introductions. "Lady
Lucia, may I present my father, Halian Corbette. Father,
Lucia—" He broke off, unwilling to tell Halian what
totem she wore. He needed to protect her. Once Halian
figured it out and made the connection to the prophecy,
he would tangle her in his ridiculous schemes. He
couldn't fail to see it, with her white and red decorations
in her human form, in the swanlike grace of her body, in
the tilt of her long neck as she studied him. Her presence
had always moved him, but in this land her natural self
became deeper, somehow, like sand settling in the ballast.

If Halian noticed his omission, he didn't mention it.
"Come, come. You look wet through. Come sit by my
fire. Tea? Bread?"

"Yes, please," Lucia said. "I'm starving."

"Starving the lady, are you, boy?" And his father gave
him another one of those looks that said he'd measured
the weight of his soul and found it wanting once again.
Coal dust on the scale instead of gold.

Corbette tightened his smile. He tried to stand between
Halian and Lucia. He had to protect her from his father's
lures. Halian had always been a good old boy, a charmer.
He would whittle out every secret until she felt as exposed as the riverbed at the end of a long, hot August.
Corbette knew she didn't have anything to be ashamed of,
but he also knew she didn't believe that.

Smoothly reaching around him, Halian hooked Lucia's

elbow and brought her to the fire. Corbette bared his teeth. "What a beautiful cloak, my dear," Halian said. "Might I exchange it for a blanket while it dries out?" And he swapped a woven blanket for the blue wool, elegantly draping it over Lucia's shoulders while she slipped the cloak off beneath. Corbette sat next to her and put one hand on her knee. Everything Halian touched turned to ash. He didn't want his father anywhere near Lucia. *Don't tell him anything*, Corbette would have sent through the Aether, but he had no supernatural gifts left to use.

Her hair was mostly dry by this time, but Halian pulled out a mother-of-pearl comb for her to work the snarls out.

Corbette's heart gave a lurch when he saw it. "Mother's comb."

"She's not using it," Halian said. "She had the most beautiful hair, Liluya did. Black as a Raven's wing with faint wash of red, like the sunset had fallen into her hair and gotten tangled in it. Alice got it, lucky girl. How is your sister?" His voice softened even more, the fondness palpable.

"She's . . ." Corbette took a long breath through his nose. She was directly in the path of the Babylonian Goddess of Chaos. *Please let her have escaped.* But he couldn't tell his father that. "When I left, she was in good health."

Halian cocked an eyebrow. "Still with that dragon? Brand, was it?"

"Yes." A deep, loaded word.

Halian hung a kettle over the fire and pulled out a loaf of bread. He offered it to Lucia first. "He'll protect her from whatever it is chasing you."

"Nothing is—"

"I know you screwed up, boy. Now tell me all about it."

Lucia still watched them; back and forth, her wide eyes darted. "It wasn't his fault."

"No?" Halian gave her another smile. "It rarely is, my lady. No one person can bear the responsibility for the whole world. It's arrogance to try. Takes a village to succeed, takes a village to fail. But try telling that to Emory. He won't hear it. Believes the ruler is the people, isn't that right, boy?"

"The ruler is responsible for leading the people. You let the enemy in through the front door."

"Can't keep them out," Halian said. "Can't spend a lifetime fighting. That's no kind of life. Peace isn't an abstract concept; it's a discipline we choose to apply to each and every decision. Whether we find it or not, what we can't do is wage our wars and then curse the gods for not bringing us peace."

"I hardly curse the gods for the Drekar decimating our people and creating endless war," Corbette said.

"No, you just blame me," Halian said.

"We could have fought them when they first arrived and finished it. We had twice as many numbers as Norgard did."

"Our ancestors tried that, didn't they? Wiped out the local Unktehila, but the dragons came back. Maybe we could've gotten rid of Norgard's Norse Drekar, but dragons live all around the world. There will always be more to take their place. We've got to learn to live together."

Corbette closed his eyes for a long moment. How could he explain to his father what his death had wrought? It would just sound like more blame, and they'd never get out of this circle of bickering. All of a sudden, he was tired. He listened to the snap of the fire and took a deep breath of cedar-scented air.

"Corbette kept the Kivati safe," Lucia said. "He made us strong."

Her defense touched a vulnerable chord in him. He cared too much for her good opinion of him. "Why are you here, Father?"

"Waiting for you, boy. What do you think?" Halian pulled the boiling water off the fire and poured it into three ceramic mugs filled with elderberry bark. He put the kettle to the side of the fire pit. Taking a flask from inside his coat, he added a generous helping of amber liquid to his glass and offered it to Lucia. She declined.

Corbette took a mug. "What, waiting for me to screw up like you did? That's a long time to wait for a chance to gloat."

"Gloat? No." His father held his gaze, eyes hard as flint. Corbette looked away. "You think you're in control, boy? The Spider holds the world together with her web. You think you could have prevented what happened? You think anything you did could have stopped your feet from leading you right to this door?" He jerked his glass toward the thick round door cut into the cedar wall. A bit of amber liquid sloshed over the side, and Corbette felt his lip curl. Halian couldn't see what Corbette had accomplished. Of course he couldn't. What had Corbette thought? That his father would change? He saw only that his son wasn't the life of the party, didn't resemble him in the slightest except that damned beak of a nose.

"I make my own fate, thank you," Corbette snarled. "Blaming destiny is just a pretty way of laying blame at someone else's feet."

"Like mine?"

Corbette studied his father's face. The shadows carved deep furrows in the tan skin, tracing his eyes and mouth not in lines of laughter, but of grief. Was this the real

Halian? The laughter just a mask for the pain? His father would have to be one hell of an actor. "And Mother's death? You still think the gods to blame for her death?"

Halian threw his glass into the fire. The liquid ignited, shooting a ripple of sparks up to the smoke hole. He stood in one smooth movement. "You don't know anything about love."

"You didn't even mourn her!"

"I grieved for your mother every day of my miserable life. But I had you kids. I had people who depended on me—"

"You gave up our land to the soul-suckers!"

"Land! Land, boy, is nothing but dirt and history. Not even a weed will grow in earth untouched by love. I'm not going to argue with you about the past. What's done is done. Move on. Leave the past to the dead. The present is for the living."

Anger rushed through Corbette's veins. He rose too, feet planted. The smoky air of the lodge filled his lungs like the water of the river. He was drowning again. "Well, you failed."

Halian took a deep breath. It sounded like the wind rattling through the mountain pass. He argued with a man long dead. There was little but smoke and shadows.

"Forget it." Corbette reached his hand out to Lucia. "Let's go. The Enkidu is putting miles between us as we waste time here."

"No." Lucia settled back against the bolster. Despite the tension simmering in the air, the heat of the fire warmed the blanket around her shoulders. She was simply too tired to get up again. "If you two are going to keep snapping at each other, I'm long overdue for a nap. Please wake me when it's over. I'm not going back in the mud just so you don't have to talk to him." She felt cozy and safe for the first time in what seemed like ages. Outside the little house might be a bleak winter of mud, but inside the light flickered off the shiny wood posts and glittered on the beads and shells of the totem masks. She clutched the hot mug between her fingers and let it warm the damp from her soul.

"The lady has a point." Corbette's father sat, his cheeks spotted with color. "Your mother would have—"

"Don't bring her into this," Corbette said.

"Sit, Emory." Halian pulled out his flask. He unscrewed the cap, but paused with the steel at the edge of his lips. Slowly, he lowered it and poured the rest into the fire. The flames jumped. "I'm sorry."

Corbette froze like a bit of mountain granite.

"Yeah, you heard me right." Halian took a deep sigh. "Enkidu, eh? Sit down and tell me the whole story. I've got sins to atone for, and I'm done nursing my pain alone in this Lady-forsaken lodge."

Corbette lowered himself to the floor. He ran a hand over his face. She'd never seen him make such an unconscious, human gesture. Everything about the Raven Lord had always been meticulous and planned. Halian was nothing like she'd expected. Charming where Corbette was intimidating. Smiles where Corbette was stern eyebrows and severe lines. Halian was a rogue and a rambler, the trickster Raven to Corbette's chief. It was like the twin halves of the Raven totem had split to make two very different, very intriguing men.

"When you died," Corbette told his father, "Norgard burned Seattle to the ground. Then he came after the rest of us."

"Alice?"

"She fled with her Drekar lover when she found out you died. She escaped the bloodshed."

"The others?"

"They scattered. You left no structure, no clear path for a new leader to take your place. We had no protocols for war. No emergency plans to care for the wounded and vulnerable. It was every Kivati for himself, easy for Norgard to pick off."

"The totem chiefs—"

"Were loyal to their own kind only. The Wolves ran to Canada. The Cougars retreated to the peninsula and the mountains. Only the Thunderbirds came together to protect those totems not strong enough to fight. Will and I fell back to Queen Anne. We held it, but we lost the lands to the north and south." Corbette's gaze dropped to the ground. His hands curled and uncurled. There was a restless energy about him. The firelight etched his face in sorrow, each line a tick of a life he'd been forced to take, a life taken from him.

Lucia had never heard the full story of the Great Seattle Fire and the beginning of the Drekar–Kivati war told with such raw despair. Kivati easily lived a few centuries to old age, but they died just as easily as humans did to a Drekar sniper or bomb. She tried to count the number of Kivati she knew who had witnessed the disaster of the fire. She knew Corbette had saved the Kivati, but she'd never given much thought to the pain he'd gone through. Things started to click in place like gears once oiled. Corbette's fastidiousness, his perfectionism, his dedication to the Kivati. The brief haunted look he'd get every once in a while that would confuse her. So much began to make sense. The Raven Lord, intimidating, untouchable, seemed to shift off like a mask being removed. And though the man left behind was just as dominant, just as powerful, he was even more intriguing than before.

"When the smoke cleared, Norgard started building his city not a Thunderbolt's strike to the north. He dismissed us—scattered, leaderless, and terror-stricken."

"He didn't know you very well," Halian said.

"I was fourteen."

"Even at fourteen, anyone with half a brain could see you'd make one hell of a foe. I did." Halian smiled ruefully. "Hell, you scared me, and I had to live with you."

Corbette's jaw tightened.

"But you brought them back, didn't you?" Halian asked.

"Will and I found those scattered and convinced them to return with the promise of safety. I've held that hill for a century. Kept that promise. Held the Drekar off and slowly won back some of our lost territory. Built up wealth and resources and political connections. Leadership"—Corbette looked straight at his father—"that's worth a damn."

"Ah, boy. Sharp a tongue as ever. But at what price? You never had compassion. Did everything the opposite of me, huh? Right all my wrongs? But where'd it lead you?" Halian waved a hand around him to the dim lodge and the softly shining masks. "The Land of the Dead, same as me. At least I've some memories to keep me warm on these endless cold nights. You don't look like you've found a single bit of softness in the long years since I last saw you. Still just as arrogant. Still angry as a young bull."

Whatever warmth Corbette had held when he'd looked at Lucia washed out of his face. She hadn't realized it had been there until it was gone, but the blackness that suffused his irises almost mirrored the dead man across the fire. Her heart broke for him, for the boy he'd been. The man he'd become had trained himself to feel nothing. He stood. "And what memories would those be? Drinking the night and day away? Playing cards while the human settlers slowly encroached on the Sacred Territories? You know what I see when I look at you?"

Lucia stood too. Both men startled, as if they'd forgotten she was there. She wished she had some gum to pop. Diffusing tensions had always been her gift, even if it meant drawing ire her way. A distraction usually worked wonders. She stretched up her arms and gave a big sigh. "All right. I feel better after that little rest. Halian, thanks for the hospitality. My feet feel good as new." The Lady preserve her if she lied through her teeth.

Halian rose too, the anger vanished, the charm back on full force. "Forgive me, gentle lady. We've been acting like a couple of young buffalos. Please, sit. Share more tea with me. Tell me the rest of the story from your own lovely lips."

She could feel Corbette vibrating at her elbow. She was sure that if he could still touch the Aether he'd be feathered by now, soaring free. There was nothing like the air beneath one's wings to find a way out from beneath the rain shadow. But landlocked, he could do nothing but hold the pain inside him. As much as she liked Halian, the barb in his tongue when he spoke to Corbette made her angry. Though she'd joked Corbette needed to get off his high horse, she never wanted to see that shame in his eyes. She could see him freeze up as every word from Halian's lips tightened the tourniquet around his emotions.

She suddenly saw the real Corbette. He had always been handsome, wise, and strong. Now she saw his complexity, vulnerability, and passion—something infinitely more devastating than the perfect ruler she'd come to respect. He was a man she could fall hard for.

Dangerous. She didn't know what to do with this revelation. "Okay, but let's make it quick. The clay man is getting ahead of us." She sat again and pulled the blanket around her shoulders. Stiffly, Corbette sat next to her. He put his hand on her knee again. Did he think she'd tell Halian all his secrets? She didn't know half of them. "As I understand it, during the Great Fire one of your Spirit Seekers sacrificed himself to save the Gate between worlds. He bought the Kivati time." She looked to Corbette for confirmation, and he nodded.

"Cheveyo," he said. "Norgard had a long wait until he attempted another break of the Gate."

"Good man, Cheveyo," Halian said.

"Norgard started plotting again after a century. He had found a piece of the Tablet of Destiny on one of his travels and was waiting for the right moment to use it. Last April, at the winter equinox and the Babylonian New Year, he found a descendant of Cheveyo whose blood he planned to use in the opening ceremony." Lucia was proud her voice didn't shake as she said the words "blood" and "ceremony." Gods, it could have been Kayla or her sister or any other woman Norgard might have picked off the street to sacrifice. But it had been her, and it hadn't been Norgard who held the knife.

Corbette watched Halian reach out and take Lucia's hand. "You don't have to tell me the details. I can see by your face the words that are coming."

"In the end, it was one of our own that betrayed us," Corbette said, the words ripped from his chest. But if

Lucia had to share her shame, he couldn't hold his own truth back. A Kivati, under his watch.

Halian raised an eyebrow. "Not a Drekar? Why're you still so hostile then?"

"Norgard set it up, but a Fox took the Tablet and followed through with his plan." Corbette's hand tightened on Lucia's knee.

"Todd Rudrick," she whispered, face white.

"The Gate between the Land of the Living and the Land of the Dead fell, releasing the demigod Kingu and an army of souls, destroying civilization as we knew it," Corbette said.

"Ah. I felt that. The Aether changed suddenly. Wondered what it was," Halian said. "This land hasn't been the same since. It's dying."

Lucia's head came up. "Dying? But it's the—"

"Land of the Dead?" Halian laughed lightly. "'There is no Death, only a Change of Worlds.' This was once a place of serenity where the dead could find peace. Now it ain't nothing but a sea of desolation."

"It makes sense," Lucia said, "the wrongness I've felt since we arrived. It's more than a living soul being in the wrong world, more than my feeling wrong for being parted from my totem. The trapped bird souls and cry of the wind over the mud plains haven't been the welcome I had expected from the Land of the Dead. It's supposed to be . . . calm. How can the Lady let it be? Why doesn't She fix it?"

"Now there's a question, isn't it? Maybe She wills it to be so. Maybe She can't. We all have our place in the Great Web. Our job to do. Our strand to play out."

"If you're going to tell me again that it's not our place to question the gods' will, I'll laugh in your face." Corbette grit his teeth. "That's exactly why I make my own fate. I've protected the Kivati to the best of my ability, and I will continue to do so with my last breath. I will never sit back and wait for the gods to decide to step in and save us while we suffer and die."

"Like your mother?"

Corbette gave a sharp nod. He didn't want to talk about her. She'd been sincere where Halian was charming. Quiet, like Corbette, but warm. He remembered so little about her, but her voice like a nightingale still haunted his dreams.

"How did she die?" Lucia asked.

"Fever," Halian said. "But I suppose you've got fancy modern medicines that might have saved her, eh?"

"Probably," Lucia said.

Halian sat back, a smile on his face. "And why close our borders to the sins of the modern world, if that means casting out the miracles too? Emory, I'd have done anything to save her. Anything. I loved your mother, and her death almost broke me. The world was a-changin'. The West was opening up, flooding with frontiersmen and ranchers. The forests falling beneath the Scandinavians' axes to feed the hunger for shingles and ships. Our ways weren't going to keep in the new century. Adapt or perish, son. That's always been the rule. The animals know it. The ghosts know it, for if they don't adapt and move on, they turn wraith."

"But at what cost?" Corbette said. "You wouldn't recognize the land anymore. Whole forests paved over to feed the humans' material greed. The rivers awash with toxins. The salmon endangered, some extinct."

"I'd do it all again if it meant having modern medicine that could save Liluya."

Corbette looked away. What was one woman's life at the price of so many? Was it worth the destruction of the earth or the long slaughter of the Kivati? Was it worth losing their sacred honor? What was the good of saving the whole, if one single life was deemed replaceable? But they spoke of his mother, not any faceless person. He couldn't untangle his emotions from what must be done for the good of the whole. And besides, she had passed through the Gate long ago. There was no use arguing over it. He glanced at Lucia, her delicate features in the flickering light, her white hair a constant reminder of his failure to save her. If it came down to her or his people, what choice would he make?

"We should go," he said.

She turned to him, and her smile was his undoing. He couldn't be impartial where she was concerned. "Let me finish the story. I'll be quick. The Gate closed, but Kingu remained in the Land of the Living. We defeated him, not knowing that the Heart of Tiamat, the Babylonian Goddess of Chaos, still remained. She found a body and the Tablet of Destiny, and rose. She means to birth a third pantheon, resurrect Babylon, and conquer both worlds. She's created an Enkidu, a clay man, to fetch the Scepter of the Goddess of Death. We need to stop him."

"So that's what he was," Halian said.

Corbette straightened. "You've seen the clay man?"

"You just missed him."

"Damn it. We need to move." Corbette rose. "Why didn't you start with that? He's pulling ahead while we sit here gabbing."

"So you're bound for the palace," Halian said. "Where the Queen resides. I can show you part of the way."

Corbette hesitated. Old habits died hard; he didn't want to be in debt to his father.

"Let me help you. I've made mistakes in the past, Emory. I won't deny it. Let me do this last thing for you."

His father looked so hopeful, Corbette felt his defenses weaken. "Yes."

Halian's shoulders eased. "Let me give you a gift, Lady Lucia. Choose a mask from my wall."

"That one," Lucia said. She pointed to the smallest mask, a palm-sized carving of a Hummingbird. Shells dotted the cedar face and thick lines of black and red outlined its half-circle eyes. It was painted green. "It won't take much room. I can put it in my pocket."

"Wise choice." Halian took the mask from the wall and handed it to her, along with her now-dry cloak. Exchanging the cloak for the blanket, she slipped the delicate mask into her pocket and joined Corbette at the door.

"Let's get out of here," Corbette said.

# Chapter Nine

Two months had passed since Tiamat seized the high ground of Kivati Hall and conquered the neighboring territories. Some Drekar had joined her; others had been captured and forced to choose. Kai stood before the Drekar's dragon-bone, jewel-encrusted throne, which Tiamat had installed in the main hall of the Kivati. It was a sacrilege. A dragon throne in Kivati Hall. A Babylonian goddess desecrating his land and his people.

But he had to pretend, to save himself, to save the Kivati, to draw Tiamat's attention away from those trying to escape, and to deflect her temper from killing more innocents. She had no care for life. None at all. So he pasted on his bad-boy smirk and played hard to get, cocky and arrogant, which seemed to work for every female, human and goddess alike. To his great disgust, his dick didn't have a problem pretending to want her gorgeous, lying Drekar tongue and her lush, serpentine body and her warm, inviting, parted thighs. The Lady cut off his head and raised it on a pike.

"Thunderbird," Tiamat purred. "Don't look so sullen." She crooked her finger at him.

He went, hating himself for it. The horizontal battle was not how he imagined dying for his people, but it was only a matter of time before his body gave out and she turned on him.

Tiamat pouted, and he brushed his hand across her breast like he knew she liked. She'd had the hall redecorated in red, resembling the finest temples of Ishtar, silk and pillows scattered across the floors, the stiff-backed chairs replaced with velvet chaises and thick bearskin rugs. Ishtar's sacred courtesans filled the room with music—harp and violin and cello—and danced for her, a seductive twirl and shimmy of their hips, but he knew in the real Temple of Ishtar there was laughter. This court, lush and hedonistic, was a shadow of the real thing. He might have enjoyed the slap in the face to Corbette's austerity, but fear wove its way through the Maiden's melody.

"I've had two broods of children," Tiamat said. "Do you like children?"

"Sure." He'd never given it much thought. Jace was the family man. Jace would have made a good father. Kai had always pictured himself the fun uncle who would swoop in to visit with mad stories and dangerous toys. But now with the very real possibility that he'd procreate with a Dreki possessed by a deranged Babylonian goddess . . . for the first time he very much hoped he was sterile. The grip of his fingers turned hard over her creamy flesh. Tiamat winced, but she liked it rough.

She traced her long nail down his bare abdomen. Her full breasts threatened to pop out of the tight band of red silk she had wrapped around them. Zetian had always had a knockout body, but she'd been cold and calculating. Tiamat in her body had the same goods, but she had an earthiness that Zetian lacked. She had no boundaries, no shame in her body or her pleasure. She liked it every way, any time of day, no matter who was watching. Harder, faster, deeper. Gods, she was hot. A whiff of her heavy perfume, and he was raring to go. Trained like a dog. Sweat dripped down his back, from his forehead, across his upper lip. He loathed himself for the way she could make him hard in an instant.

She talked incessantly. He had to work to pay attention, because somewhere in that stream of conscious thought were the clues he needed to take her down. The Kivati were depending on him. During the millennia she'd spent mute and in pieces drifting around as a phantom heart, she'd saved up every thought, every word, every shadowy feeling that she wanted to share, and they all came spewing out now from between Zetian's ruby lips. She talked all day. During sex. Even in her sleep.

The challenge wasn't so much getting her to share her plans, but sifting through the mounds of murderous garbage to the necessary information hidden like splinters of gold. He needed to know how she was moving her troops and why, not how many ways she could disembowel a general and which courtesans she'd had sacrificed back in ancient Babylon. Her train of thought—always morbid—lacked the immediacy of mortals. The here and now held no meaning for her, because she'd killed for millennia and planned to kill for millennia more.

Not if he had anything to say about it.

She dug her nails beneath the waistband of his jeans, and his dick sat up and took notice. He'd always taken the lead in the bedroom before. He'd had no idea a dominatrix could turn him on so much. She could tear him apart with one errant claw. Her ability to manipulate the Aether was better than Corbette's, better than a dozen Kivatis combined, but not all powerful. That was the only leverage they had. He just had to figure out if she was hiding some secret knowledge or power beneath the unrelenting narration of her thoughts. It would be easy to become complacent when she droned on about the city she planned to build—with gardens to rival Babylon and palaces for the many brats she intended to birth—with, Lady damn him, him.

"Kai, sweet," she crooned. "Let's try it again, hmm? I yearn to feel life quickening inside me."

He turned his grimace into a grim smile.

She mistook it for a bloodlust he didn't share. "Soon we will lead our children across the plains to vengeance. Soon the earth will run crimson with the blood of our enemies. The violence in your heart pleases me. You can let it go with me. Let yourself embrace the bloodthirst. I know you feel it." She shot out a claw from her fingertip and sliced it lightly across his naked chest. The pain was a welcome reminder—he needed to watch himself. Her tongue darted out to lick the line of blood that dripped off his erect nipple. She sucked his nipple into her mouth and his balls tightened.

"What kind of ruler abandons his people?" she asked with a characteristic jump of topic. "You should not have been subservient to the Raven. You have too much power in you to bend your will to a coward. No wonder he tried to leash you all with very human morals. You are not human." She trailed her fingers down to his straining cock and wrapped her hand around it. A low purr rumbled in her throat. She sent a pulse of Aether through him, and it blazed up his skin. His eyes rolled back, and he had to fight to keep conscious above the rising tide of pleasure.

He needed all his wits about him. He wouldn't betray those Kivati who'd escaped into hiding.

Focusing on the other sounds and sensations in the grand room helped. He dropped his hands to circle Zetian's swanlike neck. He focused on the sound of a violin playing nearby. Minor key, gypsy ode. He could get used to this, if he could pretend it was just Zetian, not Tiamat, in front of him. He might not like the Dreki, but he respected her. She'd been a kick-ass fighter, a cunning adversary, and a scorching lay. If she hadn't been Dreki, adviser to the man who'd killed his brother, maybe things could have turned out differently between them. But that chance was past. Tiamat looked out of her eyes and pulled her puppet strings. Was Zetian still somewhere inside that shell? Did she know what was happening to her, a passive observer? What a cursed hell that would be.

"You wouldn't want another lesson, would you?" Tiamat hissed.

And there went the daydream where he was engaging in lewd behavior with someone remotely sane. Tiamat had already stripped the flesh from a man's bones using nothing but Aether and one of Kai's Thunderbird feathers. It was a sight he could never forget.

The man had been a good warrior of the Kivati. Too honorable to bow to the Babylonian Goddess of Chaos. Too moral to pretend, even if it would save his hide. The hatred in his eyes as he'd hung from the rafters of Kivati Hall, bleeding and broken, had been all for Kai. He'd died thinking Kai was a traitor. Kai could only stand at Tiamat's side and watch, helpless to act just as he'd been helpless to save his brother.

Kai had to convince the Kivati, Drekar, humans, and most of all Tiamat that he'd switched sides. Even as his captured people were led in one by one to pledge their allegiance to this monster or be slowly tortured to death. Right before they died, they always turned their shocked, betrayed eyes on him. He took their hatred and locked it inside. And every death took a bit of his soul through the Gate too. For the first time he wondered if this was what Corbette had endured through a century of rigid rule—he did it not for himself, but for the belief his actions would better the whole. But Corbette always made his personal sacrifices look like his first choice; he was a better actor than Kai.

Lucia put her hand on the door handle. She didn't want to leave the warmth of the shack, but Corbette was right, the Enkidu was getting too much of a lead on them. Who knew what damage Tiamat had wrought back at Kivati Hall? They needed the Scepter so that they could deal her her final death. Still, Lucia felt like she'd been worked over by a couple of baton-wielding Ishtar Maidens. Even when she'd trained with Grace she'd never felt this tired. The fall to the water had left bruises, and the ancient mangrove forest had taken all the energy she had left. The mud waited, cold, damp, and endless.

"Let me give you some advice, boy," Halian said. "Don't refuse a gift in the Spider's realm. Don't take paths that are not yours to follow."

She could feel Corbette's already iron spine snap straighter. Just then, something buffeted into the shack. With a crash, the walls shook, and the masks tapped against their moorings. A bit of earth fell from the ceiling beams. She dropped her hand from the door, which shuddered and creaked. Someone banged on the door; it sounded like a giant.

Corbette yanked her back and put himself between her and the door. "What's waiting for us, Halian? Is this a trap?"

Halian's face fell. "No, son. You think so little of me."

"Do you have a weapon?"

"How you gonna kill something that's already dead?"

The wind roared outside. *Lucia.*

She clutched the back of Corbette's shirt. "Did you hear that?"

"Stay close to me." Corbette's hand twitched like he wanted to pull Aether to him. When he threw open the door, a wind burst through, knocking him back. It circled the lodge and banged all the masks off the walls. The fire sputtered.

*Luciiiiaaaa,* called the wind.

She found herself walking forward toward the door. There was someone out there waiting. Waiting for her.

Corbette struggled to get the door shut, but the wind held it open.

*Luuuucia, Luciiiaa.*

"Lucia, no!" Corbette ordered.

She walked past. The roar of the wind and creak of the wooden beams faded away as the summons took up residence in her head. *Lu-seee-ah.* Thick cedars had sprung up across the mud plain. The rough red bark resembled dragon skin. Brown needles piled over the ground in a thick carpet. The forest was bright after the dark of the mud and the dim of the lodge. She almost didn't see the man who stood waiting beneath the tree canopy. His red hair blended with the bark. His wiry build wasn't much thicker than the trees.

"Lucia," he said. He wore a tuft of hair at his chin. His robe—Lady save her. His white robe still bore the bursts of red at the sleeves and hem. The blood . . .

Her blood.

She stumbled back, but the door had shut behind her. She could hear Corbette pounding on it from the other side. He called out to her. Her fingernails scraped against the wood.

"Lucia." Rudrick stepped forward.

"Get away from me!"

"Lucia."

"Corbette? Corbette!" Her throat constricted. She was alone with Rudrick. Alone and vulnerable. She looked down at her wrists and found thick iron manacles circling her slender bones. "No!" She turned her back on the man who'd savaged her. Panic vibrated across the bones of her skull. Change, she needed to Change. To fly. But the Crane was gone.

"Let me explain," he said in that sly voice—the same voice he'd used to convince her to betray her people, the same cloying persuasiveness that haunted her dreams. He had seemed so logical. *Corbette has lost it*, he'd told her. *You must be strong for your people.* And she'd let herself be dragged under by that reasonable, seductive bullshit.

"Shut up!" she yelled, still trying to pry the door open. "I have nothing to say to you! You have nothing to say to me. You're dead. You're gone. Just . . . just shut up!"

"Don't you?" And suddenly Rudrick was on the porch next to her. He leaned languidly against the banister watching her with those dead eyes.

She scrambled back and fell down the stairs. The ground rose up to catch her, and thick needles softened her fall, but still it hurt. As she lay on her back, Rudrick towered over her. The memory shot in a bullet through her mind, present and past mixed together just like the Aether storm during the Unraveling. She threw her hands up to protect herself and screamed; the sound ripped through the cedar forest. Birds fell out of the trees—all different species and sizes. They called and cawed, hovering in the air.

"Corbette!" she screamed. In a great cloud of feathers, the birds rushed the shack, claws extended. Rudrick howled and fell down the stairs as he tried to get away from them. As the birds hit the door, the walls of the shack came down. Corbette stormed out, black as a thundercloud. He took one look at Lucia on the ground and Rudrick's bloody robe, and he launched himself off the porch and onto the Fox. Landing on top of Rudrick, he wrapped his hands around the smaller man's throat. They rolled across the carpet of needles. Lucia crawled away to the shelter of the nearest trunk and shivered in her cloak.

Halian came out. "Don't, son—"

Corbette got one hand free and tried to gouge Rudrick's eye out. The birds settled back in the trees, still screaming. Even the trees seemed to lean away from the fight. Halian marched down the stairs and tore the men apart. He was insubstantial as a ghost, but had the strength of an aptrgangr. Corbette went flying. Rudrick gathered himself and stood, fists ready to defend himself again.

Lucia wondered if Rudrick had the same hidden strength—if it was a property of the dead here in their Land. If he did, he might have killed Corbette. A new wave of shame engulfed her.

"Get out of my way, old man," Corbette bit out. "Don't you know who this is? He destroyed the world!"

"Be that as it may," Halian said, "this is not your fight."

"The fuck it isn't."

"This isn't your world, boy. You'll call down the Lady's wrath if you don't stop—"

With a primal yell, Corbette launched himself again at

Rudrick and threw Halian out of the way. Lucia could only watch, shivering, with a sense of being outside her body. She could see herself wrapped in the blue cloak. Helpless. Just as she'd been helpless once before. She'd imagined this moment a hundred times. What she'd say to Rudrick if she could do it over. What she'd do to Rudrick if she ever saw him again. Training with Grace, it was Rudrick her fist had planted into with every punch. It was Rudrick she stabbed, kicked, sliced, and boiled alive in every one of her waking dreams. Now here he was in front of her, and she was paralyzed. She had her chance to tell him all those perfectly crafted words, and she couldn't think of a single one.

Corbette rammed his fingers into Rudrick's mouth and tried to rip his jaw off. He couldn't see through the violent haze. Pain was a distant throb, reason a distant pulse. He'd imagined killing Rudrick in a thousand creative ways, and the lying, murdering, rapist piece of shit had the gall to show up here and attack Lucia again.

It didn't matter that Rudrick was already dead. Corbette hadn't been able to save Lucia the first time, but he wouldn't make the same mistake twice.

"Emory! Emory, let him go!" Halian yelled, and his father's voice siding with the Fox only served to fuel Corbette's rage. Rudrick had challenged his rule, violated his woman, and thrown the world into a disaster the likes of which hadn't been seen since the Great Flood.

With the unnatural strength of the damned, Rudrick managed to pull Corbette's hand out of his mouth. "Must make amends," he said before Corbette's fist smashed into his jaw. He spit out a tooth. Dead he might be, but he still felt pain. Corbette could see it in the wince of his lifeless eyes, hear it in his groans and grunts as they wrestled on the ground.

He only vaguely heard his father arguing with Lucia. *Get your tainted feathers away from her*, he wanted to yell. "Die," he told Rudrick, "in great pain."

"I did," Rudrick replied.

And then Lucia was there tugging him away, and in his surprise he loosened his hold and Rudrick got a last elbow into his windpipe. There was no more struggle after that. He needed air; Rudrick didn't. Corbette broke away, gasping for breath. Halian hauled him up and held him back. If he got his hands on Rudrick again, he'd make sure the fucker never got back up.

"Halian says—" Lucia began.

"Silence," he choked out. "Do I look like I care what you have to say, old man?"

"But he's your father."

"In name only. He hasn't been much of a father to me since I was nine." He shook off Halian's hold. Lucia stood with the cloak clutched tightly around her. She needed steel, not wool. Her eyes were rimmed like the brightness of the Lady Moon. The edges of her thin lips were lined in sorrow. She looked so much older than eighteen. An ancient, world-weary soul. Rudrick had done that to her, and for that he deserved eternal torment.

Lucia wasn't crying, but she kept Corbette's body between her and her attacker. In this he could protect her. The wind tore at the branches overhead. A storm was coming. The land seemed alive with Aether energy. It cut him that he couldn't touch it, couldn't soothe it. It felt . . . malignant.

Slowly, Rudrick rose from the ground and wiped the blood from his lip. "Let me say my piece. She freed the others. She can free me too—can't you, Lucy?"

"Don't call me that!" she snapped.

*Good girl.* Corbette straightened his shirt. The buttons had been torn off, and it hung open across his chest. One shoulder seam gaped. The threads strained like a surgeon's stitches to keep a semblance of order to his person. He felt for the raw patches along his jaw, the bruises forming across his ribs. "You are not fit to breathe the same air as the lady."

"Give him his say," Halian warned. "It's the law."

"Whose law?" Corbette asked. "You might have suffered murderers gladly, but I've run things a bit differently since you've been gone."

"The law of the dead," Halian said.

"And what law is that? Forgiveness? Not for him. He killed millions of people."

"And he'll have to answer to them too. But not to you." Halian pushed him back, leaving Lucia without a protector. Her thin shoulders shook, and her face resembled freshly peeled bone. A little cry like a sparrow escaped her throat. A sob, and then she pivoted on her heel and ran.

"Lucia!" he called after her, but she didn't turn. Her cloak billowed out behind her like wings. Her bare feet left divots in the thick carpet of needles. Lady be, he could hear her sobs echoing off the silent trees. He'd failed to protect her from suffering . . . again. He would take care of this for her. He picked up a thick log from the ground and spun. The crack of wood against flesh shot like lightning to the sky. Rudrick screamed. His form dissolved, each atom splitting off into a mass of black particles of his rotted soul. They swirled up into a funnel that twisted to the strange, starry night above. The high-pitched whistle forced Corbette to cover his ears. He shut his eyes, leaned away, and the twister passed him by. The scream faded.

"You fool," Halian said. "He'll be back."

Corbette dropped the stick. "I stopped seeking your approval a long time ago, Father."

"I haven't waited all these years to watch you throw it all away."

"You've waited? You left me nothing!" If he were whole, he'd Change to Raven and be done with it. Fly into the sky and find Lucia in an instant. Aerial view, fast pace. But his all-too-human feet had to make do, and he was forced to march away from Halian in a slow, useless retreat. "You know what? I don't need you. Don't follow me. You were a lousy father."

"Stick to the path, boy," Halian called after him. "Across the desert and sea to the palace. If you don't follow any advice, follow that one. The path—"

Corbette tuned his father out and followed the tracks Lucia had made in her flight. He missed the sea salt air, the feel of the fresh up current carrying him higher, and the thrill of the land dropping beneath his feet. Flying was freedom. Nowhere had he ever felt peace like he did far over the Pacific Ocean.

Except in the presence of a young woman who forgot herself and made him laugh. When she thought he wasn't looking, she broke his rules, mocked his orders, and ignored his edicts. They were all but incompatible, except when he stood next to her he felt the calm of the blue ocean calling to his soul, even while his blood pressure went through the roof. She was the serpent who could deconstruct his carefully planned Eden, and he'd worked so hard to keep a safe, chilling distance between them.

But his Eden had been destroyed anyway, and the only thing he had left was hope and a slender, beautiful woman who was getting away from him. He hurried to catch up. He found her because she was limping, and the torn soles of her feet smeared blood on the needles behind her.

Rushing to her, he grabbed her hand. "Lucia—"

"Is he here?" She turned, her hair twirling out in a wave of white. It framed her perfect heart-shaped face and contrasted sharply with her red-rimmed eyes. Trails of tears streaked down her muddy cheeks. Light sparked in those eyes. The banked anger flared to life, and his heart bled for her. "Is he after me?"

"No. You're safe." She sank against his chest, startling the hell out of him, and he wrapped his arms around her. Gods, how he'd wanted to hold her like this.

"I can't believe I ran. I just—it's so easy to be brave in the dark of my room, safe behind Kivati walls. I think of all these things I would do differently, all the words I would say if I saw him again, but when the moment came, I panicked."

"You were brave, Lucia. No one faults you."

"But I fault myself, don't you see?" She looked up into his face. A smear of muddy tears crossed from one delicate cheekbone to the next. "I need to fight my own battles."

"You don't have to. I failed you once, but I never will again. I swear it."

She pulled out of his arms. Cold filled the space where she had been. "I'm not some delicate pet you need to coddle."

"I never said that—"

"I will stand on my own two feet. Rudrick will come again, won't he?"

Corbette nodded.

"You have to promise me you'll let me face him."

Her skin was so youthful, but pain made her eyes old. Hardship had worn furrows between her brows. Experience had stripped the simple, the shallow, from her lovely face, replaced lovely with something deeper. Something wiser and unexpected. In a word: beautiful.

"Promise me!" she said.

His gaze caught on the parted line of her mouth. Lips swollen from crying. A salty sheen gave them luster that no chemical gloss could match. There was a drop of pain in true beauty—the shadow of a cruel world that carved out the soul to hold more.

More pain. More joy. More pleasure. He couldn't refuse her.

"I promise," he whispered, and then his mouth was on hers and the hint of salt gave the depth of realness to the kiss. She opened for him, and she didn't hold back. There was nothing proper about that kiss. He could taste her strength in the fierce mating of their tongues and teeth.

"Make me feel alive," she moaned against his lips. Her fingers dug beneath his ripped shirt and pulled it from his shoulders. He loosened the clasp of her cloak, and the blue wool fell—soft as a bird's feather, the silent swoosh of his self-control following hers out the window—and then she was exposed to him, breasts and shoulders bare beneath the wet, translucent chemise. His weight bore her down to the bed of pine needles with the cloak bunched beneath her. No more walls between them.

He scooped his hand down her front to cup one small breast. The nipple peaked in his palm. So tight. So warm. The noise she made was a moan, not a sob. Her hands trailed up his spine. Soft fingers, cool skin, she caressed his bare back and he arched into her. Threading his other hand into her silken hair, he tilted the angle of his kiss to go deeper. Her body was small and supple beneath him, just right to sink into. The smell of crushed cedar and her—*Lucia*—invaded his nose. Mud, of course, endless mud, but beneath that rose her own unique scent, and if he'd still had a totem he would have bathed in it.

But the man wanted to claim her in a different way, and her body was yielding, her mouth just as desperate as he was. He licked the sensitive inside of her lip and popped her breast out of its confines. Leaving it to the cool mercies of the air, he made his way down to her linen drawers and the slit at the crux of her thighs. She froze at the first intrusion of his fingers, but he didn't give either of them time to think. Sliding between the slick folds of her womanhood, his thumb pressed the tight ball of nerves at her entrance. With a gasp, she arched into his hand. He used her momentum to plunge his first two fingers into her wet heat, and she broke apart in a long, tearful scream.

# Chapter Ten

Lucia shook, and Corbette held her. He crooned nonsense into her ear and smoothed his hands down her arms and over the flat plane of her stomach. Her eyes burned. Her body was not her own. Little waves of pleasure pulsed out from the place he'd touched. She squeezed her thighs together against the ache. She had wanted something to block out the painful memories, and he'd done that and more.

"It will be okay," Corbette said against the crown of her head.

It was just too much all taken at once: the shock of losing her totem, seeing Corbette for the first time beneath the mask of the Raven Lord, learning of his past, the nightmare of facing Rudrick again, then, right on its heels, the fulfilled fantasy of Corbette finally—finally!—seeing her as a grown woman. A desirable woman. But now she couldn't stop shaking. Her emotions jumbled together, beating like a caged thing in her breast.

"I'm fine," she said. She buried her face against his chest so she wouldn't have to face him. His skin smelled like rugged male and a hint of copper. Too late she remembered he'd been injured and pulled back. "Sorry, I didn't mean to crush your chest. Are you hurt?"

"No." Sitting back, he slung an arm around his knees and watched the horizon. His brows were a slash of midnight. He suddenly felt miles away.

She waited for him to say something. The wind shushed through the trees.

Finally he glanced back at her. Nerves skittered through her belly. "I can't lose control again, Lucia."

"Why not?"

"I put too many people in danger."

Anger washed away her nerves. He regretted it so soon, did he? "But you have no Aether," she pointed out. "What are you afraid of?"

His eyes seemed to grow darker. She swallowed. If he still had his totem, his eyes would be pure violet. "I can't touch the Aether," he said, his gravelly voice sending shivers down her spine, "but there are still thousands who are waiting for me to bring the Scepter back to the Living World and vanquish Tiamat once and for all. What can I tell them while I dally here? That my personal pleasures were more important than their lives and freedoms?"

She'd been reduced to a dalliance. Heat flooded her cheeks. She brought herself to her feet and dusted herself off. "Responsibility. I get it."

"It is who I am."

"I know." She felt like her skin had been turned inside out. Raw, exposed to the elements. Her lips abraded from his kiss. Her flesh still sensitive from his clever fingers. But their intimacy had made him feel nothing. What a fool she was!

She snatched up her cloak, moved warily across the border into the desert, and wished she could be anywhere else.

"Lucia, I—" Corbette raised his hand toward her and then let it fall. If he didn't know what to say, she couldn't help him.

"No worries, my lord. It won't happen again." She turned and strode away, crossing the edge of the forest into a desert. The boundary between the two cut cleanly across the land as if the blade of the Sky God had sliced the world in two. On one side a dappled forest, life and a bit of light and clean-smelling growing things. On the other, sand—pure volcanic black—piled in dunes across the horizon. Prickly plants struggled their way out of the thin soil. Cactus and night-blooming poisons. In the distance she saw a red figure trekking across the sand with the fast, smooth gait of a mudslide. She forgot her hurts for a moment as hope flared. "Look!"

"Enkidu," Corbette said, and pulled himself together in an instant. "Hurry." He broke into a jog, and she followed. The shifting sands were easier on the torn balls of her feet than the forest path had been, but she was still in rough shape. Concentrating on the pain took her mind off her bruised ego. It was ego he'd stabbed, not anything more vulnerable. Certainly not her heart.

"It's moving too fast," she said. "I'm slowing you down. Go catch him."

He looked back, and she saw his need to protect her warring with his need to stop the Enkidu and save their people. "I can't leave you—"

"Go!"

Corbette finally took her at her word and started to sprint toward the clay man. He was fast and gaining on Tiamat's unnatural creature, but suddenly the ground shook. Lucia fell to her knees, narrowly escaping a mouthful of black sand. When she looked up, she saw Corbette, too, spread-eagle on the ground. The dunes had shifted and the landscape changed again. The new horizon was empty; the clay man had disappeared.

"Damn it." Corbette rose and shoved his shirtsleeves up to his elbows.

"Run. You might still be able to catch him."

"I can't even tell what direction he's gone in. It's useless if I catch him but lose you in the desert. I'll get you out of the Land of the Dead, Lucia. I swear it by the Lady."

A little shiver took her. The Aether around them rolled through his words, and even though he couldn't seal his promise with a binding oath, she knew he would see it come true no matter what.

He tilted his head at her in that gesture that said he'd been Raven far too long to be fully human, even when stripped of his totem. "How are your feet?"

"Fine." If he could ignore his injuries, she could too. She was determined to show him that she wasn't the delicate creature he thought her to be. It had been a mistake to let everyone assume she was broken after the Unraveling. She had to work ten times as hard now to prove them wrong. "Let's move. Either we beat the Enkidu before he gets to the Scepter, or we intercept him on his way back. Either way, we can't let Tiamat get it. It's the only thing that can defeat her. Every moment we spend here lessens our chances of getting back out alive." She set out across the dunes, hiding her wince at each step.

He saw it anyway, but gave her the point. Even if he regretted their "dalliance," he was now treating her like an equal. She steeled herself against any tender feelings for him. If—no, *when* they got back to the Living World—they would have to work together to stop the Kivati from unraveling. No more ancient tournaments and archaic marriage rites to make policy decisions; they'd have to

sit down and hash things out like civilized beings. Just
because their Animal counterparts would fight to the
death didn't mean that was the way leadership should be
decided. If anything, this journey without their totems
would be a good place to start a rational dialogue about
the future of the race.

She just needed to convince the Raven Lord. She
glanced over at him and caught sight of his stormy face. A
blush crept up her cheeks. Sleeping with him was definitely the wrong way to start a rational, civilized discus-
sion. She started brainstorming her argument. How could
she convince him his father was right, that the Kivati
needed to integrate with the world? It was a careful balance: to keep their ways and magic alive while joining with
humans and other shifter races to forge a new future. Either
way, this was the last time they would be alone together.

Tiamat had to be defeated, but a little piece of Lucia
didn't want to go back. She wanted more time to figure
out what made Corbette tick when he was just a man, not
the infamous Raven. She would need to know all his
weaknesses if she was going to win him to her way of
thinking.

Just when she'd steeled herself against any tender feelings for him, Corbette reached out to take her hand. His
nose seemed more hawkish than usual—a shadow of the
Raven. "Lucy," he breathed her nickname. The sound
whispered from the deepest hidden part of him, as if he'd
only spoken it in the hour before dawn in the hermit's
quiet of his own thoughts. His hands settled warm on her
biceps and rubbed some warmth into them. The friction
ignited and her heart dropped low in her belly to pulse, a
shadow of his touch back in the forest. It was a human
quality, this weakness for touch. His severe mouth parted,
and she forgot all about policy and political relations. Her

toes dug into the sand and her chin tilted up of its own accord. Her mouth softened with the memory of the friction and heat that waited on the other side of the barrier between them. His hands tightened.

And then there was a roar behind him, and the sky turned an unearthly shade of blue. Another roar like the steam from an iron horse and the screech of wheels across the rails. Corbette spun her behind him, blocking her with his all-too-human body. She had to peer around his back to see what stiffened his shoulders and made the muscles in his neck tighten.

It was a monster with the head and legs of a water buffalo and the body of a giant hippopotamus. Blue as starlight and translucent. Horns so sharp they seemed to cut the air. Its forelegs were big as old growth logs. Its whiskers of gold made it more dragon than bovine, but there was no mistaking who this was.

"The Behemoth," Corbette said, and the monster stamped the ground. It was white-hot fire, and its hooves burned the sand to glass. There was beauty in its hoof prints, swirls of color with a sparkle of Aether. It was a thunderbolt solidified, pure destruction and the righteous left hand of the Lady of Death. There was no pity in its empty eyes, just a swirling film of Aether, and she saw her own death reflected back at her.

"Run," Corbette said.

She stayed put. There was no use running. Even if she could Change to Crane, the Behemoth would follow her across the heavens. It was even less land-bound than the winged people, and it would never tire.

The Behemoth stamped again and opened its enormous jaws. Teeth the length of her leg. A forked tongue not unlike the Drekar. She was struck by the similarities, and she wondered if perhaps their two races weren't quite as different as they'd all learned at their mothers' breasts. The Damned and the Just were just two sides of the same coin.

The monster roared. She covered her ears against the sound. Even Corbette leaned back like a great wind pushed against him.

"We come in peace!" Corbette yelled back. "The Scepter. Your people need you, my Lady. Tiamat has risen and means to take over the Land of the Living—"

The Behemoth charged.

There was a great rush of burning air, and Corbette threw Lucia to the ground. Her face landed in the sand, and he was on top of her, protecting her, smothering her. She turned her head so she could breathe, and the heat scorched her eyebrows. Corbette shielded her from the worst. A hundred yards away, the Behemoth turned. Its hips swayed as it lumbered around. Behind it was a glistening lane of black glass, which still smoked.

Corbette pulled her up. "Hurry. It's coming back."

"We need help," she said. "Call your father."

"No." He walked over to the black glass and tried to reason with the Behemoth again. The Behemoth had a thick ring in its nose that smoked like the glass. It was silver, like the rings in Corbette's ears. The monster was not moved by Corbette's plea. He was going to get himself killed.

As the Behemoth charged, she pushed in front of Corbette, slipping her long blue cloak from her shoulders and holding it out like a matador's cape.

"No!" Corbette shouted.

Beneath the pads of her fingertips, she felt water. She glanced down to find the cloak was no longer blue wool, but a flowing sheet of liquid she could use as a weapon against a fire-made Behemoth. She waved it in front of the monster, and it veered to the right, leaving another smoking lane of black glass across the desert sand, missing them entirely. It slowed a hundred feet out and began to make its plodding turn.

"Give me that," Corbette said. They engaged in a brief tug-of-war with the water cape, enough time for the Behemoth to charge again. Corbette was too much the gentleman to let a woman stand in front of him, but neither could do a thing with the cape if they both stood dumbly in the line of fire. He let go.

The first time had not been bravery, but an unwitting act of stupidity. The second time was the hardest; she knew what was coming and still faced down the monster. That was bravery: knowing the worst and doing it anyway. She jiggled the sheet of water or maybe just her arms shook, and the Behemoth raced past again, again veering when she stepped in front of Corbette.

It occurred to her that the Behemoth didn't want her.

"It's after you," she said.

"Run then. I'll buy you time."

"No. Call Halian," she said. "The dead are not powerless. We need his help. Ask for it. We can escape together."

The muscles in his jaw jumped. He looked up to the blue swirling sky and called out, "Halian Corbette!" The Behemoth stamped the ground again, and another foot of sand shook from the dunes around them.

Kai stood next to Tiamat at the edge of the grand palisade newly constructed to the south of Kivati Hall. The blunt end of Mount Rainier was a smoking crater to the South. From here, he could see the slave gangs laying stone down the promenade, and, at the base of the hill, clearing the bones of buildings from the path of the long road. The slaves were human. The taskmasters were Drekar and Kivati who had converted to Tiamat's cause. Some did her bidding in the hopes of sharing her power. Most did so in fear for their lives. She had no loyalty, only a chaotic interest in what pleased her at the moment. Allies and rebels alike danced on a tightwire to stay on her good side. With her power rivaling that of ten Corbettes, no one could stand up to her. She was intent on creating a world in which there was no free will, only obedience to Chaos.

"Did you know Marduk designated the human race to work for us so that the gods might be in leisure?" Tiamat asked. She was resplendent in the morning sun. He'd lived in the Pacific Northwest his entire life, and he'd never seen so much damned sunshine. Tiamat had ordered the Kivati weather workers to blow the clouds away. Every day, he watched Theo stand facing the west and willing the clouds to part. Every day, as the sun tanned Theo's skin, the effort of holding so much sustained concentration leeched the life from his body. When he died, Tiamat would send another to take his place. But none were as strong as Theo. Except Kai.

Him, she had other plans for. But once his babe was in her belly?

The thought turned his stomach, not just because he could become irrelevant to her, but because of the abomination she hoped to conceive. A half-Drekar, half-Kivati offspring was something that the gods should never let exist. Would the soullessness of the Drekar succumb to the dual divinity of the Kivati, blessed with a soul from birth as Constance claimed? Would it Change to Drekar or totem or both? What else could a child spawned by divine Chaos do? What terrible Aether powers would it wield? Tiamat wanted to take that child and rule both the

Land of the Living and the Land of the Dead, and it filled him with fear.

Divinely fucked up. He couldn't begin to fathom the terror for the world. So far, the forced Drekar-Kivati matings that she was experimenting with had failed to produce offspring. If not for Constance's claims, he would think it wasn't possible to combine the two races. Even copulating with humans, Drekar had such low fertility rates that they were practically sterile, and not for want of trying. But who was she hiding? He found himself staring at every Kivati face, searching for a telltale slit iris. He found none.

Tiamat drew near him and snuggled into the empty curve of his arms. "You will learn to crave Chaos's beauty," she whispered. "Never knowing where your next step will lead. Never living beyond the one beautiful moment that is in your grasp." She pulled his hands around her to rub her still-flat belly. A little purr came from her throat. She was insatiable as a cat in heat, and his loathing couldn't overcome his deep addiction to her body.

He hated himself.

"I will break you of this habit of planning for the future, so you too can be free," she said.

His stomach clenched. He tried to will his body to relax around her, but it was like cuddling a cobra. She was beautiful and vain and capricious, and the only thing he could count on was that she would always surprise him with increasingly creative brutality. "I'm free with you," he forced himself to say with a smile.

"But I know your secret fears," she whispered. "From chaos comes life. So it was in the beginning. So shall it be again. Be free." She held up one hand and coalesced a brilliant blue ball of Aether. He watched her turn her gaze toward the slaves laying stone stripped from the buildings in downtown Seattle. The rising sun glinted off their tools as they struggled to re-create Babylon for her.

He knew in an instant what she planned. The moment dragged out as he watched her raise her arm and release the glowing ball toward the crumbling tower and the fifty or so slaves digging at its base. He could have knocked her arm and blown his cover. Or maybe he only tortured himself that he had that choice. The rebels and the Kivati still trapped on the hill depended on him to stay next to her. To distract her. To divine her plans and warn them in time.

But she liked to watch him struggle as his mortality stripped slowly from his bones just like the muscle and flesh from her still-living, still-breathing, still-screaming victims.

At the last moment he turned his head away. He heard the crash of Aether. Heard the roar of the toppling building. Heard the cries. The silence of death was loudest of all.

To the west, Puget Sound glistened in peaceful waves. He felt the rising tide of Aether as fifty souls suddenly ripped from their bodies and flowed into the sparkling water, westward across the sky, and through the Gate. With his Aether senses, he forced himself to watch every last one cross the barrier between this world and the next.

Three months, Corbette had been gone. Three months of blood as he searched in the Land of the Dead after some mythical instrument. If Tiamat hadn't been so sure it existed, Kai would never believe Corbette was coming back. But he'd heard her talk about the Scepter enough that he knew it could be their only hope for killing her. What was the fucker doing while they suffered and died under Chaos's wrath? He'd never been much of a religious man, but every day he prayed to the Lady that Corbette would succeed in his quest and save them all.

Tiamat turned in his arms. The glint in her eye was fierce. He knew that look. After her little display, he had to work to get hard for her.

Tiamat cupped his groin and whispered in his ear, "Come, love, rule the world with me."

Power, sex, and a beautiful woman. He might be tempted, if she wasn't a psychotic mass murderer. He imagined Zetian and that one time they'd fucked up against an alley wall. Enemy against enemy in one moment of madness. He tried to pretend she was still there somewhere trapped inside her own body, and when his dick got hard, it was all for her.

# Chapter Eleven

Corbette asked his father's ghost for help, and the knot of anger in his chest released like the snapping of a rubber band. He hadn't realized how much resentment he'd carried over from boyhood. He'd told himself for so long that nothing his father did or said could affect him anymore, but calling for Halian in his hour of need showed him for a liar. Would his father come? Could his ghost do anything to save them from the fury of the Lady's beast?

He waited a long breath, the hope that his father would come a welcome change from the anger that had rusted over his heart.

The Behemoth roared again. The discordant notes of the sound twanged and then melded together into a chorus of bells. The monster charged. As Corbette watched death streak toward him, one last image floated in his mind: Lucia on the balcony with the rain beading on her coral lips and plastering her white gown to her skin. He should have kissed her then, should have licked the water from her lips, warmed the chill autumn from her arms, and twirled her across the veranda while the rain beat out a waltz.

The heat of the Behemoth sizzled the air around them. Lucia moved to step in front of him, but he grabbed the sheet of water out of her hands. As soon as he touched it, it turned back into a cloak. It was almost comical. He tried to pinpoint the moment when everything started to go so wrong as he watched the Lady's judgment barrel down on him.

He should have forgiven Halian when he had the chance. "Please, Father." The name tumbled from his lips.

And then in the space between him and death, a Raven appeared. His father, coal black with a rainbow sheen on his feathers like an oil slick. He was man-sized, but much smaller than the great Behemoth. The blue-white fire from the creature outlined the black of the Raven in a blinding silhouette. The Raven hovered in front of Corbette, protecting him. The Behemoth lowered its head and hooked the Raven with its two razor horns. They tore through and out of the Raven's back, and then took Corbette in the face. He was consumed with fire. Blue, blue, blue, and pain. His eyes burned.

Slowly the pain faded. He lay in the smoking sand, the grit of the desert in his mouth and beneath his palms, but he was alive. His father had saved him. He could smell scorched glass, but he didn't hear the Behemoth. He didn't hear anything for a long moment, until a soft, female cry, and then small hands caressed his face. A few drops of water hit his cheek. He turned his head away from the sand to see if the sky was raining, but there was only that eerie blue above and below. No Behemoth. No Raven. No sand or sky.

"Lucia?"

"I'm here."

But he couldn't see her face. He was Raven. Sight was his strongest sense, and he was blind.

* * *

Lucia held Corbette's head in her hands. The Behemoth had vanished. She'd watched it gore Corbette in slow, agonizing motion, but she couldn't find a single mark on him. There were no wounds. No torn flesh or holes the size of an elephant's tusk. She smoothed her hands over him twice, thrice, ten times just to be sure. Still, something was wrong. He didn't get up. He didn't look at her with his usual arrogance and brush off her concern. He stared blankly over her left shoulder. Blinked. Moved his head slowly side to side, still staring. His hands crept up to cover his eyes. "What's wrong? Corbette, answer me. Where do you hurt?"

He took his hand away, and she was shocked to see a milky haze had appeared over his pupils. His eyes swirled with phantom stars just like the eyes of the Behemoth. He'd been touched by the gods. Marked, and she didn't think it had been in blessing.

"Is it gone?" he asked, voice gruff.

"Yes."

He adjusted his head in the direction of her voice, and now he was staring at her left eyebrow. By the Lady. Her heart dropped into her shoes. "You can't see me?"

"My"—he cleared his throat—"my father?"

She looked over to where the Raven had fallen. He'd Changed back to man. "He's moving."

"Go see to him." Corbette shut his eyelids. "Please."

She was afraid to leave his side, in case he died before she got back. Halian was already dead, so what did it matter if she saw to him? But she did as he asked. Gently lowering his head back to the sand, she went to find Halian. Halian's eyes were still the black void of death. She put her hand on his forehead, and he surged to a standing position.

She saw the lines of pain in his handsome face had melted away. What had the Behemoth done to him?

"It wasn't the Behemoth," he said. "Change happens in the heart."

Had she spoken out loud?

He walked to his son and knelt. Carefully cradling Corbette's head in his lap, he bent to give his forehead a kiss.

"Father," Corbette murmured.

She was intruding on a private moment, but she couldn't turn away.

"Thank you, Emory," Halian said. His dead eyes glistened. "I have been waiting for this moment for a long, long time."

"I'm sorry," Corbette said.

"I'm sorry too." They sat like that for a long breath.

"Where will you go now?"

"To join your mother. My soul passed on long ago. I am merely a projection of Halian Corbette's last ties to the Living World."

"So you're free now."

"We both are."

Lucia wrapped her arms around herself. There was a rawness in Halian's face that made her eyes itch. "I thought you were going to guide us," she said. The day had run her down, and there was no sign of the Lady of Death and her stupid Scepter. "Is the palace close? I don't know the way. How will we—"

Halian turned to her with that charming smile that made him look unrelated to Corbette. "A last gift. Over that far dune you will find a boat."

"A boat."

He winked and the edges of his form began to twinkle. His body faded in a ripple of light as the Aether Changed

him back to Raven. He hovered in the air for two long
wing beats, then rose and flew in the direction he had
pointed, west, finally slipping out of sight over the horizon. The wind blew sand from the nearby dunes, the fall
of granules a soft shushing across the glass lanes. They
looked like luges for angels. In a day or two, no one
would be able to tell what had happened here.

Corbette pushed himself to his feet. He wobbled, his
balance terrible without his primary sense. He staggered
away from her.

"Over here," she called, words echoing in the stillness.
"We need to go west. Do you hurt?"

"No." His voice was sharp. The sand shifted under his
feet, and he stumbled. She ran to him and took his arm.
He stiffened for a moment, and then allowed her to turn
him west and lead him toward the far dune.

His shirt hung open. Sand clung to the sculpted plane
of his chest and the hard pack of abs. She looked. She
could look all she wanted, and he would never know.
There was only a thread of guilt, but mostly she felt
possessive. He was blind and helpless and half naked,
completely and utterly at her mercy.

The tables had turned.

Corbette clutched Lucia's elbow as the ground gave
way beneath his feet. There were no lights and darks, no
sky or horizon. He tried to keep his head up, back
straight, but he barely knew which way was up. The world
felt small. He was trapped in a box. A coffin. The only
thing that was real was the soft woman at his side.

"We're at the top of a dune," she said. He adjusted his
idea of her position based on her voice. She was taller
than he remembered. Stronger. Unfailingly patient with

him. Inside, shame curled around his spine and slipped through the cracks between his bones. He'd never been so helpless. As they slid down the sand, he had no sense of the length of the dune or what horrors waited at the dark bottom, but he could hear the rhythmic lap of waves against a rocky shore. "We've reached a sea," Lucia said. Her voice was too cheerful. "We might be in the Caribbean—turquoise waters, warm golden sand, and a pretty little boat painted white with green trim. This will be a piece of cake."

The edge of his mouth curled. "There is no boat, is there?"

He felt the muscles in her arm tense.

"Yes, there is."

"And yet you lie so beautifully."

"Well, there *is* a boat." A small breath of air fanned his face as if she was waving her hand in front of his unseeing eyes.

"Are we alone?"

"Yup. No one else on the beach." A thread of worry undercut her cheerfulness. There might be a boat, but there was no boatman to ferry them across.

"Can you see the other side? The place we're meant to row to?"

"Sure. Maybe. If I squint, I can see a sort of island."

At that moment, he could see the attractiveness of faith. His words to his father came back to him: *I make my own fate.* But the gods had left him with almost nothing. "I can row."

"You can't see."

"You can navigate." The helplessness of it sent his blood pressure skyrocketing. If he were whole, he'd Change to Raven and fly out over the ocean until he burned off this restless energy. But he couldn't Change. He couldn't even row a gods-be-damned boat without help. His body was too tight in his skin.

She tugged his elbow. As he moved to follow, he stumbled and took them both down. He couldn't roll to soften her landing, and so landed on top of her like a whale, pushing her down into the giving sand. The ground vibrated beneath his face with the pound of the surf. He tasted salt and seaweed and rotting fish. "White sand beach, huh?"

"Yeah," she said, but she sounded winded. Her mouth hovered near his cheekbone, her breath soft on his face, her curves yielding beneath him. There was no light but touch and this woman whose siren voice called him.

Just as he'd decided to roll off her, she closed the distance. Her mouth coaxed his, tentative, inviting, and all of a sudden the world righted itself again. He might be blind, but he didn't need sight for this. The night was the kingdom of lovers. He knew Lucia's face by memory. He found her tongue and tasted her hunger.

The kiss was full of quiet desperation. Unlike the kiss in the tunnels beneath the city, this one wasn't a good-bye. Corbette's possessive hands marked her. His mouth anchored her, sweet and insistent. She could taste his fear, and was only too happy to comfort him. Blind, but not injured, she didn't feel the least guilt about taking advantage of him.

But he pulled away before things got too heated. "Lucia—"

"Let me guess: Time's a-wastin'?" She gave a wry laugh. "The Scepter, Tiamat, your eyesight . . . the list just gets longer."

Corbette sat up and turned his face into the wind. His eyes seemed to stare out to sea, body still. A sheen of sweat clung to his sculpted chest and arms. She wanted to lick off the salt. "We're not alone."

She looked up. Birds filled the skies. They perched on the beached logs lining the shore. Some wheeled overhead, chattering like old biddies. A heron flapped across the beach and landed on the boat. It gave a long, throaty caw.

"Who is that?" Corbette asked.

"A heron," she said. "He wants us to get into the boat."

"Spirits of the dead sometimes play tricks."

She studied him. The mask had descended again. The Raven Lord: cold and calculating. But she'd seen him vulnerable, and she'd never look at him without seeing the pain on his face at the Behemoth's punishment, or the pleasure of the kiss. "I've taken advantage of you," she said.

His eyebrows jumped. "Of me?"

"Yeah. Here you are stripped of your weapons and defenses, your very eyesight, and you're dependent on me to protect you," she said. His lips thinned. "And the first thing I do is kiss you like I want to tear off your clothes."

He gave a dark laugh. "Well, when you put it that way . . ."

"You really ought to know . . ." She touched his lower back, and he jumped, not knowing she'd slipped up behind him. Standing on her tiptoes, she brought her mouth to the sensitive skin right below his ear. ". . . I plan to do it again." His breathing sped up. He turned to catch her, but she darted out of reach, laughing.

His reaching hand curled into a fist, and he turned back out to sea. "What will I do with you, fair lady?

Every time I try to cast you as a damsel in distress, you turn my world on its head."

It was the most honest thought he'd ever shared with her. She rocked his world? Or she wrecked it? She'd finally tasted Corbette and all she wanted was to do it again. It was heady to know this intense attraction wasn't one-sided.

He stood silhouetted against the dark sea. So alone. Stepping forward, she took his hand. He turned into her, blind, and his other hand came into contact with her breast. A sharp frisson of energy sparked through her. Gods. It wasn't even the Aether this time.

"Corbette—"

His hand moved out to her shoulder and down her arm to squeeze her hand. He brought it to his lips. "Emory," he said. "My name is Emory." His lips were soft, gallant.

"Emory." She tried the name. She would never have called him that, not even in her dreams. This person, "Emory," had been an enigma until this trip. He'd always been the Raven Lord. Untouchable. Unmovable. Overprotective. *Emory*. The word twisted inside her mind like an eel. Kivati kids were taught to fish in the old way. She remembered being taken to the rivers when she was five. Summers in the Pacific Northwest were a crapshoot; damp more often than not, except that one glorious month of sun in August, when a person could finally dry the mold from her bones. That summer her mom had taken her to the river and shown her how to wade in to her knees, stand still as an oak tree, and wait for the little fish to tickle her toes. Quick as a thunderbolt, her mom's hand had flown into the water to clamp around that slippery fish. Lucia had practiced for hours, but still the little fish with their rainbow bellies eluded her.

*Emory* was like that. Emory, a first name, as all Kivati

had first names first, the totem added on only once they reached adulthood. She'd never been able to imagine Corbette as a young person before. He seemed dominant and domineering straight from the womb. But since they'd met Halian, all that had changed. She couldn't help piecing together the slivers of truth she knew about him—him, not the iron mantle of the Raven Lord.

"Emory," she said again. It started to feel right on her tongue.

The ghost of a smile flickered over his face. "Lead on, fair lady."

He might have been the blind one, but she was the one who stumbled across the sand.

"The boat is just this way. Watch the log . . . step up here."

"What does this beach really look like?" he asked.

"Black sand as far as the eye can see, and"—she startled as she stepped over another barrier of logs and saw the other side—"the bodies of birds."

"Just the bodies?"

"No movement, if that's what you mean." He seemed to move more easily when he could follow the sound of her voice, so she forced herself to describe the grizzly shore. "All kinds of birds. Their feathers are matted."

"With blood?"

"No."

Corbette nodded. "I can't smell any, but I'm not used to relying on my nose. Smells oily. Tainted."

"Their wings are too sticky to fly, and they're all pretty thin. Bony, like they starved waiting for help." The black boat was large enough for two. It bobbed in the water, attached to the shore by a single golden chain. "Maybe they were waiting to be ferried across?"

"No boatman?"

"No." She helped Corbette into the boat.

His mouth thinned.

"I can row," she said.

"You shouldn't have to do this alone. My arms work fine."

But he couldn't row them straight without his eyesight. "We'll get there quicker if I do it."

"How will you know which direction to go?"

"I don't know."

"How will you—"

"I don't know! Maybe we're not meant to know at this point, ever think of that? We're both blind in that way."

"Faith," he said flatly.

"Your father said it. Maybe he's right."

Corbette was silent.

Lucia touched the edge of the gold chain to unleash them from the beach, and it sparked, slithering back from the sand and untying itself from the prow of the boat. The chain lifted into the air and seemed to melt, gold undulating, reforming itself into a metallic heron. The bird flapped its golden wings and flew west. Taking a firm grip of the oars, she followed, rowing the little boat until the line of dead birds and sand disappeared behind them and all that was left was endless turquoise sea.

Grace pressed her back to the cement wall and willed her breathing to be silent. The Drekar guards passed by on the other side in a cloud of cinnamon and the heavy stomp of boots. *Three . . . two . . . one . . . go!* She took one more sweeping glance and dashed across the street to the next shadowed niche in the wall. There were no cries of alarm, just the scream of her own heart. Hunting aptrgangr had never been as challenging as evading

Tiamat's Drekar and Kivati troops. When a wraith took someone over, it wasn't the sharpest tool in the shed. She'd had it easy when Tiamat's Heart still rested inside her body. Now that she was only human, her reaction speed had decreased. She almost missed the days when it was just her against a newly possessed aptrgangr—one debilitating kick took down the body and all she had to do was brand the banishing runes into its skin to send it back through the Gate where it belonged.

But the days of aptrgangr hordes and their black-and-white, good-versus-evil status had given way to a much more dangerous gray. The lines between humans, Drekar, and Kivati had blurred, true loyalties hidden. Some were loyal to Tiamat, some to the resistance, but it was impossible to tell which were which. Spies were everywhere. Grace had no chance against Drekar or Kivati—she had to run. It wasn't a game anymore but a fight for a life free from slavery to the Babylonian Goddess of Chaos. The Drekar who hadn't joined Tiamat depended on her to reclaim their land. The Kivati who had escaped Tiamat's occupation of Queen Anne looked to her as the face of the resistance. Most importantly, her mate, Leif, her heart, needed her to survive. If she died, he died. Two bodies, one soul. They would travel together into the Land beyond, but she wasn't ready for that yet.

*I've got plans for us*, Grace thought. *We're going to finish this thing once and for all.*

She snuck across another street perilously close to the gardens being dug along the edge of the boulevard along the sea. Scores of humans labored in the hot midday sun. She wiped her forehead on her sleeve. Who'd have thought she could miss the rain so much? It was unnatural, this heat. The land thirsted. Tiamat had Kivati Aether workers turning Seattle's cool gray skies into the hot desert of the Middle East.

Closer to the base of Queen Anne, where the Needle Market still supplied food, scavenged supplies, and questionable magic remedies, Grace slid into the crowd and let herself be swallowed up. She could lose a tail as easily as tying her own shoe. Weaving in and out, hood over her blue-black hair, she eventually found her way out of the mob of downcast people to an empty alley. She stopped and watched for the messenger. This was as close as she dared to come. The crow sat on a broken pipe that stuck out of a wall six feet up. The wall used to hold half an apartment building; now it simply waited for its inevitable crumble back into the earth. She eyed the crow warily, and it tilted its head quizzically. With a little jump, the crow fluttered into the air and landed on a bent trash can next to her. It had a small scrap of paper tied to its foot.

She approached. "Blackbird, blackbird, bake me a pie."

The bird held out its foot, and she untied the note. "One for the little girl who hides in the lane," she said, dismissing the messenger, who flew off. Kivati could pass messages by piloting the consciousnesses of the birds, but Tiamat could sense that ripple in the Aether. The resistance was reduced to passing messages like this. High risk . . . typically low reward.

On the note were two words: *She knows*.

Grace felt a rush of fear, an icy sea swell over her head. She scanned the surrounding buildings for eyes and rifles aimed in her direction. Sun glinted off empty glass. The cut of shadow hid ghosts of memory. She slipped back into the crowded market and held her breath. Stalls sold sacrifices for Tiamat and less lavish offerings to Ishtar. Honey sticks, parasols, and hashish packed next to flower bulbs and divided plants that had been scoured from the surrounding countryside. Tiamat wanted to re-create the great hanging gardens of Babylon, and the people were eager to please.

*She knows*. The word repeated with each step as she dodged through the sea of shoppers, not too fast to draw attention, not too slow to draw the ire of the guards. Left foot, *she*. Right foot, *knows*. But what? What did Tiamat know of their plans? That the resistance existed? The location of their camps outside the city? They hardly knew their own plans at the moment. Taking in exiles and gathering enough food to feed the camps took most of their manpower. They didn't have the means to raid the city. They didn't have the weapons to free the human slaves.

They had to hold out until Corbette returned with the Scepter. There was no other hope, no other means of defeating Tiamat and handing her her final death. How many would die before Corbette came back? Grace couldn't think that far ahead. She just had to keep as many refugees alive as she could. Tiamat would wipe them out if she knew.

Grace slipped the incriminating paper with its elegant cursive into her mouth. She chewed and swallowed. No one would learn the identity of her informant by the slant of his handwriting.

# Chapter Twelve

"Tell me what you see."

Lucia glanced up at Corbette in the stern of the rowboat. His face was tilted up to the sky, and the angled light washed his face with a soft glow. His eyes were closed. He'd been quiet for a long time. Nothing but the splash of the oars and the creak of the planks beneath the onslaught of waves. And the birds. The birds circled overhead and called and played across the sky. She was grateful for their noise, for the sheer joy of their flight. The ocean stretched out to every horizon. It would be easy to feel lonely in a place like that. Hopeless with the endless sea. But the birds were watching, keeping her company as she followed the golden heron, and she found a certain courage in their presence. There was no point wringing her hands. She couldn't go back; she could only go forward. Corbette couldn't take care of everything; he couldn't even see. That was a lot of pressure for one soul to take and not bend and warp like wood in the flame, so she didn't take it. She let it go into the Lady's unending sea. The fear that seemed so all-encompassing to Lucia was nothing but a drop of rain when added to Her swirling waters.

Lucia cleared her throat. "There is nothing but water below and birds and sky above." She had no watch, if such a human contraption would even work in the Land of the Dead. It seemed like they'd been rowing for days. Hunger was a soft gnaw in her belly. Thirst was just another clue that she was still alive.

Corbette cocked his head to the side. It was the way he used to study the world when he was Raven, but now his eyes were closed. His brows furrowed. "I sense—" He broke off and clenched his fists against his knees.

She wanted to comfort him, but this thing between them was too new, too raw. Instead she squeezed her blistered hands around the wooden oars and pulled harder.

The gulls overhead cawed. She looked up to see a large black bird pelting through their wheeling flock. "A raven. Is it—?"

Corbette's head shot up, but his face blackened in frustration. "She's made me helpless as a newborn," he growled. "Does the Lady wish Tiamat to win? Is that it? She wants to see me fail." His body vibrated with anger. The boat rocked unsteadily.

"Now you know how I felt."

He stilled. The boat stopped rocking. He opened his mouth, but just then the raven called. Turning toward the sky, he strained toward the sound. The yearning on his face she understood all too well. He'd been bonded to his totem much longer than she had, but still, when one had dual souls bound in one's breast, it made little difference whether a century or a day. The loss of her totem was a hole in the fabric of her universe.

She turned to look over the bow of the boat. The horizon was no longer a smooth line of blue; emerald-green mountains rose straight from the sea like the spines of giant serpents. Steep, tall, and narrow, they could have been plucked from a traditional Chinese painting or the Irish's Tir-na-nog. The air thickened with melancholy. She picked up speed, pushed through the pain in her shoulders and hands, because they were so close. She was so ready for it to be over. The Lady could give Corbette his sight back and banish Tiamat with her Scepter and everything would go back to the way things had been before the Unraveling.

Her right oar caught wind and chopped across a wave. The boat jerked sharply left.

"What's wrong?" Corbette asked.

"Nothing. Just got distracted. We're almost there. The gold heron is leading us to some islands. The Palace must be somewhere up there." When they got back, she wouldn't be so willing to let Corbette marry her off. She wouldn't be satisfied until they explored this spark between them all the way until it burned to ash. She had until the end of the journey to find out if they had something worth fighting for. "It's an archipelago," she told him. "The islands are mountains—sheer cliffs that rise straight from the sea up into the clouds. Bonsai trees cling to their faces. And birds. Lots and lots of birds." She pulled faster. The boat skimmed through the choppy waves. "I think I see a passage between the islands opening up. I'm going to steer us through."

The boat slipped between two steep walls into a narrow channel where there was no light but a pinprick of sky directly above them. Water dripped from the walls. The splash of her oars echoed. The birds were suddenly silent, but she could hear the rustle of a great host of wings. She was almost grateful for the dark. "This must be the Valley of Death," she whispered. Her voice bounced off the tight passage, splintered and rose as it ricocheted up and out into the heavens. She winced. The boat hit something, and she was thrown forward into Corbette's lap, facedown. Memory ignited: heat and skin and sweat and the heady feeling of closeness. He grew hard against her cheek. His hands tightened on her arms to steady her. She wriggled out of his lap, but his hands kept her close against his chest. He pulled her up to where their lips almost met, and her breath hitched. She could close that distance and sink back beneath the waves of pleasure with him.

Lucia's breath kissed his neck. Her body was a tangle of willing woman in his lap, and there was no power on earth that could stop him from grabbing the lifeline she offered except his own stubbornness. Corbette had walked this precipice—one side reason, one side ruin—many times, but never had the latter been so tempting. He could sink into her, like his cock wanted to do, and never leave, never climb the steps, storm the palace, and finish the quest.

Now he knew how she felt?

His teeth ground against each other. With his heightened hearing, it sounded like the whirr of a stonecutter. He pushed her away from him. The boat had stopped bobbing, but the waves still knocked it against whatever was holding them back—a dock or rocks. Sounds didn't come from a single direction; everything bounced and played back, no right or left or up or down. He was dizzy with it. First sight, now sound. What would the Lady take from him next? Did She want him to crawl to Her?

He still had touch—the soft skin of Lucia's arms beneath his calloused fingers and the inviting press of her lips only inches away. He was afraid to let go.

"The gold heron has turned back into a chain. We're at

a dock," she whispered with a hundred repeating voices. The boat wobbled as she pulled her arms from his grasp. The boat jerked again, tipped as her weight left it. He felt her hand on his shoulder. "Stand up slowly. Here's the dock." She took his hand and placed it on a smooth wood plank next to the boat. "Step over the side. Hold on to me."

He climbed out, leaning on her more than he should, feeling impotent. Gods, he hated this. The boat splashed down behind him. When he regained his sense of balance, she pulled her hand away. He was immediately lost. Grabbing for her, he missed the mark and ended up tackling her around the waist. Pulling her to him, he found her face. She had such elegant bone structure.

"I'm here. I'm not going to leave you."

Never. "Good." He pressed a kiss to her, catching half her mouth at the corner.

She didn't say anything, but he felt her relax in his hold. She took his hand again and tugged him forward. "There are stairs here. Watch your step. We'll go slow."

He counted. One. Two. Two hundred. She paused now and then, and pulled her hand from his. He thought she was scouting the way, but when they started again it was still up, up, up. Three hundred. Four hundred. His toe caught a niche in the rock, and he lost track, trying not to fall.

"Let's rest for a moment," she said.

"I'm fine."

"Well, I'm tired."

They sat, his hand in hers resting in her lap. He ran his thumb over her newly chapped skin and the blisters across her palms and the pads of her fingers. Scrapes from the rock were there too—they were no longer the delicate hands of a Kivati lady. She was roughened. Each mark told a part of their journey. It was a beautiful map. His fingers moved to her wrists, where not long ago Rudrick had slashed her arteries with a sharp jade blade. He was surprised the skin was so smooth. "Your scars have disappeared."

She curled her hands into a fist, shutting him out.

"Sorry. I shouldn't have brought it up."

"We never talk about it."

"I should have been there to protect you."

"Even the Raven Lord can't be everywhere at once."

"Sadly true." The wind brushed through his hair and played over his face. He smelled the salt sea and incense—cedar, lavender, and myrrh. Their voices didn't echo as much, and his sense of direction had improved. "Tell me what you see."

She took a long breath. "We have passed some of the shorter edge mountains. The one we are climbing is the biggest. I still can't see the top in the clouds. There are small pruned trees clinging to the side of the stairs. Gold cages hang in them."

"I see." Her pauses in the climb suddenly made sense. "Are there spirits inside?"

"Some. Some of them are empty."

"And below us, all are empty now, aren't they?"

"I can't leave the birds trapped in there!"

She tried to snatch her hand away, but he wouldn't let her. "Don't be defensive. What if they're being punished—"

"Like your eyes?"

He cleared his throat.

"I can't stand to see you suffer either," she said.

"I'm not a little bird in need of protection—"

"Then climb the damn mountain on your own!"

"Lucia—" He pulled her to him. Words never heeded him around her. They always came out wrong, twisted to new meaning that he'd never intended, but he had a better use for his tongue. He couldn't stand the distance between them. Without her, he was lost. He'd been lost for a long time—far longer than their trip through the Gate. His world had shifted to orbit around this strange, headstrong young woman. The angry slant of her mouth gave way. He took little bites of her lips until she opened for him. If this staircase never ended, maybe it wouldn't be such a bad thing. He could think of worse tortures than to kiss Lucia for eternity.

"Touch me," she whispered. Taking his hand, she guided it to her breast. He needed no more invitation. There it was, just like he remembered, soft and round with a puckered tip that pulsed into his palm. He took time exploring her. Without sight, touch was his greatest weapon. Every cell of skin was more sensitive. Every whisper guided him like a strike of bright red across canvas. She was his map with her moans, her body's response. He could make her body sing with no guide but the hitch of her breath.

Soon the fear in his pulse gave way to something hotter. He could untie a corset with his eyes closed, but this wasn't just any woman. This was Lucia, and he needed to make it good for her. He needed to make it perfect. So he went slow and waited until her heart fluttered in the hollow of her neck and her moans rose higher. He freed her breasts and made love to her mouth and fit his body between the V of her thighs. Gods, he'd dreamed of seeing her face when he took her, but in this cavern of sound and touch, love had never been such a sensory game.

She pulled at his shirt, and he eased his arms out of it.

By the time he'd slipped out of his pants, she was already naked. Skin to skin, he was drowning in feeling. Lady be. He slid one arm beneath her to shield her from the stair's edge, and pulled her close. His cock throbbed against her welcoming heat. She hadn't even touched him yet, but just holding her against him was more pleasure than he could remember. His blood raced, breathing ragged.

Lucia arched off the stairs when Corbette slipped his fingers inside her. She cried out. She wasn't completely naive, but these weren't her fingers exploring sensitive places in the dead of night. At that moment, the events of the Unraveling were a distant memory. She knew that had been all about power and control. This was completely different, and she had the power, she had the control, because she could see. Corbette found his way in the dark to take her with him into a new world of sound and sensation and taste.

She didn't want to be the only one drowning. She reached out to explore his lean, sculpted body, sliding one hand into his hair and bringing his mouth back to hers. Her tongue mirrored the movements of his fingers down below: in and out, building a slow, steady rhythm. He circled, and she moved her tongue in the opposite direction, around his lips. He tasted of the salt sea air.

Suddenly he shifted and pulled his mouth away. He was breathing heavily. He shook his head, frustration in every line of his face. "If I could see you, Lucia . . . Lady be. I want to look into your eyes. I can't tell what you're thinking. Do you want this? Please." The word was guttural. His body vibrated, every muscle tense. The tendons of his neck stood out.

She'd brought the mighty Raven Lord to his knees. "Yes. Please." She needed this as much as he did.

A sharp cry, almost Raven-like, came from his throat, and then he pulled her to straddle him. She braced her knees against the stair and then he was inside her, slick and hot and full almost to the point of pain. His body shook beneath her. He rested his forehead against her lips, and they breathed together, once, twice, three times, until her inner muscles relaxed and he slid in deeper. She couldn't help the moan that seemed to come from the place they were joined right up through her torso and throat to vibrate inside her skull.

"Lady be," Corbette whispered. He tilted her hips up, pulling out in a slow, agonizing motion, and then slid her down again to the hilt. Her fingers dug into the muscles of his shoulders as sensation rippled through her core.

Eyesight was apparently not a critical part of making love, but she'd hate to miss the fierce intensity of his expression while he took her. He kept one hand on her face, and didn't miss this time when his lips found hers again. He knew her face, even blind. She wondered if he'd studied her when she wasn't looking. She'd certainly studied him. Her darkest imagination had never come close to painting this reality. He was fire and night; she was light and Aether.

Years of restraint frayed in a matter of minutes, and then she was moving her hips against his, the rub of her clit against his pubic bone driving her faster, higher. Corbette called out, a low grumbling like the mountain's roots rubbing together. The tinder struck, and sparks exploded through her nerve endings. She'd trekked miles through a place that felt so wrong—this felt so right. The dead land climbed beneath them, and their joining breathed life back into its barren soil.

When she came back to herself, she rested her head against Corbette's naked shoulder. A lock of his hair fell across his eyes. His blank eyes. She was whole, and he still couldn't see. He was completely at her mercy, and they clung to each other on a steep, never-ending staircase in a strange, topsy-turvy world. The absurdity of it made her laugh.

"Do I amuse you, my lady?" Corbette asked.

"Very much. You can amuse me anytime you like," she said.

"I wish . . ." He shook his head. "If we had more time—"

She sighed and kissed his mouth. The only certainty about the future was that it was dangerous and deadly. Corbette was not a man to build castles in the sky. "One thing at a time, my lord. *If* we get out of here alive, *if* we defeat Tiamat, *if* we have anyone left to save—"

He gripped her arms. "We will."

"Good. One of us has to keep on task." She forced herself to pull away. "We're almost there. Let's keep moving."

His eyebrows rose, but he helped her off his lap and pulled on his clothes.

There were more and more spirit birds in the trees as they climbed. Wrens and sparrows. Crows and kitty hawks. They twittered and watched and waited. Her thighs burned from the never-ending climb. Just when she thought she could climb no more, they reached the top. Her feet and hands were blistered and throbbing. Her clothes were tattered, salt and mud-stained. Her spine felt bowed by the weight of lifting one foot after the other to the top of the world. But the view from the top was almost worth it. From there, she could see two glowing orbs on opposite sides of the sky: the Lady Sun and Lady Moon, sisters to the Dark Lady. The strange, brightly colored stars fingered out like rays across the streaked sky.

She turned back to the mountaintop. "We've reached some gates. I hope they lead to the palace, 'cause I don't think I can walk any farther." The gates rose twenty feet out of the soil. Scales of bronze wove in a serpentine form across the front, and at the center jutted a giant head of some sort. The neglect was evident: spiderwebs covered every inch, as if they hadn't been open in a long, long time. She brushed the spider silk back, and found jewels inlaid in the bronze like a thousand sparkling, watchful eyes, decorative as a peacock's feathers. "I wonder how they open," she said.

"Is there a lock?"

"If there is, it's hidden in the cobwebs." She pounded on the gates, but they didn't budge. Brushing back more of the spiderwebs, she uncovered the head in the center. A giant snout, glowing eyes, and wicked sharp teeth. A dragon. She snatched her hand back, but sliced her finger against one of the fangs. Hissing in a breath, she stuck her finger in her mouth.

"What happened?" Corbette asked, instantly alert. He'd become attuned to her every tiny noise and movement. She couldn't hide anything.

She pulled her finger out of her mouth. "Cut myself. No worries. It's shallow." The dragon glared at her. "The gate is shaped like a dragon. It's a thick wall of bronze scales with a giant head in the center, mouth open. I bet we're supposed to put something in the mouth to open it. A sacrifice? Why would a dragon be guarding the Palace of the Dead?" She watched a drop of her blood glisten on the dragon's fang before rolling back into its mouth.

"Dragons have always been the ancient guardians of treasures and sacred places. The Ishtar Gates in ancient

Babylon were carved with dragons. They're immortal sentinels incapable of being bribed by humans' sad sob stories."

"But they're barred from the Land of the Dead," she said.

"They weren't always."

"Maybe they aren't meant to be forever. This makes it look like Asgard and Grace might be right—he will pass through the Gates and be welcome here." Lucia looked down at the abandoned fence, the overgrown weeds sticking out from between iron bars, the cobwebs thick across the metal spikes. "If anyone is welcome here anymore."

Corbette growled.

"They're not all evil," she said.

"Children of Chaos—"

The gates groaned. Gears screamed beneath the bronze scales. The dragon snout started to belch steam, and the scales lifted to reveal row upon row of hands cast out of bronze. Each hand held a little silver bell. They began to ring, a peal fit to wake the dead.

Corbette covered his ears. "What did you do?"

She clapped her hands over her ears too. The bells were too sharp, too high. Mind splitting. These seemed the opposite of the bells they used at Kivati Hall to keep out the wraiths; these kept out the living. Her eyes watered from the pain. The bells drove her back toward the stairs, where birds lined the trees. "Help us! Please."

In a great rush, the birds rose into the air as one and flew into the dragon's mouth. "No!" she shouted, but instead of being impaled on the fangs as she had done, their bodies fit through in a river of rainbow feathers. The gates creaked under the pressure. Protesting, the metal bent and finally gave way in a resounding crash. The bells stopped ringing. She watched the cloud of birds disappear far down the path where the turrets of a palace were barely visible.

"I guess it was a good thing I freed them," she said.

"What happened?" Corbette asked.

"The birds opened the gates for us. Come on." She took his hand and helped him through the twisted metal of the gate. "There's an inscription on the gate." She brushed back some of the spiderwebs. "I can't tell what it says. Looks like an ancient pictorial language. Babylonian?"

Corbette shrugged. "I can't help you."

Inside the gate, she found an ornamental garden with overgrown bushes and trees. Exotic flowers ran rampant over empty fountains and wrought-iron benches. Hidden in nooks were statues of long-dead gods from every corner of the earth. She pulled the Deadglass from beneath her shirt and adjusted the fit to her eye. It was supposed to see ghosts, but the garden was empty. There were no more parishioners for the forgotten deities. Spider silk traced from the tip of one statue to the toe of the next.

She imagined the garden as it had once been—vibrant, filled with birds in a rainbow of feathers, the hedges pruned to within an inch, spiral paths leading to sacred altars, music floating on the flower-scented breeze. She felt like a trespasser, and she was. What had happened to make the dead abandon it?

Dropping the Deadglass beneath her shirt again, she squeezed Corbette's hand. "We're following a long path of beach pebbles and quartz through a garden. Lady be— I can see the palace!" She let out a whoop of joy and squeezed Corbette's hand. The palace rose like a black blade from the colorful grounds. It should be foreboding, but after so many miles and who knew how many days, seeing it meant the end of the journey was within reach.

Architecturally it was a mutt: a forest of minarets and onion domes, lace-carved stone and shiny blue-black rock. It combined an eclectic mix of cultures and styles in a bizarrely cohesive whole. Her eyes couldn't focus on any one piece for very long; it was like an Escher drawing. She didn't think it followed the laws of physics. The architecture of the Living World was a pale imitation, but then it had things like gravity working against it. How many dreamers returned to build their castles and churches with the fading memory of the Palace of the Dead singing in their sleep-encrusted minds?

How it stood up, how it held together, how so many strange staircases and turrets could meld together in a harmonious whole, she didn't know. She tried to convey its image to Corbette, but words failed her. "The palace is black," she said instead. "It feels like coming home."

His head cut to her. "This isn't your home."

"I know, but that's the emotion it invokes. This sense that I want to get down on my knees and worship here— not the building, but this sense of wonder."

He tugged on her arm, reeling her in like a fish. "We will go home, together."

The finality in his voice sent a thrill down her back. Maybe he didn't intend what had happened between them to stay in the Land of the Dead after all. His lips were a smooth line of peach. Always a thin line, always disapproving, but now they softened, parting. She slid up his chest to reach them and pressed her own mouth to his. His whole body melted against her, and his arms held her close. "We can do this thing," she told him. "We're almost there. Maybe, in the way of dreams, no time at all will have passed, and we'll come out into the Living World before Tiamat ever arrives at Kivati Hall—"

"Or maybe, like Odysseus, years will have passed."

"Cynic."

"Realist." He let her go. It was cold outside the comfort of his arms. "I always expect the worst, so I'll be ready for it."

She looked him up and down. His shirt was undone, his usually sleek hair irreparably mussed. His trousers were crusted in dried mud and ragged around the ankles. Scratches marred his skin. His sightless eyes stared straight ahead.

"The worst, huh? And how is that working out for you?"

His strong fingers tapped his mouth once, and the edge of his lips curved. "Very well indeed."

She swallowed at the gravelly promise in his voice. "Let's go fetch the Scepter. There's a shower and a bed with my name on it somewhere in the Living World." She hoped he would join her in it.

# Chapter Thirteen

Kai lay next to Tiamat in the dark. A thin shaft of moonlight cut across the great silk-hung bed that used to be Corbette's. It painted a line of star-yellow over Zetian's bare torso, along the curve of one perfect breast, up the swan neck and heart chin to kiss the corner of her mouth, and hit her eyes, now closed. The rise and fall of her chest was the slow, steady rhythm of deep slumber. He lay in the dark and took a moment to watch the body of the woman outside the crazed goddess. He'd known that body, made love to that body, touched every inch with every inch of his own. Tiamat was insatiable. When she was awake, she was never still. There were no moments when he could lie like this and meditate on the mockery his life had become. His eyes slid down over her skin to where the red silk sheet just covered her belly button. Her stomach was still only slightly curved, in the normal shape of a healthy female. Would it grow round soon? Would he lie here like this in five months? Eight? Would she let him live to watch her stomach bulge out with their monster child?

If she didn't conceive, it wouldn't be for lack of trying.

Slipping his hand between the headboard and mattress, he found the hidden knife. He had to try, even if she woke before he could finish cutting off her head. But what would happen if Zetian died and Tiamat fled into another body? Kai didn't have the skills or tools to bind her and banish her like Grace did. Zetian would die for nothing. All he could buy them was a little time. He'd imagined cutting off her head as she slept countless times, but the tiny doubt that a seed might have sprouted in her womb held his hand. It was selfish, this small hope.

If Jace could have seen him now, would he have disowned Kai as his brother? Kai had saved lives by distracting an enraged Tiamat with sex and soothing the chaotic deity inside the Dreki body. But she was Primordial Chaos, and this order they'd created couldn't last. He thought of Apsu and Kingu and those brave or foolish gods who'd lain in her bed before him. His days were numbered.

Where in the twelve territories was Corbette?

Still, he didn't pull out the knife. He watched the moonlight slowly creep over her closed eyes, and she stirred. His whole body tensed. Her eyes opened. He released the knife. To cover, he smiled his lazy smile and moved his hand to draw his fingers along the curve of her belly, down beneath the sheet—

She seized his hand.

*Oh, shit.*

"Help me." The whisper was so faint he thought he'd imagined it. He was prepared for an attack, but not for what he saw in her eyes. The woman looking back at him was not the ancient Babylonian goddess of his nightmares. Her eyes were wide enough to show the whites all around. Fear made her young, a child compared to

Tiamat, but a woman he'd fought before. "Help me," she whimpered again. Her slender fingers squeezed his.

"Astrid Zetian?" he whispered back.

A little sigh slipped from her parted lips, and then her eyes rolled back in her head. Her eyelids flickered, and the presence he'd grown to loathe clicked back into possession. "You dare wake me?"

He covered his chagrin with a smooth lie. "Humans used to believe that sex by moonlight, after the first sleep, was a better time to procreate." It helped that it wasn't a lie but a superstition, and Tiamat was nothing if not superstitious. She would do anything for her third pantheon.

She relaxed back into the plush mattress. He let his fingers dip under the sheet to find her ready. She was always ready.

Zetian had been here and gone in such short a breath he could hardly believe it hadn't been a trick of Tiamat's just to keep him on edge. But the raw vulnerability in Zetian's plea was so far removed from Tiamat's imagination. Tiamat was fully unable to comprehend things like vulnerability, hope, and love. She was pure selfishness.

He rolled over her. Zetian's body was beautiful, but she wasn't in control of it. Shame settled in his stomach. It was easy to do his job when he hated her. This was wartime. This was survival—for himself, the Kivati, and anyone else inhabiting this cursed city.

But he couldn't shake her plea, and as Tiamat beckoned, he couldn't help but think of the woman who owned this body and still resided inside. Did she sleep when Tiamat was in control? Or was she trapped as an observer in her own body? Because that took the assignment to a soul-tarnishing place he could never return from.

"I grow impatient," Tiamat crooned. "If your seed isn't up to the challenge by the end of this cycle, I'll be forced to find someone more amenable." She pulled him close, bit the lobe of his ear, and then licked the blood off. "And I'll find your little friends, Thunderbird. I know you've been passing them notes. Naughty, naughty. You've been a very bad boy."

Rocks of ice rumbled in his gut. There was very little time left. All he could do was ask for Zetian's forgiveness.

Corbette walked in darkness. He followed the sound of Lucia's voice as she described the scenery of Death's garden and palace. Even though he couldn't see it, he could picture it perfectly, almost as if he'd been here before. Through the journey he'd felt an eerie sense of déjà vu, but he'd chalked it up to his Raven dreams. Never had he lost his sight in the dreams. Never had he dreamed of Lucia's delicate body above him on the steep staircase. His feelings were tangled as a spider's web. He wanted her again, but he shouldn't have taken advantage of her in the first place. Would she want a blind man in the Land of the Living? He had nothing to offer her. He'd lost his throne, his totem, his Aether, and his eyesight in one long slide into darkness.

"Do you think Will is holding off Tiamat?" Lucia asked, breaking into his cloud of self-pity.

"Will is the best Thunderbird I have. If he can't do it, no one can."

"He mentored you when your father died, right?"

"Yes. He was more of a father to me than Halian ever was. We saw eye to eye."

"Is he as strong as Kai?"

A flicker of jealousy struck Corbette. How could he have ever thought of giving her to Kai? The idea of her with anyone else flooded him with a wave of black irrationality. "Strength is useless if it can't be directed. In a fight, Kai would win, but he's hotheaded. Leadership is about putting the good of your followers above your own selfish desires. It takes trust and a certain selflessness."

"Faith," she said. "You must instill faith in your people that you will lead them to prosperity and peace."

"Yes," he said, startled, because he'd always thought that the Crane symbolized faith and the Raven symbolized power. She'd never shown much interest in being a spiritual leader of the people, and he'd never wanted to leave his rule up to such an insubstantial emotion as faith.

"I believe in you." She squeezed his hand.

He let out a harsh breath. "After all that's happened?"

"It wouldn't be faith if it was never tested."

"Gods, Lucy—" He pulled her to him and his lips found the edge of her ear. She laughed and turned her face to meet him. He caught the edge of her smile before she was opening to him, tongue sweeter than nectar, body pressed against his. Her faith in him shook him to the core, shamed him for how little he'd trusted in her before this journey. She'd surprised him with her endurance and generosity. She gave when she had nothing left to give. She believed when he'd lost all hope. "You make me want to open Gates for you."

"Despite your sacred duty to keep them closed?"

"Yes," he whispered against her lips.

"I—" She stiffened.

"What is it?"

"There's a man walking toward us."

"The Enkidu?"

"No," she whispered. "No." Her fingers dug into his arms.

A moment of happiness, and then the gods ripped away even that. He knew by the sorrow he heard in her voice what she was going to say. They'd been too lucky not to cross paths with any of their people so far. With Tiamat in the Living World, he'd been surprised that there hadn't been a flood of spirits crossing the Gate. He braced himself. "Who?"

She didn't answer. He listened to the crunch of pebbles beneath booted heels coming toward them. A man, tall, broad, by the sound of it. A familiar set of footsteps.

"Hello, Emory," Lord William Raiden said.

Corbette needed a long moment to find his voice. Lucia took his weight as he rested, so briefly, from the punch in the gut. "How?"

"Tiamat took the hill."

"When?"

"Four months have passed in the Living World."

"Four?" Corbette croaked. At his side, Lucia gave a little cry.

"Casualties?"

"I was the first."

So Will wouldn't know how bad things were. Time was even more pressing now. "Any news of the others? Have many passed through the Gate?"

"Yes. Humans and Kivati. You must hurry your quest. I'm sorry, Emory."

Corbette nodded. It was all he could manage.

Blinking back tears, Lucia studied the shade of the Thunderbird general in front of her. Same stern expression, same proud nose and arrogant cheekbones. He wore the same clothes she'd seen him in last, which meant he'd died soon after she'd left him at the Hall. Anger replaced the shock she'd felt at first seeing him. "I warned you Tiamat was on her way."

Will gave a faint smile. "She strolled in without a shot fired."

"You had time to prepare!"

"Moments only."

Corbette put a hand on her arm. "It's done. Will, have you seen others? My sister?"

Will shook his head. "I don't know. I was carried through the Gate and made my way here. The last journey one makes alone. I haven't seen Alice, but I fear for her. She's headstrong. Wouldn't bow to Tiamat even to save her own skin."

"But her mate, Brand, surely he would protect her from his dragon goddess—"

"Dragon, Kivati, Human—those old separations are done," Will said. "You didn't see her, Emory. If there is any hope for the Living World, they must forget their enmity and work together to defeat her."

"But you hate the Drekar," Lucia pointed out.

"More than anyone," he agreed. "But I loved life more, and I lost it. So you know it's with greatest gravity that I say do not shun help, no matter what side it comes from."

A weight settled in her gut. Was this what had carved Corbette into such a serious, untouchable ruler—the knowledge that he'd sent good men to their death? She didn't like it any more, but she finally understood it. Doubtful she'd have any laughter left if she'd had to do this for centuries. A grim resolve replaced the feeling of victory she'd had at seeing the palace. "We should hurry."

"Follow me," Will said. "I can guide you to the maze, but that is all."

"Lead on." Lucia pulled herself away from Corbette's comforting side and tugged his hand. "Tell us what you know."

"I know little. Only the Spider can see through her

webs into the Living World. It's better for the Dead to forget the past."

"Unless you have unfinished business," Lucia said.

"I've been waiting for you at this junction." Will gave her a smile so full of sorrow that she felt her heart breaking. "I can't be at peace not knowing if you've succeeded."

"Will we succeed?" Corbette asked.

"Only the Lady knows, but you must."

"Then fuck it—let's do this thing," Lucia said. The palace drew into view, but the lower part was still hidden by bushes and briars. "Where's the front door?"

"Through the maze."

Of course it was. As they drew nearer, the hedges of the maze drew up. Above soared Alhambra lace-carved stone, vaulted windows out of which blew sheer crimson curtains, rising to shimmering onion domes of pure obsidian. The towers wove out of thin air in places, an impossible dreamscape. Below waited a forbidding warren made of blood-red nightshade, hemlock branches, and purple sawtoothed leaves.

Suddenly the ground shook. Lucia crashed to her knees and watched the ornamental tree in front of her crack down the center and fall, straight up, into the sky. The sky was so close here. An optical illusion, but she felt like she could almost reach out and touch the swirls of color.

"What's happening?" Corbette demanded.

"Earthquake," Lucia said. "What's wrong with the Land of the Dead, Will? It's felt so wrong the whole journey. I can feel it in my bones that this isn't the way it's supposed to be."

Will watched the swirling sky. The tree passed the onion domes, hit a thick smear of red swirling sky, and exploded. Fireworks poured down over the palace in gold and green. "Same thing that happened in the Living World: the crash of the Gate destroyed the balance of Aether. The fabric of the universe ripped. Think of a woven tapestry— you pull one thread and it bunches the rest, distorting the pattern. The Spider weaves the Aether threads to hold the worlds together, but the threads on one side were all yanked out of alignment."

"But we closed the Gate," Corbette said. "Kayla took power from all of us: earth, air, fire, water, and spirit. All the Lady's sacred tools. It should have worked."

Will shrugged. "The Aether can't hold an electric charge in the Living World. What do you think it did to the Land of the Dead? All those inventions and tools you saw on the way were once someone's hopes and dreams. Now they're rusting in a swamp. Discarded like trash. People can withstand the crash of civilization, the death of loved ones, disease, poverty, suffering. As a group, they are resilient. They will bounce back with their creativity and grit. But take away their dreams, and their souls will shatter like an ice crystal. They can't make their way through the Land of the Dead to their everlasting peace. They become trapped."

"Like the birds in the cages," Lucia said.

"Yes." Will adjusted his suit jacket, and she caught sight of a large blue-black hole through the center of his chest. What had Tiamat done to him? "Don't waste your pity on me. I haven't lost my faith in Corbette in a hundred and twenty-five years. I'm not going to now. I believe in Emory, and, for good or bad, Emory believes in you. Come. The quake is over. If you don't find the Scepter and restore the balance of the Aether, Tiamat won't be the only threat rising from the dead."

Lucia pulled herself off the ground and helped Corbette to his feet. "How do we restore the balance?"

Will gave her his sad half smile. "I don't know."

They continued toward the maze. Many of the statues had fallen from their pedestals. She stepped over a giant bust of a many-armed blue elephant and helped Corbette navigate around it.

"One thing I'm confused about, Will," Corbette said. "Why did Norgard have any of the Lady's sacred powers? He and his Drekar kin were cursed. They have no connection to the Aether other than the power to Turn, and without their soul's other half they are barred from the Lady's domain. Why would he have the power of fire? Maybe it didn't work because Kayla only had four of the powers present to close the Gate."

"A better question would be, why could Lucia's blood break the Gate in the first place? Norgard waited a few centuries to find a cracked Gate and set up his plan. He had the Tablet of Destiny and he had plenty of Kivati he could have used, but he waited. Why?"

"He planned to use Kayla's sister, Desiree, or their kid for the ceremony," Lucia said. "Maybe he was waiting to have a child and wasn't able to impregnate anyone else."

"A child to mix the Drekar and Kivati blood," Will said. "An abomination."

"It would reunite the Drekar blood with the sacred blood of the Lady," Lucia said. "Ceremonially, it makes sense—"

"But your blood was the blood to open the Gate in the end, and you're pure Kivati," Corbette said.

"As far as I know," Lucia said, but she was beginning to doubt everything she'd thought she knew about herself. "My parents, grandparents, everyone listed in the family tree was Kivati. Of course, if someone wasn't, it would be considered a great dishonor. No one would talk about it." Her aunt had died escaping almost a year of Drekar captivity. What if Sarah had had a Drekar child? Would her parents, with their strict adherence to Kivati law, kill the baby or shelter it? She didn't know anymore. Why did she heal so fast? Why did she have such blue eyes? Why couldn't she touch the Aether with a skill worthy of the prophesized Crane? She knew she was Kivati, because she had two souls, but she had no idea if she had tainted blood. She found she didn't really care, except she was afraid of what Corbette would think of her. She glanced anxiously at him.

Corbette sighed. "I can see some of my policies to keep us safe have bred dangerous secrets."

"Desiree and Kayla have very little Kivati blood. They're mostly human," Lucia said. "Everyone knows Kivati and Drekar can't mate."

"Improbable, not impossible," Corbette said. "There is very little that the universe is incapable of imagining."

"You don't sound horrified."

He ran a hand through his hair, shaking his usually sleek locks back from his face. "I've had my world turned upside down. My beliefs, my staunchly held prejudices— those are slipping from me with every step deeper into the Land of the Dead. Drekar and Kivati? Will is right. Who cares about parentage or heritage? All that matters is where you stand now: for Tiamat, or against her."

Lucia let out a breath she didn't realize she'd been holding.

Another earthquake, and this time the ground seemed to tilt. Fallen statues slid toward the maze. She stumbled and lost Corbette's hand. She grabbed a tree root to keep from falling. The elephant statue caught Corbette across

the ribs and dragged him across the ground. "Emory!"
she screamed. He couldn't see to escape, tangled in the
marble arms that seemed to writhe with life.

"Lucia!" He fell straight at the maze. With a rustle, the
thorns parted to let him and the statue slide through.
She saw a dark corridor of purple leaves, and then the
bushes snicked shut behind him.

# Chapter Fourteen

Corbette extracted himself from the crushing grip of the marble and let it tumble away from him. He tried for purchase on the thorns that brushed past him in the darkness, but his hands came away bloody. Finally, he found a thick iron bar and hung on until the ground stopped shaking. Wind whistled through the branches, and he knew he must be in the maze. He felt the ground and found flat stones. Pushing himself up, he examined his surroundings with his fingers. Iron bars. Either the maze wasn't all thorns, or he'd fallen straight through into something else. Gods, he hated being blind.

*Hello, Emory.* A hissing voice sounded in his mind.

"Who's there? What do you want?" He heard the click of bars being shut. "Don't lock me in here!"

*Patience and faith, little bird*, the voice said. It seemed to come from all directions at once.

"Faith? I built an empire from the ground up and hid it in plain sight from the humans. I watched countless of Kivati blood fall to the Drekar, and still fought on to defend our sacred honor. Who are you to talk about faith? Is this faith, to risk everything and end up with nothing?"

Only the wind answered him.

"I need the Scepter!" he shouted, but the voice—the Lady or a ghost or simply a tempting dream—didn't respond. He thought of all those birds Lucia had freed on their journey here, stuck in cages like his, and wondered how long he would wait until someone came along to save him too. He didn't give up until he'd explored every inch of his cage. Barbed branches stuck through the iron bars, letting him know he was still in the maze. He tried climbing the bars, but his hands gave out long before they ended, if they ever did.

With no other options, he sat down to wait. He remembered Lucia's soft scent, her comforting touch. The way she'd ribbed him. The press of her lips against his. She made him forget his duty. Dangerous, but that was why he'd always set her at a distance. Now that he had nothing to do but wait, memories of her came flooding back. The time he'd watched her dance in the rain. Laughing with her friends on the balcony of Kivati Hall. The fear in her eyes when she'd had one of her nightmares. His arms had ached to hold her, but back then he hadn't trusted himself. Why not? When she needed comfort, how could he turn away? He'd been a cold bastard. Gods, he hoped he had the chance to make it up to her.

He heard a flapping of wings against the cage and then a screech of hinges in need of oil. "Lucia?" He pushed himself up. "Lucia, is that you?" Next to him, the Aether rolled. He couldn't help but lean into its old familiar warmth. The brush of Aether was replaced by a very real brush of fingers, soft as a babe's cheek. "Lucia?" he asked, but he got a whiff of jasmine. "Evangeline."

"Emory, you don't have to sound so put out. I thought it was you, but it seemed too good to hope." Her voice was just as he remembered it—a wry bell like the jingle of fine china. Her fingers moved into his hair. She massaged his scalp and the crease of his forehead. "You work too hard."

He pulled back. "Ever the same refrain."

She laughed, the edge of frustration like a dry creek bed. "And yet here you are, alive and landing on my doorstep. Don't you know only desperation will drive the living to abandon their world? Or did you think it was so easy to cross the boundary?" She laughed again, and he could hear her heels clicking on the stones. She started to circle him, her hand light along his arm and shoulder. She leaned into his back and inhaled deeply. "What am I thinking? Of course you thought it was easy, Emory, darling. For you, the Raven knows not the meaning of failure."

"I failed you."

She pulled away again. "I was never first place in your heart. Is she?"

"Lucia?"

"If you have to ask, then the answer is no."

"That's not fair."

Evangeline circled again. Her hand drew loops over his chest and lightly traced a line down his abdomen. "Fair? Love is not a game of checkers you can pick up and play when the mood suits you. It's a passionate abandon. You eat it, sleep it, breathe it. It's a mad poison that beats in your veins, an inescapable hold—"

"Sounds miserable. It doesn't have to be that way."

She seized the front of his shirt and pulled him down to her. He could feel the soft, sweet breath on his lips. "There is no other way. Love is an all-or-nothing game. And if you try to halve it, to stick it where it's convenient, you will end up with nothing but sand trickling through your fingers. You will find yourself a broken shade caged by your own bitterness."

"A bit melodramatic—"

"Didn't you see them? Or did only your little poppet watch while you turned your back on those trapped along your journey? Oh, no. What am I thinking?" Her laugh was dark. "Emory Corbette would never slow his mission down."

"Unfair, Evie. Jack did right by you."

"Yes." She let go and drew back. Her anger dissipated like the morning fog on Lake Union. "Jack was a kind man. Patient, caring, a soothing balm for my bruised heart."

The wind whisked through the space between them. "I didn't mean to hurt you. But I had responsibilities—" He reached out to touch her, to reassure her or himself he didn't know. He found empty air.

"Corbette, the Kivati won't die with you. But that iron ship you're sailing will lead you to a lonely grave. I worry about you, darling."

"I'll be fine as long as I can get out of here and find Lucia. Tell me, Evangeline. If there was any love between us once, tell me how to get out of this predicament and get the Scepter back."

Her sigh right against his mouth caught him off guard. "You can't have both, dear heart. Choose."

"Between Lucia's life and the fate of the world? Be serious!" *Lucy*, his heart whispered inside him. And he felt a great chunk of the mountain granite that made up his core crack down the middle. He staggered. Evangeline caught him.

"Hush now," she whispered. "You are only as strong as you need to be. Even the mountains shift over the centuries." Her lips caught his, soft as a rose petal, and memory threw him back in time. He'd never paid much attention to the shape of her mouth, to the bit of fullness in the top, to the little thrum in her throat when she kissed him. Back then, he'd only felt passion to ease the stench of war. He'd lost himself in her to erase the horrors of the Drekar from his mind if only for a night. But he couldn't give her a heart he'd already pledged to the Kivati, and in the end she'd left him.

The kiss was light. Friendship and nothing more.

"I forgive you," she said against his lips. "There is more to you than this hatred and solitude you've built for yourself. But you must open to the pain if you are to experience any of the pleasure."

Lucia found her footing as the earthquake stopped. Corbette was nowhere to be seen through the thick thorny hedges. "Will, what do I do? Where is he?"

Will's mouth was thin. "Do you love him?"

Did she love Corbette? Her feelings for him were too tangled and raw. She'd hitched her wagon to his star once, and her heart still hurt from it. "Does it matter? We need to find the Scepter and get back to the Land of the—"

Will laughed. "You sound like him now."

Lucia drew herself up. "Look, you son of a wraith, I know you've never liked me, but I'm your best shot for seeing us succeed and finding your little slice of peace in the afterlife. So either you continue to be mysterious and we waste valuable time, or you let go of your prejudices against me and help me find him."

Will's eyebrows rose. "You've changed."

"That makes two of us, ghost boy." She planted her fists on her hips. "Move your ass."

With a smile, Will bowed. He held out his hand toward

the maze. "Keep your claws unsheathed. You'll need them in the maze."

"What's in there?"

"Riddles and minotaur."

*Never ask for reason from a ghost.* She strode past. Close up, the sawtooth leaves were actually small metal disks with spiked edges that were sharp enough to cut. The maze had no visible entrance, but she couldn't push her way through. The whole thing was a metal booby trap. Wind rustled the hedges, and the metal leaves tingled like chimes. She should have noticed that it didn't smell of green growing things, but she'd been too distracted by the appearance of the Thunderbird. The section that had swallowed Corbette was a long unbroken wall of iron thorns. "How do I get through?"

"Use your key."

She shook her head. "I don't have one."

"Around your neck."

"All I have is this." She pulled the chain with the Deadglass hanging on it. "But it just sees spirits of the dead. It's useless here. I can see you just fine without it."

Will shook his head in the same disappointed gesture he'd used so often in life. "It's a truth glass. In the Living World it sees spirits. Here, you'll find it sees something entirely different. Open your mind."

She put the Deadglass to her eye and adjusted the gears. The wall of thorns came into focus. She zoomed in on the spaces between the branches. Through the glass, they weren't so tangled together. An opening, she thought. Leaning forward for a closer look, she felt herself falling. Suddenly she was passing through the spaces with a whir of leaves in her ears. She landed hard on stones. Will was nowhere to be seen. Bars rose up on all sides with the cutting edges of leaves poking through.

She turned around and there was Corbette. He was not alone. A gorgeous, leggy brunet in a shimmering aquamarine dress was kissing him. Her hands were tangled in his shirt. His hands clasped her forearms like he was trying to keep her rooted to the spot. His hair was mussed, his cheeks rosy. The woman had an impressive rack, not that Corbette could see it, but the way they were standing left little doubt that he'd sampled her wares before. Lucia had interrupted something intimate, and a blind rage descended over her. "Corbette," she growled.

The woman slowly pulled away. She whispered something to Corbette and turned to Lucia, the smile on her lips a little sad, a little angry. Lucia wanted to claw her eyes out. The woman pulled the Aether to her and it rippled across her lustrous skin, making her even more beautiful than before. The shimmer dropped away to reveal the regal elegance of a great horned Owl. She launched herself at the bars, and they bent to let her through. She flew off, leaving Lucia and a blind Corbette whose lips were still parted in memory of a kiss.

His hands fisted at his sides, and he growled into the night. Did the Owl woman mean that much to him? His head jerked in her direction. "Evie?"

By the Lady, he even had a pet name for her. "Nope." Lucia shook. "Sorry to disappoint you."

"Lucia!" Light broke across his face. She could almost believe him. The Corbette she knew had always been faithful to the Kivati, but had he ever been faithful to a woman? She'd let herself weave daydreams in the stardust of this place. Corbette had always been clear that he didn't have time for her. She'd just refused to listen.

He took a couple steps toward her. His hands swept the air. She stepped out of his way. "Lucia, where are you?"

She was thankful he was blind. He couldn't see the

220 *Kira Brady*

tears in her eyes. She lifted her chin. "Trying to find you. My mistake. I didn't realize your company was so highly sought after." A wave of hopelessness swamped her.

He stilled, head cocked like the Raven. "How long have you been here?"

"Long enough." Anger filled her, but it was too strong, like a physical wind that bowled her over.

"It's not what it looks like—"

"Evie? So that was Evangeline, the woman you planned to marry?"

She watched the emotions flicker over Corbette's face. He was usually so good at hiding what he was thinking, but now his expressions gave him away like a news ticker.

Corbette brought his hands up in a placating gesture. "Lucia—" He growled in his throat. "I don't like that I can't see your face. I can't see what you're thinking. I can't communicate without eyes, damn it!" He turned away from her and clenched the iron bars again. He rattled them, but they wouldn't budge. "What do you want from me? I've brought you through death and trapped us here, while who knows what's happening back home. Time is passing much faster there than it is here. We might be gone years before we have even a hope of defeating Tiamat. Will anyone be left alive? Am I striving here for nothing? I just . . . gods, I can't give up. Not when there is a lick of hope left that I can save them."

"No one expects you to."

A black laugh. "The Lady does." He rested his head against the bars, despair in every tendon. "Even the ghosts do."

The wind blew and hatred corroded Lucia's gut. "What did Evangeline want?" The vitriol in her own voice made her stagger back. This wasn't her. These weren't her emotions. The maze was playing mind games with them both.

It had pegged her wrong. "It's a test," she ground out. The ill wind blew harder. She was pushed against the bars by an invisible hand. The fingers curled around her throat. "Corbette!"

"What is it?" He lunged in her direction, but she couldn't speak. The hands of anger were choking her. "Lucia?" He found her shoulder in the dark and felt his way across her body. "Talk to me. What's wrong?"

She managed a squeak. If this was a test, there had to be something they could do to end it. What was the maze testing? She frantically searched her memory for clues. Since she'd fallen through the maze and found Corbette with another woman, all she'd felt was jealousy and betrayal. The wind amped up those feelings, turning them into rage and hate. Reaching her hands up, she found Corbette's face and brought it down to her level. His skin was taut across his high cheekbones. His black brows were a thick slash of concern. His black eyes swirled with a film of Aether. Frustration and panic etched his features. He cared for her deeply, and no parade of beautiful women could make her believe otherwise. This was truth.

The invisible hands let go of her throat.

"Emory," she breathed.

"Gods, I can't protect you. I'm useless—"

"No." She covered his mouth with her hand. "It's the maze talking. These emotions aren't real. We need to hold on to the truth. No more lies between us."

His head dropped to rest against her forehead. "Her name was Evangeline Arnette." He laughed grimly and shook his head. "She wanted to be my wife, and might have been, except World War II erupted and the Drekar started bombing our houses. There was always another front to fight on. Always another fire to put out." He shut his eyes.

She had to shut out the howl of the wind in her ears. It was hard to listen to him talk about other women, but Kivati lived much longer than humans. Corbette looked not much older than thirty-five, but he was closer to one hundred and thirty-five. Of course there had been other women before her. He'd had over a century of living before she had even been born. The maze sent a wave of jealousy to freeze the bars at her back. "Did you love her? No, don't answer that. Just this: do you love her still?"

"No."

"Okay." She took his hand and found freezing skin. She rubbed some of her heat back into his fingers. "I'd rather imagine you found some happiness with her than imagine you all alone."

"I'm never alone. I have the Kivati. I should have waited for you."

She rolled her eyes. "You mean for the Crane?"

"No." Corbette lifted his hand to her cheek and rubbed her lower lip with his thumb. He cared for her. The wind didn't rise with unreal emotions; this was his truth. "I never loved anyone as much as I loved the Kivati. I had too much to do to have room for a lover. And now, when there has never been more at stake . . ."

"Now?"

He moistened his lips, and fear gripped her. They'd found each other, skin and tongues and desire in the dark, but he still hadn't said he loved her. The tinkle of metal leaves hushed as the maze waited along with her. Anything but the truth would ricochet back at them, a hundred times worse than before.

Lucia chickened out. "I used the Deadglass to get here," she said quickly. "We could try it to get out. I can't see a door of any kind, but the Lady can't mean to keep us here indefinitely. There will be more tests before we make it out of the maze."

"Lucia—"

But her fear made the wind start up again. The sawtooth leaves jabbed into her back through the bars. "Let's get out of here." She pulled the Deadglass from beneath her cloak and twined her fingers with his. Focusing the small brass gears, the bars came into crystal-clear view. Every grain was illuminated, every sliver of metal a slightly different hue. A rainbow of silver, and suddenly she was falling through the bars. She squeezed Corbette's hand as tightly as she could. *Stay with me.*

The Deadglass spit them into the air, straight at the swirling sky, and then released them. Free fall. Wind ripped her stomach up into her throat as they fell toward the ground. *Fly!* her brain screamed. But the Crane was gone. She forced her muscles to relax, and their fall softened. Letting go of her fear completely, she welcomed the wind and the earth and the air. This was what the Lady demanded—for Lucia to trust the journey. They slowed to a gentle pace, landing softly between long rows of purple bushes with berries the color of blood.

"We made it—" She caught sight of a figure waiting for them at the end of the long row. Her hand squeezed Corbette's. Out of the frying pan . . . The next test just might kill her.

# Chapter Fifteen

Lucia clung to Corbette. The old familiar panic washed over her.

"Tell me," he ordered. She shook her head. "Trust me. Tell me what it is. We're in this together."

Down the dappled row of the hedge maze a dark figure waited. The domes of the palace rose behind him. The metal leaves rustled in the wind with an ominous snick-snick. The swirling light of the sky sent shadows skittering over his features, but she'd know him anywhere. As she watched, he grew. He took a step toward her. Corbette's grip tightened on her arm.

"Rudrick."

Corbette swore.

"You can't fight him. You can't see. I could . . ." The maze ratcheted up her fear. She needed to face him, but she couldn't. "We have to run."

He took a deep breath and touched his forehead to hers. "You know I would protect you with my last breath. I'd kill him again if I could. But Halian is right. We need to hear him out."

Rudrick took another step toward her, and another, and

with every step he grew taller and broader, till his head topped the hedge and his body cut out the sky.

"He's shifting."

"Gods, Lucia," Corbette said. "The way your body shakes." Together they faced the giant looming over their path. She felt like an ant at a picnic waiting to be crushed underfoot. The sky swirled behind Rudrick, pink and purple and burnt orange. "I can't make you do this—"

"Lucia Crane." Rudrick's bellow shook the ground.

"Run," Lucia said, and she pulled Corbette behind her, fleeing down the narrow path. The branches of the hedge ripped at her clothes. Behind her, the crash of Rudrick's footsteps rocked the earth.

"Wait!" Rudrick's roar only made her run faster.

Corbette stumbled behind her. She yanked him around the twists and turns of the path and knew, if she were blind, she'd never be as nimble on her feet. He kept up.

"Hurry!" she told him. She could feel the fear catching around her chest like a steel trap. The maze took her in circles, left, right, left again.

And then her luck ran out.

"No. No!" She scrabbled at the hedge that cut across her path. Boxed in on three sides by cruel metal spikes and knife-edged leaves, and from the fourth, the giant came rumbling down. Taking the Deadglass from around her neck, she pointed it at the dead end. Move. Move! Where was a door? An escape. That's what this stupid thing was good for, wasn't it? But nothing shifted. The dead end stayed a dead end, and she and Corbette trapped with it. She swallowed. Slowly, she turned and pressed against the hedge. The thorns cut into her back. "Corbette—"

He squeezed her hand. "Let me—"

"No." The whisper of the wind shushed around her,

drawing her hair out from her neck, singing in her ears in a strange, minor key. Corbette leaned into her. His shirt stuck to the sweat of his back, and his skin smelled of the run and the familiar crispness of wood smoke in autumn that was all Corbette. She inhaled deeply and entwined her fingers in his shirt. His arms came around her, but they didn't seek to confine. His protection was all comfort, lending his strength, and for the first time, she allowed herself to lean into his embrace without the fear that came with it. Corbette would never hurt her. He was not quite the same man who'd entered the Land of the Dead with her. He stood like the mighty oak: a place to shelter, to lean her weary head. The danger was all in front of her in the man who had stolen everything and ruined her life.

"Rudrick is dead," Corbette said.

"Yes."

"But not you. You're alive. You're a survivor." He kissed her just above her ear. "I hate not being able to protect you. But you are stronger than you know. I've watched you come out of the shell where you retreated after the Unraveling, and stand up to me and take matters into your own hands when you saw the need to do so. Do you know how many people would have come this far in your shoes? Many people recognize the difference between right and wrong, but few are brave enough to act on it. You are stronger than Rudrick will ever be."

She swallowed against the tears welling in her eyes. "I'm not strong."

He laughed. "Lady be, how many people aren't afraid to tell me when I'm wrong? And I was wrong, Lucia. So very wrong."

"About what?" But Rudrick turned the corner and found them, and she didn't have time to see what Corbette meant, because the giant took up the sky and the blackness swirled out from him, a radiation of despair. She fought against the memories as they welled up: the altar and the manacles and the knife. The blood and the pain and the shame.

"He's dead, Lucy," Corbette said. "He only has as much power as you give him."

She nodded and released his shirt.

"Lucia Crane," Rudrick boomed. "Stand forth and listen."

"I'm done listening to you," she said. She slipped her hand into Corbette's for strength and planted her energy deep into the earth. "You ruined everything. You lied to me—"

"I told you my truth," Rudrick said.

"But it wasn't my truth. You tricked me. You seduced me with your arguments and preyed on my insecurities and played me for a fool. And I am so angry!" Her voice rose until she screamed the last. "You hurt me!" Gods, she'd wanted to say these things for such a long time. She'd stored up words like arrows in the black of night for this moment, and she hoped they drew blood. She was so tired of his ghostly memory drawing her own. "You made me feel so small and worthless. But I'm not. I'm not." Each word loosened the clamp around her chest until anger outweighed the fear. More sky slipped into view behind the giant's head, and every word shrunk him a little more. "I've given you the power to hurt me for far too long. Well, now I take it back. All of it! I'm done cowering from you! I'm done letting you ruin the rest of my life. You mean nothing to me. You are nothing. You have nothing that I want to hear, and I reject everything you say."

Rudrick had shrunk to his normal size, just a wiry man

of average height. He was pale as a wraith. His hands hung down, palms toward her.

"You have no power over me," she said.

"I'm sorry," he said, and his voice was an ordinary voice, the same one she'd heard countless times. It meant as little to her now as it did before he'd tried to change the destiny of the universe.

"You should be."

"I thought I was doing the right thing. Just look what has come to pass under Corbette's rule—"

"Shut up. Any power you gain by taking away someone else's is cursed." He took another step toward her, and she shot up her hand. "Stay back."

"I thought you didn't fear me."

"I don't."

"I've been trapped here waiting for you. You let the others go. You can free me too. Go on, free me. I said I was sorry."

Corbette growled low. She could feel him fight himself not to lunge across the distance and punch Rudrick. The violence of him stained the air. Once, it would have frightened her, but he didn't move. She didn't think it was the blindness that stayed his hand; he could pinpoint Rudrick well enough by his voice.

"You," Rudrick spat at Corbette. "Look at you, holding the hand of your enemy. You don't even know what she is."

He was testing Corbette. Taunting him. He grew another foot. She waited for the wind to pick up and drown her with strange emotions, but nothing happened. Lady be. What was she?

Corbette's hand tightened in hers. "I'm exactly where I need to be."

Rudrick smirked. "You ever wondered why her blood

could open the Gate? Fair Lucia. Blue-eyed serpent in our midst."

Blue eyes. Serpent. Who was she? Lucia felt what little blood she had left drain from her face. Still, the wind didn't pick up. The Kivati would take the knowledge of her Drekar blood as a death sentence. She'd be worse than moon-marked. She'd be one of the untouchable. Dead girl walking. She searched Corbette's face for the revulsion she knew must be etched across it. His face was tense, but he didn't let go of her hand.

"I'm exactly where I want to be." Corbette's voice held the full force of his dominance.

Tears spilled down her cheeks. Whatever secrets her parents harbored didn't matter. Only this: the Raven Lord, dragon slayer, didn't care if she had Drekar blood. He wanted her, Crane or no, pure Kivati or no. The knowledge shook her like an earthquake.

"I can do this," she murmured.

"I know," Corbette said.

His trust melted the last shards of fear spearing her heart. She lifted her chin. "Rudrick Todd, I absolve you—"

"Good."

"—of the power to hurt me ever again. I take it all back. You are no longer bound to this place by any chains that connect you to me."

His smile flipped. "But—"

"There is nothing between us. Your actions during your life are between you and whatever spirits you hold holy. May the Lady have mercy upon your soul." Her voice ended in the deep chime of a bell. At each peal, Rudrick staggered back. His body continued to shrink. His pale skin turned the matte white of an egg, and the next ring sent a crack shooting across his face. More fractures cut his skin. The bell tolled the last beat of twelve. He screamed and shattered into a thousand translucent pieces. They flew into the air and turned into the gray wings of moths. The moth cloud rose into the sky and began to burn. Smoke rose into the orange night. Ash fell like the soft fluttering of snowflakes.

"He's gone." Lucia's voice was barely a whisper.

Corbette could hear her deep inhale catch in her throat. Her small hand pressed in his was icy. "Good." There was no pit of hell too deep for the Fox. It had taken every molecule of his self-restraint to let Lucia handle him. To expose her to her attacker and let her take the heat. Not to protect her. Not to take care of her.

*Sometimes*, his father used to say, *you gotta fall before you can fly.*

He'd always read that as his father's excuse for abandoning his people and his children. He'd heard in those words his father's reluctance to put himself out in order to protect the ones he loved, and Corbette had sworn never to do the same. He'd dedicated his life to protecting those he loved from the horrors of the outside world. He'd made a promise, and he'd stuck to it, whatever it took. But maybe in his zeal to protect his people, those walls of defense had become more prisonlike. What if it was fear, not courage, that drove him? He'd never have let Lucia face down her demons on her own if he could have fought them for her.

He did her a disservice. She was so much stronger than he'd given her credit for.

"You did well," he said.

She made a little choked noise, and he pulled her into his arms. Ah, well. So much for letting her stand on her own. He couldn't help this feeling of emptiness when she wasn't in his embrace. He couldn't help this driving need to make her happy. It had become of utmost importance to his existence, like oxygen to his lungs, and he wasn't sure where this new vulnerability fit into the impenetrable mantle of the Raven Lord. He hugged her close, needing to reassure himself that she was there and unharmed.

"Lucy," he crooned. "Light in my darkness."

She cried into his chest. He brought her down to the hard-packed earth, leaned back against the thorny hedge, and pulled her into his lap, where she settled heavily and let herself be rocked. "Look at me. I'm blubbering all over your shirt."

"Cry all you want," he said into her hair. "Let go."

"I wish I could be like you," she sobbed. "You never cry."

He huffed out a laugh. "Lady be, it isn't a strength not to cry. Strength comes from finding your balance with the universe: the joy and the sorrow, the dark and the light. There is no one without the other, nor should there be. Only in the center is there peace."

He smoothed her long silky hair and hummed a little lullaby his mother used to sing until Lucia's sobs turned to hiccups and she lay calm and easy against his shoulder. They sat in the stillness of the night for a long while, until even her hiccups subsided. She wiggled in his lap, and he knew the precise moment she became aware of him, not as a chest to cry on but as a man. The silence changed subtly. Not the soft retreat of low tide, but the gathering before the rush of an incoming wave.

He couldn't see her face, but the tension in her body told him all he needed to know.

"Corbette—"

"I can't do anything about it. Don't worry. I'd never ask for—"

"Emory." A finger touched his lips, and then her lips, soft and surprising, salty from her tears. Against her hip, he hardened further, but instead of pulling away, she adjusted herself in his lap to straddle his thighs and place the stiff heat of him right where he wanted to go.

"Are you sure?" he asked. He stopped her with his hands on her upper arms, though it pained him to do so.

"You want me even if I have Drekar blood?"

"I don't care if you're all human, woman," he growled. "I don't care if you're half hydra and sprout twelve heads. It's madness to want someone who turns my world upside down. You don't follow directions, you don't act as a proper person should, but—gods!—there is no one I'd rather take this journey with. I've lost everything I thought mattered—my people, my throne, my totem, my powers, even my gods-be-damned eyes. But I've found you." He ran his thumb across her cheeks and wiped away the tears. "Don't cry. Please. I can't bear it."

"And when we win? When you get your sight and totem and powers back and we kick Tiamat's ass? What then?"

"I've spent a hundred years fighting change. I thought I had it all and there was nothing I could do, save defeat the Drekar, that could make my world any better. I was wrong. You make it better. I never realized I was caged until you showed me the bars."

She kissed him, soft and gentle. He sunk into her embrace. Her lips soothed the rawness of his speech. Her hips rubbed against him, and he forced himself to pull away.

"I won't take advantage of a woman in distress. Don't

do this because you feel obliged. Don't do this to please me. I think the utmost of you whether you will or not. You have to know that, Lucia. I want your friendship more than I want your body. There must always be honesty between us."

"Are we friends then?" Her voice hid a smile.

He kissed her again, a light, breezy thing that was the palest shadow of what he wanted to do to her. "I'd like to be your friend."

She slipped her hand between them and down the front of his trousers. "You're right, I'm not proper. I have no qualms about taking advantage of a blind man."

He grinned. "You, mademoiselle, have me at a distinct disadvantage."

"I need you."

He sobered. Her hand still rubbed him distractingly. "And maybe there is no cure for this blindness. I'm not sure how we'll get out of this. Would you want a blind man for a mate?"

A little hitch caught in her throat. "If I'm not the fated Crane, will you still want me?"

"Gods, yes." He leaned into her and spoke the words against her lips. "There is nothing in either world that could keep me from wanting you." He leaned her down to the scratchy earth, her cloak beneath them and everywhere the scent of broken leaves and crushed earth. Something dug into his hip from beneath her cloak. "What is that?"

He felt her rummaging beneath the cloak. "The hummingbird mask. I'd forgotten about it. I wonder what Halian meant for—"

There was a flash of Aether, a searing tingle like bubbles in champagne, and then the warm weight of Lucia was gone, and he found himself alone in the darkness with only the soft whirring of wings for comfort.

At the edge of the Gas Works, behind the caved-in towers and burnt-out engines that used to turn coal into gas, Kai waited. The pump and boiler houses hid him from view, Lake Union stretched in front of him, and between the beams of the building he could see the grave markers reaching out of the muddy earth like midwinter blooms. The markers and toppled towers were all that was left to show the battle with Kingu had taken place. Might as well have given in then, because the current state of the city was a certain downgrade. Lady be, he thought he had it all then: a sweet gig where he saw action and got rewarded, but no one depended on him to make the hard decisions. Corbette called the shots and he could criticize the man in private as much as he wanted. He didn't have to shoulder the burden.

Snowflakes danced in the air, a light dusting across the top of Kite Hill like powdered sugar on a cake, but here at sea level the ground was too warm for it to stick. The snow touched the ground and dissolved. Disappeared into the earth with just a sparkle of dew. Tiamat had grown too hot in her newly created Babylon. She'd demanded cooler weather, and the Aether workers gave. Kai let his feet take root and sent his energy down into the ground, not his Aether power but simply his breath and his subconscious connection to the pulsing beat of the earth.

He opened his eyes and found the Reaper in front of him. She had her blade out.

"This is dangerous," Grace said.

"I walked. She's tucked in bed."

"She's afraid of the snow?"

He turned his face back to the grave markers. "Nausea."

"Gods damn it, Kai."

"What am I supposed to do?" He threw his hands up. "I've been placating her, buying you time. You know how many times one of the Kivati escaped only because I distracted her? You don't like my technique? Fuck you. She's got this whole plan down to the wire, and there's only one place I fit in."

"Giving it your best shot. The world thanks you."

"Don't fuck with me. Corbette was supposed to be back by now with the Scepter."

"What if he's not coming back?" she asked.

"Corbette always comes back."

"He's certainly taking his sweet time."

"He can't abandon us. Even if he's dead, his cursed ghost would be back to warn us."

"You have such faith in him."

Restless energy took Kai to the edge of the barn and back. "Tell me you have something else. Tell me you have another plan all worked out, and you're just waiting to save the day because . . . because?" He leveled the full weight of his frustration at Grace.

She looked away.

He grabbed her shoulder, and she brought up her knife. He didn't move to defend himself. The blade cut a thin line of red across his wrist. "My time has run out. It's done: she's pregnant. I can't cover for you anymore. Tell me you have a plan."

The tip of her knife lowered. "Leif has this theory."

"Your plan is a theory?"

She pushed his hold off of her shoulder. "When Tiamat's Heart was in me, she didn't have control. Leif says my soul and will were strong enough to keep her trapped, plus the runes on my skin. But it started with my soul."

"Zetian is Drekar; she has no soul to fight."

"Maybe."

"Maybe? That's why Tiamat wants the Scepter. Besides taking over both worlds, she's planning to save her children from the curse, benevolent mother that she is." The irony was chilling. If Tiamat was an ideal mother, she'd twisted every ideal of motherhood he knew. Motivations that sounded sane in a normal person were subtly rotten in her hands. She'd save her children, but kill millions to do so. She'd bear children, but only to worship her. With the knife in her hand and blood soaking the earth, she'd whisper so convincingly, "But I did it for you."

Kai turned his back on Grace. *Why did you leave, Jace? You'd have five different fail-proof plans by now.*

"Have you seen any trace of Zetian inside her body? Any thing at all? An out-of-character word from Tiamat? A—"

"Yeah." Kai crossed his arms. He didn't want to feel pity for the woman trapped with Tiamat, but he couldn't get her damned helpless plea out of his brain. Zetian might have been a bitch before being possessed, but she'd chosen to warn him the last few times she surfaced. She'd saved more than a few lives with her insight into Tiamat's brain. "I've seen her ten times. Maybe more. I think the"—he cleared his throat around the foreign word—"*baby* has split Tiamat's attention, or drawn it inward or something."

"When? Where? Can she communicate?"

"When Tiamat is deeply asleep. Sometimes she can say a bit. We have her to thank for knowing Tiamat's latest plans."

"I'll remember to tell her thanks when I see her," Grace said in a flat voice. "Can she communicate any other times?"

"Sometimes when Tiamat is . . ."

"Is . . . what? Don't make me beat it out of you."

Kai felt the side of his mouth kick up. He cast the Drekar's little human fighter another glance. "I don't doubt you'd try."

Grace crossed her arms. "So? Only when Tiamat's dead asleep and . . . ?"

Kai kicked a piece of broken concrete with the toe of his boot. "Or when she's orgasming." Lady damn him, he could feel embarrassment steal across his cheeks. "She's coming, and then her eyes widen in this pitiful, helpless look that punches me in the gut, and then it's gone, and just Tiamat, confident, arrogant, insatiable goddess witch is back." He covered his face with his hands. "My soul is marked every time. I don't want to feel anything for her, but I do." He dropped his hands. "I do. And now there's some evil spawn in her belly, and the hell of it is, it's my evil spawn. I don't know if I'm saving the world or damning it anymore. All I know is the world might survive, but I've damned myself for eternity."

Grace's nose scrunched up. "You don't know that."

He shrugged. "It's a life, and I'm responsible. Tiamat is sick with it, which makes her more helpless and more unpredictable than ever. Being helpless doesn't sit well with her. She lashes out. I don't know which way to step to keep out of reach of her claws. And she doesn't need me anymore, so that makes me irrelevant. So I want to hear you say, 'Yes, Kai,'" he mimicked a high falsetto. "'Yes, I have a plan.'"

"We're working on it."

"That's not bloody good enough."

Grace held her hands up, and he realized his anger was setting fire to the air around him. He took a deep breath and tried to find his center.

"You and me, Kai, we understand each other. I've been there with Tiamat housed inside my brain, so don't tell me I don't follow. I follow. Believe me."

"Zetian . . . is there any way to save her?"

"Zetian's good as dead, Kai. Don't go soft now."

He kicked the dirt again. "You survived Tiamat's possession—"

"What, you *like* her now? A 'soul-sucker'?"

Did he have a soft spot for a damsel in distress? Nah, he'd always been attracted to smart, assertive women. He would have thought Zetian would be the first to sign up to the Dragon Mother Goddess's cause, but she hadn't. She'd thrown in her lot with the rebels when she'd found a way, even possessed, to warn them when she could.

His silence was enough of an answer for Grace. "I'm sorry," she said.

He couldn't take the pity in her voice. "Forget it. Forget I asked. Tiamat has started killing people and trapping their souls in clay pots in her hanging gardens, so that she'll have an army ready for her spawn to rush the Land of the Dead, or some shit. I'm next. I can feel it. Don't leave me in some damned pot, Grace Mercer."

"Just sit tight. We've got your back."

There wasn't much else he could do. Lady have mercy, he'd succeeded far too well already.

Lucia gasped as the Change took her. She'd pulled out the hummingbird mask and—unthinking—had brought it to her face. So small and frail a thing it seemed, but it had survived in the pocket of the cloak through the Behemoth's

charge, the earthquakes, and the fall through the maze. As
soon as it touched her face, Aether stormed through her,
ripping her skin inside out, blasting her core self out from
this human body to flit, wings and beak and tiny feathered body, in the air. It seemed a lifetime since she'd last
Changed, and suddenly she had wings again. Hummingbird instead of Crane, but still, she could fly. She could
leave this place and return home.

But not without Corbette.

His concealing expression had settled back into
place—the cold panel of iron that hid the flesh-and-blood
man beneath. His hair was rumpled, cheeks flushed,
clothing askew and dirt smeared across his sculpted
cheekbones. His trousers still lifted in interesting places,
and she felt a mirroring rush of heat low down. Interrupted just when it was getting good. It was a pity to leave
him like this.

His head turned an inch as he listened for her. "Lucia?"

She couldn't answer, but she flitted near his head and
hoped it was enough of a clue for him. Then she let the
wind bear her up. It sung to her of the mountain passes
and the fresh buds of spring, of the ice crystals that
chimed from the rooftops and the crisp creak of bare tree
limbs in the fall, of the steaming corn of summer and the
deep freeze of midwinter.

And then the Aether, like the rising sun, lit a path for
her across the sky. She'd missed this—the connection to
the very fabric of the universe, the steady pulse of the
heartbeat of the earth that rang across the shimmering
strands, the shining water flowing through her as her
body melted and reformed in the Change to totem half.
She shot into the air and left Corbette far behind.

She remembered the first time she'd flown with the
wings of the Crane. A brash thirteen-year-old, she'd

thought she knew everything with the arrogance of youth. But she'd never touched the sky until the third night of her vision quest. The Lady had come to her in a dream with the tip of a long white feather and painted her skin the color of snow. She'd taken her own blood to mark Lucia's temples, and that's when Lucia had known there was no going back. The pain of the first Change, and then the pleasure of rising above the tree line to soar with the stars in the sky. Wild and free, the way the Lady had intended her children to be.

In the middle of the maze, she spotted a strange tree reaching toward the sky. The blossoms on its branches sent shivers down her back. She flew toward it for a closer look, and a wall of fire shot up from the ground. The wall of flames blocked her from the tree on all sides. But she could see through the orange and red sparks that the blossoms were not normal blooms. In the center of each five-fingered sawtoothed leaf blinked an eye. Human eyes. Animal eyes. Beady black spots of insect eyes and the giant organs of whales. She knew what she had to do.

Lucia flew back down to Corbette and let the Aether roll through her. The Hummingbird wings melted to human arms and skin. The twig legs and talons lengthened to slender human thighs and calves and tender bare feet. The long, pointed beak shrunk to a human nose, still a trifle over long. She dropped to her knees as the Aether left her. The mask fell to the ground. The emptiness of her totem's abandonment struck her anew. Frantically, she reached out for the Aether again, but it blew through her outstretched fingers. It wouldn't come to her call.

"Lucia?" Corbette's voice was sandpaper.

"I'm here. I know where we need to go. The mask let me fly, but . . . ."

"But the Aether left you once you took it off."

"Yes." This sorrow he would understand.

"And now, I suppose, you're naked as a jaybird."

Heat suffused her skin from her roots to her toes. She cleared her throat. She needed Aether to pull clothes from the Aether.

"Ye gods," Corbette sighed. "I've never wanted for eyesight more."

# Chapter Sixteen

Lucia led Corbette into the center of the maze. She'd memorized its shape on her flight, and now the twists and turns seemed as natural to her as breathing. With him at her side, there was nothing she couldn't do. Turning the last corner, they arrived at the tree surrounded by a circle of fire. The flames leapt right out of the ground, but didn't burn the grass or leaves. No heat, just a steady white-orange flame. The tree had almond-shaped leaves with serrated edges and silver-petaled blossoms that opened and closed with the snapping of the wind. They glittered with the iridescence of an unearthly magic.

"What do you see?" Corbette asked.

"A tree in the center of a wall of fire. At the very center of each tree blossom grows an eye. The petals open and close over them like eyelids. They're watching us."

"Eyes." His excitement was palpable. "They're watching for evil. Wait a moment." He tugged her hand and she found herself wrapped in his arms again. His hold was unbreakable, almost too fierce, far beyond gentlemanly. He could crush her if he wanted, even without the Aether. His body contracted with physical power, even sightless, even stripped of his totem. Her heart tripped in her chest. This was the true Corbette—an untapped reserve of power that he kept carefully leashed. Maybe it wasn't his design to control all those around him, but rather his need to control himself, this wild heart of him, to spare them all his overwhelming nature. "Your heart is racing. Do I frighten you?"

"No." But she could tell from his flared nostril that he smelled her lie.

"I can't see you. Not the emotions flickering across your face, not your body language. But I can feel your shiver when you're pressed against me like this. If you ran, I couldn't follow."

"But you would."

He bent his head and took a deep breath at the base of her neck. "Does that alarm you?"

"No."

"It should. I don't trust myself around you. If you want to run, this is your chance. Now, before I get my eyesight back. Now, run, hide. No looking back. No regrets."

"You give me an out now? It's far too late for me."

His arms tightened around her. She might have been hurt that his words let her go, but his body told a different story. His hard length dug into her hip like a running iron. His brand would forever be on her soul. "Are you sure?"

"Emory—"

"Be sure. Be very sure you know what you promise."

"Would I abandon you blind to the carrion crows? Do you think so little of me?"

"No. But it would be a greater mercy to leave it at this for both of us. Don't pity me, Lucy. Don't stay out of some sense of obligation or kindness."

"You're a damn fool." His breath on her neck tickled.

He nipped her skin right over the nerves running down her neck, and the sensation shot down her body to weaken her knees. She locked her legs to keep herself upright. "The tree is only a few feet away."

"Be sure," he repeated and let her go.

She wobbled a step before finding her balance in the sudden cold. Corbette was an element all on his own. She could give him up about as much as she could give up oxygen, but she knew what he meant; there would be no half-truths between them. His uncompromising nature demanded all or nothing. "You're not the only one with demands," she said.

"Good. Demand me anything, Lucy."

"A kiss."

His lips quirked. "For luck?"

She had to swallow against the sudden fear that he wouldn't like what he saw when he finally had all his strength back. She needed luck. Luck to get out of here with her heart intact. Because once Corbette was whole, what could keep him at her side? "I won't be second to anyone." The demand tumbled out. "Not even the Kivati."

He stilled. "Neither of us is completely free."

"You told me not to stay out of a sense of duty, but you can't do the same yourself."

"Don't ask me for that."

"You said anything."

He covered his eyes with his palms and rubbed. She could feel the struggle tearing at him. Gods, she wanted to spare him the pain, but she couldn't take this decision from him. She couldn't accept anything less.

"And what of your sister?" Corbette asked. "Your parents? You want me to leave them to fend for themselves? To let the demons and demigods, Drekar, and wraiths separate us and pick us off, one by one? To let our people scatter to the four winds and disappear into human society? Children and grandchildren become less than they could be as the blood thins, until none are left who can Change as our Lady intended? Until we are no more than human, one body, one soul, with only the memory of our time touching the sun left to comfort to our root-bound feet? No. I don't think you would prefer that. I don't think a woman who frees the souls of darkness would willingly strip her people of their sacred power. It would be a cage, Lucia. A prison for the likes of us. No animal survives in captivity with its soul intact."

She took a step back from him. Of course he was right. She didn't want to leave her people unprotected, but she was afraid. The Crane was supposed to lead them, but she felt unequal to the task. If he wouldn't leave the throne, then the only way they could be together was if she became a leader of equal power. Could she do it? The edge of her nose prickled, and she wiped it on her cloak. She wouldn't cry. "Wait here," she told him. "I'll find you new eyes, my lord."

"Lucia—" He held out his hand, but she was done talking and she wouldn't beg. She turned her back on him and pulled the Hummingbird mask from her pocket. The shock of Aether when it touched her face was a live wire through her body. Her limbs twisted and turned and she sprung into the sky on wings softer than air. The thrill of flight, the feeling of right that came from reconnecting to the soul of the universe, the wind in her feathers and rush of speed. She would take this away from her people? Already there were those who couldn't Change, and she'd seen the broken jealousy in their eyes.

Could she take responsibility for protecting that magic for the entire Kivati? Was she strong enough to match the power of the Raven Lord? Pushing away her frustration, she flew at the higher branches of the tree. But the fire circle roared up, knocking her back and singeing her tail feathers. It wouldn't let her pass.

What was she missing? She tried again, and again the fire rose up. She zoomed straight up until the air grew too thin and her lungs ached, then dive-bombed down, trying to reach the tree from straight above. But the fire had no upward limit, and it threw her back. She spun in the air and plummeted toward the ground, slowing her fall at the last moment with a flurry of wings. She landed in the ground and the mask fell off in a rush of Aether. It took a moment to find her balance again.

"Lucia, are you okay?" Corbette's hands fisted at his sides.

"I'm fine. I can't fly over. I can't reach the bush."

"It's another test."

"The gods give us all the tools we need to pass, don't they? Why would the Lady set us up to fail?"

"Why indeed."

She picked herself up and brushed the dirt off. The fire warmed the air, one small consolation for her naked skin. "Trust," she said. "I don't think I'm meant to do it alone. What if you try the mask?"

"And I try it alone? If it's meant to test our trust, we must do it together."

"But there is only one mask."

"Maybe we're not meant to fly over it."

"Through it?"

"Why not?"

"Walk through fire?"

He laughed. "I've followed you this far. What's another sheet of flames?"

Lucia pulled the Deadglass from the chain around her neck and looked at the fire. It saw the truth and the tree saw evil. Was the truth evil? The nature of truth wasn't so black-and-white. The truth could be freeing. It could also be life-shattering. What truth did being the Crane ever bring her? Here she'd found some measure of peace, as if the land meant for her to come and claim it, as if the caged inhabitants were waiting for her to set them free. What if Grace was right, and the prophecy had nothing to do with the Kivati and everything to do with the spirits who lived in the darkness of death?

She adjusted the Deadglass until she could see each sliver of sparking fire jumping and dancing and writhing in the devil's dance. Up close, the color separated out into a rainbow of dots, blues and purples mixed with greens and teal and strawberry maroon. Like a Seurat painting where the individual dabs of color tricked the eye to see the bigger picture, a picnic on the Seine instead of a canvas of tiny dots. She searched the wall of color for an opening of some kind. Adjusting the gears again to zoom in, the Deadglass separated the dancing dots of flame further. She zoomed in again, and again the colors spread. It was a trick of the eye, she knew it, and yet the Deadglass told the truth. There were separations between all molecules, even so tiny as an atom, and in that space ran the Aether, massless and measureless and true as the ocean was deep. What proof did she have of the Aether, except what she'd seen and touched and felt to the hidden core of her being? Human scientists were dead certain it didn't exist, but deciding something was irrelevant didn't unmake it. No amount of wishing could make the world spin round in the opposite direction, and yet here in this impenetrable wall of flame, the Deadglass showed that in between the molecules of fire, there was all the space she needed to slip on through.

Fear was a distant buzz. She squeezed Corbette's hand

and embraced the disruptive creativity of the Deadglass. The colors pinwheeled. The slivers of fire flared as she stepped to toe them. *No*, she ordered, *obey my command*. And they flickered and cursed in the kaleidoscope, but she seized those spaces between and slipped through, pulling Corbette behind her. The heat of the fire engulfed them. Her skin screamed out at the nearness of it.

In the next breath, they were through.

She stood shaking on the other side. The Deadglass dropped back to lie between her breasts. Letting go of the mindfulness of change released the fear too, but there was no turning back. She didn't let herself turn around to see the wall of fire. She didn't give herself time to imagine what might have happened if she had let doubt win the battle. This quest wasn't over.

"What do you see?" Corbette asked.

"The tree grows up from a circle of clover. The eyes are too high up to reach. I'll use the mask." She found the Hummingbird mask in her pocket and put it on again, the Aether more real than ever as the Change burned through her. All the eyes in the centers of the flowers were different shapes, sizes, and colors. Some tiny, some huge, some slit in a cat eye, oblong and round, with pupils and without. There were bulbous frog eyes and hexagonal insect eyes and tiny black dots. No two seemed the same, but she found two that were at least human. The petals opened for her as she hovered over the blossom and stuck her long needle beak to the center of the eye. The Aether shot in a tingle up her beak, and the eye disappeared from the center of the flower. She came back down to where Corbette stood, stoic and calm but for his clenched hands, and touched her beak to the center of his eyeball. The Aether left her in a rush.

Corbette staggered back. Hurriedly, she flew to the tree

and speared another eye. She brought it to Corbette, and
the shock of Aether threw him to the ground. His eyeballs
jittered back and forth as if he were having a seizure,
before both eyelids opened wide and a beacon of light
shot out from each pupil. Then he closed his eyes again
and the light was gone. He sat up and stared at his hands,
turning them over to study the nails and the palms and the
small birthmark at the base of his thumb.

Lucia let the Change hit her again and the mask fell
off. She landed on her knees beside him. "Did it work?"

Light shredded the blackness. Color: searing reds of
the fire; purple-bronze of the maze; the swirling golds
and cobalts of the strange Van Gogh sky; his hands, a
cooler tan, marked with ten thousand miles through a
war-torn world. He curled his hands into fists and uncurled them, watching the skin slide effortlessly over
muscle and bone. Strength coiled there. The power to kill,
Aether or no. The force to keep shape-shifters in line and
carve a kingdom from the rubble of the last. His own
hands, his iron grip a tool to mold the universe to his will.
But now they were so much more. In the dark, they'd been
his eyes, his lifeline to the world around him. He'd used
them differently. Gently. Tentatively. They'd allowed him
to focus on Lucia's soft body on a deeper plane.

His body was whole again. Not the full breadth of the
Lady's gifts, but his physical human form was completely
his. He'd never appreciated it as he did now. Power ran
through his muscles, strength as he flexed, the ability to
run and fight and fuck. Nothing could stop him now that
he could *see*.

He looked up from his hands and saw Lucia. "Lady
be. Beautiful."

A light pink washed over her elegant cheekbones. Her white hair cascaded down to cover her breasts, which hung free in the firelight, but it wasn't long enough to hide below that, where the smooth curve of her belly flashed white and the soft V at the base of her thighs glinted with the light pelt of her femininity.

"If this very vivid dream is just another figment of my imagination, I hope to never wake up." He swallowed. He'd learned her scent and touch and taste while he was blind, cataloged her every sound. But as sight, his strongest sense, came roaring back, he felt as if he were seeing her for the first time. Beautiful, not for the gentle innocence as he'd once thought, but for the ancient wisdom in her eyes, the grit hidden beneath her elegant skin, the confidence she'd earned with each step into the Land of the Dead. "You'd tempt a dead man."

Her gaze dropped from his face down to the front of his trousers. "You seem very much alive."

"Gods, yes." There was a deeper sense about her, like a young plant that had taken to the soil and shot down new roots. "Forgive me. I can see I was wrong."

"About?"

"I had some notion that innocence was fetching. That I should shield you from the world to preserve that carefree light of you. To keep you from becoming hard, cruel, like I had become. To keep you always safe, but that safety would seal you off from experiencing the fullness of the world, the sadness of the world." Unable to help himself, he reached out and slid his fingertip along the smooth curve of her jaw. She had a tiny beauty mark to the right of her ear. Her lobes were detached, and a tiny bump of skin curved from the tip of her ear like the memory of some elfin ancestor. He pulled her hair back on the other side and found no small bump. They were mismatched, those ears. He'd never seen a more perfect pair.

She crossed her arms over her chest. His attention was drawn down to her perfect breasts, small and high, a handful, nothing more. "So now that I'm not innocent?"

She drew a smile from his lips. "You are a thousand times more bewitching. Damn, but I was an idiot. Hey, now." He lifted her chin. "I can finally see you. Don't hide from me."

"I'm naked."

"That fact has not been beneath my attention. Your body is beyond comparison." He tucked her hair behind her ears. "But hear me, love, were you a misshapen troll, you would still be more beautiful to me than moonrise." His hunger grew. A wild thing, it was possessive, dominant. He'd always tried to shield her from the untamed part of him, but that was when the Aether and Raven had run beneath his skin. Now he could see he was just as much a danger. His senses were on overload, and he craved Lucia like the Lady Moon called to a marked Wolf.

And she knew it. She uncrossed her arms and let her hands fall to her lap, where they twisted together.

"Are you afraid?"

A little smile played at the edge of her mouth. "Terrified."

He let his hand drift down over the edge of her jaw and along her neck, enjoying the way his touch made her shiver. His fingers played along the curve of her delicate shoulder and down her arm. She had a few freckles here too. Restraining himself, he leaned in and kissed one. Gently, gently. He would burn every mark on her into his memory to light his dreams.

Beneath long white lashes, her eyes flicked to his

crotch and back. Her breath hitched in her chest. "So now that you can see . . ."

"I mean to take advantage of you." He let his lips trail down to the racing pulse in the thin skin of her wrist. Her pounding blood made his breaths come harder, faster. The hunt, the race. The sweet takedown of his prey. Closing his eyes for a moment, he reined himself in. The iron control he'd cultivated for a century had been irreparably damaged on this journey. Could he even go back to the Living World and not be a threat to those around him?

"But the Scepter, the Enkidu, Tiamat—"

He placed his finger over her lips. "I can't promise you tomorrow. I can't protect you from what comes next, because I don't know what we'll face. The only guarantee I have is that the worst is to come." He took her hand. "If I could guarantee your safety, I would. You have to know that. I would do anything to see you safe. But I was wrong. I was arrogant. I know now that I can't control the future any more than I can change the past."

Lucia blinked, a sheen in her eyes. "I don't want empty promises."

"The only promise I can make you is that whatever we face, we will face it together. I'll not leave your side come hell or high water." Tiamat would have to exterminate his soul entirely; if there were even a spark left, he'd come back to Lucia. Leaning forward, he kissed the tear that had escaped to trickle down her pale cheek.

"And now?"

"Tiamat can wait. I'm bloody scared of losing you." The maze was quiet; he heard only the snap of the nearby wall of fire and the gentle buzz of the night. "We have a few minutes together before the next task. Spend them with me." He forced his body to relax, to appear unthreatening even as adrenaline pumped through him. "Please."

A slow smile spread across her face. It eased the fear he saw mirrored there: miles to go, battles to fight. It wouldn't be an easy victory even with the Scepter. "A few minutes, huh? Promises, promises."

He had to laugh. "My lady, let me show you just what I can do with a few minutes. I promise to make them ones you'll never forget."

She took his hand and pulled it to her breast. Her hand crushed his, hard, around her soft flesh. "Don't hold back. Don't be gentle."

"You don't know what you're asking—"

"If I'm going to be true to myself, it's only fair you do the same. No more hiding. You say you see me, but what about you? You're a dominant man, Emory, even without your animal side. I can take it."

Corbette dropped his hand from hers and stood up.

Disappointment flashed over her features, but she firmed her shoulders. "Don't hide from me, Lord Raven."

"Lady be, and you'd think I was doing it just to torment you. Don't you see? These shields are all that keep me together. I am not human."

She rose too. The sight of her naked skin and those mile-long legs made him want to sink into a kneel and beg her to have mercy on him. But she asked for something he couldn't give. "You have no Aether to speak of. You can't lose control and hurt me—"

"I can't?" Anger growled in his throat. He took a step toward her, toe to toe, and let her feel the energy coursing through him. "This oh-so-Aetherless body isn't powerless. I can't fry you to bits, but I'm still more than capable of breaking you in two."

"I trust you."

"You're a fool."

"Maybe you're right. But better a fool than a coward."

She stared up at him, feet planted, lit from behind by the wall of flame, and naked as a jaybird. She looked like an avenging goddess. "I trust you. Let go and show me the beast inside. Break it all down for me, for if we are to go anywhere from this point, there can be no lies between us. I won't return to the way things were—"

"I would never ask you to.

"—and so here is where I make my stand. Show me your worst. Show me your best. Show me all that is in you and all that you could still be, but don't protect me in the dark any longer." There was weariness in her eyes that tore at him. She'd shouldered so much of the burden leading him here, navigating over the sea and up the mountain, banishing Rudrick without his help. He wanted to hold her and take away some of the pain, but she wouldn't let him. "Don't make me less than I am. I deserve better."

He swallowed hard. If he thought letting her lead him through fire was a leap of faith, he'd been wrong. He hadn't seen the fire, and so had little fear of the unknown. But this—he knew the deep madness inside himself, and that wild abandon scared him more than an army of Tiamat's racing across the mountains. "Yes." The word grated through his system and cut every control he'd bound himself in on the way out. It freed him. "Yes. You do."

Her inhalation brought the tips of her rosy nipples into contact with his skin. It was the lightest touch, but enough to snap the last restraint inside him. He leaned down and took her mouth. Let go? She would regret those two little words. Holding nothing back, he let her see the full force of his power, the full might of his body, the intense need she kindled inside him, and his intent to let this fire rage through them until they were nothing more than smoking husks.

Sucking in her bottom lip, he slid his teeth along the sensitive skin. With a little moan, she melted into him, her curves molding perfectly to his hard body. It stoked the fire in his veins. How could he have ever thought he wanted a wisp of a proper Kivati lady? The Spider had sent him exactly what he needed—a woman who could meet him as an equal at every level. Lucia bended like a willow, and the last vestiges of his fear gave way to something sweeter: the knowledge that she could take everything he could give and still not break. He'd been too blind to see the gift right in front of him. Thank the gods for second chances.

Corbette slid his hands over the curve of her ass and lifted her to fit snugly against his hard cock. He let his tongue make love to her mouth while the V of her thighs rubbed against him. It was a preview. A promise. She melted beneath his onslaught, sending a thrill of domination through him. *This*. This is what he needed: to take her with everything in him until he was wrung dry.

He reveled in the damp heat and the smell of her feminine arousal that bit the night. "Gods, Lucy. Get on your knees." Her lips were swollen, her cheeks flushed. He wanted to watch her take him in her mouth and feel that soft pink tongue and the back of her throat. A question danced in her eyes. "You said to show you all of me. The gloves are off. I'll have your surrender."

She hesitated only a fraction before sliding down his body and dropping to her knees, her face turned up to him exposing the long line of her throat.

"Trust me to take care of you, Lucy. I'd never hurt you." He unbuttoned his trousers. She watched his fingers move and swallowed. "Trust me to see to your pleasure."

He dropped the pants over his lean hips, baring himself to the wind, to the heat of the fire at his back, to her piercing gaze.

The reflection of the flames danced in her eyes. "I trust you."

"Open your mouth." The tip of her tongue darted out to moisten her lips, and even though the dominant part of him wanted to assert his control, that small vulnerable move broke him. He dropped to the ground in front of her and seized her biceps. "You are magnificent." He took her mouth in a soul-searing kiss and chased the question from her eyes. She met him, tongue for tongue, thrust for thrust, driving him higher, winding him tighter, until his body vibrated and the sky started to spin. He broke away, chest heaving.

"Was that a test?"

"Touch yourself." He brought her hand down to the crux of her thighs and laced their fingers together. Together, they spread the soft curls and found the small nub of nerves hidden like an egg in the nest. He brushed his knuckles over it, feather light, and her body shuddered. "That's it, love. Gods, you're so wet already. Come for me." He guided her hand to slide her wetness across the lips of her femininity, circling around but not entering the place she wanted. She tugged her hand in his toward her entrance, but he only smiled and held back. He took one of her fingers and pressed it to her core, slowly, slowly, gliding it around and across, teasing her until the glade was permeated with the scent of her arousal.

A frustrated moan broke from her throat.

"You will come when I say you can come." He hoped she heard the deadly intent in his voice, because she had let this monster free. He would show her what it meant to love the true heart of the Raven Lord. He settled her fingers to press the bud and with his other hand he pinched her tight nipple. Her body jerked forward. "Not yet," he ordered. "Not yet."

"Please—"

He let go and pulled her fingers away from her core. "Do you want me?"

"Yes." The word was a moan.

Laying her on her back, he replaced her fingers with his own. "Then surrender." He bit her breast lightly and then kissed the brief pain away, ran his tongue along her navel and over the soft curve of her belly, all the while keeping pressure on her clit. He could tell she wanted to move. She fought the control, an instinctive need to see to her own desire, and he couldn't fault her for that. He admired her strength, her ability to stand on her own two feet. But in this—in this he would teach her body to obey him. He would light a fire of need in her that would heed no one else. He would feed those flames until they consumed her, and then he would drive her over the brink until she craved only him. Until her body remembered down to its last atom that only his touch could bring it that ultimate pleasure. Until she collapsed, happily sated by his hand alone.

# Chapter Seventeen

An onslaught of sensation, trembling limbs. Lucia had craved to be taken by the Raven Lord with no holds barred. No retreat, no half measures. She would never be able to hold her head up in the Land of the Living until she looked into the black heart of the man and knew she could hold her own. But, oh, there was no going back from this razor edge.

Trust, it came down to, was a fragile word. She'd ordered him to stop fighting his nature, and now he held her on the cusp of something vast and wonderful. His thumb pinned her like the talons of a hawk. His scent, crisp rain and rich earth, seduced her nose. The press of his knee between her spread legs and the heavy fall of his muscles as he lay half over her were enough to send her head reeling.

And then he shifted his body lower and replaced his thumb with his tongue. Her hips launched off the ground. He settled his hand over her navel and pressed down. Anchoring her, he feasted, touching, tasting everywhere and everything except the empty place that clenched for him. She writhed, every nerve begging for release.

"Not yet," he breathed against her curls.

She whimpered.

His mouth left her, and he sat up, eyes midnight black, sculpted body carved of firelight and madness. "Turn over," he ordered.

Limbs like jelly, she struggled to make her body obey. He didn't help, but watched, his eyes touching every curve and valley of skin. Stripping her of all secrets. She was no more than blood and bone and endless need. With her ass in the air, her vulnerability shifted to the surface of her brain once again. But as the bubble of conscious thought lifted and broke, she found she didn't care. *Please*, she moaned in her mind, and further words were untouchable. Aching, she stretched back, offering herself to him in unspoken plea. He wound his fingers in her hair, pulling back almost to the point of pain, anchored her hip with his other hand, and filled her with one long, blinding drive. A scream rent the night, and it might have been her own, but all she knew was the feeling of fullness, stretched to the limit. Her inner muscles clenched around his intrusion, every nerve ending blazing.

"Not yet." His words were a distant roll of thunder, but her body obeyed. "Not until you let go of every last scrap of fear. Not until your body trusts me as much as your reasoning does. Not until you submit—not out of fear, but out of the knowledge that I will fulfill your every darkest fantasy and bring you skyrocketing back to the light. You are Lucia Crane, the Harbinger, a goddess who walks the Living World, and you are mine." He pulled out and thrust again on the beat of that last word, and his possession twisted her to a blazing plateau. The world dissolved into colors: silver and ember and deep cerulean. Her skin thinned to parchment with every stroke, until the color of her own soul rolled out of her in a cloud of powdered paint.

"Now!" he ordered and thrust, and she broke apart in one shining nova of a dying star.


Kai walked through the Needle Market, barely seeing the mostly empty stalls and the handful of anxious shoppers bidding hungrily on scraps of last year's food. As he passed a grimy black tent that reeked of vinegar, Constance slipped next to him.

"I got your note," she said.

He didn't answer. He stopped at the tent and surveyed the stall stacked with jars full of murky greenish liquid.

"Pickled spleen," the shopkeeper barked out from where he stirred a steaming pot of vinegar over a fire. Above his head sat a row of pickled fetuses. "Five gold pieces."

"Human?" Kai asked.

The shopkeeper squinted at him and nodded. Maybe he'd lie to the next customer, but not to Kai.

Next to him, Constance fidgeted. Her nervousness made him angry. He turned his back on the shop and strode down the line of stalls. "How did you find out your half-Kivati, half-Drekar baby had a soul?" he asked.

Constance tripped. "Not here. Not—"

He spun and grabbed the front of her shirt. "Enough hiding already. I know Lucia isn't your child."

"No!" Constance spluttered, but Kai shook her once, and she dropped her head. The Needle Market patrons looked the other way. No one would lift a hand if he broke her neck right there. That thought was enough to sober him, and he set her down and took a step back. He breathed deeply through his nostrils and tried to find some semblance of peace.

"Come." Constance tugged his elbow and led him off the main drag. "Sarah," she whispered. "She's my sister's child. Sarah escaped her Drekar kidnapper, but she died giving birth. Died in my arms with my promise to protect her child. Her last words to me were, 'Call her Lucia, for she is my light.' How could I turn the baby away after that?" Her voice was choked with unshed tears. "Any Aether mage could tell the child had a soul, so who would know she was half-Drekar? There was nothing to give it away. I knew the safest spot for her would be in Corbette's fortress. She should have been safe! But the Unraveling—" Constance dropped his elbow and raised her chin. "She is my child even if she didn't come from my womb, and I won't rest until she is home safe again."

Kai had never seen a light so fierce in Constance's eyes, and he didn't doubt her pledge, Tiamat be damned. "I just want to know if the baby in Tiamat's belly will be a soul-sucker."

"You can't know. You can't predict what form your child will take, and it doesn't matter. The only choice you have is this: will you claim the child as your own, or will you abandon it to certain misery and death?"

Kai took a step back from her. Could he love a child who had the power to destroy worlds like its demonic mother? What would Jace do? The Lady have mercy, but he didn't know.

Finding the end of the maze from the tree of eyes was simple. Corbette walked hand in hand with Lucia. The palace was even more fascinating than Lucia had described. The towers seemed to shift in the air as they drew

near. It was so familiar and yet unreal. He'd been here
before in dreams, different parts of nightmares from his
childhood, hotter snatches of memory as a teen, the long
burn of the Drekar/Kivati war that preyed on his sleep as
the rising body count kept him tossing and turning late
into the night. He recognized the twisted black towers and
the poison blooms of the garden, the impossible architecture driving his eyes away, the carved gargoyles perched
along the gutter, and the whirling black birds in the skies
overhead. The strange sky lit the onion domes from above
like fireworks.

"I've often wondered if artists have found inspiration
in the Land of the Dead," he said. "I didn't think there
were that many mortals who could traverse the realms."

"Maybe they came in dreams."

"Yes. Have you dreamed of this place?"

"Yes. Nightmares more than dreams. People reaching
out to me. Their hands clawing at my clothes, pulling me
back. I could never escape them." She wrapped the blue
cloak around her body.

"And now?"

"Now I think perhaps their hands weren't reaching out
in anger. Maybe they didn't want to hold me back, but
sought my help."

Corbette gave a sharp nod. "I dreamed of this place,
but only just recently."

"Has your dream come to pass?"

Not all of it. But he couldn't hide the knowledge from
her. She'd stripped him bare.

"I see," she said. "And the worst is yet to come. Let's
get the Scepter and see what we can do."

A gauntlet of black suits of armor lined the path to
the wide front doors. As they passed, each in turn
pounded his pennant on the ground three times. Corbette

braced himself to be stopped, but nothing else happened. Close up, he could see the walls of the palace were covered in a thin sheet of spider silk.

The doors opened silently for them. Inside was again the place he'd been in dreams: the endless hallways he'd raced down with some unseen assailant at his heels, the line of mysterious doors that never led back home. Paintings covered every inch of wall in thick, ornate frames. He had the sense that he recognized the artists, but these paintings were all unfamiliar. They depicted everything from legend to ordinary, everyday people. Pastoral scenes and battles, mothers and children, burlesque dancers and animals. No order, just endless color and movement.

"It's as if all the art museums in the world were squished together and housed at the Louvre," Lucia said, "except without a curator. I could spend eternity here and never grow bored."

A long pause. "Perhaps that's the idea."

The halls were filled with birds. They swooped down the long hallways and perched in the candelabras. Watching, waiting, and silent.

After what seemed like forever speckled with wrong turns and dead ends, Corbette and Lucia found the doors to a grand hall where servants in black livery waited to let them in. Their faces were completely blank—no eyes, noses, or mouths, just a flat stretch of skin across their skulls. They took hold of the handles and opened the doors.

Color. Corbette saw nothing but color. All patterns, all shades. A kaleidoscope of polka dots and stripes, prints and solids. So bright, it took his eyes a long moment to adjust. Then he saw the people—men and women in masks and gaudy costumes spinning across a wide dance floor. Their clothing spanned all eras, but

was alike in the flashy colors and eclectic patterns found
in nature. Purple polka dots on a rose skirt with a saffron
striped bodice. Seersucker pants and gold chains. And the
masks—every shape and style, wood-carved, wire and
plaster crafted, feathers and sequins and elaborate
headdresses of bone and taffeta. A woman in a simple
Grecian-style white gown wore a five-foot headdress of
crimson feathers with a small eye mask carved of gold.
Real bone horns protruded just below the explosion of
feathers. Not all were beautiful—another wore a gorgon
head of snakes.

A man all in green wore a head that was twice too
large for his body and shaped as that of a bulbous frog.
His eyes were wet. He blinked at them in a slow, steady
appraisal. "Intruders," he croaked.

"Guests," said the snake woman.

The dancing and talking ground to a halt. Those nearest drew back. Corbette noticed the walls and ceiling
hung with cobwebs. The candles flickered with black
flame. The elegantly dressed people were familiar but not,
their elaborate masks transforming them into something
beautifully monstrous. An accusation in their eyes pricked
his conscience, but for what, he didn't know. They tittered
behind fans. Corbette was too old and hardened to care
what the polite society of the dead thought of him. He
glanced to Lucia. Her back was straight as an arrow, but
she held herself more confidently than she had in Kivati
Hall. Something had changed for her, and he was proud.
She was more than a match for these cockatoos.

"The living have no place here," the Frog said.

Corbette stepped forward. "The Raven has always
been welcome on both sides of the Gate."

The Frog's head jerked. His tongue shot out and

snapped back as if he tasted their scent on the air. "I see no Raven. Just a man."

"Where is the Spider?" Corbette demanded.

"We don't want you, faithless one," the Frog said.

"Faithless?" Corbette repeated. Fury seeped across his vision. "We have passed the Lady's tests. Jumped Her hurdles. But She punished me for trying to save my people? Tiamat is taking over the world, and you do nothing!"

The dancers hissed.

"You have learned nothing," the Frog said.

"I've kept the faith alive for more than a century. The Kivati are whole only because I fought off our enemies and upheld the old ways. And what did I get for it? The crash of the Gate ruined the land, decimated my people, and now Tiamat has risen to enslave us all, while you drink and dine and dance—"

"*Your* people?" The Frog croaked a laugh, and the crowd echoed him. "Ah, but there you are wrong. Tell me, who holds together the threads of the world? Who created the Aether to tie the universe together when the birds of torment tried to rip it apart? And who welcomes Her children home at the end of their journey, here to Her bosom, here to rest in Her halls? Do you?"

"So She only cares for the Dead now?" Corbette's voice was flat. "And the dead have turned their back on their brothers and sisters on the other side."

"Still so arrogant," the Frog said.

"And right," Corbette growled.

"What a room full of cowards," Lucia said. "Dancing? Drinking? Are you all blind to the horror that's risen in the Living World?"

"Am I blind?" A girl stepped forward from out of the crowd. She pushed up a mask made of crow feathers to reveal familiar Kivati features and the proud nose of the bird tribes.

Beside him, Lucia gave a small sob. "Georgie," she whispered.

He remembered her friend. She'd died in the Unraveling.

"Am I blind?" A man stood forward and pushed up his mask of eagle feathers. Another Kivati. Another name on the long list of casualties that woke Corbette in the middle of the night.

Another stepped forward, and another. Men and women who'd died in the Great Seattle Fire stood next to others who had perished in the battles afterward. He saw faces he'd not seen since boyhood. People whose old black-and-white tintype photographs hung in Kivati Hall, and he'd given them no notice, but here they were in "living" color. The victims of the Unraveling walked forward and nodded in turn.

Last came the newly dead. Corbette could name them all. Lucia held tightly to his hand, and he was grateful for her strength as one by one his murdered friends revealed themselves. These were the surprises. The ones who'd come through the Gate behind him. Lady be, so many. How could such an atrocity go on and the Spider do nothing?

Will stepped forward and threw back his mask of silver and vermilion. His feathers soared above his head, casting giant shadows on the walls. "Am I blind?" he asked. "The dead who look back never find peace. The dead who walk the shores of the living have signed up for eternal torment. Are you a king to us all, Emory Corbette, or only to those who haven't passed through?"

Corbette straightened. "I would lead you all, if you'll have me."

\* \* \*

Lucia wiped the tears from her eyes. So many dead. So many with hope in their eyes looking to Corbette to lead them. But lead them where? The room sat hushed, waiting.

*Who will lead them?* a voice hissed in her mind. Like the wind in the Valley of the Gods, it was split into a thousand hissing sounds, bouncing into her head from all directions.

She couldn't tell who spoke. *Corbette will*, she thought as she searched the room. The high gothic ceilings disappeared beneath a murder of crows. Silent as the grave, they wheeled across the room, biding their time, beaks sharp.

*But who will lead him?* the voice said again. *The blind leading the blind will not move far, and the world calls for balance. The Aether is unraveling.*

Lucia finally pinpointed the direction of the voice. Across the sea of color, the far wall hid in shadow. She studied it, and the shadows shifted. A monstrous creature came into focus, and it was all Lucia could do not to scream. Black as obsidian, her abdomen stretched halfway to the gothic arches that held up the ceiling. Her legs were thick as light poles and hairy as a Newfoundland dog. Lucia had mistaken the legs for pillars when she'd first come in. They bent at the level of the window tops and plummeted back to earth. But her head sucked in Lucia's attention, even though a thousand voices screamed inside her, *Don't look into her eyes*. Which eyes? How many eyes? Their silver depths drew her in like funhouse mirrors and reflected herself back at her in a hundred variations: young, old, thin, fat, pretty, hideous, injured, whole, glowing and white as the grave. But in each one, something deeper than any of those shallow appellations applied to human skin showed through. There was a continuity of spirit—bright, sparkling with

Aether. Lucia wasn't the same woman who'd walked through the Gate, but her spirit was recognizable no matter the shape. A feeling of destiny struck her. She'd been here before, and she would come again when the world needed her.

*Me?* she asked the Spider. *I can't do anything about the Aether. I can hardly control my own Change. Corbette is the most powerful—*

*Unity*, the Spider said inside her head, *balance. Your blood unites us. Your blood destroyed us. Together, you can weave the threads back together. Hurry, child. Sing the song of making.*

The voice reverberated in her bones as if it was drilling into her back teeth. Lucia's jaw shook. Song of making? Was this another test?

Corbette pulled her to him. She'd forgotten him entirely, but his hand in hers was an anchor, and he used it ruthlessly to yank her into the circle of his arms. The vision of the Spider was replaced by his welcoming chest. The scent of cedar calmed her racing heart. He wrapped her in his arms and crooned into her hair. "What's wrong? Tell me."

"Do you see Her?"

"Who? The Lady of Death?"

Lucia nodded. "At the end of the room."

"I see only webs and shadow."

"She's trapped in the unraveling Aether webs."

"How do we free her?"

"I don't know."

His arms tightened. "Lady Spider," he called. "We need the Scepter of Death. Tiamat has risen. The world cries out for you once again."

The crowd rattled. The frog man stomped forward.

"Leave us. You upset the dead with your presence. We don't wish to be reminded of all we have lost."

Corbette gave him the Raven's death glare. The musicians started up again, and the host of dead donned their masks and picked up their skirts to swirl about the dance floor. After a moment, Lucia couldn't tell they were masks anymore. The violins screeched a minor key waltz. The flames in the candles grew taller.

The doors opened again, and the Enkidu stumbled in. Skin red as clay, eyes a film of white, he looked the worse for wear. He was missing a finger on his left hand, and his movements were rocky, like he'd injured his right leg.

Lucia wondered what tests he'd been sent on the journey here. *Help us*, she tried to send to the Spider, but the Lady didn't respond.

The Enkidu advanced. Corbette tried to block his way, but the clay man picked him up and threw him aside like a sack of potatoes. Tiamat had imbued him with some of her strength, and Corbette couldn't match it. The Frog moved aside with a short bow, and the Enkidu slipped into the crowd of dancers.

"Why are you helping Tiamat?" Lucia yelled at the Frog. "Why would you choose chaos?"

"Only chaos brings the true diversity of life," he said cryptically. "We do not interfere with the affairs of mortals."

Rising, Corbette ran after the clay man. He tackled him from the back, and they crashed to the ground, locked together. Corbette held on as if he could squeeze his opponent to death. Twisting in his grip, Enkidu socked him across the jaw. Blood splattered the ground.

Lucia rushed over and dug her fingers into the Enkidu's eyes. She tried to pry away his head, but the man wasn't human. He knocked her back, and the two men rolled across the floor, leaving a trail of crimson. She searched the surrounding faces for help. The masks stared back at her. There was no mercy in the dead.

The blood on the parquet floor started to bubble. Steam rose, and the stench of rot. Lucia backed away. "What's happening?"

"An unmaking," the Frog said.

Her stomach clenched. "What happens when someone dies in the Land of the Dead?"

"They cease to exist."

"Like when a Drekar dies?"

"To be unmade is the ultimate punishment. The gods showed no mercy to Tiamat's dragon spawn."

"But Corbette—"

"The Lady's threads hold the world together, but the crash broke them apart. You must reweave the web."

Lucia stared at him. "I don't know how to do that."

The Frog shrugged. "Then your lover will no longer exist in any world."

"Tell me! What is the song of making? How do I sing it?"

"Listen," he said.

She focused on the sounds around her. Beneath the hum of violins, she caught the crackle of the fire, the chuff of gowns and slippers across the floor, the tap of fans and light jingle of bells on costumes. Overhead, the glide of wings through the air. Deep beneath her feet, the heartbeat of the world. It rose into the walls, *thump thump, thump thump*, and settled into her bones.

Closing her eyes, she shut out the screaming colors of the ballroom. In the dark, blind, her hearing sharpened. She could feel the Aether threads stretching through the room, flowing to the beat of the phantom heart. Where did it come from and where did it return to? The sparkling water bore the taint of the Unraveling, like oil on the tide. The warp and weft of the universe in a liquid essence, like time, it had no beginning and no end. How did she fix it? How could anyone expect her to know how to do this? It was too vast, too important.

Corbette cried out. She was pulled from her exploration, fear drowning out her senses. He needed her. Her, with her mixed blood, Kivati and Drekar, two ancient enemies united in one small body. She held her palms up and closed her eyes again. Soft power, Grace had called it. Wisdom and compassion. Violence couldn't fix the Aether—it could only unravel it further.

Focusing on the deep heartbeat, she matched her pulse to its stronger pull. Blood, bone, and flesh, all these were transient, fleeting properties. She dropped her awareness of those things, and was left with the blinding light of soul. She felt invisible wings of Aether spring to life from her back and the spirit of the Crane flow over her. She joined her soul with it. Not two souls sharing one body like before, but one soul, united, lighting up the world.

The burst of power radiated out in every direction. The ground shook. The musicians faltered; dancers were thrown to the ground. The very foundation of the palace began to crack.

Across the worlds, she heard Tiamat shriek.

*Out of chaos came life*, Lucia thought. She opened her mouth and began to sing. The song filled every corner of her soul and spilled out to light the corners of the room. It burned away the cobwebs and melded the cracks together. Shadows fled as the light burst out in a fire of sound. At the far end of the room, her song lit the grand dais where the Spider waited. She flickered, clean Aether swirling around Her monstrous form, and the hideous legs collapsed. When the dust cleared, a woman lay across a throne carved of ebony.

Lucia came to the end of her song. There was a great rushing in the room as all the Aether retreated like the tide releasing the beach cove, and then it came raging back in, directed, hungry.

# Chapter Eighteen

Pain tore through Corbette's head. He bled freely, leaving a trail of bubbling red in his wake. The Enkidu was as strong as an aptrgangr, but even harder to kill. He crushed Corbette's rib cage into his lungs. Only Lucia's voice kept Corbette from succumbing to the blackness. Her song coiled around him, reknitting his bones and tissues as they were broken. He wrenched his elbow beneath the clay man's neck and broke the creature's hold.

"Emory!" Lucia cried, and Corbette moved just in time to avoid another attack. Bloody hell. If he could touch the Aether right now, he'd blast that sorry piece of rock right back to his gods-be-damned maker.

Dancers rushed from the floor, straight past him, blocking the Enkidu from another volley. They mobbed the side of the room that had been lost in shadow. His view was blocked by a rainbow of skirts and polished boots.

Lucia pushed through the crowd to his side. She knelt and wiped a bit of blood from his cheek with the edge of her cloak. He caught the glimpse of her pale, naked limbs beneath the blue wool.

"I'm fine." He let her help him to his feet. "What happened?"

"The Spider was trapped by the tainted Aether. She's free now. Everyone is going to see her." Lucia's gaze was steady, her face betraying none of the shock he felt.

"How did you do it?"

"I don't know."

"But you knew the song? It was inside you, and the journey unlocked it? Was it a memory from past lives?"

"It's everywhere. I just had to listen." She flashed him the smile of a woman with secrets to keep. There was no sign of the innocent girl she had once been. And—gods—the experienced version made his knees weak. Was there anything he wouldn't do for one kiss? "We need to get to the Lady before the Enkidu does."

"Right." He curled his arm protectively around Lucia and pushed his way through the crowd. She felt right in his arms. A missing piece of his life slid into place, soothing something inside him that he'd not realized was agitated. Even without the Aether, without his totem, she made him feel whole.

The Queen of the Land of the Dead wore all black, from the long straight hair to the tight bodice and wide skirts. Her skin was bone, her hair ebony, and her lips the color of blood. The effect was stunning. She should be beautiful, but her beauty was the beauty of death, terrible and sad and irrevocable, and he wanted to turn his eyes away. On her finger she wore a thick silver ring that matched the nose ring of the Behemoth.

The clay man pushed through the crowd ahead of them. She watched him, still as a block of ice. In her lap lay a gold bar that was the length of Corbette's forearm and encrusted with black onyx. On one end was a knob with a needled point; the Scepter of Death was a spindle and distaff. He could feel the threads of Aether pulling toward and around it.

The clay man bent on one knee and came to rest in a full bow.

"Who sends the dead to the dead?" the Queen asked. Her voice was the deep rumble of the earth. Corbette felt himself instinctively curl around Lucia at the sound of it. It spoke of the hibernation of winter and the quiet suffocation of plants in the long snow.

The clay man spoke. "Tiamat, Goddess of Chaos, sends you a message. She demands the return of her children's souls. She demands justice on those who wronged her."

Corbette stepped forward, Lucia still tucked against his side. "Tiamat is a sadistic goddess who seeks nothing more than rule of all the Worlds. She will come for you next, and the Dead shall know no more peace. You can't give her what she wants."

The dark Queen shifted her infinite gaze to him. He couldn't stand under its weight. Helplessly, he let go of Lucia, crashed to his knees, and bowed, just as the dead man beside him. "And who dares order me in my own palace?"

"You have forsaken the living," Corbette ground out.

"And who are you to speak of forsaking duty? You, who have forgotten what it means to serve?"

Corbette's head whipped up. "Me? I've served your children my whole life. The Kivati are everything to me. I would give my life for them."

"And here you are in death of your own accord, yet your people are no freer, no safer for your sacrifice." She raised the Scepter and pulled the spindle from the distaff. Aether spun out between the two halves. "See the world continue on without you." The spinning threads wove out from the spindle into the air in a shimmering picture. He saw Kivati Hall. Sun shone on the yellow facade and the new wide brick road that started from its new giant gold doors. On the steps stood Kai, a stern smile on his face, and next to him stood a beautiful Zetian. Her long black hair was twisted up in combs of gold and jewels, and her red silk gown trailed on the steps behind her. Her hand rested over the pronounced curve of her belly.

"No," Corbette said.

"Did you think the world would fall apart in your absence? You are not so crucial a stick pin."

Corbette inhaled sharply. The emotion was a sucker punch in the gut. Instinctively, he reached out to the Aether, but it ignored him. A soft touch on his shoulder brought him back. Lucia.

"She's not showing you the whole truth," Lucia said. "Show him the whole."

The Queen smiled. "All of it, little Crane? Do you have so much faith in him already?"

"Yes."

Somehow, Lucia's belief released the Queen's hold on him. Corbette stood. Lucia slipped her hand into his just as the Queen in black gave way like an Aether vision breaking, and the giant body of a monstrous black spider took her place. *Good Lady, no.* But he held his ground. "How did you know?"

Lucia shrugged. "I see her as she truly is, even without the Deadglass."

The Spider was all-encompassing. True terror, but she faded back into the mask of the dark Queen again. The woman smiled. After having seen her true self, Corbette couldn't help picturing that smile full of venomous fangs. The Queen's beauty was terror. "But you meant something else, yes? Harbinger, we have been waiting for you."

She raised her distaff again, and again it spun Aether out into a vision of the Living World. This time the sight roared down the new road to downtown, where human slaves toiled in the biting winter air to build a new hanging garden at the edge of the sea. Overseers, both Kivati and Drekar, held whips and marched down the lines shouting orders. "See, Raven? She rebuilds her idealized society, her memory of her golden age. She is not so different from you."

"But he is," Lucia said. "He protected the humans."

The Queen's face darkened. "He sent many through my Gates in his war with Tiamat's children. It's not enough to have good intentions if one's means betray the ends. How many have you killed, Crane, in seeking your justice?"

"None."

Corbette cut in. "If protecting my people from the Drekar attacks is wrong, I reject your idea of justice." Lucia's hand tightened in his.

The clay man stood. "Tiamat is willing to trade for the Scepter in the old tradition."

"And what are you willing to trade?" the Queen asked Corbette.

"What old tradition?" Lucia asked.

"Balance, child of two worlds," the Queen said. "There must be balance in the universe. When Ishtar traveled into the Land of the Dead, she made the blood trade to keep the scales balanced. She exchanged her husband, Tammuz, for herself and was granted release from my kingdom. Did you think there was free passage through the Gate? You, of all people, should know better."

"You won't let us leave? With or without the Scepter?"

"Do you want to go without it? You should never have come if your quest was so frail a calling."

"What is Tiamat's trade?" Lucia's voice rose. "The life of this man? He's already dead!"

"Blood sacrifice," the Enkidu said and jumped. One moment he was frozen in a half bow, and the next he'd thrown himself at Corbette. Corbette fell beneath the impact, and they rolled to the floor. Corbette fought off the attack. He could hear Lucia screaming and the murmur of the crowd. But he couldn't match Tiamat's servant in strength. He started to lose consciousness.

Suddenly Will was pulling away the Enkidu. "I've got your back, kid. No matter which side of the Gate." Unlike Corbette, Will had the strength of the dead. He succeeded in pulling the clay man away and punched him in the face. With a roar, he dove after him, and the two went at each other like a couple of rabid dogs. Will's shape morphed faster than a flick of light and suddenly a Thunderbird hovered in the air. His talons seized the Enkidu and threw him across the room. He followed, giant wings sending the candles sputtering and blowing the curtains off their hangers. There was a loud thump and the scuffle of further fighting from the back of the room.

Corbette picked himself off the ground. An icy calm washed over him. He knew what the Queen wanted. He could see it in the unwavering black of her eyes. There was no room for adjustment, no room for persuasion or lies or manipulation. "A life for a life, is that the trade?"

The Queen's voice hissed with a thousand echoing tongues off the high ceilings overhead. "Yessss." The mask shivered, overlaying the truth of the giant Spider across the woman on the bone throne. "Balance."

He took a step forward. "I accept."

"What?" Lucia asked.

"The Scepter belongs to Tiamat!" the clay man screamed from the back of the room, followed by the shriek of a Thunderbird, but Corbette kept his face turned to the Spider and let his resolve steel his voice. In his acceptance, everything else fell away. So small a thing, this surrender. So vast a power. Lucia had taught him so much.

The Spider's voice rang in his mind. *The blood exchange is irrevocable.*

"My life for Lucia's. Let her go. Take me instead."

"What? No! Emory. Don't do this." Lucia tugged on his arm. "Please, no. Take me. The Kivati need you. Didn't you see the vision? They will all die without you! You are their only hope—"

"No, love." He trapped her hands in his. Gods, she was beautiful. Light radiated beneath her alabaster skin. Her white hair streamed down her back. Tears rose in her wide blue eyes. Dragon blood, Kivati blood, it didn't matter. She was his to love and his to lose. He brushed away a drop of water that threatened to spill over. "I can't promise you forever. I can't promise you it will be perfect, or that the world will be saved. But I can give you this: life. Please." He kissed her—too briefly, but all the more sweetly for it. "Live, my lady. If you still want me at the end, I'll be here waiting for you. There are no good-byes."

"How can you give up on us? How can you just walk away?"

"I'm not."

"The Raven Lord I know would never give up!" She pulled one hand free and hit him in the chest.

He captured it and laid a kiss on her palm. "I'm sorry I was such an ass. We could've had more time."

"We can still have it now! Don't do this." She turned to the Queen. "Please. Please don't ask this. Haven't you taken enough from us? Do you have no mercy?"

The Queen turned her head to the doorway, where the

Thunderbird and the Enkidu still fought. Already dead, death was no ending for their fight. "The balance of the universe must be restored. That is mercy, so that all creatures may live in peace. Your actions helped sever the weave and weft of the Aether, and your actions now may restore it, but nothing worth doing is free. So tell me, Light Bringer, will you be the key to salvation? Or will you be the ruin of your brothers and sisters, leading them into chaos?"

"Look at me, Lucy." Corbette took her face. His hands shook. "They need you out there. Take the Scepter and go. Defeat Tiamat. This is your destiny. This is the battle of the prophecy, but the prophecy never said if you win or lose. I'm not the one to do it. I'm just a small bit player in the game. I helped you get here, and now it's your time to go on. You can do this. I believe in you."

"I don't want to go without you." The shattered look in her eyes cut him as if he'd eaten broken glass.

"I know." He kissed her again, poured all his love, all his regret, all his hope for her into that one last kiss. Her lips were demanding beneath his. No soft surrender here, just passion and the fierceness of the end. He pulled away, breathing ragged, knowing if he went any further he would never be able to let her go. "Lady have mercy on us both."

The Aether curled around him and pulled them apart. This time he didn't try to pull it inside him. It was a false god, that rush of power. All he needed stood in front of him, and he was letting her go.


Lucia knew panic like nothing she'd experienced since the Unraveling. Corbette was abandoning her after all they'd been through and every fiery kiss they'd shared.

He would die, while she lived to take the Scepter back into the Land of the Living. Didn't he know there was nothing left for her back there without him? This journey seemed to have been orchestrated for one outcome. The spirits had been waiting for her. The land welcomed her. The signs were everywhere—she belonged here, not Corbette. "Don't be such a fucking martyr. I never asked you to die for me."

"I know."

"We'll find another way." She reached up and wrapped a hand in his shirt. His eyes widened. "Dying is easy, and you've never taken the coward's way out. Don't start now. I need a man who has the courage to live. Not to live *for* me, but to live *with* me, facing the good with the bad."

"You think I wouldn't choose that if I could?" he growled.

"It's been the Kivati or me all this time, and now you change your tune? Now? When our people need you more than ever? Finish what you started." She released him, her throat too tight to get another word out.

He stumbled back. Big, strong, confidant man that he was. His shoulders curled in on him. He rubbed the left side of his chest. "Damn it, Lucia. What would you have me do?"

"Live." She wished she could soothe the pain from his eyes, but she had nothing left. He wouldn't leave willingly.

"So be it." The Queen's voice echoed in the room and a phantom wind ripped the tapestries from their moorings. "Emory Corbette, son of the Raven. You may have what you came for. Use it wisely. You have three days."

"No!" Corbette cried. The Scepter appeared in his hand. Aether twisted around him, buffeting his body with its magic light. He rose in the air until the tips of his toes left the ground. A giant Raven—translucent, more nightmare than bird—raced across the great room with its wings spread and talons out. It shot straight into Corbette's chest. A bomb of light exploded from his body as the totem reconnected. His limbs shot out, his head dropped back, and his mouth opened in a cry of agony. Light shot from every inch of skin and with a great ripping sound, he Changed. The man dissolved to feather. The brooding nose lengthened and sharpened to a beak. In the great bird's talons hung the Scepter, still weaving the Aether on its spindle point.

"Emory!" Lucia cried. But the Raven didn't look at her. It launched itself straight up to the high vaulted ceilings. At the highest point, the rafters closed around a smoke hole open to the sky. The bird shot straight through the hole and disappeared from sight. There was nothing left of him. No feather, no light, nothing but the shriveled pieces of her heart. With a slow, zombie lurch, she turned to the Queen. "He got what he came for."

"Yes. And you made the trade. The balance of the Universe is intact."

The buzz of the courtiers started up around her. The high tinkle of laughter and the low buzz of conversation returned to normal. How would she survive in such a place? But this had been her choice. She'd told Corbette to go back and finish what he started.

But she'd become so used to having him by her side, the physical loss felt like she'd severed a limb. How many times had she glanced over to see his expression? How many times had she stopped to touch him, to take his hand, to reassure herself that he was whole and with her? What had started as the overbearing mask of the Raven Lord had crumbled to reveal the very real man beneath, and that man had grown more precious to her than breathing.

Good thing she needed neither blood nor breath in the Land of the Dead.

In the corner of the ballroom, the Thunderbird and Enkidu still fought. Will had stepped up in the nick of time. She couldn't let him be unmade. The crowd parted for her. The strange, unreal animal heads, hands, and hooves stuffed into elegant formal wear had lost their ability to intimidate her. Let the dead mock her. Their pity couldn't touch her. She'd had the love of a good man, and there was nothing they could say or do to take that warmth away from her. The aisle opened straight to the fight. The Thunderbird was barely holding on, half his wing hanging at a crooked angle. The clay man dug his heels into the parquet floor and tore a piece of flesh off Will's neck with his teeth. The Thunderbird screamed.

"Stop it," Lucia ordered. "Stop it!"

They didn't heed her. She focused on the Aether swirling through the room, no longer tainted, no longer tangled in webs sticky with the Unraveling's darkness. Her Drekar blood meant that she'd never been able to manipulate the Aether like she should, but she could feel it now, a comforting thrum of power. Perhaps the Kivati way didn't work for her, but she'd never tried the Drekar way. She'd picked up a few more things from Grace than just fighting. Next to her stood a lady with the head of a rainbow pheasant. In her goat hands she held an elaborate fan with a mount of sage green lace and blades made of finger bones.

"Excuse me," Lucia said. She ripped the fan from the woman and broke it. The finger bones had been sharpened at the end, and she tore one out to use as a carving tool. Grace had special instruments for her runes, silver needles for inking and a running iron to brand, but Lucia suspected that the true magic behind it was intent. She'd never been so focused in her life. All the anxieties she'd had back in the Living World had been stripped away. She knew with absolute certainty that she was the Crane. Though mortal, she'd journeyed through the Land of the Dead. She'd sung to clear the Aether and freed the Spider. There was no self-confidence she hadn't earned with the scrabble of her nails and the spilling of her own blood.

Using the pointed end of the bone blade, she carved a rune into her left palm. A stream of crimson flowed down her wrist. The pain was a distant hum; she was too focused on calling the Aether to fill her rune to notice it. As she finished the last line, Aether rushed her. Her palm became a beacon. She focused the Aether and then directed it in a killing beam toward the clay man. The stream hit him like a fire hose and shot him ten feet back against the far wall. He screamed as the Aether pinned him.

"Tiamat took your life in exchange for your service," Lucia said. "She made you immortal, but you are locked in unending slavery." She held her bloody palm higher. Red dripped from her elbow. "I offer this sacrifice, blood of the Drekar and Kivati, to undo the evil that was done to you. Your soul is free to move on."

The red drained from the Enkidu's skin, leaving a corpse behind. She lowered the stream of Aether, and the body collapsed to the floor. A sparkling cloud of soul light rose from it and was washed away by the river of Aether flowing about the room.

Tiamat shrieked. One moment she was ordering the lashing of an overseer who'd failed to deliver his section of hanging gardens on time, the next she dropped her head back and screamed. The sound broke a nearby window. Kai thought his eardrums would be next.

"That bitch!" Tiamat roared. She fell against a giant pillar of stone, slamming her growing belly into it.

"Careful of the baby!" Kai said.

She pushed him away. "Stop hovering like a damn mother hen. I've birthed two pantheons—*ahhhgg*." Her face drained of color, and she clutched her midsection. "Make it stop!"

"You weren't in this body before," Kai said. He slung his arm under her shoulders and helped her up. "You need to lie down." *Traitor*, he could hear his dead brother's voice in his head now. It would be a mercy to all of them if she died in childbirth. He'd tried to think of the child as a monster, but it was still his. He'd started this charade to save his people, but now he stayed just to watch over one small life. A life that shouldn't be loosed on the world. Tiamat's spawn.

It was still half his.

He helped Tiamat past the prostrate overseer, a Drekar named Grettir who'd certainly deserved the punishment she'd been about to give him—not for his project lateness, but for working his slaves to death. Kai forced himself to pass the helpless humans, hate in their eyes as Tiamat leaned on him.

"The Drekar blood should heal," she whimpered. "Why does it hurt so?"

"You are strong, but even a queen must rest."

"She killed my Enkidu. I will flay the skin from her bones!"

"Stress will make it worse—"

"We will retaliate!" Tiamat pushed off him and tried to stand. She punched her fist in the air and a blast of blue fire shot heavenward. "No more mercy to Her Kivati children. The chosen ones should always be mine. This

is what I get for weakness—betrayal. It will stop now."
Her anger singed the air.

Kai held his breath. He was Kivati. Would he be the
first to die? But she'd said "we," and he knew with a sink-
ing feeling that even the Goddess of Chaos had forgotten his true loyalties.

The blue fire shot across the long brick road in the
direction of Kivati Hall, and he read death in her eyes.

She was too distracted to notice him sending a message to the crow hiding in a nearby tree. The crow lifted
into the air and took off through the new gardens in the
direction of the ruined city. Whatever Kivati it came across
would stand a chance. They had to get out before Tiamat
found them.

But—brief mercy—Tiamat collapsed again, hand
across her belly. He would buy his people as much time
as he could before she made it back to the hall. Hopefully
it would be enough.

# Chapter Nineteen

The Queen of Death rose from the throne of bones. She was petite, shorter than Lucia, and her ebony hair touched the backs of her knees. Moving gracefully as a shadow, she descended the steps to face Lucia and took her hands. Surprisingly, her skin was warm. "There, there, child," the Queen crooned. "You have come too far to lose your faith now."

"What will happen to him?"

The Queen smiled. "Would you care to watch?"

"Is that what you do? Sit here in your hall and spy on the Living World but do nothing to help?"

"Ah, that. That is the great curse of free will. Would you care to live in a world where the gods made all the decisions? What would be the point of living, if there were no actions or reactions, no joys or sorrows that were yours and yours alone? No, sweet Crane, that would be no kind of life. So here I sit, and watch, and suffer along with them. To know the future, but have no say in it. To be able to do nothing but watch my children from their first baby steps to their last suffering breaths and finally welcome them home at the end of their all-too-brief journeys. Sit with me, dear one, and watch the webs unfurl."

Lucia followed her tug back to the throne and sat at her feet. The Queen swept her hand to the side and webs of Aether descended all around them, caging them in, glistening with dewy lives. Her vision adjusted to the chaotic jumble of images, and she gasped. It was the whole world laid out in threads of light, humans and supernaturals, animals and plants. The world had survived far better than she had feared. Everywhere creatures of the earth were pulling hope out of the rubble and fashioning a new way of life in the altered landscape. Joining forces with former enemies. Building cities out of the bones of the old.

"If Tiamat wins, she won't stop at Seattle," Lucia said.

"No," the Queen said. "My sister is not one to stop until she beats down the Gates between worlds."

"You're in danger here. Doesn't that make you want to fight back?"

"And what then? Should I stop when one goddess falls, or must I stay vigilant while every demigod and power-mad creature picks up arms against me? They would be right to fear me, and they would fight first for survival, and then because they know no other life. But fighting isn't the only way. Violence will never be strong enough to hold together the threads of the universe. Violence is a brittle thing, easily made, quickly broken whenever enough brave souls rise up together to oppose it. There are bigger divides between the hearts of man than there are between the Lands of the Living and the Dead. Hate and violence can't bring them together."

"Only love," Lucia murmured.

"Yes. Love is the web that connects us all, god and mortal alike."

"Who does Tiamat love?"

The Queen smiled. "Now you're asking the right questions."

"Show me Tiamat, please."

The Queen waved her hand and the webs surrounding them zoomed to the Pacific Northwest, then the Puget Sound, then the stretch of land encompassing Seattle, Lake Washington, and the Eastside suburbs. The picture narrowed in on the former suburb of Redmond. Smoke rose from a sea of tan houses even as the skies let down a torrent of rain. Drekar flew overhead blowing streams of fire across a forest of army-issued tents. Men, women, and children ran through streets clogged with debris. The storm had flooded the roads knee-high with rapidly moving water.

Lucia clutched the arm of the Throne. "Who are they?"

"The survivors from Tiamat's initial takeover."

"We must help them!"

The Queen shook her head. Her eyes were sorrowful, but she only moved the picture to find a beautiful woman with jet-black hair and the violent joy of true bloodlust. Flashes of lightning illuminated her crazed expression. Tiamat's hands were red to the shoulder, her face splattered with her victims' blood. She swung a rusted scythe through the fleeing refugees and laughed as they fell. Behind her stood Kai, hair plastered across his forehead from the rain, eyes full of abject horror. He made no move to stop the carnage.

The thin, high wail of a baby sounded over the screams. Tiamat paused, scythe raised. Slowly, she turned toward the noise and waded through the bloody waters to find the child on an overturned VW bug that was half buried in the hillside. A woman's body lay in the mud next to the car's tires. Retrieving the baby in her blood-soaked hands,

Tiamat raised the babe to her breast. Her croon could be heard over the storm and the cries of the refugees.

Lucia stood. "Please, let me help them. Someone needs to warn Corbette!"

"Watch, little Crane, as darkness covers your world."

The burst of Aether pushed Corbette out through the Palace roof and tumbled him through a hole in the very top of the sky. He spilled out into the Living World in the black of night. No matter how hard he tried to fly back to that precise rip in the Aether, he couldn't find the way. He'd got everything he'd ever thought he wanted: the Scepter, the key to saving his race and assurance his name would go down in history as a great king.

The gods were laughing somewhere in the sky. All he wanted was Lucia, and she was as untouchable to him as a snowflake captured in his palm.

The night was tropical. This time of year in the Pacific Northwest should be wet and damp. There wasn't a cloud to be seen. Had Tiamat done this? Or was this weather the work of one of his own under duress, or a traitor who'd followed Chaos to more favorable shores? Flying over Lake Washington, he gave the city a wide berth. How he wanted to see Tiamat's damage himself. How he needed to storm into Kivati Hall and take back control, but maybe his time in the other world had changed him. He was not indestructible, he was not all-powerful, and he'd left the most important part of himself back with the dead.

By the Lady, he would go back for her. His talons tightened around the Scepter. With a deep croak from his Raven throat, he closed his eyes, hovering, and listened to the night. So quiet. So peaceful, he might never believe the slave pits he'd seen in the Spider's webs. The soft flow of Aether directed his thoughts, and he followed it, smooth eddies curled across the sky away from the dark city. Before his journey, he might have tried storming Kivati Hall alone. Now he knew better.

The Aether stream brought him across Lake Washington deep into the tentacles of abandoned sprawl that made their way up the mountain foothills in the Issaquah Alps. He wouldn't give the area a second glance, but the Aether spurred him onward, and then he saw the first crow and knew his people hid somewhere in the empty tan-washed landscape. The crows guided him the rest of the way, up into the wild parts of Mount Si. He Changed beneath Haystack Rock, pulled clothes from the Aether, and found himself at the center of a ring of blades, arrows, and shotguns.

"You picked a bad place to land, friend." The decidedly unfriendly voice came out of the dark woods.

Corbette didn't move to defend himself. "Peace."

"You're no friend to Drekar."

"I'm no friend to Tiamat." He held up the Scepter. "I'm here to talk to Asgard. I need his help."

The hush had the peculiar taste of sorrow.

"You're too late." Another voice in the dark, this one he recognized. Grace Mercer pushed aside one of the swords aimed in his direction and entered the clearing. "It's okay, Vern," she told the swordsman. "The day Corbette joins Tiamat's Court is the day the Frost Giants descend from Jotenheim."

"Miss Mercer."

"It's Asgard now." She'd aged since he'd last seen her. He'd never had much dealing with the shadow walker, but he'd seen the thick file his people had collected on her, especially after she'd started teaching Lucia how to fight. Her blue-black hair was drawn back in tight braids,

and her eyes—old before her time—were creased at the
edges with sleepless worry. She wore a light gray tunic
and black leather pants tucked into boots. A red sash tied
at her waist held the sheath of her dagger. A swirling mist
of Aether drew through the runes carved along the blade.

"What happened to your husband?"

"Two days ago Tiamat attacked our camp. It was a
massacre. Leif gave himself up to buy us time."

"But she wouldn't hurt her kin."

Grace looked away. "She's scheduled a public execution for the third day of Nisannu."

"Not till spring? The vernal equinox is—"

"In five days. You've been gone a long time." Grace
turned and led the way into the woods. Her soldiers
dropped into line behind him, but more than a few kept a
sharp grip on their weapons. He followed her along the
path that cut close to the side of the mountain. To the left,
the ground dropped away in a fast slide to certain death.
The pointed tops of evergreen trees speared up from the
forest floor.

Nisannu—the Babylonian New Year festival around
the beginning of April. Five months after he'd left.
Strange how time across the worlds didn't match up. To
him, it felt like he'd been gone a week, except his body
and mind were morphed. His perception of the world
skewed to a different star. Maybe it wasn't so strange to
believe that time had passed. He'd changed a lifetime's
worth. The air of this world was heavier. His body moved
more slowly, and as he picked his way across the steep
bank, he gave thanks that the Lady had restored his totem
at least. If he fell, he could save himself with the Aether.
It came when he called, curling around his fingers like an
old friend. Once, he would have thought the return of his
powers would be all he needed to be complete. He pulled

his hand from the lulling tendrils. A fickle friend. Too little, too late. He couldn't beat Tiamat with his own Aether power, but as the strands slid through the point of the Scepter's spindle, he knew someone who could.

Grace let him through a hidden entrance to a cave. He had to duck to squeeze through the opening, and the damp of the inner walls slicked unpleasantly on his hands and chest. Inside, the cave opened up into a series of narrow tunnels. It was an old mine shaft with the iron bones of a pulley system and dangerous holes that dropped hundreds of feet into inky black. Here in the outer cave, he saw stockpiles of weapons and civilians in training. Men, women, and children huddled in the glow of the biodiesel lamps with the blank eyes of shock etched on their faces.

"We had five thousand," Grace said. "Survivors, escapees. We had water and shelter and food. Our location was betrayed. This is all that's left." She swept her hand across the refugees and warriors who were loading baskets of supplies into a pulley system and lowering them into the black abyss. Farther down, humans climbed into a rickety coal car and descended below. Five men strained against the ropes as the human cargo slowly lowered down.

"How many do you have?" he asked.

"We've split up. It was a bad idea to have such a big camp—hard to hide so many people—but Tiamat wasn't interested in us at first. She had plenty of manpower and subjects to build her new Babylon in Seattle. We didn't plan on growing so big, but there were too many refugees too quickly. We got careless when she left us alone. We didn't have many other options. All our energy was focused on getting fresh food, water, and shelter. On getting thousands of starving, scared people through the winter." Her tone was sharp enough to cut.

He held up his hands. "I'm not judging."

She held her face in her hands and took a long breath. "I blame myself."

"Who betrayed you?" He would find the man and deliver him to Grace. She had the right to serve the killing blow. It was only justice.

"Kai—"

"Kai?" He would kill the Thunderbird himself.

"No, no. Kai told me she knew. I don't know who told her, but I didn't move fast enough. I was too worried about his other info."

"Has Kai turned traitor?"

"Let's talk somewhere private." Grace motioned for him to follow her back to a makeshift room where old beams had been nailed together to block off the section from the outer cave. A few battle-worn men who were there when they entered picked up their maps and left with a deferential nod. She collapsed into a chair. The wood squeaked beneath her weight. She was too thin. He could tell their supplies wouldn't carry them much farther. He settled across from her on a crate. The table held more maps of the city and countryside. Kivati Hall had been marked in red, with the surrounding area colored in. The line had been redrawn a number of times. Tiamat's territory was expanding.

"Kai got stuck on the inside when she came," Grace said. "A lot of people did. If it weren't for Kai, a lot of your people would have never made it out. Some turned, of course—"

Corbette growled.

"—but a lot more made it to us than we had hoped.

He's in deep, don't get me wrong. He's in trouble, and he knows it."

"Tiamat is pregnant."

The tense line of her mouth confirmed it. "It's what's kept Kai alive all this time. She wanted to combine blood-lines to make a stronger third pantheon. Once she has her new army, she's going after the gods who wronged her."

"And you know he isn't on her side?"

"She took a liking to him. It's the only way he's been able to play her this long to get people out and informa-tion to us."

"Fatherhood can change a man."

Grace studied him. "I'd have thought you'd be livid over the prospect of your precious Kivati blood being joined with that of the soul-eaters."

"I was . . . wrong. I should have lent your husband and his Drekar army my aid, judged him by his actions in-stead of those of his brother." Corbette forced himself to unclench his fists. This was harder than he thought. "I'm sorry."

Grace sat back. "Does this sudden change of heart have anything to do with a pair of bright blue eyes?"

"How long have you known?"

"I suspected there was something else going on with Lucia. I taught her to fight. Her bruises and scars heal just a mite too fast." The Raven shot into his eyes, and Grace threw up her hands. "Whoa, there. I didn't harm your girl. I taught her to defend herself. A few bruises were more than worth it. You wouldn't want me to give her the confidence without any real skill, would you?"

Corbette forced himself to relax. The Raven beat its wings inside his breast. He needed Lucia next to him, not worlds away. "Regardless, Lucia isn't the immediate child of a crazed god. Tiamat's heir will be a demigod with unimaginable power."

"Maybe. There's no way to know. So what are you going to do about Kai?"

"I'm more concerned if we can trust him. Tiamat must die and her child with her if we have any hope for a future."

"I agree. Where is Lucia?"

Corbette stood. He paced the room, a nervous, uncontrolled gesture he'd always despised in other people. It showed his weakness, but he couldn't help himself. From outside the room came the scrape and shuffle of supplies and people being moved through the cavernous, dangerous mine shafts. Inside, the single biodiesel lamp cast shadows across the walls. Illustrations of key Tiamat supporters, Kivati and Drekar and human alike, were pasted across the rough boards. A few had black lines across their faces—victories for the rebels, but Corbette couldn't help thinking, *More good men lost*. Two long lists of names in tiny script took up the far wall. He was afraid to read them though he knew, if this were his battle station, what he would find. The men and women who'd bore those names were even now being welcomed by Lucia in another place, another window out of time.

He tapped the Scepter against his thigh. Was it worth it? All these names, all these innocent souls saved in exchange for just one? Once he would have given an unequivocal yes. He couldn't bring himself to justify it anymore. *Lucia*. He would have given his own life a hundred times over for hers.

"So?" Grace prodded.

"The balance of the universe required a trade."

"You didn't . . . no, you wouldn't. Lucia gave herself up for you, didn't she?"

"It was supposed to be me," he growled.

She nodded. They understood one another. There was more to this war than the fate of the universe. "The gods never play fair, do they?"

"Let's hope they have more at stake in righting the universe than they let on. Tell me some good news."

Her eyes took him in, from his scuffed boots to his wrinkled shirt missing buttons. "You have the Scepter."

He waited a long moment for her to elaborate. Silence. "And that is the full extent of your plan?" He itched to lean across the table and snatch the maps up. This ragged excuse for an army called out to him to save, but he knew he had no standing here. In Grace's eyes, he'd abandoned them. Five months was more than enough time to lose hope that he was ever coming back. Their trust must be earned.

Leaning both hands on the edge of the desk, she dug in until her fingers turned white. "You have the Scepter. That's what you went for, isn't it? That's the only thing that can take away her Godhead and unmake her. She sent the clay man—"

"The Enkidu failed. Where is Tiamat holding your husband?"

Her bone knife appeared in her hand. She impaled it into the map straight through Kivati Hall. "The new seat of Babylon." Her eyes shone with tears.

"We'll get Asgard back."

A sob met him.

"It'll work out—"

"You can't fucking make it so just because you want it!"

"No. I don't have all the answers and I don't have the power to mold the universe to my will. But I have faith, and I have hope, and I have a woman waiting for me in the Shining Land who won't welcome me back with open arms if I fail in this mission."

Grace raised both eyebrows. "One day, when Tiamat isn't about to destroy the city, I gotta hear this story about you guys in the otherworld."

Corbette smiled. Gods, he wished he were still back there. Even blind. Even totem and Aether-less. At least there he had Lucia. "Can you still get messages to Kai?"

"No. And you can't use the Aether. She can sense it."

Corbette sat again. "Let's start at the beginning. Perhaps if we put our heads together, we can defeat Chaos once and for all."

"And Lucia?"

"Once we defeat Tiamat, whether I'm dead or alive, I'm going back for her."

Kai slipped through the magnolia trees in the grounds of the new Palace of Babylon, formerly known as Kivati Hall. He couldn't think of the former. Couldn't imagine Jace here, shaking his head at Kai's surrender. Or worse, Jace—straight-as-an-arrow Jace—broken under Tiamat's thumb. Kai had always been able to bend the truth, as he did now, hiding like a coward in the grounds. He rubbed his eyes with the palms of both hands. He hadn't slept since the massacre of the rebel camp in Redmond.

"Come along, warrior," she'd said with those lips that were Zetian's and those eyes that were purely ancient evil. Naively, he'd followed, realizing too late the subject of her journey. The crow he'd sent didn't have enough time to warn them. No time to stop her. Nothing he could do but watch. The Lady have mercy on his thrice-damned soul. Jace would have died long before this. Small comfort that Jace wasn't here to suffer, that Jace wasn't here to fix this, because it couldn't be fixed. At least the Enkidu was dead. Small consolation, when she'd vented her wrath on the innocents who'd fled. All those men and women he'd helped to escape. And now the hope of the resistance—Asgard—was locked in the basement cells.

Good thing Kai had spent some time in his youth acquainting himself with the cells down there. He pulled out his knife and pushed through the bushes to the thick limestone blocks of the building's foundation. He hoped Asgard was in Kai's old cell. The stucco between the blocks had never been repaired. It was still gouged out in the thin place in the wall where the renovations for the conservatory had cut up the ancient building footprint. This part of the wall had been fixed during Corbette's father's time, and Halian never cared much for spending money on something no one would see. This secret spot was all old brick. He found the spot and scraped off a bit of paint with his knife. Yup, exactly how he remembered it. He tapped the brick three times with the hilt of his dagger and waited. Eventually, he heard an answering tap. *Please let it be Asgard.* The brick started to jiggle as the inhabitant pushed from the inside. As soon as Kai had a bit of space, he squeezed his fingertips around the brick and pulled. It required a little leverage with the blade of his knife to remove the moss and mold that had gathered in the cracks. Finally the brick slipped out. He gave a silent apology to his brother. Jace had whittled this hole to pass him food during one of his teenage imprisonments. Kai had promised to seal it back up, but he'd never gotten around to it.

"Regent?" Kai asked.

"Did Grace escape?"

Of course, the first thing the man would want to know. "Yes. Are you injured?"

"No."

"Sorry, stupid question." The Drekar's magic blood would heal every wound Tiamat's guards inflicted on him. He could be tortured for eternity and never kick it. "You've got three days." Until the execution.

"Will she use my death to fuel a spell? Make another clay man?"

"Maybe. She's closed me off from her plans. She's beginning to not trust me."

Asgard was silent for a beat. "You should leave."

He would to save his own life, but, "I can't."

Another beat. "You can't save the baby."

"If Grace could exorcize Tiamat, then Zetian—"

"She's not Zetian anymore. Let her go."

Kai smacked one fist against the brick and leaned his head against it. "I can't leave them."

"Listen to me, Thunderbird. Zetian is a female Dreki. She has no soul. Tiamat's soul is all that's nourishing the fledgling in her womb."

"Fuck it. There's got to be some way."

"There is only one. You know of my bond with Grace."

"Hell, no." Kai drew back from the wall. Rumor had it that Grace had bonded her soul to Asgard, so that they shared it, one soul, two bodies. When one died, the other went too. Asgard had given up his immortality for her, but she'd given him something more precious—the ability to pass with her through the Gates into the Land of the Dead. Kai would rather die than share one of his souls with a soul-sucker. He didn't think Zetian and the baby deserved to die, but to be trapped with her for eternity? No. "Why would you want Zetian to get a soul anyway?

Didn't she try to kill your woman? You should be asking for her blood—"

"So you've seen pure evil in her and still won't leave? I won't argue with you. I can't think of a worse punishment than being trapped in your own body with Tiamat at the tiller. Zetian was no angel, but far be it from me to damn someone else. I'll leave her judgment to Freya."

Kai tugged on the bandoleer across his chest. "What do you need? You have three days. Dawn at the public square." If the rebels were going to make their move, that was the best time for it. He knew Asgard understood.

"I'll be ready."

"I'll try to come again."

"Kai . . . thank you."

Kai fisted his hand above the hole in the brick. "She'll come for you."

"That's what I'm afraid of."

The edge of dawn was a slice of soft gray across the horizon. Corbette motioned to the warriors behind him, and they moved as one across the open street to the shelter of the next shell of skyscraper. This was the last line of broken city before the clearing, where Tiamat's gardens sprouted up from terraces of porcelain and glass mosaic tiles, and palms grew to the hanging baskets overflowing with purple, green, and white. He could sense the trapped souls left to fester in the baskets. Gods, if Lucia were here, she would have stopped to free them, but he couldn't ruin his element of surprise. Babylon Square lay two hundred meters into the greenery. A patio on the edge of the crater, just above the crashing sea, the square sported a raised dais in the center surrounded by fountains carved with dragons and scorpion men. The green boulevard lay quiet as a sleeping python. Though Kivati earth workers had managed to coax abundant plant life from the cold, ashen ground, no birds sang in the leafy branches.

Corbette and the Kivati with him couldn't rely on the sight of bird guides. The Drekar and humans might be used to this arrangement, but without his spies, Corbette felt blind again. His hand clenched around the hilt of his sword. He missed the soft hand leading him through the darkness.

They'd taken all the rebel warriors with them from the mines, all except ten who guarded the children and injured. Corbette had argued, at first, that the women should stay back too, but Grace had given him a look all too close to one he'd seen from Lucia, and he knew he was being an old-fashioned ass.

"We have every right to fight for our freedom," Grace had said. "This is our home, too. Our blood is just as good as yours to be spilled for the privilege of calling it ours."

She'd made him ashamed, because what reason did he have for holding her or Lucia back like a delicate hothouse orchid? Just this overdriving need to protect what was his. Even though half the warriors who crept to the brink through the fog with him were not of his blood, he'd still marked them as his. He led them to their deaths; their lives were in his keeping. It was a lot of responsibility to risk so many for the good of the whole, but he'd never had a problem making hard decisions before.

*Faith*, the Spider Queen would say.

*Faith*, Lucia whispered to his soul. The Lady wouldn't have sent him back with the Scepter if all hope were lost. They had a good chance to defeat Tiamat if they could catch her unawares.

Grace led a contingent on the other side of the road. Her black and gray worn fatigues blended with the concrete jungle but not the green one. She wore a stripe of black paint beneath her eyes and a sour expression. Corbette waved two fingers, and the tattered rebel army slipped into the green. They had no supplies or fancy uniforms, but each had a weapon and the clear knowledge that this was their only shot. By the time the sun rose over the mountains, either Tiamat would be dead, or they would.

The path was clear until the bricks of the boulevard. Tiamat had ordered the public execution to show her subjects the price of disloyalty, but in a last bid of quiet rebellion, many had stayed home. A long procession announced the affair with great solemnity. Drums, followed by a long line of lords and ladies of the Kivati. Their faces were pinched white as they waited for their former enemy, the Drekar Regent, to die. Tiamat, mother of all dragons, wasn't merciful to one of her children. The threat was very real to those who'd placed their marker in her camp. She left no room for forgiveness. Next came the slaves in two long lines down the side of the brick. They lined up along the edge of the square to watch.

Then Leif, dragged in chains by two of his own—Thorsson and Grettir. He'd been stripped to the waist. His pale skin showed no marks, but his eyes were haunted, the irises slit. At the dais, Leif turned his eyes on the western line of the distant Olympics, his back to the shimmering edge of dawn. Behind him strode Kai, forced—or volunteered?—to be the master of ceremonies, his face black as his formal dress. On his face Corbette recognized a singular determination, the iron jaw that came from doing the right thing no matter the personal cost. No sign was left of the reckless young Thunderbird who'd defied his liege and stolen countless hearts. Corbette had been guilty of thinking the wrong brother had died, but Jace Raiden would never have pulled this off. As long as Kai's loyalties were still intact, he'd survived longer by Tiamat's side than any of the rest could have. But was he still Corbette's man?

Behind him came the Drekar, an uneasy bunch about to watch their Regent's demise. At the end of the procession, slaves carried a golden litter fit to convey a queen. The small box of the carriage was big enough for Tiamat to lounge comfortably. The sides were closed. Twelve slaves, oiled up with nothing but golden armbands and loincloths, carried the litter on their shoulders by long poles. They set it down in front of the dais. The red curtains were drawn tight against the night. Corbette couldn't see inside, but he guessed Tiamat lay there watching her handiwork.

Kai tied Leif to the dais in the center of the square. Once the stage was set, the Thunderbird motioned for the drums to stop. "The High Goddess of Babylon, Tiamat, Primordial Chaos, Empress of the New World, hereby declares the traitor Leif Asgard, son of Fafnir, Drekar and former Regent to the crown, no longer worthy of his immortality or the love of his divine mother. He has colluded with the enemy, killed members of the goddess's royal guard, and plotted against her life and health. He is hereby sentenced to death by beheading, ending his mortal and immortal life. How do you plead?"

Leif rattled his chains as he tried to straighten. He was chained on his knees in front of a large block of cedar. Torches lit the corners of the dais and cast his face in pale, ghostly planes. "I renounce Tiamat's right to the Living World. She is no goddess of mine."

Corbette expected a tantrum from the litter, but none came. The gentry shifted. Buckner was there clutching the arm of his willowy mate, Lady Acacia, who held a sleepy blond toddler in her arms. The portly Coyote Spickard leaned on a cane. His leg had been taken in a Drekar raid. More of Corbette's people, each one with a reason to stay behind in the reach of the mad goddess, were there. Corbette studied the faces in the dim light. He didn't see the hatred and anger he'd expected as they stared at the doomed Drekar leader. Only weariness. Only fear.

A couple hundred downcast souls waited in the predawn. Kai pushed Asgard's head onto the chopping block. A hush settled, marred only by the wind ringing the bells that hung throughout the gardens. Kai picked up an ax.

Corbette rose out of the bushes with the loud caw of the Raven slicing through the air. He held the Scepter tightly in his grip. His warriors poured in on either side, birds shooting into the air to dive-bomb from the sky, the fleet-footed Changing mid-leap. The guards fought back. The slaves gave a halfhearted defense, more from fear of the monsters charging them than loyalty to Tiamat.

Changing, Corbette now held the Scepter with Raven talons. He flew over the skirmish to the dais and ripped the ax from Kai's hands with his free claw. He Changed to man, pocketed the Scepter, and hefted the ax in his hands. Kai stood back. He made no move to repossess his weapon. Corbette swung the blade and chopped through Asgard's restraints.

The Dreki jumped to his feet. "It's a trap. Get out! Go. Go!"

# Chapter Twenty

Corbette looked back across the skirmish to see most of the crowd waiting patiently while the guards fought off the attack. On the far side, a Thunderbird ripped off the silk curtains of the litter. Empty. Crows rushed it, and the gilt-covered wood toppled, breaking against the stony ground. A cloud of ash spilled into the air. Expanding, it engulfed the Crows, blinding them. The warrior-birds shrieked. The odor of singed feathers filled the square.

"Warriors, stand your ground!" he ordered. "Guard the civilian retreat!" Spinning, he caught sight of Kai watching something in the distance. He followed his gaze to a massive storm cloud bubbling through the sky toward them. Lightning crackled and lit the cloud's interior. Inside flew fifteen creatures he'd never seen before: leathery wings of a bat, sculpted silver-skinned torso of a man, and ink-black legs of a giant squid.

"Storm demons," Asgard said. "Children of her second pantheon. Get our people out of here."

In the center of the storm cloud flew Tiamat in Zetian's dragon form. A smaller dragon, she had red wings, three horns, and whiskers of gold. Her normally silver scales glowed blue with condensed Aether. Thunderbolts crackled from her long spiked tail. The boom of the thunder rolled in her voice, a cackle that hit the backs of his knees and threatened to melt the strength right from his bones.

Corbette motioned for the rebels to fall back, but the civilians, slaves, and guards descended into chaos. Some of the Kivati in the square ran. Some just stood there and watched death roll in. Tiamat's loyal men still fought his warriors. "Grab the vulnerable and get out!" he yelled. He seized the Aether and snapped it through every connection they had, alpha to pack, pulling the strings to the fabric of their twined souls. "Move! Now!" They staggered. A few were jolted out of their shock and ran, but others were too old or young or sick to get out of the way and were mowed down by the crowd. Corbette watched a clump of human slaves stampede toward Buckner and his family. His wife clutched the toddler as the baby screamed, her face hidden in the child's hair. Buckner tried to block the crowd with his body.

Corbette grabbed a ripple of Aether and threw it at the family just before the mob hit them. The sparkling water looped around them in an infinite river and deflected the tide of bodies around them. "Kai, help me."

Kai took one last look at the goddess bearing down on them and his face creased in anguish. He clamped it down and Changed, Aether rolling over his body like a blanket, dropping away to reveal a giant bird with a twenty-foot wingspan and terrifying hooked beak. He took to the battle and attacked the guards, buying the rebels time. Asgard Turned too, and he met his former subjects in the air. Glittering scales rained down on the square as claws and teeth clashed.

Pulling the Aether to him, Corbette reveled in the shock of it, the wild abandon that flowed through his

veins when he let go of his need to control it. He was a
beacon. The Aether flowed to him and down his arm into
the Scepter of Death in his hand. Unhooking the spindle,
he drew the Aether out between it and the distaff. A crystal
thread sprang to life. It shone with the blue fire of the
gods, the same brilliant blue that made up the Behemoth.
Corbette knew his warriors were no match for the storm
demons, but the Behemoth would be.

*Blessed Lady, aid me in my hour of need*, he prayed.
She wouldn't have sent him back with no hope of survival. Closing his eyes against the storm rolling overhead,
he focused on the feel of Aether pouring through him and
the Scepter. Instead of trying to control its wildness like
he used to do, he let go of his fear and let the spindle do
its work. *Have faith*, the Spider had told him. Here in the
darkest dark there was nothing else to hold him up but his
faith, and he found it was more than enough to keep him
moving forward. The crackling Aether thread spun out,
and he felt the shape of it flow into the body of the Behemoth. The crash of thunderbolts from the storm
demons hit the ground around him. The air charged, the
smell of singed flesh and earth rising from the square.

He heard a familiar roar and opened his eyes to see the
blue line of the Behemoth pull from between the spindle
and distaff. The wood of the dais caught fire beneath its
hooves. Corbette held as the flame crept toward him. De-
taching from the line of spun Aether, the Behemoth
pushed off into the air just as the storm cloud descended
on the square, cutting out all light but the blue of the
shooting thunderbolts. The Behemoth attacked the storm
demons. The irises of the silver-skinned men glowed red.
They released an inky black cloud in their wake, just like
the squid they resembled. The ink seemed to burn those

caught. The Behemoth scattered them, just in time to save the masses from being trapped.

Tiamat flew over the battlefield screaming. She attacked Asgard in the air, her dragon form half his size but lit up like a Christmas tree with snapping thunderbolts.

Corbette scrambled back from the burning wood and jumped into the fray.

Lucia rose from her seat next to the Lady of Death. She walked through the glowing Aether webs and they reformed behind her. On the other side she found the lords and ladies of the dead watching the same grizzly sight she had been. Their animal eyes glistened. She searched the faces. "You all have blood relatives fighting in that square." Her voice wavered. She cleared her throat. "We are not that different, the living and the dead. We are united by memory, by hope, and by love. Our children and grandchildren are counting on us to leave them a better world. Is this the world you want to be your legacy?" She waved her hand at the battle behind her. The blast of thunderbolts couldn't drown out the screams. "Is this destruction and terror what you envisioned for your people?"

The Frog stepped forward, all obsequiousness. His tongue shot out. "But, Lady, what can we do? We're dead."

"The dead are not powerless," Lucia said. "The Aether that holds together this world is the same Aether that holds together the one you left behind. It's the same Aether that weaves through your soul and the souls of those fighting Tiamat for their lives. You have wings. There is nothing to stop you from traversing the worlds and flooding the battlefield with your presence. Remember what it is to love someone."

"So easy to send us into battle to die in your place," the Frog said.

"I'd go myself in an instant if I could!"

"Nothing is stopping you."

"I—" Lucia considered it for a long moment. If she could sing a song of making, what was stopping her from making herself a pair of wings and leading the charge into the Living World? Certainly not permission. She turned to look at the Queen to find She'd turned back into a giant Spider. In Her eyes, Lucia saw every potential outcome: if she stayed, if she went, if she lost, if she won. There were more possibilities than mirrored eyes, but because she had free will, she had the power in her own two hands to seize her destiny.

*Choose well*, the Spider called in her mind, thousand tongues clicking.

Lucia turned back. She felt the old fear of never measuring up give way in the face of the certainty that what she was doing was right. She was the Harbinger. No one could stop her. "Rise up, beloved ones. Join me. We fly in the face of chaos. We fly to victory." She opened her mouth and song poured out. The notes sounded like the chimes of bells, and as they vibrated in the air, she felt the Crane solidify out of the Aether. It beat its great white wings and settled with the warmth of embers in the chambers of her heart. She pulled the Aether around her and felt her body dissolve. In the last peels of music, her new form burst forth. White feathers of peace, not surrender. Red splash at her temples. She called with her Crane voice and the assembled dancers began to Change too. They rose up into the air, a flock of birds from all corners of the globe, united in common purpose.

*The Universe must be balanced*, the Spider said.

*I'll send you Tiamat in my place*, Lucia promised. *It's time she pays the piper.*

Corbette slogged through knee-high carnage. Though the Behemoth fought the storm demons, some had detached to wreak havoc on the rebel troops. Human warriors worked on getting the civilians out of the thick of battle while Kivati and Drekar loyal to the rebels attacked Tiamat's soldiers. In the sky, storm demons battled Thunderbirds while opposing Drekar forces chased each other through clouds brimming with lightning. Rain hammered down, turning the garden paths to rivers of mud.

Without a miracle, they would lose.

Corbette drew the Aether through the Scepter and shot it at Tiamat. The dragon screamed, opened her jaws, and breathed a long burst of fire across the ground. Corbette had to dive out of its path. The Scepter gave his Aether powers enough of a boost to fight her, but she still had the upper hand. He needed to ram the pointed distaff through her heart and squeeze as much Aether as he could through her body. If she didn't land, he wouldn't get the chance. Every blast seemed to piss her off, and her Drekar blood healed almost as quickly as he could shoot.

He needed help. *Kai*, he sent through the Aether, *gather the aerials. To Tiamat!*

Thunderbird, Eagle, Owl, and Crow extracted themselves from other parts of the battle and swooped through the air toward the goddess. They converged on her, ignoring the fire of her Drekar and the stinging black clouds of the storm demons. She screamed and tossed Thunderbolts in all directions. Feathers singed and fell. Avian bodies sizzled and dropped like stones. More replaced them. Kai launched himself across Tiamat's muzzle and dug in his talons. Blinded, she couldn't stay aloft. The ball of scales and feathers and fangs hurdled toward the ground.

Corbette sprinted to them. He had to get to Tiamat before she recovered. With a roar, she threw Kai off. He crumpled to the ground with half a wing torn off. Tiamat Turned. The brilliant blast of Aether blinded the battle-field, and in the brief moment of peace, Corbette heard the rush of thousands of wings.

Tiamat stood in Zetian's skin, naked but for the Tablet of Destiny hanging around her neck. She glowed in the heat of the fires. Her black hair crackled back from her face. Her smooth skin showed not a scratch. Her eyes were wild, irises slit. "Face me, you miserable coward!" she screamed. "You think you can best me with my sister's toys? You are nothing! Marduk and an army of gods couldn't cage me forever. I will crush you and every member of your miserable race!"

"Including the child in your womb?" Corbette asked.

Her gaze locked on him. She covered her belly with a hand. Her lips drew back from her teeth. "My new pan-theon will be unstoppable. Double souls with the fire of the gods at their fingertips." She sauntered toward him, ignoring the blood creeping to her knees. "We will rule as we were meant to—the earth will cower before my children and the humans will serve us. Chaos will reign. That could have been you, Raven, but you were too much my sister's lackey to see it. If you had vision, you might have owned this land. But you failed. Compassion makes you weak."

He'd let her draw too close. He raised the Scepter and pulled the Aether to it, but she tossed a thunderbolt at him, and he had to dive out of the way. The blue fire seared his left arm. A moment of *oh, shit*, and then the pain shot through his body. His fingers fell open, and he dropped the spindle.

Tiamat dove for it. They collided. Her body was smaller, but she held the unnatural strength of a goddess. Her round belly pressed between them. He tried to use her unwieldy balance against her. She clawed across his injured arm, sending pain shooting up his nerves. Biting his lip, he locked his arm around her to prevent her from reaching the spindle. He still held the distaff between them—if he shifted he could jab it into her belly, but he hesitated.

Turning one hand, she dug her claws into his back. He shut his eyes against the pain. Her breath was hot on his ear as she whispered, "Mercy makes you *weak*." She yanked her claws across his shoulder blade, tearing muscle, and it felt like fire ran beneath his skin. His left arm fell limply to his side. Pain rushed to his head, and he almost blacked out. With a laugh, she pulled away and straddled him. She kicked the spindle out of reach. He pulled Aether to knock her back, but he needed both parts of the Scepter to magnify the force. She sucked in his blast and molded it into a ball of condensed Aether. He watched the blue light flare between her hands, spinning out in a shimmering orb. So beautiful, the light of a galaxy within. She raised the ball, prepared to crash it down on his head.

Could the distaff alone deal Tiamat her final death? Wrestling it one-handed from between their bodies, he prepared to try.


Kai lay half in the mud, one wing mostly gone, life leeching out of him as thunder shook the sky. He wondered if it would hurt this much once he passed through the Gate. He was vaguely aware of Tiamat screeching somewhere nearby.

*I've failed*, he thought. He liked life. Liked fighting and fucking and drinking craft beer. The things he'd miss in the Land of the Dead . . . well, it didn't matter anymore. He was dying, and Tiamat still lived. It turned out, though he would deny it to his last breath, now that it came to the end, he was a bit afraid.

"Kai."

Someone tall leaned over him, talking to him, sounding urgent. Someone with a short crew cut and a hawkish nose. It wasn't possible.

"Kai. Get up."

"You bastard." Kai coughed and blood filled his mouth.

"Our parents were married, brother."

Kai managed to sit up. His vision wavered as pain engulfed him. Blackness threatened, but he shoved it down. The blood and the pain were everywhere, woven in his skin, injected into the marrow of his bones, flowing freely down his back. Every breath produced a sickening gurgle. "Jace?"

His brother's form seemed faint around the edges, but his hand was as firm as Kai remembered it as Jace helped him out of the mud. Kai stood, and everything he'd saved up over the last year to tell his brother tumbled out of his head now that he finally had his chance. All he could say was, "I missed you."

"I'm not here to collect you. Not yet." Jace smiled and pulled him in for a hug. Kai felt tears that had nothing to do with his injuries collect on his cheeks.

"Gods, I missed you," he said again.

"I never really left," Jace said. "There is no death, only a change of worlds."

Kai pulled back. The sounds of battle still reverberated

in the air around them. If Jace was here, that meant his work wasn't finished. "Tiamat?"

"We'll do this together, just like we used to do. The world still has need of the Raiden brothers." Jace clasped his forearm, and Kai felt Aether flow into his body, strengthening him, healing some of the worst of his injuries.

"I've got something to tell you, bro. Zetian is pregnant with my kid."

Jace just nodded. No condemnation like Kai had feared. No disappointment that he had knocked up a goddess and one of their sworn enemies. "You saved a lot of lives. I'm proud of you."

Kai swallowed.

"This job is a ball buster," Jace said, "but if Tiamat succeeds in taking down the Gates to rule both worlds, there won't be any place left sacred. The Raven Lord needs our help."

Kai turned to see Tiamat standing over Corbette with a blazing ball of Aether over him. "Let's do this thing." He steeled himself. Jace stepped into him, becoming one, and his spirit infused Kai with the strength of his love. Kai had to take another breath. He felt like he could move mountains. "Zetian and the baby?" he asked.

*Trust your gut*, his brother's spirit whispered in his head.

Corbette watched the blue fire ball shimmer over his head and struggled, helplessly, to move from beneath Tiamat, but she had him fast. A second before she could release the ball, he heard someone shout, and Kai came bursting out of nowhere. Kai tackled Tiamat around the waist and knocked her off Corbette just in time. The ball of Aether broke apart, and both Tiamat and Kai went up in flames. He could hear Kai screaming as the residual energy burned the skin from his body.

Freed, Corbette steeled himself against the nauseating smell of burnt flesh and prepared to move. Every inch of his body hurt, but so much adrenaline rocked his core that he could power past the pain. With a last, desperate burst of energy, he lunged for the spindle with his uninjured arm.

"Ah, ah, ah!" Tiamat said as she emerged unscathed from the fire and jumped nimbly from the ground. She crushed Corbette's hand with her foot, and threw the burning Kai a pitying glance. "Such a waste. He could have enjoyed immeasurable power at my side, but he was always loyal to you," she spat. "What magic is this that men would die for you, Raven? Can't they see how weak you are? So much potential, yet you squander it. You will never measure up."

"And yet, you're jealous," Corbette growled. Her face reddened and her nostrils flared. He'd hit the nail on the head. Blood and sweat dripped across his vision. He strained his crushed fingers and brushed the spindle. "Why is that, Tiamat? Power of the gods, and yet you envy poor, weak mortals like us." She ground her foot into his hand. Corbette grit his teeth as a spasm shook half his body.

"I have everything I want, worm. My children love me—"

"Your children fear you. Not the same thing at all." He tried to pull another blast of Aether, but she only laughed as she soaked it up like a living sponge. Every burst made her grow stronger. A blue light flared around her head until her slit irises reflected it. He was going to lose. She was going to kill him. Would she leave anything left of his soul to journey back to the Land of the Dead?

*Lucia, forgive me*, he thought.

\* \* \*

The Crane swooped through the smoke hole of the Palace of the Dead and into the Land of the Living with a host of spectral birds at her tail. They flew in from the west, over the storm-tossed waters of Puget Sound, straight to the heart of the new Babylon Hanging Gardens. The battle raged across the unnatural oasis, brother against brother, Tiamat's loyal against those who fought for freedom. The centuries of bloodshed of the Kivati-Drekar war were a distant memory; now Drekar, Kivati, and human fought side by side against the forces of Chaos. *She's unified them*, Lucia thought.

Storm demons chased the Behemoth across the black skies. Thunderbolts rained down, fire of heaven to purge the battlefield of souls. The trees and hanging baskets burned merrily. Smoke clouded the air and screams rang from the distant mountains.

Lucia followed the currents of Aether to the center of the square. Against a backdrop of flame, Tiamat stood over a prostrate Corbette. Aether wreathed her head. The Scepter lay in two parts at her feet. Nearby, a burned man rolled on the ground. Lucia stretched her neck to the sky, opened her beak and gave the long bugle call of the Crane. The birds at her back took up the call. Together they rushed Tiamat just as the Aether at her head condensed into a ball of fire.

Her first thought was, *This is going to hurt*, but it was her old conditioning. The ball was Aether and she was Aether and the threads that held the universe together were Aether. They were the same—connected. Instead of bracing for impact, she welcomed the condensed energy and absorbed it, letting the shock of it reverberate through her wings and out into the current of Aether she rode. It dispersed on the waves of shimmering water.

Tiamat didn't have time to retaliate as the flock of souls poured through her chest, knocking her back. She fell. Birds flew out her back and looped in the air to pour through her again. Her body shook with the impact of hundreds of ghosts. Their effort immobilized her.

Lucia landed next to the spindle and let the Aether flow through her to Change her from Crane to woman. Bending, she picked up the spindle and turned it over between her fingers. She could feel the way it had been made. The Aether was pulled through the carvings on its surface much like the runes on Grace's knife.

Corbette pushed himself to his feet. His left arm hung limply at his side. Dirt and blood covered his body. She couldn't tell how much of the blood was his. "Emory!" She flew to his side.

"Lucy. You came."

"Always." Gently placing her hands on his shoulders, she gave him a searing kiss. "Let's finish this."

He held the distaff in his right hand. She held up the spindle. "We need to put it on the other end," she told him. "One side to create, one side to destroy. Balance." She screwed the spindle to the black end of the distaff and gave it back to him. The sharp point glistened as Aether swirled around it.

"Tiamat," she said. "It's time to move on and leave this world to your children. You are hereby relieved of your life and banished to the Land of the Dead into your sister's keeping. May the Lady have mercy on your soul."

Corbette raised the Scepter.

"Wait." The burned man clamped his hand on Corbette's ankle, and Corbette paused with the Scepter poised to strike. Lucia realized it was Kai. With that much burnt muscle and so little skin left, he should be dead, but she could see a halo of Aether ringing his body. Something supernatural was keeping him alive. "The baby. Mercy—"

"There is only one chance," Corbette said. "You know what you're asking?"

Kai nodded. "Please."

"So be it. On the count of three."

Kai pulled himself to Tiamat and placed his hand over her belly. Lucia could think of only one thing he might be trying: binding himself to Zetian for all eternity. Grace and Leif had done it, but they had love going for them. Was there enough connection between Kai and Zetian for it to work? With the skin blistering across half his body, he had a one-way ticket through the Gate himself whenever that supernatural halo that was keeping him alive abandoned him. To her surprise, the halo flowed into Zetian's belly. With her newly strong Aether senses, she could almost see the third spirit weaving itself through the baby's life strings.

"One. Two. Three." Corbette swung the Scepter down through the Tablet of Destiny, which shattered, and plunged it into Tiamat's heart. The goddess screamed. Blue fire shot out of her body, through the Scepter, and into the sky, a beacon of Aether blinding the battlefield. It was beautiful and terrible all at once. All fighting stopped; the only sound was the call of the phantom birds. In another flash of light, the spirit birds shot out of Zetian's body and flew up along the beacon of blue fire. A crash of thunder shook the field, and the fire cut off from Zetian's body, leaving her a worn husk but for the threads of softly glowing Aether that Lucia could see wrapping her and Kai together. The spirit birds caged

Tiamat in the middle of their flock and escorted her across the sky. With a roar, the Behemoth chased the storm demons after them. They reached the Gate just as the first rays of sun burst over the Cascade Mountains, and disappeared in a golden flash of light.

# Chapter Twenty-One

Tiamat's army foundered after the death of their leader. The Behemoth chased the storm demons beyond the Gate. Some of the Drekar who'd fought for her fled. Corbette took a moment to watch the tide of battle turn in their favor before pulling the Scepter out of Zetian's chest. Unless he cut off her head, her Drekar blood would heal her. He hoped for Kai's sake that Tiamat's possession hadn't destroyed her mind.

"What will we do with her?" Lucia asked.

Corbette studied the Dreki for a long moment. She'd been lovely, ruthless, and dangerous even before Tiamat had taken over her body. He wondered what Kai had seen in her to make him risk everything to keep her alive. "When a man saves another's life, he becomes responsible for it. If the binding worked, Zetian will be able to use Kai's soul to keep the baby alive. They'll be trapped together for all eternity."

"It worked."

He raised an eyebrow, but saw no reason to doubt her. "We have no way of knowing what powers the child will have. Will it Change to dragon? Or will the Lady gift it with a totem when it comes of age? Will it rival Tiamat in her ability to manipulate the Aether? Will it use its power for good or evil? Is chaos in its nature, or can nurture give it a shot at a normal life? Have I spared its life only to have it show up on our doorstep as the next violent, power-hungry demigod bent on destruction? Just as my father once did for Norgard, allowing the viper into the nest with the hope that he wouldn't bite—"

"Peace, peace." Lucia slipped the Scepter from his hand and laced her fingers through his. She rested her face against his chest. He laid his chin on the top of her head, welcoming the comfort she offered. "These are tomorrow's troubles. Mercy is never the wrong choice. I love you more for it."

"Lucy—" His voice broke. "I never thought I'd see you on this side of the Gate. I planned to go back for you."

"I know. You're predictable like that." He could hear the smile in her voice.

He kissed the top of her head. "Predictable, huh? And can a woman who loves change and surprises be happy with a predictable man?"

She raised her head from his chest to catch his lips. She tasted of smoke and Lucy. If this could be his reality, he'd never change a thing. She broke away. "Only if that man is you, Emory Corbette."

Deeper in the gardens, the fight went on as rebel troops rounded up Tiamat's guards and pursued those who'd fled, but the square had calmed. His men began to gather around them to see the shell of the woman who'd tried to take over the world. Corbette held his hand up. "No one touch her. Get a medic. See to Kai." His Thunderbird hadn't moved since the binding except the faint rise and fall of his chest.

"You need a medic," Lucia said. "Your arm is a dead weight."

"I only need one for this."

"For what?"

With Kivati, Drekar, and humans drawing near, Corbette dropped to his knees. He took her hand with his good one. "Lucia Crane, will you be my mate? Will you let me shelter you when you grow cold, feed you when you grow hungry, comfort you when you grow weary? Will you let me change with you through the years, bearing children with you, as the Lady wills it, and growing old with you? I can't promise you perfection, but I can promise that I will love you with every last breath in my body."

"Emory—" Tears filled her eyes.

"Will you let me love you in this world and the next, forever bound not by magic, but by the strength of our love?"

"Yes. Yes!" She threw herself at his chest, and without the balance of both arms, he fell backward with her on top of him. She rained kisses across his face, eyelids, nose, and forehead, before finally coming to the place he wanted her kiss most. He tried to show her the depth of his feeling with his lips and tongue. She met him, an equal, taught him what she liked, brought him to the edge of reason.

Slowly, he became aware of cheering around them.

Lucia sat up, her cheeks pink, her face bright with a smile. "Decorum, my lord."

"To hell with it." He pulled her back to him and kissed her again. He'd been wrong to doubt the Lady's path for him. Through hell and back, Lucia had guided him. There wasn't another soul he'd rather have at his side. He was truly Lady-blessed. The Aether flowed gently around

them, clean and sparkling once again, and he felt his
totem stretch its wings to embrace the soft white wings of
the Crane. For however long the Lady gave them, he
would cherish every moment with Lucia now that he'd
found her.

Kai woke in the infirmary at Kivati Hall. Kayla Friday,
healer and mate to the werewolf, stood over him with his
wrist between her fingers. "Will the patient live, nurse?"
he croaked.

She cracked a smile. "Seems like it. I'll tell the men to
lock up their daughters."

He closed his eyes again. "They're safe from me," he
whispered. Searching inside for his brother's spirit, he
found only the warm memory of his brother's love. Jace's
spirit was gone. Back through the Gate? They'd see each
other again; Kai knew it. He found his totem, whole and
hearty, as well as a thick stream of Aether that pulled his
soul across the room to a heavily padlocked door. He
didn't need to ask what was through that door. The
sparkling water connected him to Zetian as clearly as his
arms still grew from his torso. The binding had worked.
Their life forces were woven together. He could sense
how his light brightened the corners of her shell and
flowed through the babe in her womb.

The baby's own soul reached out for his own, and his
heart flipped in his chest.

His baby, with a soul like a Kivati, not an empty
Drekar, just like Constance had said. But he could feel
there was something unnatural about this child. Monster
child. Tiamat's spawn.

The baby tugged on his soul again, and he felt love
rock through his chest so fiercely that he almost fell off

the bed. *His* child. He would move heaven and earth for the little one.

"How do you feel?" Kayla asked.

He was silent. A Kivati bound for eternity to a Drekar. It was . . . improbable. He felt like some of his brother's blessing was on them. Jace had helped it happen, and, well, while his baby was in Zetian's womb, he would risk everything to keep her safe. Was there anything left of Zetian after Tiamat possessed her? He'd never been a coward. Rolling to his side, he pushed himself to a sitting position. "Everything seems to work." He held up his hands. There were no burn marks. The skin of his face was smooth beneath his questing fingers. A cold realization flooded him.

Kayla confirmed it. "Drekar blood. It seemed a shame to waste your pretty face, considering. You don't mind?"

He shook his head. "Too late for pride. Besides, the Kivati already hate me."

"If that were the case, you'd be locked up for your safety too."

Kai shot the door another look. "I thought she was considered a danger—"

"People still see her as Tiamat, or at least the baby as Tiamat's direct heir. There have been multiple attempts on her life. The door is locked from the inside."

"What's going to happen to her . . . us?"

Kayla squeezed his shoulder. "That's up to you. But . . ."

"But we can't stay here."

"No. Tiamat killed a lot of people while she wore Zetian's skin. No one is going to forget. It's not safe for her here. If you want the baby to have a chance . . ."

"We gotta get out of here." He rose to his feet and swallowed. He'd been born in Seattle. Sure, sometimes he'd dreamed of escaping the rain and traveling the world, but when it came down to it, the Pacific Northwest was home. "Timbuktu, here I come. This one-cow town was getting a little crowded anyway."

Kayla put a hand on his arm, and he gave her a tight smile. "Lucia said the world isn't as ruined as we first thought. There are wide stretches of civilization, and if Asgard is right and the Aether is fixed—"

"It holds an electric charge?"

"Yes. We can rebuild technology. It will take time."

"But there's hope."

"There's always hope."

Was there hope for him? He could take Zetian and the baby away from here and travel the world. Where would they go? Who would welcome the spawn of Tiamat once they found out the child's origins? They could never stop running. That kid better grow up fast and grow up mean, because he or she was in for a long, hard road. Hiding. Fighting. He rubbed his temple. What a life. "Thanks, Kayla." He took his first step toward the locked door, and the connection through the Aether pulsed. He could feel Zetian waiting for him. The hundred yards down the rows of infirmary cots felt like a hundred miles, but then he was at her door. He knocked. "It's Kai."

He heard the creak of a bed and footsteps to the other side of the iron door. It was the safe room where they usually kept dangerous occupants—moon-mad wolves and predators so out of their minds they couldn't shift back to human. He expected her to give him lip—Zetian had never made it easy for him even before her possession—but the door opened quickly after the clink and whirr of a dozen locks.

Zetian appeared. She wore a long white shift that clung to her growing belly. Her dark hair hung unbound, setting off too-pale skin and those wide cat eyes that were so often glaring haughtily at him. Now they only looked lost.

"May I come in?" Gods, he'd fucked her six ways to Sunday, but this felt like a blind date. The gulf between them stretched out. How much did she remember of her time imprisoned with Tiamat? He felt his face flush.

She opened the door wider, and he stepped in. Shutting it behind him, she moved all the locks back into place. He had a moment to survey the forest-green padded walls. The sturdy iron bed was bolted to the claw-scraped granite floor. Some creature comforts had been added to make the room less bleak: a checkered quilt, a washbasin, and a green Tiffany lamp. A stack of books sat on the bed, one opened and placed spine up to mark her page. He took a step closer to read the title. *What to Expect When You're Expecting.* He quickly looked away.

"Thank you," Zetian said.

Turning around, he couldn't do anything but stare at her. He'd done a lot of fucked-up shit in his life, but what had happened between them took the cake. She was *thanking* him?

She cleared her throat. "You saved my life."

"I'd been planning to get down on my knees and apologize—"

"No." A bit of her old confident swagger flared to life in her eyes as they slid down his body. "Believe me, you were the only bearable part of the whole ordeal. It was my own fault Tiamat took me."

"You shouldn't blame yourself—"

"I welcomed her with open arms. Her power was— glorious. But it was never mine to use. Anyone else would have died with her. Corbette should have run me through with the Scepter. But you bound yourself." She gave a rueful little laugh. "Stupid. I'm stuck with an arrogant

Kivati Thunderbird for the rest of my life. But . . ." Tears filled her eyes.

"Don't cry." He hurriedly searched for a tissue, but the pockets of his hospital scrubs were empty. "The Zetian I knew never cried. But—?"

"You don't understand. I've had centuries here. Yawning, empty years of wars and power struggles. I've done terrible things. Much worse than you, young honorable thing that you are, can ever imagine. I destroyed beautiful things just because I could. But you took away my eternity. Because of you I'll die, when you do. I don't have endless, lonely years to fill. I have a brief span, a laughable handful of years—"

"I'm not going to die tomorrow," he growled. "I'm only thirty. I could live another three, four hundred years—"

She laughed again, a high chime that shot straight to his cock. "Infant."

He straightened and gave her his best bad-boy smirk. "Oh, I'm all man, baby. You need a reminder?"

"Yes."

He'd been bluffing, but the heat in her eyes was all Zetian. It sent his blood raging south as Tiamat never could. The woman was in possession of her own body, and she wanted him. Still, he hesitated. "You don't mind being trapped with me for eternity?"

Zetian had never been one to wait for what she wanted. She closed the gap between them and tore open the front of his scrubs. The smile on her face said she liked what she saw. "Because of you," she whispered, "I'll get to see the blessed land beyond." She took his mouth, and the spark between them flared to life.

He'd never been able to get enough of her body. They had all the passion of a love-hate relationship, but now it meant something. It was like the first time all over again, except this was the first of forever. They had chemistry. They had style, a no-holds-barred attitude and a penchant for giving the finger to authority. With the bump of her belly between them, he could hardly forget they were already bound by blood. The Aether wove between them, a bond no man or god could break apart. What would the future hold? Could he keep his mate and child protected far from Kivati territory? Could he keep Zetian satisfied for a lifetime of being bound to one man? He didn't know, but the challenge of it would keep him entertained for centuries.

He met her tongue thrust for thrust and molded his hips to hers so she could feel the bulge of his erection. *Infant, my ass.* He'd show her he was man enough to match her ancient experience any day. Bring it.

The coronation ceremony took place outdoors beneath the glow of the Lady Moon. The Kivati attended in their totem forms. Crows covered the trees and gabled roofs. Cougar, Bear, Fox, and Coyote paced the wide grassy lawns of Kivati Hall. Even the Wolves had journeyed down from the Great White North to attend. No Kivati living would miss the chance to see the woman who had brought the Raven Lord to his knees or the prophesied Crane who had led them out of darkness.

There were no lights but the stars. The Milky Way stretched across the heavens like a river of Aether. The Kivati were at home in the darkness. From the earth, the deep heartbeat of the Lady thrummed in the soles of their paws and talons.

With a cry, a giant Raven launched himself from the top of Kivati Hall to a place of honor at the edge of the grounds overlooking Puget Sound. Cries rose from the assembled animals—howls, growls, and guttural songs. The cacophony would drive a stranger into the night screaming with terror, but Lucia heard each note like a symphony of earthly song. These were her people. They looked to her to lead them, to protect them, and to inspire them. They would defend her to their last breath. The weight of that responsibility would have sent her running before, and it had. But she welcomed it now and wrapped the edges around her like the blue cloak she'd once worn. She belonged here—her toes sending roots deep into the fertile soil, her wings stretching to the stars above.

Beating her wings, she flew in a circle over the assembly with a nod to each of the Lady's four sacred directions. A Thunderbird perched at each compass point with their House crowded in front of them, all except the south, where Will's place remained a gaping hole. The Southern House was a mass of angry, hurting animals. Their leader had died, and the strongest fought for dominance to take his place.

She saw her sister and parents in the crowd and brushed her wings over them. They had reunited and told her everything. She wanted to know more about Sarah, her birth mother, but there would be time later. The Lady had blessed her when Constance and Milton had taken her in and hidden her parentage. She gave another bugle call, and the cries of her family rose into the black night to join her. Landing on the east side of the lawn next to the Hall, she let Aether spark through her and she Changed. Her white feathers turned to snowy hair and moon-pale skin. She didn't pull clothes from the Aether, but stood before her people naked as the Lady had made her, her chin up, her eyes looking across the growling and pacing predators to the giant Raven who waited at the cliff's edge. Lifting his head to show the shaggy feathers at his neck, he raised his wings and gave a loud throaty caw. The Animals repeated his cry.

Lucia took a step forward and the crowd parted for her. A female Wolf jumped in her path, hackles raised. Lucia snapped her teeth and the Wolf slunk away. A Crow dive-bombed her from the air. She grabbed the bird's wing and, using its weight against it, tossed it into the crowd. One by one, each Animal tribe sent an emissary to block her path. Each one she bested, until her skin was slick with sweat and claw marks covered her arms. By the time she'd faced down the last, a Bear, she'd reached the end of the path. The Raven cawed again, and as one, the land totems knelt on their front paws and the air totems bowed their heads.

The moon, hovering at the edge of the Olympic Mountains, illuminated the Raven from behind. Aether shimmered over his translucent feathers, and then the totem dropped away to reveal her last test: a man, lean but muscled, with severe nose and brow and violet-ringed eyes that demanded obedience. Power crackled from his bare skin. A saner person would run.

Lucia licked her lips.

The ring of violet around his pupils thickened. His voice, when he spoke, was hoarse. "Lucia Crane of the Kivati, Harbinger, Light Bringer, what do you seek?"

"I seek to lead these people."

"And what makes you worthy of such a task?"

"I have faced down each totem and shown them the fire in my heart. I have walked through the Gates and flowed on the Aether between worlds. I have battled the birds of torment and I've named the four Sacred Houses as my own: The North." The new head of the Northern

House, Douglass Raiden, spread his giant wings and set a thunderbolt ripping toward the sky. Those in his house repeated his shriek.

"The East," Lucia said when the noise died down, and an emaciated Theo let his cry rend the air. It was the most heartbreaking sound she'd ever heard. Though wounded from his time enslaved to Tiamat, Theo hadn't broken. His Eastern House staunchly supported him on his slow road to recovery. They opened their beaks and muzzles to scream into the night. Gods, what would they have done if Theo hadn't made it? The Kivati had already lost so many of the leaders they relied on to keep order: Jace in the Unraveling, Will in Tiamat's rise, and Kai, soon to flee east. Theo was the last experienced Thunderbird general. They would need him as they forged a new destiny.

She didn't turn to look at the empty spot where the oldest, most experienced Thunderbird should've sat. "The South," she cried and let her own bugle call ring out to take the place of the one whose memory they mourned. The Southern House drowned out the calls of the previous two houses. Their pain rent the night.

Corbette held her gaze, and she read her own sorrow mirrored there. They wouldn't forget Will's sacrifice.

Finally she called the last House, which sat uncharacteristically silent for the band of merry rogues who called it home. Kai hadn't announced his plans to anyone but Lucia and Corbette, but his people could feel the winds of change pulling their fur and feathers in the night air. The Western House's answering call was a long howl of anguish. Kai was leaving, and they knew it.

Corbette raised his arms to encompass the gathering. "You've called the four houses, and how do the people answer?" Cries from every totem went up. The earth shook with the noise. When it had died down, Corbette lowered his hands and held them out, palms up, to Lucia. "Do you seek the madrona throne?"

She hesitated briefly, and then let a smile play along her lips. "It would be the perfect time to do it," she murmured so that only he could hear. "With Thunderbirds too weak or absent to offer checks and balances to my power, I could rule unopposed."

His nostrils flared, but still he held his hands out. "You could do it, if you wanted to, my lady."

She laughed and accepted his hands. "I know."

"I couldn't lift a feather against you."

"Because you love me?"

"Yes." His voice was hoarse. "I love you, Lucia. And I know you would rule with mercy and grace, a better ruler than I could ever hope to be alone." He pulled her to him. The scent of him made her mouth water. The touch of his skin against hers struck a spark of Aether down the length of her body. She was just as much at his mercy as he was at hers. They'd found the other half of their missing puzzle pieces: salvation and kryptonite.

"Then rule with me," she whispered into his ear. His arms came around her, holding her close. "Be my vengeful right hand, and I'll be your forgiving left. Together we will build the Kivati stronger than ever before."

"Together," he repeated. Aether whipped around them, a clean flow of pure energy that radiated through their connected bodies and out into the animals surrounding them just as the Lady intended it, the Aether connecting the earth and all her harmonies. Balanced.

"I swear to the Lady and on Her sacred powers to do Her work in the world, to serve the Kivati as I serve Her, and to love you and cherish you with my last breath." She felt the Aether seize her words and draw them out into the furthest corners of the universe. It was a binding pledge.

Corbette's hold on her tightened. He raised his voice so that all who gathered could hear him. "I love you, Lucia Crane, and I promise to serve at your side, honoring the Lady and our people, nurturing this love. I've been given a second chance to love you, to live with you in the Living World. Gods know, I don't deserve it, but I swear I will spend the rest of my days making every last moment count." He ran his fingertips lightly over her cheek, a reverent touch, wonder in his eyes. "All the mistakes I've made led me right here to you. I wouldn't take back a single one."

His lips descended on hers, and the Aether tied around their heartstrings, binding them. Lucia welcomed the bright flow that connected her to the man she loved. Behind her, the Kivati raised their voices in song.

The madrona throne had been the seat of the Kivati leader for centuries. It was a squat chair grown out of a madrona tree by some long forgotten Kivati craftsman. Corbette stood in front of the throne and studied it. Behind him, workers removed the last traces of Tiamat from the room; the red velvet curtains and chaise longues from the House of Ishtar made their way to the surplus storehouse for repurposing. Once Corbette would have burned everything Tiamat had touched in a mad flash of anger, but he recognized the uselessness of that now. Textiles and working furniture needed to be preserved and recycled no matter whose blighted hand had tainted them.

But the madrona throne, with its centuries of history and tradition, had outlived its usefulness.

"Burn it," Kai said.

Corbette looked up to find his Thunderbird general and a steamer trunk. He eyed the trunk with distaste. "Leaving so soon?"

"We've overstayed as it is."

Corbette gave a jerky nod. He clasped arms with his friend. "I wish there was another way—"

"Don't get sentimental on me, old man."

"Where will you go?"

"East." Kai's eyebrows furrowed. He glanced down at the trunk. "We're taking it one day at a time."

Corbette released his hand. "And you can't tell anyone your destination, I know."

Kai slowly shook his head. His mate and unborn child would always be in danger from those who feared Tiamat and those who sought her powers. "Asgard's heathwitch, Birgitta, has connected us with her network of witches. They're midwives who know how to birth a dragon. This baby has a soul, but it's not simply Kivati. Whatever it comes out as, they're the best shot we have."

"Good."

"And if you need me for any reason—"

"You can never come back."

"I know." Kai took a deep breath. "So what will you do with the throne?"

Corbette turned back to it. The deep reddish wood had been worn to a glossy sheen, but talon and claw marks marred the surface. "I think the past should serve as a reminder to the future. We'll move on, but we'll never forget."

"Someday I wanna hear what happened to you two in the Land of the Dead," Kai said.

Corbette smiled. "I don't kiss and tell."

"Never mind then." Kai chuckled. He clasped Corbette's shoulder. "I'll be on my way."

Corbette reached beneath his shirt and pulled out the Deadglass on its chain. He turned it over, remembering how vital it had been to him and Lucia making it through the Land of the Dead. He held it out to Kai. "Take this."

"I couldn't—"

"Take it. I have a feeling it might come in handy wherever you're going." Corbette dropped the brass spyglass into Kai's hand. Kai nodded his thanks and pocketed it. "I'll see you again, brother."

"I'll hold you to that," Kai said. "In this world or the next. And if a kid with my rugged good looks ever lands on your doorstep—"

"I'll treat him as my own," Corbette promised. "Tiamat or no, he will be Kivati."

"Thank you." Kai's voice was hoarse. He strode away, and Corbette wished him well. He hoped, for all their sakes, that the child would have no god powers. Being half-Kivati, half-Drekar would be a hard enough road.

His sister, Alice, and her mate, Brand, brought in a skinny madrona sapling, its root ball bound in sackcloth. "Where do you want it?" Alice asked.

"Put it on top of the throne and cut the bindings, please." Corbette was making a concerted effort to include Alice's Dreki in Kivati life, inviting him to social events, volunteering him to serve on the new Kivati-Drekar committee, even soliciting his opinion on state matters. Perhaps he was overdoing it, but he had a century to make up for. To his surprise, he actually liked Brand once he gave him a chance. The man had a core of honor, and his art wasn't half bad either. Most importantly, Brand made his sister happy. In the end, that was all that mattered.

Alice cut the bindings, and the cloth fell open, spilling dirt around the legs of the throne. "Now what?"

"Patience, sister. Let an artist work." He reached out

his hands and called the Aether to him. It flowed around the long-dead throne and into the living cells of the young tree. Slowly the roots began to grow. They followed the contours of the old throne and plowed into the floor-boards, seeking the fertile soil beneath the Hall. The throne room had nothing beneath it but the Lady's earth, and the tree connected, sending its roots deep. He'd had this idea since passing through the primeval mandrake forest in the Land of the Dead. The raised roots of the madrona covered the old wood, not imprisoning it but drawing strength from the traditions of the past.

He sent the river of Aether to wind around the trunk next, and the tree's branches flared out as the trunk divided into two parts. The twin trunks curved to form matching seats, then swerved back toward the ceiling in a wide rising sun pattern of trunk, branches, and leaves. The fresh red wood reminded him of the fire he'd walked through with Lucia to get his eyesight back. As he sat on the new throne, one half of the ruling team, it would do him good to remember that justice was blind.

"Where are you taking me?" Lucia asked as Corbette tied a silk blindfold across her eyes.

"Do you trust me?" His breath tickled the sensitive skin on her neck.

She felt a rush of heat head south. "Yes."

He took her hand and led her out of their room. "Did you know in ancient times kings cemented their rule through public displays of sexual prowess? Animal species still do it. Only the alpha pair may mate."

She stopped walking. "No."

He laughed and tugged her hand. "It's the truth."

"Not 'No, I don't believe you.' No, I'm not having sex in public!"

"Do you trust me?" She could hear the smile in his voice war with his instinctive need to command.

She stuck her nose in the air. "Yes—"

"Yes, but . . ."

"Yes, *and* I'm not having sex in public."

He chuckled. "Follow me to destiny, Crane," he purred, and the seductive promise in his words made her pulse accelerate. She couldn't see with the blindfold. If he led her in front of all of Kivatidom and made love to her in the open, she wouldn't know. If he kept teasing her with his scent and his voice, she wouldn't care.

She quickly lost her sense of direction as he tugged her down dark corridors. The scent of the sea mixed with the biodiesel smoke as they passed through what she assumed was the main entry hall. Rain beat against sky-lights high overhead. The comforting rhythm added to the allure of the night. Her limbs relaxed.

"In here," he said. His voice echoed in the large space they'd entered.

"We're in the throne room, aren't we?"

He swooped her legs out from under her, and her surprised breath left her in a huff. "I have to work harder, I see." His words vibrating in his chest pressed against her side. Her nipples tightened. "Why don't you direct me, Lady Crane? I am your servant tonight."

Lucia licked her lips. "Kiss me."

He feathered kisses across her forehead, right along the edge of the blindfold.

"Lower."

Lifting her skirts, he kissed her knee and untied her garter with his teeth. He tore off the silk and trailed his tongue down her bare shin.

"Higher."

He nosed her skirts higher and blew along the sensitive skin of her inner thigh. She squirmed in his embrace. Carrying her, he kept her distracted with his tongue just inches away from where she wanted it. Swiftly he set her down on a hard, smooth seat of some kind. She felt out with her hands over the gnarled, flowing wood. She found living bark beneath her fingers, but the tree had been directed to grow into two sturdy seats. Only a very powerful Aether worker could direct a living thing to grow as she willed it.

She opened her mouth to ask, but he hadn't forgotten her last command. Spreading his large hands on her thighs, his mouth met the seam of her silk panties. A little moan broke from her throat. His hot, wet mouth quickly soaked the silk. Her head fell back against the tree. It was remarkably comfortable, and she was struck by how well he must know her body to have crafted the seat so perfectly for her.

But she shouldn't be surprised. He played her like a lute. His hands pinned her wide against the throne, and although she was calling the shots, she was completely at his mercy until he decided to end this torment. She threaded her hands through his hair. The tie over her eyes made every other sense sharper. Her own musk mingled with the scent of cedar and madrona and fresh rain.

"Please," she said when she couldn't stand it anymore. Every nerve was wound tight, but he licked her softly, gently, drawing out her response.

"Command me."

Her laugh was a touch desperate. "You can't even stop being domineering when you're ordering me to command you!"

"Do you mind?" He slipped a finger beneath her

panties and into her. Her gasp was enough of an answer. She couldn't deny it. She tried to move her hips closer to his hand. "Ah, not yet. Command me, please."

"Make me fly, Lord Raven."

Suddenly his hands were gone. Her skin chilled in the cool night air, and then he was pulling down her bodice with his teeth, exposing her breasts. He tore off her silk underthings and bared her to the world. She heard the slide of his belt through the buckle and the fall of his pants to the ground, and then he was inside her. He pressed her against the back of the madrona tree as his hips filled her with a steady rhythm. His lips caressed one peaked nipple, then the other, and she knew she wouldn't last much longer.

"Kiss me," she ordered. His mouth on hers pushed her over the edge, and he followed her soon after.

He trailed light kisses across her jaw and down her neck. "I love you."

"I love you too, Emory."

He untied the blindfold and pulled her up to see his handiwork. "What do you think?"

She lounged against him and took in the beautiful work of art he'd built out of the madrona tree. The old throne peeked through the roots of the new, living double throne. The branches stretched to the ceiling like arms of a giant held out to embrace the world. "It's amazing."

"Together," he said. "I meant what I said."

"I never thought you'd give up power for anyone."

"I'm not. I'm stronger with you, love. What's best for the Kivati and for me is you. There is no partner I'd rather have at my side. No matter what comes next, I know we'll face it together and win."

Inside her, the Crane crooned, happy and at peace for the first time. *Stay*, the Crane whispered. *Stay*.

# Epilogue

*Seventeen years later*

The train arrived in a cloud of steam. Rain struck the windows, fogging up her view. Jacinda wiped the glass with her sleeve and tried to see the mysterious city she'd dreamed so much about.

"End of the line!" the conductor called.

She picked up her backpack and joined the queue of passengers hunting for their umbrellas and travel bags before stepping into the late afternoon drizzle. She took a deep breath of the salt sea air and coal, and turned to get her first good look at Seattle. King Street Station was at the south end of town. The skyscrapers she'd read about in old books were nowhere to be seen; the new city grew in short blocks of reclaimed asphalt and brick. Trees lined the wide muddy roads. People hurried through the streets to get out of the rain.

She wondered for the hundredth time if she'd made a mistake. After ten weeks of travel, Seattle didn't seem too welcoming. A fresh start, she'd thought. A chance to find out where she came from and who she was. But the city was gray and the mountains were gray and the skies were gray. It didn't look familiar at all.

All along the train, porters pulled trunks and supplies from beneath the passenger cars. Some travelers eagerly sized up the city, just as she had done moments before. Others looked back in the direction the train had come with a resigned sort of longing etched on their faces. There were two sorts of people who fled west: those looking for adventure and those running away from something. She still wasn't sure which category she fit into. True, tales of the supernatural creatures that owned the Pacific Northwest had fueled her daydreams. Even the humans were said to dabble in magic. Everyone was a misfit out west; it was a place to belong, especially for a strange girl with no people to call her own.

At least that's what she'd told herself when she'd set out with a backpack, her father's old brass spyglass, and not much else.

Jacinda passed groups of reuniting families. Strangers waited at the station with signs that read, SMITH and VANDERLUND. No one waited for her. She almost turned around and got back on the train, but the remaining money sewed into the pockets of her pants wouldn't get her farther than the Cascade Mountains. Tightening her hold on her backpack, she forced herself to keep walking through the station with its gorgeous tiled floors and old world chandeliers, and out the other side into the rain. The street was full of bundled-up people hurrying to get where they were going. She didn't see a dragon or unnaturally large animal anywhere. So much for living in the open.

"Now what, Jacie?" she asked herself. The fear crept into her eyes, and she could feel her pupils slitting, the violet filling in. Out of habit, she pulled her sunglasses out of her shirt pocket and covered up. Seattle might be a supernatural city, but the rules had been drilled into her since birth: *hide what you are.*

Suddenly the clouds parted, and a shaft of sunlight broke through into the street. A young man dropped the hood of his raincoat and turned his face up into the light. His hair was the precise color of the sun; his face gorgeous as rays illuminated his perfect, sculpted cheekbones and mischievous smile. Gods, what would it be like to have that smile turned in her direction?

And then he turned and saw her. She braced herself, knowing what she looked like: hair and clothes mussed from weeks of travel; patched backpack; too-big sunglasses, so out of place west of the Cascades. But his eyes said he saw none of that. He gave her a long once-over, and as she watched, his irises narrowed like a cat's. She sucked in a breath.

"Well, hello," he said, voice like chocolate. Through the rain, she caught the scent of cinnamon. Her heart sped up. "I'm Viggo."

"Jacinda," she said. Seattle suddenly looked a lot more interesting.